A.J. AYENI

The Zaragoza Chronicles: Beginnings

First edition

Contents

Leave A Review!

It would **mean the world** to me as a self-published author if you **rate and post a review** of *The Zaragoza Chronicles: Beginnings* to Amazon, Goodreads, and wherever you bought the book.

Your review will **help others** decide whether to read this book, and your rating will help it soar to the **#1 spot!** Thank you so much for your support!

Scan the QR codes below or type the link into your browser.

Leave an Amazon review

Leave a Goodreads review

https://tinyurl.com/goodreadstzc1

https://tinyurl.com/amazontzc1

Find the Hidden Easter Eggs!

Throughout this novel, you'll find several Easter eggs or references to "nerdy" pop-fiction such as TV shows, books, songs, and/or characters. If you think you stumbled across one, connect with me!

via email at hello@ajayeni.com

or Instagram: @aj_ayeni

for a chance to win a prize, ranging from naming a future character to some cool TZC-specific merchandise!

Good luck, may the force always be with you.

(and no, the Star Wars references don't count :)

Preface

I wrote this book for many reasons; perhaps, the foremost was to remind people of a certain truth. The truth that despite our inherent differences and beliefs as a species, we are still indeed the same species. Sharing the same hopes, fears, goals, and aspirations. Oftentimes, we forget this and digest media, which only reinforces our differences, be it for monetary or social gain. My life has been enriched by meeting remarkable people hailing from all parts of the world, and I have no reason not to believe that this will ever change.

Furthermore, I truly believe in the sayings, "You must be the change you wish to see in the world," and, "Do or do not; there is no try." Although from two radically different sources, they undoubtedly share the same sentiment. I wrote this book to remind people that it doesn't take superpowers or *special gifts* to make an impact; all it takes is ordinary people who can find the courage to make a difference in the world.

P.S. This is my first novel, so I may have rushed things a bit. If you spot any typos or errors, email them to me at hello@ajayeni.com

Prologue

"So this is how liberty dies. . . .with thunderous applause." One of my favorite quotes of all time spoken by the fictional Senator Padmé Amidala in the fictional world that is Star Wars. Fictional indeed, but no less true. What would the child version of me say now? Now that my reality mirrored those stories of old. Now that my friends and I were faced with our own rebellion. We didn't have the illustrious Jedi come to save us, but we did have each other….

-Femi Alakunle

Chapter 1: New Beginnings

It all started when I applied to the prestigious and highly competitive Zaragoza New Beginnings Scholarship to fund the rest of my Ph.D. program in paleoclimatology. The ZNBS, unlike other scholarships, was guaranteed to be fully funded, not only through college but also throughout any future scholastic pursuits any of its recipients undertook. As if that weren't enough, to sweeten the deal even further, all ZNBS recipients were guaranteed a job at the Zaragoza Consultancy Agency: a firm that people have literally killed for, just to land a job there.

There was a catch, though. The scholarship was exclusively offered to students with various dimensions of differences, be it ethnicity, gender, sexual orientation, and perhaps most interestingly, personality disposition—which at the time of applying, gave me quite the chuckle because how could they verify that? I didn't grow up exceedingly poor, thanks to my ever-hardworking, *no-chill-having* Nigerian parents, but on the other hand, it wasn't *Coming to America,* either, and I was definitely no Eddie Murphy courting Shari Headley.

Obviously, accepting the scholarship was a no-brainer,

especially considering that I had aspirations to use its benefits generously and fund my post-doctoral research using the ZNBS, as well. Growing up, I've always had ambitions to become a world-renowned TV personality paleontologist, but the increasing cost of schooling proved to be a formidable adversary. But now. . . .now I had the opportunity to fulfill one of my lifelong dreams; all I had to do was accept the scholarship and fly out to the Zaragoza Estate in Spain to complete my three-month orientation. If I'm honest, the most persistent hesitation I had against accepting the scholarship was this: *the orientation*.

Not only was it weird to complete an *orientation* just to accept a scholarship, but I also didn't know anyone else who had been awarded the scholarship to ask what the orientation would include. "Oh well, it's a once-in-a-lifetime opportunity to become a young, black David Attenborough! Moreover, who doesn't want to *mess around* in Europe for three months, anyway?!" Those were the words I told myself, and shortly after, I was surfing the web for plane tickets to the Navarre region of Spain. An area that sits on the southwestern border of France. The Zaragozas were believed to have lived in that area since the time of the Kingdom of Navarre and have been influencers in both countries for centuries. Likewise, the Zaragoza Consultancy Agency (ZCA) even had relaxed relations with several wealthy nations in exchange for key investments, among other strategic *favors,* I'm sure.

Needless to say, I was very intimidated to be heading to the home of such an acclaimed aristocratic European family. Hell, the only thing I knew about the region was the bull-running spectacle that took place in Pamplona.

Compounding my frustration of trying to portray myself as this worldly *Nigerian American scholarship recipient,* it was practically impossible to find any pertinent information on the family that would aid in this effort. They tended to be very secretive about their affairs, other than the slew of low-key philanthropic donations that were occasionally traced back to them. Unbeknownst to me at the time, there was a very good reason why the Zaragozas chose to live in relative anonymity instead of basking in their ancestral authority.

The most prominent member of the family was, *unsurprisingly,* the current patriarch, Pierre-Antonio Zaragoza. For a powerful family historically known for operating clandestinely, Pierre was a stark contrast to his family's reserved demeanor, especially known for his outspoken views about all matters of affairs, extreme hobbies, and extravagant quarterly soirees. Pierre was primarily responsible for all the information currently known about his family. Unapologetically benefiting from the hundreds of years his family had been operating in the area, Pierre was able to found his multi-trillion-dollar consultancy firm, the Zaragoza Consulting Agency, the company that hosted the scholarship I was granted.

Of all of his peculiarities, one of the most interesting aspects of Pierre was his self-professed love for astrology. In fact, some tabloids even reported that all his business dealings were based on astrological information, such as how and when to make any significant business transactions. Given that he was the CEO of an already exceedingly rich conglomerate, it was hard to confirm or deny if his astrology beliefs played any part in his success. For me personally, I always wondered how good his astrology would fare for him if he had not been born into one of the most influential families in the world, worth hundreds of billions, even before his parents had that initial thought of engaging in coitus.

Following in prominence, status, and age came Pierre's sister, Julie-Marie Zaragoza. Where Pierre was brash and heavy-handed, Julie took a more measured and calculated approach to run the ZCA as its chief financial officer, which was perhaps another reason why the company was so successful, astrology-related or not. Julie had all the attributes traditionally associated with being a Zaragoza, personality-wise and physically. I'd always heard that if she had not studied economics, Julie would've been a shoo-in for any major European fashion house as a runway model, with her long, toned legs, violet hair, and eyes greener than the lush forests of the Basque country.

Honestly, another reason, perhaps more serendipitously for me accepting the scholarship, was having the off-chance of meeting Julie and showing her how she needed a *real man* like me to show her what was what! Perhaps it was a bit of *astrological intervention,* but what I didn't know at the time was how close I would actually get to realizing this fantasy.

Chapter 2: Castillo De Zaragoza

As I previously mentioned, the one true requirement of being awarded the ZNBS was to successfully attend a three-month orientation at the Zaragozas' ancestral estate, aptly named Castillo De Zaragoza. I always thought it was a bit ostentatious to actually name a home, let alone after your own family, but hey, this was Europe, where wealthy families have had ancestral homes for centuries—and this wasn't any ordinary family. I will never forget what it was like when I first arrived at the Castillo. The massive medieval castle loomed over the immediate region like a sentinel always on the watch and ever present. Its front façade was as menacing as its tower spires, which seemed sharper than knives.

Once inside the Castillo, I arrived at what most resembled a scene out of *The Hunger Games* mixed with the Summer Olympics opening ceremony. I saw what must've been hundreds of different flags from various nations, a full orchestra performing a multitude of harmonious national anthems, as well as a great diversity of people that would've made Captain Planet proud! For as beautiful as their Castillo was, I couldn't help but think that lipstick on a pig was still, well. . . .a pig. The Castillo was far from ugly, but the old foundations, questionable archaic architecture, and stuffy furniture left a little to be desired for my modern tastes.

When I heard that the scholarship was awarded to only two people per country, I had always assumed it was some kind of marketing ploy to help ZCA shareholders sleep easier at night, knowing they were helping some underprivileged kids across the world—though I admit I was wrong. I thought growing up in New York City would offer insight into diversity, but as my uncle always used to tell me, "Femi, there's levels to this game of life," and nationality-speaking, I had just arrived at the next level.

After checking in at the main office on the Castillo's *ground floor*, I reported to my assigned dormitory. There was no mention of any roommates, but I soon discovered that I would be sharing my orientation experience with three other scholarship recipients: a like-minded and similarly built, stocky guy from Taiwan named James; a petite, red-headed, and often socially inept but endearingly so girl from Norway named Sarah; and finally, a tall chap from England named Paul who seemed to always know what to say. James and I hit it off well, which I had a feeling we would. Sarah was nice enough, but she was difficult to get a read on at first and mostly kept to herself (which didn't bother me too much because James and I talked about martial arts and video games most of the time).

And then there was Paul: most interesting of all. My first impression of Paul was that he came off as being *very English*, always talking about football, his intense love of room-temperature ales, and moronic yet extremely comical stories of how his frequent inebriation led to the most outlandish events. In regard to his storytelling, we were never really sure if he was telling the truth or not, but his aptitude for tale-spinning was so great that it didn't really bother us. The stories always gave us a sense of vicariousness that was sorely needed in such an ordered environment. However, Paul's most captivating trait was his encyclopedic knowledge of the most mundane topics ranging from the native birds of the Galapagos Islands to the ancient dynasties of East Africa. No matter how much we *called his bullshit* (I mean, fact-checked him), he was always right. Paul was just one of those guys who was so smart, yet so nonchalant and happy-go-lucky, that his presence gave everyone he interacted with a sense of vague familiarity, which no one explicitly stated but was felt and appreciated by all.

The *official* ZCA-mandated reason for having these roommates was to have someone to go through the orientation process with and confide in. I didn't know if they were serious or not, but the ZNBS mission statement in their glossy brochures even stated, *'To have a brother and/or sister that you could always rely on.'* In the beginning, the last part didn't make any sense to me, and I thought it was some corporate PR gimmick companies used anytime they paired diverse groups of students together.

The first thirty days of orientation were straightforward, with a series of aptitude tests and classes about how to properly conduct oneself in school, life, and business. A recurring thought that I couldn't shake was how important these courses would've been if they were actually taught in university. I guess the Zaragozas thought of this, as well, and decided to incorporate it into their curriculum to fill the void that higher education leaves out, purposefully or not.

The second part of orientation flowed seamlessly into more philosophy-oriented classes that I initially found to be quite thought-provoking and much more interesting than the stuff that was lectured in my intro to philosophy class back in my freshman year of university. The very first lecture we had was debating the virtues of the Abrahamic religions (Judaism, Christianity, Islam) compared to the Eastern and usually polytheistic religions such as Buddhism, Hinduism, and Shintoism. A significant portion of class also delved into more of the *fringe religions* by today's standards, such as Paganism and Satanism.

Granted, I didn't pay as close attention to these lectures, primarily due to my lack of interest in these religions and probably my belief that their followers were crazy and being contrarian just for the sake of it. As our discussions continued, it became increasingly hard for me to support the traditional Abrahamic religions due to how much war these religions have caused over the years. My ignorant but everlasting take on these religions was that there was so much ambiguity and hypocrisy in each of their holy texts that the whole thing just seemed silly to me. The whole notion of God saying something in one book, yet contradicting Himself, Herself, or Itself in the next, just seemed ironically human to me. That's, of course, considering this omnipotent and omnipresent force one day took time out of their busy schedule (conceivably on a Sunday), and said, *"You know what, let's create this all-powerful book that only my creations with the ability to read can live their whole lives by, and any deviations from this material will result in eternal damnation. Yep, sounds good to me!"*

The more probable story may have gone something like this: One monk probably started to write down some stuff he heard from the village storyteller, just to have another monk arrive from a neighboring village paraphrase and write down the same story in a different way—this process continuing over millennia with different monks writing new material that completely negated what a previous monk just interpreted and wrote! Not only that, but it always seemed weird to me that this all-powerful and all-knowing God allowed for so much pain and suffering in the world of his *children*. Not saying that divinity and anguish are mutually exclusive, but it was my opinion that believers of these religions casually gloss over how fucked up the world that their God created is. But hey, what do I know? I stopped going to church as soon as my *uber*-religious parents respected my decision to stop attending.

As the orientation courses dragged on, the philosophy of religion courses started to delve into the more mystical aspects and dogmas of these religions: such as the belief in a hell, or underworld, demons, spirits, and other things of the like. I enjoyed these classes because those topics were the aspects of religion that excited my fantasy-filled mind. Despite how scary they were, they usually made for good horror movie backstories. After all, Revelations, the last book of the Old Testament, always read to me like the screenplay of a supernatural anti-hero film directed by Michael Bay. However, poor James didn't share the same sentiments I did.

Being raised in a super Christian Taiwanese family that even rivaled my family's firm Catholic beliefs, it was an understatement to say that he had his fair share of apprehension when studying for these classes. "I get trying to make us more worldly and refined, but what benefit is there to learning about this filth?" James lamented to us after a lecture.

"I'm not entirely sure, but it is interesting, don't you think?" Paul added. James wasn't having any of it, though, and promptly went to bed that night with little social interaction with any of us.

I specifically remember the lecture about the origins of demons and demonic possessions. James disliked it so much that he actually walked out of the classroom, curtly denouncing not only the lesson, but also the ethics of the *former* priest giving the lesson.

It started like any regular day. Reverend Bertram, or "Rev. Bert," as we liked to call him, came in, slammed his antique and dusty King James rendition of the Bible on his robust wooden desk, and began his lecture.

"Do you all know where the word *demon* comes from? The revered said arrogantly." No answer from any of us made him specifically call out to one of his usual suspects and, unfortunately for James, he was one of them. . . ."Ah, James, my dear boy, do you know where the term comes from? Surely, a devout Catholic like yourself must know," he said.

"I don't, Reverend, and to be honest, I'm not comfortable discussing this topic at length," James politely responded.

"It comes from the Greek word d*aemon,* meaning a divine power. And why would such a word devolve into its current malevolent meaning, young James?"

Becoming increasingly agitated by the priest's incessant questioning in quite the rude manner, James snapped back, "Is there any particular reason why you keep calling on me, *Bert*? Surely you must have better things to do?" James said, storming out of the room.

"I keep calling on you. . . . *James*, because with that name, I deem it important that you know the *significance* of that name, but also of the parts of your faith you appear too fragile to confront in their entirety." Reverend Bertram said.

Without hesitation, James stormed out of the classroom. Giving the Reverend a menacing scowl the whole way through.

Looking back at the situation, I think that was the first time I ever saw James visibly upset. Out of fear of having him dismissed from the program, Sarah, Paul, and I went out to bring him back to class, which drew little resistance from him because the next lesson, naturally, was about exorcisms. I found it amusing that he wasn't okay with discussing demons, but he was perfectly fine when these very same demons were being extracted from their human vessels! But on second thought, for me and any other kid who innocently surfed early 2000s cable, only to be surprised by the classic namesake movie and the infamous *crab-walk* scene, exorcisms were seen as cool!

For James, though, it had to do with the whole good-prevailing-over-evil thing that made it okay for him to come back to class. Paul and I were more similar in the sense that we found it humorous that we were in a classroom discussing topics that we typically only saw in movies. To be fair, though, I think Paul found everything humorous, which added to his gift of putting everyone at ease with his natural, nonstop joking. From occasionally calling Reverend Bertram "Reverend Butt-tram"—quickly enough to correct himself, while making an outlandish sound like he was clearing out an extremely hoarse throat—to making funny faces while Rev. Bert was turned away facing the board. Paul was always able to calm down James in subsequent lectures regarding occultism.

After courses ended at around 5 p.m., each scholarship recipient was to report to the Castillo's main dining hall for dinner. Although the food was always amazing and impeccably prepared, the dining atmosphere was severely lacking. There was always an air of not being able to openly discuss the topics that we were most interested in during the day. Not that it was openly mandated that we couldn't talk about the classes of the day, but along with having lecturers hover over us as we ate, the ambiance of the dining hall gave off this distressing impression that extracurricular banter was not encouraged—from the timeworn and stuffy wooden floorboards that looked like they never left the Dark Ages to the portraits of long-dead Zaragoza family members that adorned the walls, constantly gawking at us without rest.

"Hey, why do you think they put these pictures in the dining hall?" Sarah was the first to ask, mouth full of spinach. We mumbled something inaudible, but once she had mentioned it, that was all we could ever see. . . .

Not letting the Castillo's outdated interior design deter us, we usually gossiped throughout our quarters and the common spaces that the lecturers rarely visited. We started having what we called the *Fireside Chats*. Not only because of their similarity to Franklin D. Roosevelt's version of discussing the current state of affairs, but also because the chats always took place near a fireplace, either in a common space or in the cavernous dormitories of scholarship recipients. A theme that was often mentioned was a philosophical one, unlike the topics we discussed in class. Rather than discussing the philosophy of religions and ideologies, we often talked about the philosophy and reasoning of why an international group of scholars from various dimensions of differences—but with great academic aptitude—were asked to complete an orientation just to receive a scholarship?

Of course, we all understood that this scholarship had the ability to change each of our lives forever, but it still didn't register to us why we had to learn about the differences between a djinn, a spirit, and a demon. We often surmised that they were just trying to supplant our critical thinking abilities or see how we would react to being taught different ideologies. But then, there was one student named Raphael, the third scholar from America. . . .

Now, you have to understand that normally this would have been prohibited since the ZNBS was strictly limited to only two citizens from each country, and there was already another American girl who was awarded the scholarship after me but before Raphael. . . . However, an exception was made for America, which I assumed was due to Raphael's Indigenous American background. This exemption at the time didn't make any sense to me. Why was America granted the only exemption to having more than two recipients at a time? Were the Zaragozas drinking the *American Exceptionalism* Kool-Aid, too?

I first became aware of Raphael at the initial Fireside Chat before we even called it that. After the philosophy of religion lecture with Rev. Bert, Paul, James, Sarah, and I went to our usual hangout spot in one of the common rooms near our dormitory. Scholars usually gathered there to pass the time between lectures or whatever else we had to do that day and talked about our day and our backgrounds. Surprisingly, I overheard another American accent coming from the common room, which made me curious. I vaguely remember seeing a third name beside the American list on our acceptance letter, but I thought it was an error and dismissed it. An error, it was not, and here he was, the closest person to the fireplace, luscious locks and all, currently discussing the infamous Reverend Butt-tram, as Paul liked to call him.

"Yeah, I don't know about you guys, but there's something definitely off. Not only about that guy, but this whole fucking place," Raphael said. I was intrigued by what he was saying, so I stepped in closer to the fireplace to hear him better.

"You're American, too?" I asked him in a pitch I didn't recognize my voice could make.

"I guess you can say that. You must be Femi?" His reply must've gone in one ear and come out of another ear that was not on my body because I completely ignored him and continued on with my questioning.

"But how? There's only supposed to be two of us!" I said.

"I'm not sure, dude, but here I am, and to be honest, that's probably the least strange thing about this place. . . ."

"What do you mean?" I genuinely asked.

"Come on; we get accepted into the world's most prestigious scholarship, hosted by the world's richest family who controls the most powerful company to, perhaps, have ever existed on Earth.. . . What would they want to do with us?" Raphael asked me.

"Well, we are super-smart and highly driven!" I replied half-sarcastically, swinging my arm with bravado.

"Yeah, perhaps, but it still doesn't explain how for such an acclaimed family, barely anything is known about the scholarship and even less about its prior recipients."

I didn't want to admit it, but he was right, and I wanted to pick his brain even further.

To me at first—and I'm sure to a lot of the other recipients, as well—Raphael came off as a stereotypical representation of an American Indian young man. He had this wavy jet-black hair that flowed magnificently down his shoulders, which reminded me of a curvaceous river. Its lustrous elegance was usually tied up in a ponytail, further accenting his prominent jawline. Furthermore, he always dressed in a manner that incorporated some element of turquoise and silver. Raphael was proud of his culture and wasn't afraid to show it. Given that I had more in common with him than I did with the Nigerian scholarship recipient, Tolu (who later became a dear friend), I discovered that Rafi, as he preferred to be called, was one of the smartest and most perceptive scholars at orientation. Not only was he scholastically smart, which was obvious if he received the scholarship, but he was also intuitively intelligent: a quality I always liked to adorn to myself but saw in spades within Rafi.

For instance, although he did not speak much in groups, I often saw this look in his eyes, a quiet intensity that spoke volumes about what he thought about the current topic being discussed, even if he remained silent on the matter. Moreover, whenever he did speak, I noticed that others quickly stopped whatever they were talking about to listen to what the *wise and stoic Indigenous American sage* had to say, though this title was bestowed upon him more out of jest from the snarky scholars.

Unlike most of my peers, I sincerely thought Rafi was wise beyond his years, and I definitely spent more time with him than any other person outside of my roommates. Out of curiosity, I asked him to take a Myers-Briggs Type Indicator (MBTI) personality test, a test I became familiar with back in university. As I expected, we both belonged to the same personality type: INTJ (Introversion, Intuition, Thinking, Judgment). In the original interpretation of the test, the INTJ was a person who gains energy by being alone (I), prefers to focus on big overarching ideas and their theoretical underpinnings (N), makes decisions that are grounded in reason and logic (T), and finally, typically plans out their lives in an ordered and structured way as opposed to going off of impulses (J).

The point I was trying to make without going on another tangent was, where others saw Rafi as this stereotypical shamanistic, millennial hippie-type, I saw him as a kindred spirit whose opinion on the reasons for us undergoing all of these classes about religion and spirituality were probably more accurate than what any of us thought at the time. We all thought that the courses were meant to expand our minds to different kinds of beliefs regarding the supernatural world, and for us to be more worldly in our affairs, analogous to how the Zaragoza family was involved virtually in every sort of business industry, ranging from horticulture to nanotechnology. But it turned out that Rafi had an entirely different theory. . . .

Rafi believed that this could all be part of an indoctrination policy to make us more susceptible to not only believing everything Pierre and Julie-Marie had to say but also to proliferate their message to others who could/would not be as easy to reach geographically, socially, or politically. When I ruminated over this theory (at how outlandish it first seemed), it started to make sense to me. So much so that it sent a chilling, serpentine shock down my spine.

I mean, let's think about it objectively, as any logical person here would. You have a full-ride scholarship exclusively for persons belonging to a minority status of some sort in each of their respective countries, but are also very smart and have access to the sort of people that would benefit greatly if they received some form of mentorship or assistance, be it financial or plainly practical. By excluding members of society who have cruised on life's proverbial Autobahn, the Zaragozas effectively have access to the vast majority of the world's population who are not as fortunate—through a sub-population of scholars who have emerged out of these neighborhoods on academic merit, but who obviously still have ties with their communities, and let's face it, are increasingly likely not only to return to these communities to help them in any way they can, but also hold authority in informing their neighbors on how to emerge out of their own unfortunate circumstances. . . .

The more I pondered Rafi's theory, the more I tried to resist its plausibility. I reasoned to myself, "This is crazy, and maybe the other students were right about Rafi, and he's just playing up this whole *Wise Shaman* act. Additionally, at no point were the Zaragoza family espousing any of their ideas or personal beliefs to us, to which Rafi countered with a sly grin, brushing his hair out of his face, "Maybe they're just gauging how susceptible we would be in the first place."

My logical brain vehemently persisted in trying to disprove this conspiracy theory. I mean, everyone here is equally as intelligent and capable, and they all laughed at Rafi's theory, but why couldn't I shrug it off as easily? As a natural skeptic of the altruistic intentions of exceedingly wealthy people and businesses—such as offering a scholarship that could literally change the lives of the world's most downtrodden community members—I always had a feeling that this scholarship was too good to be true, and here was a theory that postulated just that.

"Yeah, it seems too good to be true because it actually is," Rafi warned.

I didn't want it to be true, but the more this idea danced on my mind, the more it bothered me, the more I tried to make sense of the whole thing, and eventually, I bought into the idea. . . . The way these people operate is on ROI; there always has to be a return on investment. *Always.* Besides, if you're a member of some of the most impoverished communities in the world, who are you likely to believe has your best interests at heart? Some rich douchebag who has more money than they know what to do with, or a person who also came from your community and not only made it but is willing to help you achieve your dreams, as well?

On the flip side, for a corporation looking to expand its operations and scope of influence, wouldn't you want to grow your consumer base to a sizeable population of untapped potential that conveniently represents most of the world? Through this scholarship, you already have direct access to some of its most influential members.

When I spoke like this aloud, it seemed like a no-brainer, but I guess that's what Rafi was trying to tell me the whole time. Still, though, I wanted to get the opinion of my roommates, so I sent out a text message telling them to meet Rafi and me at a secluded park not far from the Castillo, right after lectures.

"Who the *fook* is this guy?" Paul said, surprisingly being

the first roommate who arrived.

"This guy's name is Rafi, and there's no need for that type of language, dude," Rafi coolly replied.

"Oi, sorry mate, just so many faces to get used to in this place," Paul quickly apologized.

"Rafi meet Paul, Paul meet Rafi. He's the third American recipient and has an interesting theory for why we're here," I said. Not wanting to re-introduce everyone once they arrived, we waited for Sarah and James.

It was weird to see all the people I was closest with now all in the same place, but weird in a good way.

"Hey, guys, so this is Rafi. He's another scholar from America—the third, in fact; I met him in the southwest common room a few days ago."

"What does he have to do with us?" James said, out of breath.

"Third? I thought there were only supposed to be two?" Sarah said, tying her shoe against a nearby tree.

"All great questions, and I promise to get to all of them," I said, standing in the middle of the circle they formed. Understandably, everyone was angsty. We'd only been at the Castillo for a few weeks, and trying to keep up with orientation was already stressful enough.

"Have you all ever wondered why the ZNBS is only for scholars who don't belong to the *majority status* of their countries? Why it's being awarded by literally the richest assholes on the planet?" Rafi asked as he paced back and forth, his hands crossed behind his back, looking intensely into each of our eyes when he passed.

"Um, yeah, but it's a no-brainer: to reap the massive tax benefits of hosting such a scholarship while being able to espouse philanthropic beliefs, duh!" Sarah mumbled in one breath.

"Wow, I don't know how you said all of that without taking a breath, but yeah! What she said!" James eagerly added.

"Yes, that's very logical and most plausible, but isn't that what they would want you to think?" Rafi said, staring into every crevice of Sarah's Norwegian soul. I pressed my hands into my cheeks, anticipating a feeling of dread when it came to Rafi's first impression.

Please don't go off sounding like a crazy person in front of my roommates, whom you've just met! I thought. But he continued, "I'm not one for conspiracy theories either, ma'am, but if they're so charitable, why is there barely any information on the prior cohorts? How are the Zaragozas clouded in mystery but still the wealthiest family on Earth? I mean, get real guys—and girl); we're the most brilliant minds on Earth, yet no one thinks anything is fishy here? We all know when there's smoke, there's fire. . . ."

"Dude, we've just met you, and you sound pretty crazy, but that's an awesome head of hair you got," James said bluntly, genuinely enamored with Rafi's hair. He said it so bluntly and deadpan that we burst out in laughter, Raphael included!

"Look, I know how this sounds, but as you all probably know, my people are well aware of the consequences of being too trusting, especially with whites—no offense, Sarah and Paul."

"None taken," they both replied with a nervous chuckle.

Rafi smirked and continued, "All I'm saying is, learning about all this occultism, the blatant secrecy, the fucking architecture in this place, it just feels very indoctrination-like to me, and there could be more than meets the eye. You all may not completely believe everything I'm saying, but I know I've piqued your interests."

Rafi was right; they were definitely interested, no matter how convincing their initial poker faces were. It was starting to get late, so we returned to the Castillo, but this was not the last time we discussed Rafi's theory.

Sarah, James, and Paul were a whirlwind of emotions when processing what Rafi told them but ultimately agreed that it could *potentially* be plausible, to quote from Sarah directly.

And where were Rafi's roommates during this whole debacle? It's not that Rafi didn't trust his roommates, the only twins in the program, Bei-Xian and Cai-Chun, but like most of the other students in the program, they had little time to ponder the intentionality of our *saviors,* the Zaragozas, plus this portion of orientation was soon ending and *the Trials* were fast approaching. No one knew or had even heard anything about what these Trials were going to be, only that this was the portion of orientation that had the highest drop-out rate. Coupled with everything that we've experienced in orientation thus far, plus knowledge of Rafi's theory, my mind was now racing faster than a horse at the Kentucky Derby about the possibilities of what would soon transpire over the next few weeks.

Waking up at the ungodly hour of 5 a.m., eyes still half-closed, I rushed out of bed to get my hands on the free breakfast that was offered every morning. Although the breakfast lasted until 10 a.m., the most succulent sausages and fluffiest French toast were usually gone way before then, leaving only burnt pieces of toast and an overripe assortment of fruit. Before leaving the dorm, James was already having coffee at the breakfast counter and asked me to wait for a second.

"Jesus, James, why are you up already?"

"Firstly, please don't use His name in vain, and as you can see, I'm having a coffee. But more importantly, I'm using this new conditioner your buddy, Rafi, told me about!" James said.

I apologized and chuckled at the last bit, then started to wonder when James and Rafi even started to talk, let alone recommend each other hair products! In the middle of reminiscing at the comment James made about Rafi's hair in the park, he spoke again, "Listen, Femi, I know I said he sounds crazy, but he's actually pretty clever. I didn't realize it, but he's in my modern ethics lecture, and we got to talking after class. Did you know he was a dual physics/philosophy major back in undergrad and is earning a doctorate in both, at the same time!?" James said in awe.

"No, James, I didn't know," I said, trying to mimic his deadpan intonation from the park.

"Well, yeah, he is. He's definitely still a weirdo, but a pretty smart weirdo."

"*JAMES*, I know this; that's why I wanted you all to meet him. Now, what is this about? Because there's a fat stack of vanilla-infused French toast that's seriously calling my name right now!" I said.

"I'm sorry, dude. Where was I going with this—ah, right! I just wanted to ask if you really believe this conspiracy stuff because the more I think about it, the more plausible it starts to sound to me. . . ." James and I were perhaps about to have a heart-to-heart moment, so I put my hunger pangs aside and sat with him and had coffee instead. I tried to never miss a chance to have a real conversation with a companion.

"Tell me, buddy, what's really on your mind?" I asked James candidly.

"Well, you obviously know about my disdain for Rev. Asshat."

"You mean Rev. Bertram?"

"Yeah, that guy," James said, rolling his eyes. "Well, my whole thing is, in twenty-four years of being a devout Catholic, I've never heard a holy father speak like that. . . ."

"Like what?" I inquired.

"Well, that blasphemously," James said tersely. "But it's not just that, though. I vaguely remember when I was about fifteen years old, our economy was on the brink of collapse. I remember a Spanish family coming to Taiwan and donating a shitload of money, and pretty much revived our whole economy overnight."

"Well, what's strange about that?" I asked.

"What was strange was that despite being a huge fucking deal, the press it received was not congruent to how momentous the occasion was, almost like they didn't want it to be known. . . ." James said uneasily.

"The wealthy like to be anonymous, don't they?" I said as I took a swig of my freshly pressed Colombian roast.

"Yeah, they do, but I don't know. If there's anything that Catholicism instills in you, it's that nothing good comes for free. " James said gravely.

"Tell me about it. Well, I'm just glad you're starting to see things from our perspectives. Don't get me wrong; I'm not fully convinced yet, either, but what I do know is that there's definitely something else going on here. " James nodded.

I returned his nod, thanked him for the talk, and dashed

off for breakfast.

After the occult lectures ended, we enjoyed a weekend of rest in which we were able to relax a bit before the Trials commenced. During this downtime, there was an air of optimism around the Castillo that was infectious, to say the least. Though we were all deeply perplexed as to the meaning of the courses that had just ended, you could sense that everyone was happy to have it behind them. Surprisingly, we were allowed a week off from the Castillo if we chose to explore the surrounding areas of Spain and France, which greatly delighted Paul, who had this notion that French girls couldn't resist a witty and intelligent Brit.

Unfortunately for my ears and me, his extreme confidence actually proved to be true, as he typically had women swoon over him everywhere he went. I doubt this has anything to do with his nationality and was more likely attributed to how comfortable he made everyone feel around him, no matter their background.

If there was anything mystical about the happenings at the Castillo, it was how Paul could work a room despite cultural and even linguistic differences! I was often jealous of this skill of his, and after a drunken night near the border of Spain and France, I sheepishly admitted this insecurity to him after some help from golden liquid courage.

In typical Paulistic fashion, he looked to me with his usual George Clooney-esque half-smile and said, "Oi, mate, it doesn't matter what you look like to these birds—or to anyone; the only thing that's important is how well you carry yourself. That only comes from knowing that regardless what happens, you'll always be okay on your own."

If memory serves me correctly, at that moment, I broke

down and gave Paul a big hug and told him how much I valued his friendship, which I always denied *ever* happened any time he wanted to *take the piss*.

Despite my *intelligence*, I was never a super confident kid growing up. I had always ventured to bolster that confidence by practicing martial arts or indulging in my musical and literary interests that provided me a sense of self-reliance, and only made me realize just how true Paul's words were that night. However, the fun was soon coming to an end, and we were all to report back to the Castillo on Sunday night, the eve before the First Trials were set to commence.

Chapter 3: Pierre's Wish

Promptly at 8 a.m. on Monday, we were awoken to the sound of Pierre's booming voice on the PA system announcing that we should report to the great hall for an important speech that he, *the great Pierre Zaragoza*, was going to deliver himself.

Everyone was ecstatic, as this would be the first time we had any significant interaction with the patriarch of the Zaragoza dynasty and the person directly responsible for why we were all there.

I remember exactly how I felt when I reported to the great hall to hear Pierre's speech, filled with a host of emotions ranging from excitement to anticipation, sprinkled with a bit of fear. When Pierre finally appeared on the stage to deliver his speech, I had this overwhelming uneasiness that this speech would forever dictate the rest of our lives.

As the final students trickled into the narrow corridor that gradually expanded into the great hall and arrived at their seats, Pierre began. As any great orator would do, he first began by welcoming us into his ancestral estate and repeatedly exclaiming how elated he was to have us there, with a devilish smile reminiscent of how one would smile when they knew something others didn't.

As he stood firmly behind the podium encrusted with his family's coat of arms, I couldn't help but realize how great a likeness he had to all of the modern depictions of Dracula that I've seen throughout the years. He had these piercing green eyes that penetrated right through your soul, jet-black hair styled in a cut resembling Caesar himself, and an impeccably tailored, three-piece charcoal suit accented with a red tie that would make Giorgio Armani proud. His tone and pronunciation flowed smoother than the calmest river draining into an ocean, and his words were sweeter than a freshly baked glazed donut.

Years of schmoozing perverted politicians and corrupt CEOs really paid off as his gregarious personality never felt out of place, effortlessly giving the recipients a sense of belonging in the presence of such an acclaimed business magnate since those fructose-filled words were all directed at us.

After Pierre welcomed us warmly, he began to tell us how important family was to him and how this scholarship's orientation was not hosted in his family's Castillo in vain. He explained that we should not feel like *just* a group of scholastic overachievers aggregated together due to our inquisitive minds. He told us that we should instead feel like one great family and that we were not here by mistake. It was a nice thought that I could be related to a multi-trillionaire, though the thought quickly evaporated to be replaced with Rafi's theory. *What if Rafi was right? What if the Zaragozas were trying to indoctrinate us?*

My mind was like a tennis match, going back and forth

between Rafi's theory and my default logical-reasoning state of mind. Flashbacks of the intro to public speaking class I took in university soon emerged, where I was taught that creating a friendly and familial rapport with your audience members is foremost in priorities. *Surely what Pierre was doing is the goal of any great speaker,* I thought. Nevertheless, Pierre continued on about how much families should trust each other and that no bond is stronger than that of a familial bond.

If there was anything I knew about family and elders coming from a Nigerian perspective and from the perspective of many first-generation Westerners, it was that siding with the family's wishes was *always* expected to take priority over rationality because, well, duh, it's your family, right? At this moment, the notion of indoctrination via familial bonds once again reared its ugly head into my consciousness.

Unsurprisingly, when I turned to Rafi, who was only a few seats away, I noticed his *I told you so* face. Not only because it seems like I was the only one who was not taught how to effectively smirk, *it was funny to me that I missed this foundational male life lesson,* but as Pierre became more forceful with how we should also see ourselves as *true* brothers and sisters to one another, my chuckles were soon replaced with a forlorn look of melancholy. The final portion of Pierre's speech was the most alarming when he stated, "The bedrock of any strong family is trust, absolute trust."

I'm not sure what it was about the words *bedrock* and *absolute*. . . . They had this effect on me that came off as not only authoritarian but also like the words any despot would use during the penultimate speech that cultivates the mood for impending inauspicious activities. Pierre then went on to say that by always being a man who practiced what he preached, he would like to give us insight into what had made the Zaragozas so powerful for centuries. There were only two caveats: The remainder of the speech would be given tomorrow, and we each had to sign a non-disclosure agreement (NDA), which would be the *First Trial*, whatever that meant.. . . .

If there was ever a time when I thought Rafi was some sort of reincarnated Indigenous American prophet, then this was that time. As day one of Pierre's speech came to an end, we all reported back to the residential quarters of the Castillo, each scholar's face beaming with joy and excitement over what they just heard. But I could see that Paul, James, and even Sarah were beginning to feel that the possibility of Rafi's theory was perhaps not as far-fetched as they previously thought.

As we got back into our room, Rafi included, he immediately exclaimed, "See, I told you so! The whole thing is about them brainwashing us!" However, this time the backlash on how absurd this idea was did not come as readily. We all spent the night pondering what the second part of Pierre's speech would entail. Although we were nervous about what he might possibly say or do, I must admit that I found our hypothesizing quite fun, and we got a kick out of coming up with even more ludicrous potential scenarios.

Since it was his theory, Rafi was the first to give his opinion on what he thought was going on and said that the next likely scenario would be some sort of offering to the Zaragozas to prove that we are, indeed, loyal family members and are willing to do whatever it takes to prove this.

For a guy who was routinely known as the *conspiracy*

theorist, this actually seemed a likely scenario that followed the logical chain of events of where we were. Resuming his role as the class clown, Paul stated that to prove loyalty, we would have to compete in a *Fear Factor*-esque competition that would prove familial ties through the shared experience of eating the testicles of some acclaimed Spanish bull or drinking its semen. As funny as his comment was, it was still in the back of everyone's mind that some sort of action would be taken on each of our parts to show fidelity to the Zaragozas' cause, and we only had to wait until morning to find out.

As I attempted to sleep throughout that night, my mind continued to race as to what the next morning would entail, drenching my body in a cold sweat that lasted through the long, dark hours. This restlessness was exacerbated by the persistent sound of something scratching and shrieking out on my balcony, desperately wanting to get in.

Making my way to the balcony to locate the source of the horrible noises, I discovered an injured gray-winged, white-bellied Alpine swift that must've fallen out of a nearby tree and suffered what looked like several broken bones, including its left wing. I knew it was a swift bird due to some zoology courses I took in graduate school, but I was alarmed that a bird that was supposed to be in the Arctic around this time was still in Spain.

Troubled by what to do, I quickly searched for advice on how to take care of a bird in this state. In the end, I took the poor little creature into my room and fed it small pieces of sliced bread that I had lying around. Luckily for my little friend, I couldn't finish my late lunch. I tried to bandage its fragile broken bones before placing it in an old shoebox stuffed with cloth to keep it warm. Keeping it warm wouldn't keep it alive though so I also poked the box with small holes for it to breathe and wished for the best.

When we awoke the next day, there was a palpable feeling of confusion as to what today's speech would be about that encompassed all the residential halls. To our great chagrin, instead of giving the speech in the morning as Pierre had done before, it was announced that his second and final speech would be delivered in the evening with an official time not to be announced until the late afternoon.

Though some could have interpreted this as a good thing, giving us the whole day to attend to whatever we wanted to do, this only amplified my anxiety. I had all day to ruminate over those uncomfortable feelings, instead of just getting it out of the way first thing in the morning.

With this newfound freedom, I stayed in my dormitory for the better part of the day, taking care of my new avian friend (still in bad shape, emitting intermittent yelps throughout the day). Around 5 p.m., it was announced over the intercom that we were to report to the great hall at 6:30 p.m. As all the scholars made their way into the great hall once more, the previous multitude of emotions we felt before coagulated into a single one: **fear.**

Looking just as dapper as before, only this time sporting an all-black suit with a single ruby for a button over a black turtleneck, Pierre took the stage at exactly 18:48 hours, or 6:48 p.m., a number I found to be strangely specific to start a speech that was so important. Not exactly 7 p.m. or 6:30 p.m.

On closer inspection, I realized why I found the number to be so peculiar. In a twenty-four-hour time span, the eighteenth hour of the day is 6, and 18 plus 48 is 66. Ultimately resulting in 666, the number of the beast—and of the classic Iron Maiden jam. Was Pierre a fan of classic heavy metal?! Probably, but that wasn't the point! The point is that he made the conscious decision to take the stage at a time most arguably known for being the numerical symbol for the Devil or the Antichrist.

Once I noticed this timing, the only way I could describe how I felt was analogous to the feeling when the body goes into fight-or-flight mode. The amount of adrenaline coursing through my veins must've been equivalent to what a race car feels right after it has been topped up by nitrous oxide, if this were an anthropomorphic race car, of course.

Although I'm making jokes about the situation now, there was nothing funny about the way I felt during this extremely unlikely coincidence. Instead of sitting with my roommates for the speech, I performed a quick visual search to find Rafi, who I was sure felt similarly to the way I did. It didn't take long to find the only student wearing a maroon-colored buffalo vest adorned with turquoise jewels, and luckily for me, his roommates were also sitting elsewhere.

As soon as I arrived to take the seat, for all his strength in character, Rafi's face couldn't even hide the smugness of being validated. As soon as he flashed those pearly whites, I knew that he knew that *I* knew that his theory had legs.

"You caught it, too, eh?" Rafi asked still grinning. "The strange timing that was a horribly veiled attempt at starting at 666?"

"Yeah, I caught it," I sighed.

"You know what this means, right?" Rafi said.

"I think so, but even if I didn't, I'm pretty sure you're about to tell me." I said slightly annoyed.

Rafi then placed his hands underneath the old wooden chair he was sitting on and scooted it closer to me.

"It means that even if we're wrong about the Zaragozas trying to indoctrinate us, they're definitely still up to something, and if any cohorts don't see it, then they're just choosing to be ignorant."

Again, I wanted to believe Rafi, desperately. It's honestly what felt right, but still, my logical mind fought to its dying breath. "The Zaragozas couldn't really be trying to usher in a new world order through minority empowerment. . .could they?"

My senses were hyper-tuned to every syllable, every vowel, and every consonant coming out of Pierre's mouth to properly take in any sort of metaphor, simile, and/or double-talk of anything remotely nefarious. Not sure if it was fortunate or unfortunate, but my innate deductive abilities would not be needed for the next couple of sentences spoken by Señor Zaragoza.

I will never forget those words till the day I die. I guess for me, that day was now what psychologists call a flashbulb memory: a memory that is so firmly grounded in your hippocampus that not only can you remember the memory itself but also how you felt at the moment, the thoughts bathing in your mind, and even the exact clothes you were wearing.

As we all took our seats for the second and final portion of Pierre's speech, he came out with what I like to think, *hope,* was a glass of wine. He cleared his throat the same way one does when attempting to appear subtle, although the attention they seek is anything but, and makes you wonder if there was any actual phlegm to clear out in the first place or if he was just making it known that he was now in control of the environment. Whatever his reason, it worked well and we were now giving him our complete and undivided attention.

"Scholars, graduates, future leaders of the world, every one of you is here for a specific purpose. Hand-chosen by my sister and I, for your unique talents and superior intellect!" Pierre opened.

"I welcomed you into my home, not because I couldn't afford to host each of you in the finest hotels across Europe, but because I truly believe you all are my family, my children, and my legacy. Not only is it my annual dream for every one of you to reach your highest potential, but it is also my dream for each of you to help me transform the world into one where peace and prosperity triumph over dread and despair. Though the road for this world I envision may be long and arduous and may require sacrifices and changes of allegiance, I promise you, my dear children, if you follow me on this road, if you remain loyal to the cause, you all will be granted gifts beyond your wildest dreams. Join me, join my family; let us make this bond permanent. *En sangre de mí para ti, de ti para mí. . . .*"

Pierre's atrocious attempt at humor may have reached some of the scholars when he said that he could afford to *host us at the finest hotels across Europe* with a devilish grin. For me, the only salient part of his speech was when he ominously and casually mentioned the changing of allegiances, sacrificing, being granted *gifts,* and most portentous of all, making the bond permanent. "In blood from me to you, from you to me. . . ."

I had been hoping that my intro to Spanish class would pay off one day, and boy, oh boy, I sure wished it would've been to order some sort of exotic delicacy in the mountains of Chile instead.

The very second Pierre Zaragoza ended his speech, what looked like monks straight out of the Dark Ages, each adorned in dark-hooded robes and grasping what seemed to be a scroll of some sort, suddenly appeared in the great hall. At this moment, I, by chance, glanced over to Pierre, still standing behind the podium, looking happier than if it were Christmas morning. I watched as he took a sip of his mysterious drink enclosed in a jeweled goblet and announced, "My sweet children, 'tis the time to truly marvel at the strength and splendor that comes with being a Zaragoza! Today I share with you the secret to our long-lasting wealth and power. Today is the first day of the rest of your lives, and today, each of you is born again. But first, I need you all to do something for me to prove your fealty. I need you to sign a non-disclosure agreement."

As Pierre's words slowly started to devolve into a language spoken centuries ago with words like *'tis* and *fealty,* those thoughts of potentially believing Rafi's theory and what the Zaragozas truly wanted from us went from lukewarm to nuclear fusion-like temperatures quicker than people abandon their New Year's resolutions. . . .

I figured the thought process for some of the other scholars was: *Sure, we have to sign an NDA, but this man and his family are the wealthiest people on Earth. Of course they wouldn't want to share the secrets of their empire with just anyone!* This predictably makes sense that no super*(natural)* villain will ever make their evil intentions so easily documented and traceable for the masses to consume.

As plausible as it seemed to sign an NDA before delving into the secrets of the Zaragoza wealth, I wasn't buying it, and thankfully, some others weren't, either. After Pierre announced that we'd have to sign the contract before continuing any further, he allowed us to return to our residential quarters for one hour to decide whether we wanted to continue with *orientation* by signing, or abandon the ZNBS entirely and immediately be sent home.

To this day, I'm not entirely sure what drove me to make this decision—call it innate intuition or just watching too much television—but once I returned to my dormitory, I checked on the bird that I rescued a couple of days back. As anticipated, it had passed away sometime not too long ago, given that its little body was still a bit warm.

Though I felt horrible about what I was thinking to do, I tried to tell myself that the bird would've been happy to return the gratitude to the person who gave it a few more days of life. Reaching for the science toolkit we were given during the lecturing portion of orientation, I retrieved a syringe and extracted a few milliliters of blood from the little birdie and placed it in several vials for safekeeping. While excessively rich megalomaniacs like Pierre love to talk in extended metaphors and similes, I took ". . . in blood from me to you and from you to me . . ." quite literally, which I'm sure he did, as well.

Not wanting anything disastrous happening to anyone I cared about in the Castillo from them donating their blood to the Zaragozas, I reached into my left pant pocket, pulled out my phone, and hastily looked for the group chat we were all in to alert Sarah, James, Paul, and Rafi to come to my room for an emergency, immediately. I knew it would be hard to explain to them that, "Hey, guys, I have a feeling that the next part of orientation will involve us donating our blood and possibly selling our souls to the Zaragozas, so fuck that, and instead of donating your own blood to stay in the ZNBS, let's use this bird's blood!"

Fortunately for me, given everything that occurred thus far—including the mysterious monks that apparently possess teleportation abilities, or more likely, emerged out of some hidden wall—none of this seemed too odd to my friends. Plus, I even had Pierre's verbatim words to go off for additional evidence. If it weren't for Rafi, none of us would've even had the foresight to think in this manner. He was the first to concur that the next portion of orientation would involve us donating something to Pierre to prove ourselves to him and his sister, which made convincing the others much easier.

I didn't have much time to explain my rationale to my friends, but I didn't want to appear like I was hiding anything, either. "Wait, wait, wait. We don't even know for sure if he literally meant for us to give him our blood. It could just be, you know. . . .symbolism," Sarah said, trying to be the objective one of the bunch.

"Yeah, that's plausible, too, but wouldn't you want to be safe rather than sorry?" Rafi interjected nonchalantly, helping me organize the vials on my desk.

"She's right, though, Femi; we don't know for sure if he wants to take our blood. Perhaps you two are having too much fun playing occult detective," James chimed in sarcastically.

Annoyed at all the inaction and talking, I stopped what I

was doing to nip the situation in the bud quickly.

"Listen, you two. Of course I don't know what the Zaragozas are really up to, or what Pierre meant when he literally said from my blood to you and whatnot. All I know is that I have these vials of blood, and on the chance that those hooded cultists want to extract my blood, I'll at least be in the position for an alternative, understand?!"

"Jeez, mate, 'roid rage much?" Paul exclaimed. I found his remark funny, but I couldn't bring myself to laugh this time because shit was getting real, and I wasn't going to be the one to slow down the momentum we currently had.

While handing out each blood vial I had collected from the bird, I could tell that despite what I thought was an encouraging speech, Sarah's disposition was rapidly changing for the worse as this conversation, and orientation as a whole continued. She went from being this prototypical Scandinavian girl who was calm and reserved in appearance, mannerisms, and speech to one who was disheveled, easily distracted, and at times appeared to be manic.

Although we all came to the Castillo expecting a relatively normal scholarship awarding ceremony and perhaps learning a bit about the Zaragozas' history by attending some lectures to gain a more *worldly perspective* needed to be associated with such an acclaimed family. However, when things started to get a bit more *inexplicable,* the gang and I—Rafi included—didn't even realize we were adapting accordingly to how the orientation was playing out. However, Sarah wasn't faring as well as the rest of us, and when I gave her the vial to use, I could tell that she was becoming more and more distraught.

Sarah tried to match the composure and levelheadedness

that we all exuded, but her face broke out in what I could best describe as a nervous and unsure smile that eventually progressed into a faint laugh that screamed of tremendous apprehension. As I handed her the vial, her palms were freakishly sweaty, which did not correspond with the temperature in the room. Even if the rest of us were as cool as cucumbers, It didn't feel right proceeding with this course of action until Sarah's fears were properly addressed. To assuage any feelings she had about the current state of affairs, I asked her if we could talk privately. Looking into her honey-brown eyes, I could tell that she was greatly moved by this request.

Pulling her aside, we went into her bedroom, that was across from mine. I took a deep breath and asked her in the calmest voice I could muster, "What's on your mind, Sarah?"

After taking a few seconds to gather her thoughts, she flashed me with her golden browns, and in her soft Norwegian-accented English, said, "I don't know how much more of this I can take."

I asked her to elaborate on what she meant and she didn't hesitate to tell me. All she wanted to do was to come to Spain to finish the orientation, obtain the scholarship, and to complete graduate school to financially support her family back home in Norway. She had never asked to be a part of any global supernatural conspiracy theory about world domination.

I felt for her. I really did. Norway in any form of media usually has to do with being the *world's happiest country* or having the lowest crime rates in the world. However, Sarah told me that this glosses over the fact that poverty still exists in such an acclaimed country, even if it's not widely reported. Sarah came from the eastern part of Oslo often associated with immigrants, though her family was ethnically Norwegian. Being 'fully' Norwegian, Sarah's family was assumed to be wealthier and reside in other parts of Oslo, particularly the west. Needless to say, Sarah's family was not well-off, compounding the stress that Sarah experienced.

"You just don't understand, Femi. Whenever I travel, people look at me and think that I have it all together. Yes, I earned the grades needed to distinguish myself from my peers, and it has led to great distinction, but my family isn't the studious type, and hard work is more valued."

I tried to understand the sentiment, but she was right; I couldn't. My parents always instilled in me that education is the one thing that people couldn't take away from you, no matter what shade of flesh you possessed, no matter your religious or sexual proclivities. But in Sarah's case, her family wasn't necessarily wrong, either, nor were my parents. Yes, they were correct that nobody could ever take your educational credentials, but what they forget to mention was that they couldn't take your trade skills either.

"Maintaining this double-image has always been a burden for me, and the ZNBS was going to allow me to gain some congruency in my life: Scholar plus scholarship equals good-paying, safe, and secure job; *that's all I ever wanted*," Sarah shrugged melancholically.

I related to her in feeling like she was not living up to the person she *was supposed to be* and tried to reassure her. "Listen, Sarah, this is something I learned the hard way and still even sometimes forget, but you can't compare yourself to anyone but yourself because nobody's situation is identical. The life you so desperately want, maybe, just maybe, isn't the life for you. And if it isn't, you have to be okay with that, too, because this is the only chance of life that we get, *that we know of, at least.* Just do what feels right," I said, playfully jabbing her in the arm. I could tell from the slight glimmer in her eyes that she appreciated the sentiment, and my quirky, physical-based humor put a big smile on her heart-shaped face.

All this time, I never really put much thought into why Sarah was so reclusive. But given her background of where she was from in contrast with who she believed she was, I figured that she thought whatever cognitive dissonance she was feeling could be mitigated if she just put her head down and gained the scholarship's funding.

Fortuitously, after that evening, Sarah and I got much closer.

After trying to lift her spirits, I got back to the matter at hand and tried to explain to her how she had to be strong about going forward with orientation and to the possibility of exposing whatever was going on with the Zaragozas—not only for the sake of all the people here but potentially the fate of the world, depending on how elaborate Pierre and Julie's plans were. Mentioning this, I saw Sarah's eyes starting to lose focus once more, her body twitch a few times, and the same nervous smile from before made a grand reappearance. But after a while, the whole gang came in and each gave their reasoning why they believed going forward on this path was imperative.

I told her my story of never feeling good enough or comfortable in my skin and how if we went through with this, not only would it be for the greater good of the world, but would also help me realize that I did possess inner strength and should be proud of myself for doing my part for humanity: a bit selfish, yes, but who isn't!

James then gave his spiel about how any good Christian would want to expose a potential demonic conspiracy and how proud his priest father would be of him if we could succeed in this task.

Rafi came next and talked about how everything was taken from his people by the ever-industrious Europeans and their descendants, Spanish conquistadors that could have been very well ancestors of our *altruistic* benefactors. People who didn't mind a bit of exploitation here, and a bit of genocide there to benefit their own slimy interests. By bringing down the wealthiest European family in the world, he would be doing his part in getting retribution for all Native peoples in the Americas and abroad.

Rafi's reasoning was definitely more compelling than mine, which made me jealous that he was so righteous and had the insight to think in such a way. That reptilian snap judgment of being envious was quickly replaced once I thought about how moronic it was to compare the reasons for wanting to do good in the world. *"Doing good and being good isn't a contest. You just do so for goodness sake,"* I had to remind myself.

Last but certainly not least, Paul gave his reasoning behind why he was taking part in all of this. He stated that all his life, he had always been thought of as the intelligent slacker who just goofed off all the time—the person everyone knew had potential, but just gave up.

Judging from the rare pensiveness on his face, I could tell Paul was about to share something with us that he had never shared before, and considering how quiet the room went, the others picked up on this as well.

With what looked like the weight of the world on his shoulders, Paul somberly told us that he was not always the joker we saw before us. Growing up in South London, he had been constantly surrounded by crime, gangs, and the violence that often ensues when these elements are present, though he was never actually a part of these activities, nor present in them.

Sharing his backstory for the very first time, we all listened intently to how Paul told us that growing up he was hardly the class clown he is now and was actually quite studious until the day he lost his close friend, Charles—or *Choz,* as Paul referred to him. Paul and Charles lived across the street from one another in the South London town of Croydon, and their families had known each other for years, which made Paul and Charles feel more like brothers than friends. Growing up in an ethnically mixed neighborhood and being some of the few remaining working-class white British families in his part of the neighborhood, Paul and Charles were often bullied for their background and thus experienced disproportionately more discrimination than some of their darker-skinned counterparts in the neighborhood.

To circumvent the constant harassment, Charles ended up joining a gang from a nearby neighborhood that had more white British inhabitants in an effort to have increased protection against the relentless bullying he was experiencing. On one unfortunate afternoon after school, Charles was facing more harassment than usual, which got so bad that he threatened to "call up" his *crew* from the neighboring manor to deal with the local gang. Though this was stated in an effort to discourage the boys from further taunting and roughhousing, this comment only enticed them more, and the pushing and shoving soon escalated to punching and kicking. . . .

According to Paul, he arrived at the scene shortly after the violence intensified. Not being the smooth-talker he is today, he tried to convince the neighborhood kids to stop beating on Choz, which had no effect on them. Only after a passing adult threatened to call the police did the kids pounding on Charles snap out of their rampaging trance, but not without leaving a menacing warning:

"This isn't over, you colonizing pieces of shite. You'll wish you never joined that other gang. . . ."

At this point in the story, Paul was visibly shaken and stirred, and his face was redder than a Bloody Mary. Paul's eyes began to swell, an obvious attempt of holding back inevitable tears. I interrupted and told him that if he was not comfortable, he did not have to finish the story.

He shrugged me off and told me, "Oi, what *kinda* gobshite starts a story without finishing it, mate?" Even in his visible discomfort and pain, Paul was still playing his role as the court jester, leaving me stunned at the strength of his character.

Resuming his story, he told us that about a week or so after the threat was initially given to Charles and Paul, it was actualized. . . .

On a rainy bank holiday afternoon, Paul and Charles decided to go to the nearby kebab spot for their usual lunch of two lamb kebabs with chips and a pair of orange sodas. Unfortunately for the two of them, the aforementioned gang also had the same idea for lunch. As Paul and Charles entered the store, the group of hooligans were just finishing their meals, and as soon as the two parties locked eyes, Charles and Paul immediately dashed out, ensuing a chase that they were never going to win, with the five-to-two odds being firmly against them.

As the troublemakers closed the pair off in a nearby alleyway, they kept repeating, "Oi! Where are those lads now? Where are your lads now, bruv?!" Exhausted from the constant provocation, this time Choz decided to fight back and shoved the boy who threw the first punch a week ago into a trash can, or *rubbish bin,* as Paul called it.

Paul threw himself to the floor to display how the gang member fell into the bin from Charles's forceful push, leading the other members of the gang to, almost in unison, recite with a menacing grin, "You'll regret that, *Charlie.*" After making the thinly veiled threat, the recently binned *tough guy* brandished a butterfly knife and starting to sing a variation of the lullaby "London Bridge" but exchanged the words *London Bridge* with Paul's and Choz's name, unnerving them even more.

As Choz and Paul watched the knife being whipped out, they both quickly apologized and promised an end of troubling the gang members, an empty promise they wouldn't have the chance to fulfill. Two of the gangsters grabbed Charles, whilst another two held Paul against the fence across from the brick wall where Charlie was being assaulted.

"Choz and Paul are falling down, falling down, falling down . . ."

The knife-wielding youth sang whimsically, edging ever closer to Choz. Paul started to crack the lamest knock-knock jokes trying to diffuse the chilling situation, occasionally getting some sporadic laughter out of the less-hardened gang members, solely due to how bad his jokes were. As the knife-wielder started to realize that Paul's jokes were winning his gang over, he ordered his cronies to gag Paul with some of the crumpled-up, grease-laden napkins they just used at the kebab shop. Once Paul's mouth was gagged shut, the knife-wielder whispered to Charlie, "*This is where you fall down . . .*" and repeatedly pierced the blade into Charlie's abdomen no less than fifteen times, erupting into screams of ecstasy every time the blade penetrated his stomach as his cronies still held him up against the fence, muffling his screams with their sweaty, adrenaline-filled palms until they slowly stopped, and the life vanished from his cerulean eyes.

Sunken, shocked, and scared, Paul looked over silently as his best friend died right in front of him, the hoodlums still laughing hysterically over the act they had just committed. As they ran off, the leader of the gang shouted in the distance, "You're alive because you're funny, bruv, but don't ever show your face in the neighborhood again, or you'll *fall down,* too!"

When Paul finished his story, his face was redder than a fire truck, and the tears he once successfully held back now came rushing out like an avalanche, cascading down his face and body. We all sat there, frozen with the story Paul had just shared with us. No one could have imagined that *life of the party* Paul was a victim and witness of such senseless violence. As we all attempted to console our friend, now sobbing ourselves, Paul said in his trademark sans malice acerbic tone, "Oi, why are you lot crying? I'm the one who was there!" Getting us to laugh and cry at the same time, which must've been quite a bizarre sight if anyone witnessed it.

After we regained our composure, Paul looked over to

Sarah and told her that he did not tell us his story so we would feel sorry for him or anything he had been through. Stating, "After all, we've all been through some traumatic stuff. Otherwise, we wouldn't be here. We can use it as fuel to continue to see this whole ordeal through, for us to do our part to rid the world of nonsensical violence, malice, and evil."

My ever-racing and often insensitive mind thought that all of these words essentially meant the same thing. But I quickly realized, being the *master of words* that he is—Paul probably thought that, too—and given the gravity of what he just told us, he was just trying to drive the point home, which is a task he definitely succeeded in. Don't get me wrong, though, I'm sure all of our stories were captivating enough for Sarah to realize exposing a potential plot was bigger than any one of us, but that became especially salient after Paul's story.

I could see the vigor renewed in her eyes and could tell that we could count on her continuing along on this journey of ours. Our friendship became much stronger after that day, and the only thing left to do was to wait five more minutes until we had to report back to the great hall for the conclusion of the First Trial and go from there.

Once we each had a vial of the poor bird's blood that sacrificed its life to probably save ours, we headed back to the great hall to sign our NDAs. By the time we reached the hall, the weird vibes that started with the arrival of the strange cultists not only persisted but were amplified, not coming as much of a surprise to my friends and me. However, instead of standing alongside the walls of the great hall like they previously were, each apostle was now lined up in an orderly fashion behind tables that had the scrolls now placed atop them.

Chapter 4: Sangre

As we edged closer to the tables, we noticed they were arranged by orientation group. This wouldn't be a problem since Sarah, James, Paul, and I were in the same group. The problem was that Rafi was not, and this realization had me very worried.

Why isn't he with his orientation brothers and sisters?
Why did they come together?
What is his relation to this group?!

All possible questions that we could be asked by the creeps in robes, questions that swirled around in my head, jettisoning me through a whirlwind of emotions. I started to sweat feverishly and had trouble putting coherent sentences together. My mind's eye kept flashing to scenes of me being executed for such treachery. I mean, come on, when a guy uses words that modern dictionaries define as being *archaic,* how can you not think that execution is the only reprisal for such actions? Though it was probably just my anxiety shifting into overdrive.

I tried to slow down my racing heart by inhaling large amounts of air through my nose and exhaling quick breaths out from my mouth. I felt myself reclaiming my rationality in the nick of time because we were rapidly approaching the next table. My friends also noticed we were to arrange ourselves by dormitories, and I sensed a similar note of panic. To help them avoid the ordeal I had just internally gone through, I told them to not worry. We would just tell the apostles we had found another *brother* with whom we shared a deep bond. Unlike my previous behavior, my reasoning was not erratic. I thought this would be convincing enough since the Zaragozas' whole premise was based on loyalty and staying true to *family*. The fact that we were all very carefully selected only strengthened my theory. I hypothesized it would be foolish for them to disapprove of any scholarship recipient that made it this far for just wanting to go through orientation with someone outside of their own dormitory.

The next problem would be how to remove the bird blood vials without arousing suspicion. We were now at a point in the line where we could see exactly how the process played out from the groups in front of us, helping us formulate a better plan of action to fool the apostles. From our point of view, it looked like each of the robed clerics would say something to each recipient, to which the recipient responded and then pricked their thumb and subsequently placed that thumb on the scroll, cementing their loyalty to the Zaragozas. So far, my hunch that Pierre's previous speech talking about ". . . from my blood to you, and you to me" was unfortunately correct. . . .

To be honest, I hoped deep down that this was just another use of a hyperbole and no exchanging of blood would take place, but as the saying goes, "Failing to prepare is preparing to fail." We were definitely prepared for this stage of orientation, even if we wished that we were not.

The next thought that crept into my mind was how he would give his blood to us. *Lord, I hope we wouldn't have to undergo some weird blood transfusion-type of experiment and suddenly turn into gargoyles!* My fantastical mind continued with potential scenarios ranging from drinking the blood of Pierre or Julie, vampire-style—by biting into their necks to extract their crimson life force—to preparing a blood soup for us from the blood of past Zaragozas stored in some freezer hidden in the Castillo.

When my mind returned to normal, one thing I could not understand was how willing the other recipients were in continuing with a scholarship that felt more like an initiation into an ancient and all-powerful cult.

I mean, I understand the whole coming-from-nothing story for a chance to become great with the full support of the most powerful family on Earth. In my ignorance, perhaps I only thought I understood. Not realizing the full impact of such an opportunity. How could I? Unlike some of the other scholarship recipients, though I was a minority in my country, we were solidly middle-class, not lacking any creature comforts, let alone basic necessities. Being from a country where my very existence makes me stand out, I did not take into account recipients from other countries where their dimensions of difference were not as clear as phenotypical differences. It would make it that much harder to differentiate yourself from your fellow nationals, apart from finances, and often times, differences based on disabilities or personal beliefs, such as religion or sexual identification. So, a chance to truly change your standing in life and achieve all your dreams just through a prick of blood and stated allegiance to a family worth trillions of dollars was maybe not too crazy a thought, after all.

Anyway, I digress. I had more pertinent things to think about, like figuring out how to get to the next part of orientation covertly without anyone knowing of our little avian friend's donation. Paul's idea of how to go about this was perhaps the most entertaining:

"Oi, why don't we just cause a large commotion by one of us pretending to fall ill, resulting in all of us helping out in order to take out the vials and quickly just sign the sodding scrolls!"

Although we all got a good laugh out of this plan, it was extremely impractical for a myriad of reasons. . . . The main reason was that such a big commotion would surely bring more attention to us than anything else, causing each action we performed going forward to be carefully scrutinized. Even though it wasn't remotely helpful or conducive, it did help lighten the mood considerably, which was probably Paul's ingenious plan, after all. *I could never tell with that guy.*

James's idea was a bit more clandestine, though I still had my doubts nonetheless. "It's simple, listen—all we have to do is tell the apostles that one of us has a severe phobia of bleeding in front of strangers and would rather do it near people we trusted!" It wasn't that James's idea wasn't plausible; every day there seems to be a new phobia of something extremely esoteric in nature. But my main concern was that if we were to carry out this plan, it would raise too many questions from the cultists in front of us and eventually the Zaragozas themselves, which could potentially come back to bite us in the ass.

His idea did however, inspire Sarah to develop her plan that incorporated aspects of James's *phobia plan*. "Wow, is that really all you *geniuses* can come up with?" Sarah mumbled. "Once we get to the table, we just tell the apostles that we are all extremely close to each other and wanted to do *everything* in orientation together because we already feel like a family. We would politely ask to stand to the side for a moment to all draw blood from each other and then sign the scrolls and return to the table." The beauty of this plan was that it would demonstrate the very qualities that the Zaragozas seemed to cherish most, but also give us enough time to take out a vial for all of us to sign.

As we approached the table, footsteps in unison, we tried our best to look absolutely confident in what we were about to do, making sure that we didn't look awkward to raise suspicion. Flawlessly executed, the plan was successful! We gave each other a celebratory hug right before we popped open the vials, which undoubtedly made our *family unit* case much stronger. Since none of our own blood was drawn, we didn't even bother to actually read what the scrolls said, but we had a good hunch that it was nothing delightful or pleasant.

I did manage to make out a portion from the extremely small font about "*being gifted special abilities if deemed worthy,*" which I just disregarded as superfluous jargon for being gifted with either monetary compensation or other material things from the enormous wealth the Zaragozas possessed. Oh, how wrong I was. . . .

As the lines became shorter and shorter, more and more ZNBS recipients returned to their seats to await the final portion of Pierre's speech that could not be completed until everyone signed the NDA, and by extension, the blood-loyalty scrolls. When the last recipient returned to her seat, Pierre promptly returned to the stage, looking more regal than we've seen him thus far. It was almost as if each signature reinvigorated his entire essence, as if each drop of blood added to his vitality, renewing him from the inside out. The dark and subdued tones of his previous outfits had been replaced with hues associated with victory and royalty. Hues of purple and gold appeared throughout his puffy get-up that looked straight out of the fifteenth century. He also now sported a strange medallion around his neck that seemed to sparkle like a candle, even in the dimly lit great hall. Not only was his attire altered, but his language had also differed. Gone were the grim and primeval words, and in their place, words that were laced with all sorts of positive imagery such as *enchanting*, *glorious*, and *fruitful.* If the Pierre before we signed the scrolls was a black-and-white picture, this Pierre was a full-color Instagram filter with the saturation dialed all the way to eleven.

It was the final portion of Pierre's speech that stood out the most for me, and it began, "My glorious and beloved children, today you may not realize it, but each of you has just made the first step in ensuring that your birth families are well-taken care of for the rest of their natural lives. By signing these agreements, you have cemented that your prospects in life will forever be fruitful and pleasant. Gone are the days of turmoil, conflict, and despair. Instead, each of you will now find that the destitute situations you found yourselves in before have been replaced by those that are enchanting and ever-lasting for as long as you choose them to be.

"Trust is the single most important thing to my family, and now *our* family. Following this tenet, I expect each of you to be nothing but truthful to not only me but also to your brothers and sisters sitting to the left and right of you. Out of utmost respect for this most sacred vow, it is time to tell you all how the Zaragozas came to be the wealthiest and most powerful family in the world.

"I would love to tell you all that our wealth has been accumulated strictly due to our excellent business acumen throughout the centuries. While this is still true, and my intelligence rivals even that of my greatest ancestors, it does not tell the whole story. The fact is that we were initially blessed with this wealth and now wish to share this blessing with all of you. However, in the same way that we had to do certain things to make sure our wealth and fortune would be maintained continuously for generations, *we will expect each of you to do the same....* Though some of you may be familiar with the term *blessings* in a more vague, nebulous, and ephemeral way, we can assure you our blessings are quite tangible and distinct. Not to undermine any of the religious undertones that some of you may have associated with the word and the things that come with it, we just prefer our *blessings* to have more immediate manifestations, and we now wish to impart the very same things onto you.

"*Bien!* Now that the pleasantries are out of the way, it's time to explain exactly how these *blessings* work. To put it in terms you all can clearly understand, we Zaragozas have the power to be extremely persuasive, and when I say persuasive, I mean *that we get what we want, exactly when we want it.*"

I was always bad at hiding my emotions and now, well, now my mouth was opened wider than a Swiss tunnel at the revelation of what Pierre was telling us candidly, in the most braggadocious of tones. Looking around, I could see faces ranging from incomprehension—similar dispositions to mine—to what even seemed like unabashed ecstasy from a scholar whose eyes were almost twinkling and could barely sit still. Enthusiastic about what, I couldn't say precisely, but it must have to do with the possibility of gaining powers to potentially brainwash, which made me wonder if some recipients were in on this whole potential ploy, too. I doubted this and just attributed it to smart people finally getting the chance to not only be highly intelligent, but also highly influential in ways they were perhaps not before.

Once I gained a sense of everything that was occurring before me, Julie-Marie suddenly appeared on the stage, standing alongside her elder brother. I hadn't seen her since the beginning of orientation, and the saying, "Absence makes the heart grow fonder," might as well have been common knowledge because my heart sunk into my stomach when I laid my eyes on her. Though the crush I had on Julie was akin to a childish one you have when you find a teacher or babysitter attractive, for a moment, I could've sworn that she returned the eye contact that I was showering her with and even turned over a subtle, yet seductive half-smile. I'm not sure if I imagined this or not, but the second I realized it, I immediately broke eye contact and resumed listening to Pierre's speech to act as if I didn't notice what I thought I saw.

Pierre was doing his usual ramblings about how he used his unique talents, apart from his *gifts,* in specific situations to help shape the ZCA into what it is today.

What really caught my attention, though, is when he said,

"The source of these blessings was a munificent, yet merciless, *supernatural being. . . .*"

Sadly the whole supernatural thing did not surprise me at all. What did surprise me was that at no point in his speech did he mention who or what this being (or beings) were—probably in an attempt to save face and put the more religious-minded scholars at ease if this being's nature was not something that they were comfortable being associated with.

No matter his intentions, they worked since no one batted an eye when he made this statement. The final portion of Pierre's speech went into the types of *gifts and talents* we would develop, now that we were also Zaragozas. This segment must've brought him great delight since he could not stop smiling shortly before and after each word, as giddy as a schoolgirl, in ecstasy with the sound of his voice.

"My children, you may wonder how these gifts will manifest in each of you. Worry not! You shall all inherit the primary power of persuasion, the true hallmark of a Zaragoza, the ability to take what's rightfully yours. Not only that, you shall also receive abilities that are unique to you specifically. You may not have known it throughout your twenty-odd years of life, or even when you first arrived at my family's Castillo, but deep within each of you is a great power that has lain dormant by those who do not wish to see you at your full potential. . . . But your full potential is all that we wish for each of you to achieve!

"In the coming weeks, you all will start to experience changes, which at first may frighten you, but as the lowly caterpillar becomes the radiant butterfly, these changes mark the beginning of your future and well-deserved greatness!

The only thing left now to unlock these dormant powers is for each of you to drink this potion that my family has prepared for thousands of years. Worry not; your health is of utmost importance to me, and this beverage will not cause any ill effects, but quite the contrary. . . . Once you drink it, you will be free to leave the great hall and hold your heads up high, as you will be a full member of this great family.

"To show appreciation for your loyalty to our family, you will each be given five thousand euros and a week off to explore Europe, but once you report back, the Second Trials will commence, which will require the use of those specific abilities. . . . Be well, and be great, my glorious children!"

As Pierre's speech came to a close, the cultist fanatics previously located behind the tables seemed to vanish from this location. They were now bringing out buckets of a boiling hot beverage, which smelled like a combination of honey, oats, licorice, and cinnamon. Though the smell of this mysterious beverage was pleasant, the thought of what else it contained disturbed me immensely. Unlike the signing of the loyalty scrolls, the consumption of this beverage could not be fabricated. No bird was going to swoop into the great hall and drink this potion for me! Thinking of ways to once again fool the apostles only led to great frustration, to the point where some recipients probably noticed me aggressively pulling the hairs from my beard, probably thinking I suffered from trichotillomania.

Hair-pulling aside, I was no closer to cleverly getting out of drinking this brew, which could have served a myriad of purposes for why we had to consume it. Was it to augment whatever properties granted to us by signing the loyalty scrolls? Did it serve as some sort of confirmation method to see if we had actually signed the loyalty scrolls? Or was it even more sinister than that, and was actually a time-triggered contingency plan to execute anyone who did not remain loyal to the Zaragoza family? Conspiracies cycled through my mind ceaselessly, like a hamster on a wheel, fueled by amphetamines. Whatever the underlying reason was, I knew one thing: there was no getting out of this one. I took the cup assigned to me, shook it around a bit, channeling my inner James Bond *(Timothy Dalton, of course),* and in unity with the other scholarship recipients, we raised our glasses to Pierre and Julie on the stage and exclaimed, "Salud," as we all downed the mysterious concoction together.

Fortunately, whatever it was, actually did taste quite good. This was, perhaps, the only consolation I could offer myself after ingesting something given to me by a family that just bluntly told us that they parlayed with supernatural beings that granted them *favors*. . . .

Shortly after ingesting the Zaragozas' potion, I noticed myself getting drowsy. In fact, I noticed all of the recipients getting drowsy around 9:30 p.m. I'm not sure if it was a coincidence or not, but if I were to put money on it, I would say probably not.

I wondered if this was the time we would be executed.

My fears spiked, battling with my rising urge to sleep. Unsure of where my roommates were, I returned to my dormitory to find all the lights were off, so instead of making the usual small-talk about the day and any new suspicions any of us had, I went straight into my room and collapsed.

To this day, I'm not sure if what happened next was either a very lucid dream or if it actually happened at all. . . .

As clearly as I can see the trees outside my window, I

could see none other than Julie-Marie Zaragoza at the foot of my bed. An astonishment on its own, but it was what she was wearing that truly had me transfixed—a garment most comparable to what Salma Hayak wore in *From Dusk Til Dawn*, snake and headdress included.

I tried to wake myself up, going through all the usual routines, pinching myself, moving around, and even slapping myself, all to no avail. Julie giggled at my unsuccessful attempts of trying to wake up. Mimicking the movement of the python that was now on the ground, Julie swayed her way closer to me until her lips were close to my ear, softly saying that this was, in fact, reality, and she *knew everything*. . . .

Putting on my best face of pretentiousness, crossing my arms and looking away, I exclaimed, "And what is it that you *think* you know, *she-devil*?!"

In a low and sensual voice that sounded like it was coated in syrup, Julie said that even without the mystical powers granted to her, she could tell from a mile away that *I desired her*. . . . Amazed at how calmly she made this comment, I quickly countered, "How? You have no proof. I don't even know you!" I exclaimed.

Julie smirked, flipped her hair to expose the side of her neck, looked away for a second, then looked right into my soul and said, "Do you really think I didn't see you gawking at me when I was on stage with my brother? Even an idiot would know that when I smirked, *I was acknowledging your gaze*. . . . Not only that, but I also know one of the reasons you accepted this scholarship was to have the opportunity to potentially court me, am I right?"

There I laid, paralyzed by the words that were just emitted

from Julie's impeccable rosé-colored lips. *How could she know? How did she even see me in the crowd? Did she possess telepathic powers, too?!* All of these thoughts rushed through my head as she stood there in what I can only imagine was the pleasure one experiences when they know something that you do not, reveling at the image of your mental cogs running at full capacity. How could I deny this to her? Something that I truly felt, even if it was just lust?

Attempting to flip the proverbial table on her and to make her second-guess her self-assuredness, I retorted, "You're crazy, and I feel no such thing for you, she-devil!"

Well, either she found me to be the greatest comedian in the world, or she had absolute pity for what I had just said. She replied with the type of hysterical laughter that is usually accompanied by tears. This definitely killed any attempt of arrogance that I could muster, as it was clearly evident to her that I was, indeed, lying. Once she regained her composure, she again leaned into me and whispered in my ear, "What if I told you *I felt the same way the second my eyes met yours?"*

I couldn't believe what I just heard and impulsively blurted out, "I beg your pardon, lady?!"

She didn't hesitate to make herself clear: "What if you being here is not only about receiving our generous scholarship. . . .?"

She ended the sentence with a soft kiss on my cheek as if it were the punctuation mark on a highly tantalizing sentence. My body abandoned me, and it felt like I was melting, blood rushing to the smaller head as my brain started to give in to something that was once thought of as only a fantasy. Examining my current condition, Julie-Marie smiled and winked and told me that I could no longer deny what was in my heart and *pants*, and in a moment of weakness, I sheepishly asked what I had to do in order to live out this fantasy to its fullest.

She said simply, "Remain loyal not only to my brother and me but to your newfound brothers and sisters. Most importantly, stay loyal to *the cause*, and we could live out this fantasy of *ours*. . . ."

She disappeared as quickly as she had appeared, which, I have to admit, was quite rude of her. Still not entirely convinced if what I had just experienced was reality or fiction, I knew that if it felt real, it didn't matter if it wasn't; I heard the message loud and clear, and it had me second-guess everything in a heartbeat.

Chapter 5: The Party

The next morning, I awoke to my roommates already having breakfast and, of course, Rafi was there as well, which brought a comforting feeling knowing that everyone I trusted was here around me. Starving, I quickly jumped out of bed and joined my friends in the dormitory's common space.

Ever the clown, Paul gregariously said, "Oi, mate, only the early birds get the worm!"

On any other morning, I would have returned with some snappy retort, but still being perplexed about the happenings of the previous night, I sighed and simply replied, "Fine, I'll get something for myself."

Paul sensed that something wasn't A-okay with me, apologized, and brought me a sausage and egg croissant with a steaming mug of my favorite, Earl Grey tea. I was greatly appreciative of the type of friends who innately knew when to *push and pull,* which suited my introverted nature.

After I finished my breakfast, I went to shower to feel refreshed and try to forget about what happened last night, to no avail. Unable to get Julie's image and what she said out of my head, I tried to preoccupy myself with different thoughts and asked what my roommates and Rafi had been up to last night.

"Well, after we drank their potion, we headed to the game room for a round of table tennis," Rafi answered.

Here they were, getting all warm and fuzzy to the person ***I*** introduced them to! And to think they initially thought he was a weirdo!

Confused, I asked, "Weren't you all suddenly drowsy last night, though?"

"Not at all!" James answered on their behalf. "After drinking the potion, we were all amped to go out and do something. We tried looking for you but figured you had other plans, so we met up with Rafi and met some other cool recipients, too."

Questioning my sanity, I exclaimed, "But how?! I saw all of the recipients getting drowsy just like I did, and went to bed!"

Sarah asked if I was okay and if maybe I was taking recent events too hard.

I went into the bathroom, cupped some water in my hands, and splashed it onto my face. I knew I wasn't going crazy . . . or at least I was pretty sure? Did the potion affect all of us in different ways? Did I imagine other recipients getting drowsy to subconsciously justify myself going to sleep so early? No, it couldn't be. I know what I saw, I know what I felt. It was real. . . .

Regaining my composure, I invited Rafi, Paul, Sarah, and James into my room and told them that I had to tell them something. They knew I was serious from my demeanor, so they all came without hesitation. Once we were seated, I told them exactly what happened after I drank the mysterious concoction.

"Guys, I swear to you, once I drank the potion, I got super sleepy around 9:30 p.m. and saw other recipients get sleepy, too. I didn't really think much of it and just assumed it was a way to have us all sleep around the same time since so much happened in the day, and the Zaragozas probably wanted us to sleep soundly before our week-long vacation started. When I got back to the dorm, all the lights were off, so I figured you all didn't make it back in yet, so I just went into my room and fell asleep. Normal enough, right? Well, the weird part was, I saw Julie-Marie Zaragoza appear at the foot of my bed and—"

"Wait!" James interjected. "She was in your room? Near your bed?! Sounds like some sort of erotic dream. We all know how much you like her. How is that weird?!"

"Be patient!" Rafi interjected.

"Yeah, let him finish," Sarah added.

"Thank you, but yeah, I was getting there, James. Anyway, I thought it was a dream, too, so I tried to wake up; I even tried slapping myself. The thing is, though, nothing worked and she wouldn't disappear from my sight. She even mocked my attempts at waking up. What kind of dream is like that?"

"Mate, you sure you're okay? You look all out of sorts," Paul said, his face scrunched up as though I looked like death itself.

"Yes, I promise, guys, there's nothing wrong with me!" I screamed, growing agitated from all the accusations and insinuations. "The point of this story is not Julie appearing near my bed; it's what she said to me. . . . She basically told me that *we* could be together if I stayed loyal to her, the family, the cause, and you all."

"Be loyal to us? She knows us about our little gang, too?" James interrupted again.

"No, dude, I meant *you guys,* as in all of you, as in all the other ZNBS recipients! She said especially my *brothers and sisters*, but I was just paraphrasing. . . ."

"How the fuck does she know you're into her?" James said in an enthusiastic yet slightly terrified manner.

"Yeah, that's what I don't get, either. I mean, yeah, when Pierre gave his speech, and she came on, I did look at her for a second or two, or three, and I thought I saw her smile back at me, but obviously, that was just by chance, as she could've been smiling at anyone and everyone. But she told me in my dream, or whatever that was, that she was acknowledging that she saw me looking at her."

"That's some freaky shite, mate, I gotta say," Paul added.

"*You think*? Ahh, I thought everything that has been occurring in this haunted household was quite normal, in fact," I sarcastically quipped.

Being the voice of reason, Sarah stepped in and said, "Guys, you all tried in your own ways to motivate me to stay the course and remain strong, no matter what strange stuff has happened or will happen. Yet, you can't believe when Femi is saying that the second-in-line for the Zaragoza family fortune—who just so happens to be ridiculously hot—doesn't have some sort of power to manipulate after her brother *just* told us that the main hallmark of being a Zaragoza is persuasiveness?!"

"Thank you, Sarah," I exalted. "Yes, it is a bit convenient that Julie, the woman I had a crush on, appeared in my dream, or whatever that was, but out of all the weird shit that has been

happening here, you guys are really calling me out on this?!"

"He's right," Rafi said after remaining silent for a while. "We can't count anything out when it comes to the Zaragozas. Their connection to evil is very strong, and that could possibly be clouding our minds, and by extension, our judgment, as well. I mean, even Yoda and the entire Jedi Council couldn't detect that the most powerful Sith Lord known to man was the leader of their treasured Republic. We need to be extra vigilant from here on out. If that drink we consumed made Femi drowsy but didn't affect us in the same way, who knows what lingering effects it could possibly have on us?"

"*Finally some freaking support,*" I murmured under my breath. "I have a proposal. It may sound crazy, but hear me out, okay?"

"We're all ears, lover boy," Paul said, throwing a mocking salute at me.

"Good one, Paul," I swiftly said before he could add anything further to his comment.

"Instead of traveling around Europe for our week off, I say we explore the neighboring towns and villages and see what or who we can find that might have deeper insight into the Zaragozas. What do you all say?"

Unsurprisingly, Paul went first. "I have to be honest mate, I was really keen on going to Paris. I mean, fucking hell, we have five thousand euros to burn!"

"Yeah, I second that. Let's live a little before we have to come back to this freak show. I know how much it means to you to get to the bottom of this conspiracy, but who knows the next time we'll have this much free time to do whatever we want, and in Europe, no less?" James followed.

I understood where they were coming from; ever since I sprung Rafi's theory on the gang, it had been quite the whirlwind of events. So, I waited a few seconds to see if Rafi or Sarah were going to say anything before I tried to plead my case. I took their silence as indifference and went ahead.

"Guys, I know what I'm asking from each of you is inconsiderate; heck, I know I shouldn't even be asking this in the first place. But ever since Rafi and I brought this theory to you, you all have been nothing but supportive in helping me figure out what the fuck is going on here. Unfortunately, I'm going to have to make that hard ask once more. In the same way that we may never have the chance to explore Europe with free money, we now have the one-time opportunity to get out of this Castillo and talk to the neighboring towns to see what they know.

"Moreover, we even have some cash to bribe the truth out of them, if need be! I'm truly sorry I got you all into this, but we, and only we, have a real chance to right this wrong that has been going on for God knows how long. It really is up to us, and we've invested so much into it already. Why give up now?

"I implore you all, please do this with me." Trying to gauge the room's atmosphere was a bit difficult, as everyone stood there quietly and attentively, not entirely sure if they were convinced by my plea or just sick of my ramblings about justice yadda yadda.

Luckily, I did not have to wait long, as Rafi was predictably the first one to come stand on the other side of the room where I was. What came next was more of a surprise as Sarah approached with her head down but took surefooted steps. I was not sure if her head was down due to being fatigued by all of this or because she did not want to make eye contact with the others.

Nevertheless, her actions spoke louder than any words could, anyway. I took her hand to make her feel more at ease, which she responded to with a firm grip of mine. Shortly after, James joined us as well, and only Paul was the odd man out.

We didn't wait long for Paul. In typical fashion, he made light of the previous tense situation by laughing it off, saying with a groan then a cheeky smile, "Who needs Paris when you have elderly Spanish townspeople?"

Not wanting to be the ultimate Buzz Killington, I tried to at least get the gang back into good spirits before we ventured off into town on an aimless adventure.

I vaguely remembered overhearing Pierre and Julie talk about going on an important business trip, just as our unofficial vacation was supposed to start, and I didn't have to wait long before what I thought I had heard was confirmed.

Not long after we concluded in our room, we overheard what sounded like a half-dozen SUVs enter the Castillo's main entrance to pick up the Zaragozas and escort them to their private airport about ten kilometers away from the estate. It was official, then: We had the entire Castillo to ourselves, meaning only one thing—well, actually, a combination of many things that lead into the one thing: *p-a-r-t-y!* Or in other words, use this opportunity to get to know the other scholars who were sharing the Castillo with us. Because if there was one thing that would help us reach out to more scholars, it would be free alcohol!

I didn't realize how little I knew the other recipients outside the group due to how close our gang was, so this was the perfect opportunity for us to get to know some of the other young adults who were sharing this mansion with us. The first two people I thought of were the other American in the program, Grace, and Tolu, the Nigerian recipient.

I knew little about Grace—only that, unlike me, she was from the West Coast. California, I believe it was, and that she was Asian American. It wasn't hard to find Tolu, as his dorm was only a few doors down the hall from mine. Tracking down Grace was going to be harder since I barely saw her throughout the program and didn't know in which part of the Castillo her dorm was located.

When I approached Tolu's door, he was on his way out with his roommate, Amir, an English-born Lebanese, dual M.D./Ph.D. postdoctoral student that I met during one of the banquets the Zaragozas hosted for us when we first arrived. Amir was a soft-spoken guy who always gave me a good vibe. Already a freshly graduated medical student, his demeanor came off as empathic yet self-assured—no doubt qualities that would help him mature into an excellent doctor with commendable bedside manner. But Amir was also a Ph.D. postdoc, so he was as cerebral as he was caring.

"*Amir, baby!*" I said, gesticulating to him like my name was Fabrizio instead of Femi. When we first met, we were sitting next to the Italian recipient, Luca, and our thing was to always mimic his mannerisms and intricate hand gestures whenever we saw each other.

"Ahh, Femi! *Como va?*"

"I'm sorry?" I said.

"It means 'how are you' in Italian!"

"Oh, well, I guess I wasn't sitting next to Luca long enough to actually learn Italian," I joked. Catching up briefly, I asked

Amir what he and Tolu were going to do for the evening. Amir replied that he and Tolu were going to one of the many recreational rooms to play table tennis with a few other recipients. Seeing this as a prime opportunity to practice my left-handed backhand serve as well as inviting more scholars to this last-minute soiree of mine, I asked if I could tag along, and he cheerfully agreed.

Tolu was an interesting guy, the kind of guy, I think, who would've been completely different personality-wise if he were born in a different place. Tolu was the kind of guy who was super serious in his studies, which didn't surprise me based on how hard my Nigerian parents pushed academics down the throats of me and my siblings.

There was also a softer side to him, too. Tolu had eccentric (by traditional Nigerian standards) hobbies and interests. He was fanatically into ice hockey and maple syrup; he must've been Canadian in a past life, although I'm not sure how well his bald head would fair in Canada's climate.

What I didn't know about Tolu was that, although he worked hard, he played even harder and even carried a flask of Scotch with him, which lined up nicely with my evening plans of collective intoxication.

Amir must've gotten to Tolu's flask early because once we started to play, his usually fast-paced and explosive style was replaced with one that was more relaxed—so relaxed that he even missed the ball with the paddle a few times.

"Miss any more shots by that much again, I'll probably have to record it and make it viral: 'English doctor who is ridiculously horrible at Ping-Pong.' I can see the headlines now," I teased.

"A sudden interest in things that are alive for a change, is it, then?" Amir said with a wry smile right as the minuscule orange ball whizzed past his face.

"I would focus more on the game than on my degrees!" I retorted.

We played a few more matches and had a few swigs out of Tolu's flask. With some extra motivation from the Scotch, I climbed on the pool table across from us and yelled in typical American fashion, *"Who wants to get fucked up tonight!?"* Being in a room full of acclaimed scholars and researchers did not prevent the customary response of thunderous applause and jubilation, which only meant one thing: full steam ahead for the party!

In the room adjacent to us were halves of the Japanese, Panamanian, Australian, and Finnish ZNBS recipients who I did not know at all, but they all seemed to be nice enough and even offered to help me in terms of getting the invites out. Keito was a Japanese guy of Ainu descent, the indigenous people from the part of Japan that bordered Russia. Before meeting him, I did not know that this ethnic group even existed or what they would look like, but Keito was a handsome and nice enough guy. He reminded me of what a Japanese movie star would look like if they had the grizzly appearance of an outdoorsman, equally rugged as he was easy on the eyes.

Keito played a key role in arranging this get-together. You see, for some unknown reason, Keito knew where the communication room for the whole Castillo was, and this would be the perfect time to use its resources to make sure everyone in the Castillo was on the same page.

After emptying Tolu's flask, Keito, Tolu, Amir, and I went to the comms room and boldly activated the PA system to issue our announcement: "Girls and guys of the Castillo, I don't know each and every one of you, but I think it is high time that we had a break from all this ZNBS shit and drink till we drop. Who agrees? If you're down to have a good time, let's meet in the great hall in about two hours, and bring in this vacation properly!"

Although I didn't exactly know who was in support of this impromptu party, I could vaguely hear thunderous applause after I'd said, "Who agrees?" which I took as a good sign!

The next item on the list was going to be figuring out the situation regarding food and drinks. The service staff had their own quarters in the Castillo. They usually remained on the grounds just in case the Zaragozas had any impromptu gatherings coming up or if they had to attend to some wealthy businessperson or royal dignitary. The only thing was I didn't know if we had access to the same sort of services offered to Pierre and Julie-Marie. Again, in my mind, weren't we all considered family?

Maybe it was half due to the Scotch whiskey and half to not wanting to disappoint my friends, but I took a deep breath and mustered up enough courage to actually enter the service quarters and ask the majordomo if we could have some hors d'oeuvres. The majordomo oozed an intimidating presence standing at least 6' 9". He easily towered over everyone I've seen thus far in Spain—and everyone I've *ever* seen, to be honest! He was also a particularly slender man, accentuated by his extended gait that always looked like he was walking in slow motion. His face didn't do him any favors; his piercing gray eyes, enclosed with the smallest of pupils, made it look like he was devoid of any emotion. He was absent of all hair except a thinning hairline and a pencil-like mustache that would make any French private eye proud.

He looked at me, eyebrows furrowed, squinting, head slightly tilted as if I had asked him to give me his pants or something. His reaction worried me and I feared that my glorious plans of hosting the best party the Castillo had ever seen were imploding before it even began.

As I began to walk away, the majordomo stopped me and yelled in a surprisingly soft voice, "Wait! I was just wondering what we could serve up for you children, as I'm sure your tastes aren't as refined as Señor and Señora Zaragoza."

I didn't really take this as an insult since he was probably right, nor did I care because I just wanted something delicious to eat, no matter how expensive or cheap it was. After going back and forth about what his staff would prepare, he came to me with only two requests. The staff would stop serving food past 11 p.m., and after the party, he and his staff would be allowed to drink once they were done.

I initially took these requests as a joke. I thought, These requests weren't a problem at all. Does this guy even know how to play hard to get?

Not giving him a chance to negotiate, I smiled, reached out my hand, and made the agreement official with a firm but not overbearing handshake. Minutes after the deal was finalized, I realized I hadn't mentioned *drinks,* yet one of the majordomo's requests was that his staff would be allowed to drink. This excited me because that meant *drinks,* whether stated or not, would be provided. I didn't make a big fuss about going back to him to talk about specifics, the logic being if the drinks provided are good enough for the CEO and CFO of a multi-trillion dollar company, they should be just fine for us!

After everything was pretty much set in motion, I first went back into the comms room to thank Keito, Amir, and Tolu for all the help along the way promising that we should all get closer to each other. They agreed and stuck around in the room for a bit, fiddling with all the gadgets and gizmos in the communications room, while I hurried back to my dorm to see how my friends would react to my impromptu party.

"Hope you guys are ready to get *wasssteeddd* tonight!" I said, swinging my tongue out.

Without missing a beat, Paul said, "I've been waiting all week for this, mate!"

It made me happy that there were no hard feelings about getting them to come along with me, rather than enjoying their much-needed vacation around Europe. I took this as a sign that I could really trust these people, which made me feel really optimistic about the whole ordeal. James and Rafi couldn't believe that I had arranged the whole thing in less than an hour. But in all honesty, it wasn't that hard, given that the Castillo pretty much did the work for me. I was just the catalyst to set the reaction in motion.

As we were all cleaning up and getting ready for the party, we could hear people scurrying down the halls, most likely trying to get their preferred spots in the great hall before the party officially started. For a moment, I felt overwhelmed by the number of footsteps that I could hear. "Fuck. What if this gets out of hand, and I get expelled from the program?" I said to myself.

Surely the Zaragozas will know that I was the mastermind behind this whole thing; I had been on their intercom, for goodness' sake! Nevertheless, it wasn't anything a few pre-drinks couldn't solve and before 10 p.m. arrived, we were already on our way to the great hall to have a night I hoped we would never forget. As we entered the great hall, a mixture of deep house and trip-hop music was blasting not so loudly that you couldn't have a conversation but loud enough that you knew tonight was just about drinking, mingling, dancing and, most importantly, not thinking about the consequences of any next-day hangovers.

Focusing on every minute detail, I forgot to think about the most important duty of all. Who would be handling the music? Luckily for me, the ever-astute majordomo and his staff had set up all the audio equipment, and Amir took it upon himself to be the resident DJ (which was very much appreciated).

True to his word, the majordomo had his staff walking around serving an assortment of delicious finger foods. To my amazement, even champagne was being offered, definitely making the affair that much classier. As the night and drinks went on, I lost the group and found myself wandering through the crowd, hearing a range of different languages and dialects being spoken. The strange experience of being inundated with so many different sounds so quickly made me feel like I was on something stronger than just alcohol. But it was a good feeling to see all of these nerds letting loose for once.

Looking to regroup with my friends, while stumbling through collections of human semi-circles, I got my back slapped and sprinkled with comments such as, "Great party, man" and "Perfect timing," and my personal favorite, "*Thank God for American parties*!"

After wandering around aimlessly looking for my friends,

I faintly heard my name being called behind me. It was none other than Grace, all 4' 9" of her. "Femi! I've been looking for you—"

Before she could finish, I interrupted her. "Grace! I've been looking for you, too!"

After exchanging pleasantries, I was really interested in what part of the Castillo she stayed in. So I asked rather abruptly—due to which, thinking back on how glazed my eyes looked, she probably thought I was asking for a more carnal purpose. . . . Whatever she thought my reason for asking was, she replied kindly and without suspicion, "Oh, I live in the southwest quarter."

"Ah, that makes sense," I said. "That's why I've never run into you. I'm in the northeast quarter, so we probably don't even take the same corridors!"

"Yeah, that probably explains it," she said, spinning the mini umbrella in her neon-colored beverage before she went in for a sip.

"Well, I hope this isn't awkward, but what are you?" she asked with a blank stare.

"Huh?" I responded. Genuinely confused for a second or two and then slightly insulted, I realized she was asking for my ethnic background since a prerequisite for the scholarship was being a minority in some sense that could be proven and accepted. "Oh, right, right. I'm Nigerian American," I tried to say coolly, like I understood the question right off the bat.

"Oh, that's interesting that they allowed a Nigerian American in, considering how overrepresented you all are in higher education and professional services—not only in America but also worldwide—but that's nice. Congrats!" Grace said.

I looked at her in a puzzled way, and if I weren't drunk, I would've probably taken some more offense to the comment. "Well, what do you mean? A minority is a minority, no matter how much their specific ethnic group pursues higher education, no?"

"Yeah, no, you're right. I'm just saying, I would've thought the Zaragozas were aware of other ethnic groups in America that weren't already so well-represented. . . ."

Interjecting because I wanted to move the conversation along and didn't want her to ruin my buzz any further, I finally asked what her ethnic background was. Obviously, I could see that she was of Asian ancestry, and I didn't want to be one of those douchebags who just automatically assumed she was either Japanese or Chinese, even though I had quite a few Asian friends and could readily see the distinctions between each country. It didn't matter, though, because Grace told me that she was Hmong American.

Hmong American? I thought. I've never heard of such an ethnic group before. In hindsight, maybe she was right because my minority status was, in fact, *triumphed* by Grace's background. Insatiably curious to learn more about Grace's ethnicity, I asked who exactly were the Hmong people? As I asked this question, I could immediately tell that she was comforted by my inquisitiveness. The snarky demeanor that perhaps served as her shield gradually diminished as she slowly started to let her guard down.

"Well, let's just say we're the Asians who benefit from no sort of Asian American model-minority privilege bullshit, and in a lot of cases fare even worse economically than many African and Hispanic Americans."

Ah, even worse than us Black people, eh? Didn't know it got any worse than that in America. I chuckled in my head. "Tell me more," I said as I leaned in closer to her, trying to establish some sort of familiarity so that she felt comfortable enough to speak freely.

"Well, yeah, our people primarily emigrated from Northern Laos by way of Southern China during and after the Vietnam War because we sided with the Americans and needed refugee status once the war was over."

"Wow, I didn't know that."

"Yeah, unfortunately, not a lot of people do. Despite looking at us and supposing that we benefit from *Asian American privilege,* it actually makes the situation worse because we lose out on a lot of aid that could really benefit our community by people just thinking we're one large monolith of successful Asians."

Wanting to learn more, but still desperate to find my friends, I told Grace that I had to meet up with my friends but to not be a stranger. I said we should catch up again soon, and she returned a politician-like smile that I couldn't tell was genuine or not, and said, "Sure, I would like that."

Don't get me wrong—I enjoyed what little conversation I had with Grace. Learning about new peoples and cultures is always very stimulating for me mentally, but I was in the mood just to have a good time. Using critical thinking skills was not on the agenda for tonight, and to my great disdain, getting so serious actually sobered me up. Not only that, though, for her diminutive frame and her high-pitched voice, I couldn't shake the feeling that Grace was actually a wolf in sheep's clothing. In a sense, we all were, but for some reason, my intuition told me to be careful about how much I shared around her. . . .

Looking to quickly regain the optimal level of inebriation that I had been enjoying, I returned to the punch bowl. I topped off my red plastic cup with a curious mixture of what tasted like whiskey, rum, and berry-flavored mixers. As I turned around and began walking toward the last place I remembered seeing my friends, I ran into Rafi.

"Dude, where have you been? We've been looking for you!"

"I've been looking for you guys, too!" I replied with a bear hug.

"No worries. We actually broke off from the great hall, and we were hanging out with some other recipients in the lounge. Follow me. I'll introduce you!"

As I followed Rafi, I couldn't help but feel proud that the party was a success, and I was overcome with a momentary feeling of euphoria that amplified the effects of the alcohol.

Once we arrived at the lounge, I saw Paul, James, Sarah, and some other recipients I did not recognize playing some sort of role-playing board game that looked pretty fun. Seeing a free space near Sarah, I made my way to occupy the seat when I was greeted by a boisterous, "Hey, look who it is!"

Looking at the faces of the recipients that I didn't know, I could tell from their wide eyes and puzzled smiles, they were actively trying to figure out who I was, too, and what my relationship was with the people they have been spending their evening with. I extended my hand, politely greeted everyone, and then asked how they knew my dorm mates. The girl sitting near Paul spoke first.

She told me that her name was Athena and she was from Greece.

"With a name like that, how could you be from anywhere else?" I teased, which made her crack a warm smile at me.

"I'm Femi, nice to meet you. I'm the guy who tried to set this evening up."

"Well done, man. I knew it was only a matter of time before someone set this up," said the West African-looking guy who sat across from James.

"Ha, thanks, buddy. I really thought we could all use it, considering all the shit we've been through thus far. By the way, what's your name?" I asked.

"Kofi. My name is Kofi."

"Let me guess: You're from Ghana, right?"

"Yep, you got it. How did you know?" my new friend asked.

Unable to control my laughter and being a bit disinhibited from the series of mystery alcohols I'd been downing for the past hour, I responded, "Well, just like your friend, Athena, here, your names are a dead giveaway from where you two are from."

Kofi had these massive brown eyes that looked like psychic crystal balls painted brown. His eyes even had the same brilliance those crystal balls had, which made looking at him for prolonged periods a tad uncomfortable.

Last but not least, definitely in terms of presence, was a guy and a girl who were passionately making out in the corner. "And who might you two be?" I yelled on purpose to make them uncomfortable.

Paul jumped in and said, "That's Aiman from Malaysia and Sofie from Romania."

"Well, I'm glad if my party did one thing: It brought two strangers together romantically," I joked. I asked what the next game would be since the role-playing board game was coming to an end. At least, I thought it was, judging by the way James aggressively swiped all the pieces off the board and yelled, "Excelsior!" which I thought was kind of a weird thing to say, but at least he was happy, right?

Once the awkward silence of not doing anything started to settle in, Sarah astonishingly stood up and said, "Why don't we play a drinking game?" which caught those of us who knew her completely off guard.

Staying true to his nature, Paul was the first person to show his eagerness by excitedly jumping and exclaiming that he knew just the game to play!

The idea of playing a drinking game was also enough to get Aiman and Sofie to give each other their faces back, which was greatly appreciated by everyone in the room, since the extended make-out session was pretty uncomfortable.

"Well, what are we gonna play?" asked Rafi.

Paul returned with a college drinking game staple: "Never Have I Ever."

The way the game worked was that a person says the words "Never Have I Ever" followed by something that they have not done, in the hopes that someone else has done whatever was stated, forcing them to take one sip or gulp (*depending on who you're playing with*) of their alcoholic beverage. Additionally, each participant has to hold up one of their hands, palm extended, so that they can bring a finger back into their palm and drink each time they have done whatever was just stated. Many game strategies exist, and some people purposely ask questions that are very sexual in nature. They attempt to draw out those who are more sensually attenuated, and to add another layer of intrigue to the game by seeing what your co-players have or haven't done.

As with any drinking game, there are always those who never quite understand the game's principle of getting everyone drunk, except yourself, and ask questions that have been completed by almost everyone. Either that or they just enjoy making themselves drink, as well!

NHIE was always one of my favorite games, and my go-to strategy was to always be the provocateur and ask the most esoteric things, providing deeper insight into my nature. After Paul explained how the game operated, it was quite clear that Kofi and Athena didn't exactly understand how to play because they kept asking questions about things that they had already done. But as I stated earlier, either they could've done this on purpose to further intoxicate themselves, or they just played naïve extremely well. No matter their reasoning, we always got a kick out of re-explaining the game to them in an increasingly comical and monotonous tone.

Continuing a night of surprises from Sarah, we were all quite impressed when some of the questions such as, "Never have I ever skinny-dipped," "been in a parachute," or "been to a strip club," made her put her fingers down. As the game continued, it was becoming rather apparent to all of us that there was more to Sarah than we were initially led to believe. Here we had thought of her as this shy and demure Scandinavian girl whose only wish was to keep her head down and steadfastly pursue her goals. Yet, after a couple of drinks, this image of an adventurous and free-spirited girl who didn't mind accepting a dare started to emerge. James and Paul mocked her for a bit, stating things such as, "Where has this Sarah been hiding?" and asking whether she was one of those undercover sexual deviants, which could've come off as a bit impolite if they hadn't known her so well.

Not wanting them to have the last word, she calmly

responded with a cool wink, topped up with an even cooler remark: "And here, I thought you guys were smart enough not to judge a book by its cover. "

As the night was winding down—and after numerous drinks, getting to know some of the wildest things we each have done and trying to drunkenly remember the rules to various card games—we decided to eventually call it a night. First off was the newly created couple of Aiman and Sofie, who I thought would've disappeared long ago to discover the rest of each other's anatomies.

Next to bed was Rafi, who wanted to wake up early to catch the sunrise while jogging around the estate's immediate surroundings. Quite a noble feat after a night of drinking, and I vaguely remember being so amazed by this goal that I perhaps stated I would join him.

Athena was off to meet up with her compatriot, Krystos, who was still in the great hall with the other Mediterranean students. Kofi, James, and Paul went off to see if they could procure recipes for the evening's hors d'oeuvres, no doubt embarking on a drunken adventure that would soon become a tale. This latest turn of events left Sarah and me as the only remaining recipients in the lounge.

After sitting for a while in only a mildly awkward silence this time, I asked if she would like a nightcap. Maybe it was lost in translation or just attributed to us thinking about different usages of the phrase, but as I said this, I noticed her pale Norwegian cheeks suddenly blush, matching the red blouse she had on. I thought that perhaps she was embarrassed to have one more drink, considering that we all drank rather heavily already. Not long after, I realized my usage of the word probably differed from what Sarah was thinking when she snapped back, "What kind of girl do you think I am, Femi?"

Flustered and not wanting to send any mixed signals, I quickly tried to clarify the misunderstanding by stating I was only talking about one more glass of whiskey before heading off to bed. She smiled, agreed, and stated that, despite new revelations by us discovering that she was more *liberated* than we previously thought, that didn't mean she was easy.

I was almost laughing, not because anything she was stating was explicitly humorous *(though, in a sense, it was)*, but mainly due to the fact that in all this time, it had never occurred to me that Sarah was not being her full authentic self with us, for whatever reason.

After extensively pleading my case that my request was completely innocent and not wanting to ruin our friendship, Sarah came closer to where I was now seated. Looking at me, she pressed her hands into my cheeks and said, "No one has ever believed in me the way you do. You're a great friend, Femi." She gave me a soft kiss on the forehead, took one final sip of her glass, and left the lounge.

This left me completely befuddled, since I didn't know if Sarah was developing feelings for me, or if it was just a case of drunken spontaneity. Whatever the case may be, there was a part of me that enjoyed the moment, even if it was just ephemeral. By the time I exited the lounge, it must've been around five in the morning because I could see the sun starting to rise through a nearby window.

The great hall was already tidied up, leaving no trace of the vivacious activities that had taken place just hours before. I put a mental reminder to thank the majordomo before departing for our local adventure. Were it not for him and his staff, the event would've surely been a bust, possibly leaving my friends feeling a bit dejected before going on our *local adventure* (as I was starting to think of it), without even enjoying a night off from our investigation.

Chapter 6: The ZRC

Before heading up to my room, I heard a sound of what I could only imagine was someone either vigorously exercising in place or jumping up and down at the crack of dawn—the former being more likely.

I decided to investigate and found that being true to his word, it was none other than Rafi, getting ready for that run that I was supposed to accompany him on. Mocking my current condition, Rafi sarcastically asked if I was still up for some *light cardio*.

"Sorry man, I—"

I tried to laugh it off, but before I could finish my sentence, Rafi interjected, chuckling and saying, "Looks like you had a pretty late night, brother; let's take a rain check. I don't want you vomiting all over my new sneakers, anyway!"

Too tired and hungover to mutter anything meaningful or coherent, I responded in the first way that came to mind: snapping my fingers and doing the *finger guns thing* and telling him that he was the best.

He smiled back and jogged out of the main entrance and cried, "Yeah, I know," in the distance.

When I returned to the dorm, I entered to see James, Paul, and Amir passed out on the common room sofa. I didn't understand why Amir was in our room as opposed to his, but I figured whenever there's one drunk Brit, another couldn't be too far away!

I was too dog-tired to bother removing the clothes and other various items from my bed before sleeping, so I just passed out on top of them and the rest was history.

Waking up about six hours later, I was surprised to hear the amount of commotion that was taking place in the living room. *Am I the only one who was drinking last night? How the hell are these people up and about already?* I thought. I then realized that they hadn't shared the burden of planning the previous night that they all so enjoyed, fittingly justifying my late-starting day.

Feeling groggy, disoriented, and still having a faint taste of alcohol on my breath that made me gag, I headed first to the bathroom to brush my teeth and shower, hoping that it would relieve some of the discomforts I was feeling. As I exited the shower, I could hear what sounded like Sarah and Paul shouting my name. Not having time to properly dress, I stepped out in my bath towel to see what couldn't wait for me to get dressed.

Being the solid friends that I knew them to be, I arrived in the kitchen to the perfect hangover cure of a greasy cheeseburger prepared with the finest blend of Argentine brisket and short rib, accompanied not only with steak-cut fries, but also with a generous serving of miso soup. If this meal were a superhero, its arch-villain would no doubt be vile hangovers! Tears of joy came streaming down my face, which Paul and James quickly teased me over. I couldn't care less; I had a hot and delicious meal right in front of me that I had done nothing for and the time to devour it was now.

After scarfing down the hefty meal, I then asked if they had eaten, to which Sarah responded, "Yes, we all had the same thing while you slept."

Paul responded with a cheeky, "Oh, now you ask about us!" making me spit out the Singaporean lemon iced tea that I was downing the meal with.

Feeling full and now ready to take the day by its horns, I quickly stood up, forgetting all I had on was a towel, which dropped off me, revealing my birthday suit to all of my friends, Sarah included—another moment that made me the *butt* of future jokes, pun definitely intended.

Returning to my room to finally get dressed, the enchanting yet tryptophan-laced meal pulled me into a food coma that lasted about two hours, helping me to catch up to my normal eight and a half hours of sleep, but delaying my day further into the mid-afternoon.

Feeling well-rested and still quite full, I *finally* dressed myself and went into the common room to watch some TV before getting started with the day's activities.

Unexpectedly, in the common room, were also Amir and Tolu alongside the usual bunch of Rafi, James, Paul, and Sarah. I didn't understand what was going on, but by the contemplative yet forlorn looks on Amir's and Tolu's faces, I knew that it could only mean one thing. . . .

The gang had told Amir and Tolu about our theory regarding the Castillo, and by extension, what the Zaragozas as a whole were up to. . . At first, I was apprehensive about anyone outside of our little group knowing what we thought the Zaragozas' underlying reason for hosting the scholarship was—a thought that I relayed to the group after asking them to come into the kitchen to discuss the possible ramifications in private.

"What the fuck were you guys thinking? We can't just let anyone and everyone know what we think Pierre and Julie are up to! Not only is it dangerous for us, but we are also putting them in potential grave danger if at any point suspicions are raised!"

Sensing that I had started to spiral out of control, Rafi calmly put his hand on my shoulder and told me to relax. "We can trust them," he said smoothly.

"And how are you so sure?" I immediately shot back.

"Well, last night while you were still in the lounge and we left, Amir and Tolu joined us back here to hang out."

I genuinely liked both Tolu and Amir, so I didn't want to make a scene within the range of their ears, so I asked my friends to join me in my room to finish the conversation.

"Annnnddd? What does this have to do with telling them our secret?" I demanded.

Chiming in, as well, James added, "Femi, they actually had their suspicions, too, and basically asked us what we thought!"

Starting to calm down, I finally listened closely to what my friends were trying to tell me, rather than just hearing it. "Jesus, how did this come about, though?" I said with a heavy sigh.

"As all things do, my friend: with a bit of alcohol, of course!" Paul answered. Admittedly, his answer was funny, but I did not want to give him the satisfaction of seeing my teeth.

"But no, seriously, how?" I asked.

"I'm serious, as well, mate."

My friends' demeanor removed all signs of doubt and uncertainty that I had, from how intently Rafi looked into my eyes, barely blinking, to how slowly and methodically Paul was speaking to me, contrasting greatly from his usual cadence that was more varied for comedic effect.

"Look, Femi," Paul said. "Once we left the lounge, we came back here for more drinks, and Amir was the first to ask if anyone else thought the unusual content that was covered during orientation—coupled with the weird drink we had to consume, as well as the monks showing up—was a bit strange and occult-like.

"Furthermore, he told us that he and Tolu have had these thoughts for a while. Once that was revealed, Rafi came out and told them that not only did we agree with them, we told them what we believe is actually going on, alongside the motivation behind it and all."

After hearing everything the gang had told them, it seemed that Amir and Tolu were convinced that we could be onto something and wanted to offer their assistance, in whatever capacity they could.

Feeling relieved that at least my friends trusted these two—especially Rafi since the whole thing was based on his theory—I agreed that we should bring them into any potential plans. The only condition I had was that before bringing any more new recipients into our plans, we had to unanimously agree first.

The idea of expanding the members of our little group was exciting and terrifying at the same time. If this didn't end well, it would absolutely devastate me, knowing that I had a role to play in anyone's unfortunate demise. . . . At the same time, though, increasing the number of people who supported our theory also made us stronger and more credible to future members. But more importantly, it made us better able to take on the Zaragozas as a united front.

"Well, if we're increasing in members, we need to make it official, right? We need to have a name, something people could get behind," said James.

"Well, any ideas then?" I asked.

"What about the ZEF: the Zaragoza Evil Fighters? The acronym sure sounds cool when said like a word," Paul said.

"Nah, sounds too video-gamey," Sarah said, and we all agreed.

"I have an idea; let's call it the UFZD: the United Front of Zaragoza Deniers!" James said giddily.

"That's a mouthful," I replied. Finally, I asked, "What about the ZRC?"

"Sounds cool, but what does it stand for?" Sarah asked, but before I could answer, Rafi swiftly responded:

"The Zaragoza Resistance Coalition."

"How did you know I was going to say that?" I asked Rafi, and he casually shrugged it off and called it a *lucky guess*.

After Rafi answered Sarah's question for me, there was a palpable sense in the room that our little theory was suddenly more than just empty words whispered near a fireplace; it was becoming something that united us. It became a cause, and eventually, maybe even a movement. . . .

Once we concluded in my bedroom, we stepped back out into the common room to greet Amir and Tolu, who were still on the couch, staring at each of us all doe-eyed, as if we were their parents and were about to announce our divorce.

"Relax! Everything is fine," I said, trying to reassure them.

This did little to assuage their anxieties, as their creased eyebrows and melancholic faces were an obvious tell that their apprehensions still existed, and they could not believe that everything was, indeed, okay.

Moments later, Rafi emerged into the common room, as well, and made a grand ole speech about what we are doing and why we are doing it. Paraphrasing, he said something along the lines of, "Doing it not for ourselves, but for the billions of people negatively impacted by the decisions made by the Zaragozas and their business associates. By fighting them, we fight the very system that creates people like them, ensuring a fair chance for everyone to succeed, wealthy or not. We do this from the inside of the Zaragozas' empire, for we are the ZRC, the Zaragoza Resistance Coalition!"

Rafi's lofty speech did achieve its intended effect of riling up Amir and Tolu into feeling like they were officially involved in something bigger than themselves. No doubt, they surely were. I, personally, just didn't want them to lose sight of the fact that not only were we going up against the most powerful family in the world that controls a multi-trillion-dollar global enterprise, but also supernatural forces that we did not fully understand. . . . Not wanting to ruin morale when that was all we had at the moment, I let it be and kept these thoughts to myself.

Motivated and eager to find out what the next steps would be, Tolu asked what would be the first order of business for the newly formed ZRC. Not feeling the same sense of trepidation in telling the new members of the ZRC what our next steps would be, I bluntly came out with it: "We're all forgoing our week-long vacation to visit nearby towns and villages to see if anyone can give us more information on the Zaragozas' history."

This revelation surely zapped the fervent enthusiasm Amir and Tolu previously exuded. Nonetheless, they begrudgingly accepted this course of action, perhaps not wanting to show infidelity on the very first day they were sworn into the ZRC.

Since today was Sunday, and the first official day of our vacation started tomorrow, we collectively decided that today would be spent on preparing ourselves for whatever may happen on our journey. One of the biggest concerns we had was how we could communicate with the locals, since, to my knowledge, none of us spoke Spanish. However, James said that he spoke enough Spanish to get by, and being our only hope, we had to take his word for it since we didn't really have a choice, anyway.

The rest of the day was spent catching Amir and Tolu up on all the weird things that we observed and comparing our thoughts with theirs. On the matter of the mysterious beverage we had to consume, we all had the same thoughts in that it was a way to perhaps eliminate or control those of us who fell out of line with the Zaragozas—although Amir was the only one who thought it was just some old family recipe that consummated our entry into their family.

However, none of us could make sense of the strange *acolytes* being present and the scrolls we had to sign with our blood. Hesitant to ask what they did for the scrolls portion of orientation, I beat around the bush and stated something in passing along the lines of, "How weird were those scrolls, am I right?"

I guess I didn't want to feel guilty about not giving them access to the bird's blood we all used to sign. Laughter from Tolu helped ease this situation a bit, but at the same time, it made me wonder what was so funny about anything I had said. . . .

"Well, Amir and I overslept and missed a bit of Pierre's speech, and by the time we got to the great hall, we saw people pricking themselves and signing those papers. We said fuck that, ran back to our dorms, and whipped up some fake blood to use," Tolu said.

"Wow! You guys really did that? What made you think of that?" I said, sighing with a sense of relief that they did not use their own blood, either.

Tolu answered, "As you might know, Femi, signing anything with blood in Nigeria is a sign of you giving yourself, or worse, your soul to someone else, which is a big no-no for me!"

Amir also chimed in, "Mate, you don't have to be from Africa to know that signing a sodding scroll with your blood can't mean anything good!"

"Truer words have never been spoken!" James added.

Not wanting to get off-topic, I asked Amir and Tolu what they used to make their fake blood. From the way Amir sat up straight in his chair, raised his glasses, and adjusted the collar on his shirt, I could tell we were in for some boastful claim about how he thwarted the Zaragozas' blood-thirsty monks, cultists, or whatever the fuck they were.

"Well, mate, the thing is, I love to bake, and I worked at a haunted house when I was eighteen."

His fellow countryman, Paul, blurted out, "Oi, what in the bloody hell do those things even have to do with one another, mate?" which was hilarious, but from the way Amir perched up after Paul's question, I knew that he had an arsenal of answers for any potential questions levied against him—and I was right. . . .

Mocking the tone and language of a self-righteous English professor, Amir said, "Well, I'm glad you asked, young man. What they have to do with one another is that any baker worth his salt knows to have some corn syrup and food coloring for many baking recipes—the same way any person who works in the *scaring business* knows that these very ingredients are also used to make fake blood!"

"Well, that sure is impressive!" Rafi replied, feeding right into Amir's ego. But to be honest, we were all impressed by such a quick and decisive decision.

"And that's how we thwarted those sodding hooded-heads," Amir finished. "What did you guys do?"

James couldn't help but burst out in an animated laugh. "Let's just say we didn't use fake blood, but not necessarily real blood, either!"

"What's that supposed to mean, James?" Tolu asked.

"Let's just say someone gave us a timely donation," Sarah said in the jokey same tone as James, leaving Amir and Tolu with the same clueless expression, not expecting this conversation to go down in this manner. Nonetheless, it was highly entertaining to see how confused Tolu was, but it was also especially sweet watching Amir trying to comprehend what Sarah meant, probably thinking that *he* had come up with the most genius plan ever.

Unable to keep the ruse going on any longer, I explained to them that we got our blood from an injured bird that was outside my bedroom window.

"You killed a bloody bird, you monster!" Amir shouted at me in a humorous and overly outraged tone.

In an equally overly dramatic voice, I countered, "Of course not. It was injured. I tried to nurse it back to health, but unfortunately, it died. How's that for a monster, asshat?" After we had our laughs about who was more adept at asinine name-calling, we all thought what a coincidence it was to all use a substitute for real blood and only hoped that other recipients followed suit.

We stayed in the common room for a little longer, exchanging theories on what the Zaragozas were up to, ultimately reaching the same conclusion that whatever it was, it was nothing good, and we had to uncover it. . . .

One may wonder what seven bright scholars with even brighter futures—due to the Zaragozas—had to gain in exposing our benefactors. Well, to us, it was quite simple. Directly and indirectly, we all knew what it was like to have a system work against us, be it structural classism, racism, or other forms of institutional discrimination. If the system were perfectly fair, scholarships like the ZNBS wouldn't need to exist in the first place. What the Zaragozas were doing, although altruistic on the surface, was actually exploitative and only vested in their own interests, no matter how lovely their words regarding us as a *family* were. By offering the scholarship to disadvantaged communities, they naturally would expect something in return of equal or greater value. The mutual disgust of such a malicious and deplorable act alone would have had us do it all over again.

We didn't know it then, but this fact would be one of the defining traits of all members of the ZRC.

We concluded the night trading tales of our various cultures, beliefs, ambitions, and motivations, further strengthening our bond. We would finally set off the following morning for what would be the first day of exposing the Zaragozas' plot and exploring local villages and towns to see what information we could find on this most *illustrious* family.

* * *

Although the Castillo was on pretty remote grounds, there was a nearby town about five miles away that we could get to rather straightforwardly; this would be our first stop. When we arrived at the village, the first thing that came to mind was just how *modern* it was to be in rural and sleepy Northeastern Spain. From the modern cars to the bustling shops with name brand products and boutique stores that looked like they arrived from Madrid and Barcelona rather than other nearby villages, one thing became instantly clear: the Zaragoza influence was strong here, and getting any residents to *spill the beans* on their wealthy patrons would prove to be more difficult than we initially imagined.

Remarkably, there were no town beggars, and everyone seemed to be in relatively good health. As we ventured into the outskirts of town, the presence of the Zaragozas still loomed, albeit not as evident as in the city center and its immediate surroundings. We approached what seemed to be a mom-and-pop shop specializing in shoe repairs to see if we could get any information out of the elderly couple. Not wanting to frighten or overwhelm them, Rafi, Amir, Paul, and Tolu waited outside, while Sarah, James, and I went into the run-down yet homey store.

James approached first, speaking quite impressive Spanish: "Excuse me, Señor and Señora, do you mind if we talk to you for a bit?"

"In regard to what?" asked the elderly man. Although he looked like he was pushing his mid-seventies, he still had a full head of wavy dark-brown hair and a thick handlebar mustache that had streaks of black sprinkled in.

I guess hard work keeps you young, *I thought.*

"Well, we would just like to know how you like it here and what you think of the Zaragozas," James replied.

Immediately, the man froze up a bit, and his hands started to tremble as if we had asked him what he thought of the devil himself. Straightaway, he asked us to leave his store without explanation, saying only that they were good people, but that it was time for us to vacate the premises, now.

Our friends waiting outside knew that something went wrong from how abruptly we left the store. I told them that they were frozen with fear at the first mention of the Zaragozas' name and promptly asked us to leave.

"Did he give a reason why?" asked Amir.

"Nope, but I noticed the woman reciting the Hail Mary prayer under her breath while squeezing two pairs of rosary beads once I mentioned the Zaragozas," James said.

"Jesus H. Christ, what the fuck have we gotten ourselves into?" cried Paul.

"Relax, man. What did you expect to happen? These guys have international clout; how did you think locals who live mere minutes away from their estate would react?" I answered.

Paul replied with an unconvincing, "Yeah, I guess you're right. . . ."

"We didn't expect any of this to be easy, guys. We all knew exactly what we were getting into when we agreed to go along with this plan. If we shudder at the first sign of resistance, how do we expect to take them down?" said Rafi.

Trying to let cooler heads prevail, I interjected, "We just have to keep asking people until we get something. Look at the bright side: At least we are certain that people are hiding something, right . . . ?"

We walked around the outskirts of town a little while longer, looking for other stores that might not have benefited from the Zaragozas' enormous wealth and influence. We stumbled upon a small shack where a bearded bald man in his late sixties was peddling small wares. He was quite jovial and welcomed us warmly, *"Amigos! Bienvenidos! Vengan aquí, vengan aquí!"*

Not knowing what was being spoken to us, we asked James to step in to translate for us.

"He's asking to come over," James said.

I thought that if we patronized him, he would be more candid about telling us what he knew about the Zaragozas. Therefore, we proceeded to purchase some of the small knickknacks he had for sale which, I must admit, were actually quite refined in both material and craftsmanship. As I reached into my wallet to purchase a small pendant for my leather chain, Rafi slapped my hand away, making me drop my wallet in the process. "No, don't buy from that man!"

Bewildered by his erratic behavior, I asked him what the hell that was for. He then pulled out of earshot from the old man and whispered to me, "Dude, this is it, this is an opportunity to be able to identify ZRC members!"

I didn't fully understanding what he was trying to tell me, so I asked him to elaborate. "Think about it. If we all wore a unique bracelet or pendant on our chains, it would be a way to identify those of us who wanted to take down the Zaragozas.

"Furthermore, by purchasing a few more, it could be a way to initiate new members without having the founding members always present. If we codified some rules and beliefs that all members had to abide by, we could greatly expand in numbers!"

As absurd as it sounded, it actually was a decent idea. If we could grow in number and have more influence, it would greatly increase our chances of success. Additionally, by having a set of regulations that we had to abide by and new members only being initiated by existing members, it ensured that we would not allow people to slip through the cracks. Perhaps the most salient reason of all was to have a piece of identifying jewelry that would immediately recognize those who were with us versus those who only claimed to be so. I was convinced, and we proceeded to purchase five various jewelry pieces depicting a phoenix, which was going to be the symbol to officially represent ZRC membership.

Naturally, this greatly excited the old man, and he was overjoyed with such a large purchase and was pleased to produce more if we so needed. Apart from being a nice, distinguishing feature to be used by us, each piece had impeccable craftsmanship, and we were also happy to reward a fine craftsman for his work. Sarah and I took a phoenix pendant, while Rafi and James took a ring, and finally, Amir and Paul took the bracelets.

Now that we were all adorned in the old man's handiwork, he had no qualms about engaging with us further and was even quite talkative about how he started making jewelry.

Though his story about first making unique flatware from various metals found throughout the region was indeed quite interesting, the sun would be setting soon, and we were desperate for some answers.

James used this as a segue into asking if he had ever produced any flatware for the Zaragozas. Prideful of his craftsmanship (as he should be), he boastfully stated that the Zaragozas wouldn't trust anyone else for their utensils. James then went on to ask if he still produced materials for them, to which his response was more muted.

"Unfortunately, the workers that I employed went off to work in the bigger cities, leaving me unable to produce the large quantities that I used to. It forced me to stop working for the Zaragozas," the veteran jeweler said.

Not sensing any shame or ill feelings about previously working for the Zaragozas, we asked James to push him further to see how he truly felt about his previous clients. "How did you feel about them as people, though?" James asked.

The jeweler's face became riddled with apprehension, as all of his frown lines and wrinkles became readily apparent. The once jovial and ecstatic old man started to put up his guard and tried to quickly change the subject. "Look, all I can say is that I definitely felt uneasy setting foot in their Castillo. Whatever they were a part of, I did not want to be associated with, so I focused on my work and left as soon as I could. . . ."

"A part of what exactly?" James inquired.

"My friend, I am a Catholic man, and my faith has gotten me through a lot. But for some reason, any time I dealt with a Zaragoza or went to the Castillo to deliver any products to them, the solace and serenity offered to me by my faith seemed to be placed in a void. The things that I sometimes heard coming out of Pierre and his father's office, the mysterious flying beasts that I would sometimes see perched on their towers. . . . I'm sorry, I wish I could explain it further, but I cannot.

"Out of gratefulness, I have shared these thoughts with you children—thoughts and words that I would not dare to think or speak. But for some reason, I felt compelled to tell you these things. Alas, I have already said too much, and I am afraid that I can no longer be of assistance to whatever mission you find yourselves embarking on.

"All I can say is that you should be very careful in what you are pursuing; there are forces that you all do not understand. Be very careful, indeed. . . ." the old jeweler warned.

Promising to heed the old man's ominous warning, James relayed to him that we would be careful and that we hoped he would find comfort in the fact that we also believed that the Zaragozas are involved in nefarious dealings. We thanked him for all that he had shared thus far.

Before we departed, the kind old man told us to look for a Señor Gástonio de Guzmán in the neighboring town, informing us that when he used to work for the Zaragozas directly, he always went through de Guzmán to arrange the logistics of any sales he made to the Zaragozas and that it *wouldn't be hard to find him,* as he put it.

We then parted ways with the jeweler, but not before telling him that we were forever grateful—not only for the jewelry he provided us but also for the words of wisdom and guidance that he shared. He asked to give each of us a hug before we left and told us, "May the holy spirit of Jesus Christ always be with you all."

We finally left the old man's stall and returned to the city center to discuss everything that was just told to us. We eventually found a small coffee shop, not too far from the initial shoe repair store that we visited. We thought that it would be an ideal place to plan our next steps, especially since we were the only patrons present, apart from an adorable older woman who served us our caffeinated beverages and immediately returned to the back once our coffee and tea were served.

"We're really onto something, aren't we?" Paul exclaimed.

"Yeah, I guess we really are," I answered.

"I didn't expect us to get so far so soon," Amir added. "Which leads us to our next issue: Where exactly are we? We've met an old man who used to make eating utensils for the Zaragozas, who has now led us to yet another old man called Gástonio."

"We don't even know where he lives or what his association to the Zaragozas is or was," said Tolu.

"All of this is true. All the more reason why we need to find this Mr. Gástonio de Guzmán. I mean, we already know in which direction this small town is," I said.

"I say we head back to the Castillo, think about what we'll say to him, and go from there," James replied.

"Yes, I agree," said Rafi.

"So, are we all on the same page about where we go from here?" I reiterated.

The fact that no one replied after I said this let me know that we were, indeed, all on the same page, and the next morning, we would venture out into the next town in search of Señor de Guzmán. We finished our drinks, discussed how lucky we were to find the jeweler, and how due to meeting him, we were on our way to discovering a person who used to directly work with the Zaragozas, and by purchasing his jewelry, he allowed us to really feel like a unified team, greatly improving ZRC morale now and in the future.

Not ready to depart for the Castillo just yet, we ordered pints of the local beer, in addition to some homemade empanadas that the kind woman prepared especially for us. We figured that it probably wasn't often that the owner had so many foreign visitors, which made her delighted to see her store occupied. The appreciation was reciprocated as her shop provided us with not only food and drink but, most importantly, privacy. . . . Though we could've asked the lady for information on what she knew about the Zaragozas, we believed it best if she didn't know the purpose of our visit, for the security of all.

"What if that guy was only jerking our chain and was actually lying about everything he told us?" Paul asked.

"What would he have to gain from doing that, though?" asked Sarah. "I mean, I don't know about you guys, but all that talk about religion and how uneasy he felt any time he interacted with the Zaragozas, people don't usually joke about stuff like that."

"Plus, why would he mention Gástonio if he was trying to throw us off?" James inquired.

"Not saying I agree with you, James, but just playing devil's advocate: What if it was because he, this Gástonio guy, is still working for the Zaragozas, and he was something like their enforcer or private detective?" I added.

"That could be true, but I think it's unlikely. Gástonio is supposedly an old man. Not only that, but he's not even living in the closest nice town economically supported by the Zaragozas. Instead, he lives in the smaller, more destitute next town over," Amir pointed out.

"I don't know about you guys, but to me, it just sounds like an old man who is trying to get away from the sphere of the Zaragozas' influence without entirely leaving probably the only place he's ever known," said Tolu.

Trying to get out of the realm of conspiracy theories, I stated something along the lines of, "None of this matters, and the only thing that *does* matter is that this man is our only lead and whatever his intentions are, or past affiliations to the Zaragozas were, we had to find him, period."

We all agreed and, on that note, decided that it was probably time to head back to the Castillo before it got too dark outside.

The path back seemed much longer, but that was probably due to the contents of the strong home-brewed alcohol we just drank. This got Sarah to thinking, though, that perhaps we should find a faster way to get back to the Castillo from wherever we would be coming from.

"You think we could rent a car?" Amir asked. I'm not sure if he was joking, but I sure hoped he was because it was truly a moronic suggestion, considering how remote all these locations were. "I sort of remember seeing some bicycles in one of the garages at the Castillo. I'm sure those are probably for the scholarship recipients, right? I mean, technically, we are family, no?" Paul said sardonically.

"Once we get back, let's check it out and go from there," I responded.

By the time we finally got back to the Castillo, it was already nightfall, and we were all pretty tired from the adventuring we had just completed. The fatigue must've clouded our minds because once we got back, we forgot to check on the bikes, and all returned to my dorm, Amir and Tolu included, to pass out.

There's no rush; the bikes will be there in the morning, *I thought as I fell asleep.*

* * *

The next morning, I awoke feeling well-rested. I got up earlier than usual to prepare breakfast for my friends. Feeling grateful for the breakfast they provided for me back when I was extremely hungover from the impromptu party, I thought they would appreciate it if I reciprocated their kind gesture. The only problem was that there were no more supplies in our refrigerator. The best idea I could come up with at the time was to go into the Castillo's main kitchen to see if the in-residence chefs could lend some ingredients, or even better, help me prepare some food.

Remembering me as the host of the party that they thoroughly enjoyed, as well, they were more than happy to assist me in this endeavor. They even taught me a new way to prepare an omelet, which always comes in handy. After the meal was prepared, I brought it up to my dorm, dressing it up with some cilantro garnishing, and I even served it on a silver platter. I said to myself, "Even if this is the most unappetizing meal they ever tasted, they damn well better appreciate the lengths I went to in preparing it!"

However, this was not something that I had to worry about.

Just the aroma of succulent sausages accompanied with the always enticing scent of a cheese omelet perfectly seasoned with sea salt & Malabar black pepper. A mighty meal more than capable of waking even the most somnolent.

James was immediately interested in what I was doing, as he was the first to come out of the room, greeting me in his usual sarcastic manner, "Making up for the breakfast we made for you eh?"

I chuckled and told him to shut up and just enjoy the breakfast, to which he was more than happy to oblige. Shortly after, the rest of the gang woke up and joined him for breakfast. Even Tolu and Amir were able to smell the breakfast's alluring aroma from across the hall and joined in the meal, as well, leaving no one out, except me, of course. I couldn't care less because little did they know, shortly before their feast, I had my own private breakfast prepared by a professional!

Once the gang was finished stuffing their faces, we were fueled up and ready to embark on our next adventure. First task of the day: See if the bicycles were still in the garage and then head off to find the mysterious Señor Gástonio de Guzmán, who supposedly had the answers to all of our questions. Arriving at the garage, we were pleased to see several bike racks filled with what must have been over 100 bikes in pristine condition, just ready to be ridden. It only took a few minutes for each of us to select the right bike suited to both our style and proportions.

However, there was one secret that I was actively withholding from the group, not thinking we would actually get the bicycles. The fact was, I didn't know how to ride a bike, and I was not sure how long I could keep this ruse going.

"Hurry up, Femi, choose a bike already. We have to go!" Sarah instructed.

"Just a second; I want to make sure they have a single-speed!" I mumbled.

"You just passed three single-speeds. Just choose one already!"

"Ah, yes, but the first one looked too slow, and I didn't like the color on the second one," I said.

After a while, however, the jig was finally up, and Rafi questioned if I actually knew how to ride a bike. Replying pretentiously, I stated in a mobster-inspired, faux Italian American accent, "Of course I know how to ride a bike. Who doesn't know how to ride a bike? Can you believe this guy?" I emphasized to an imaginary mobster.

"Then go ahead, ride it around the garage, tough guy," Rafi replied, mimicking my fake accent. After failing to come up with a clever response, I didn't want to waste any more time lying to my friends and admitted that I did not know how to ride a bike. . . . Ready to receive the onslaught of a mixture of outrage and shock, I took a deep breath and sighed, and almost on cue, I was bombarded by a barrage of questions thinly veiled as insults!

"You don't know how to ride a bike? *Seriously*?!"

"Where was your childhood spent, *underwater*?"

"You never wanted to learn?"

Most brazenly, Amir even asked, "*Well, what did you do as a kid*?!"

Used to hearing every one of these questions a thousand times (except the underwater one made by Sarah), which did make me laugh, I stated in the most robotic voice I could muster, "I didn't bother to learn when I was already driving by age fifteen. Furthermore, it's not like I didn't want to, but the opportunity never came up since I didn't really grow up around people riding bikes beep-borp. . . ."

Assuaging any potential reservations about how we were going to proceed with the day, I informed them that despite not knowing how to formally ride a bike, I have *attempted* to ride one before, semi-successfully, and reckoned it may only take me a few more hours to be able to ride effectively enough.

Proceeding to the activities of the early afternoon, which was spent by each of them offering me their unique insight on how to keep the bike upright.

"Kick off with your strongest foot!"

"Don't think about balancing!"

"Don't look down!"

"Just let it come naturally!"

Growing tired of both the incessant advice that did not seem to be working for me and this tone they shared as if they were all multiple Tour de France champions, I insisted that for the sake of time, we should just start riding for the village. If I slowed behind them, they should just continue riding. Luckily for me, they agreed, which permitted me to ride at my own pace and to finally be free of their *infinite biking wisdom*. It wasn't easy, but after around thirty minutes, I was able to ride continuously without placing my feet back on the ground, gradually increasing my confidence on the bike, and thus my ability.

Chapter 7: Gástonio

We arrived at the town we had visited the day before, shortly after my confidence peaked, and took a break to grab coffee at the small shop we visited yesterday.

Once again, the lady granted us ample caffeine and discretion while we outlined exactly what we would be asking Señor Gástonio de Guzmán. Though I was sad that we stopped riding soon after my riding acumen started to flourish, the thought of having a chai latte quickly ameliorated the feeling. The first question I thought we should ask him was to assess his relation to the Zaragozas and what he formerly did on their behalf. . . .

We hoped that it would be a previous association, but if it were still ongoing, that would require us to perhaps seek out another person to help us with our investigation. Secondly, the plan was to ask him random questions about the supernatural and occult to see if anything stuck or if we could get a reaction out of him.

About twenty-five minutes after we finished our beverages, we arrived at the small town where supposedly Señor

Gástonio de Guzmán resided. If the town closer to the Castillo was Metropolis, then Gástonio's town was surely Gotham. No, there weren't any jokers or masked vigilantes leaping from rooftops, but this town was definitely more dilapidated. Though for its lack of luster, the city had a certain charm that beguiled its present condition. There were still hints of a picturesque time of old where the town would've been marveled for its architectural details. Stoic archways that stood in front of buildings looked like portals to another dimension. Ancient Roman roads with weeds covering almost as much surface area as the stone itself. Roads that perhaps a certain Roman Emperor with an uncanny resemblance to Pierre Zaragoza probably used to travel on. The town had its quirks but was far from quirky.

It wasn't particularly hard to find this Gástonio de Guzmán. The first person we encountered and consequently asked was a middle-aged woman who cheerfully guided us to his house. Call it a gut feeling or my introverted intuition kicking in again, but by the way this woman talked about Señor de Guzmán, we assumed that he was at least a decent man who was respected in this village. We simply asked the woman for a man named Gástonio when her eyes lit up and she told us that he was a good man who cherished everyone in the town like his own children. "But please, be patient with him," she said with a stern stare.

This gave us a hunch that he was probably not still employed by the Zaragozas. *How could a man who is spoken of so highly be associated with such a revolting family*? The thing on everyone's mind was, what did the last part of her sentence mean? "Please be patient with him." Did Gástonio, for all his good deeds, possess a fiery temper? Did he have some sort of deformity? Questions abounded, but we had to find out for ourselves what she was alluding to.

"Even if the Zaragozas are so glorified abroad, surely these locals truly know of their real dealings, right?" Tolu asked.

"I think even if all we hear about this Gástonio de Guzmán are positive things, we still need to be wary of his associations with the Zaragozas, past or present," Rafi warned. *I agreed.*

Given the excellent directions we received from the kind lady, it didn't take us long to find "the home whose facade was outclassed by its landscaping," as the lady specifically hinted. The more that I learned about Gástonio, the more I admired him. I mean, after all, a person who doesn't have much but still takes pride in the appearance of his home must be a man with integrity; at least, that was my hope.

James, as he should be, was the first to approach the oversized, rounded, gray wooden door. He clenched his left fist and knocked three times.

"Siii?" we heard an old man wheeze out.

"Good afternoon, sir, we are looking for a Señor Gástonio de Guzmán. Do you know where we could find him?" James replied in his finest Spanish, trying his best to mimic the local accent to hasten familiarity.

"If it's de Guzmán you seek, he will be right down," a voice cried out from behind the impressive timber door.

We waited a few moments before the door swung open. *For such a respected man, he must not have received too many visitors,* I thought. We could hear him shuffling about in the circular hobbit-like house, like he was tidying up, but we could also hear him talking to someone before he unlocked the door.

The first thing that we realized was that despite his obvious advanced age, Gástonio had a boyish charm to him that was evident despite his weathered appearance. It was also evident that he must've been quite fit in his youth, as years of physical training had permanently left his traps, lats, and deltoid muscles well defined for a man his age. He even still had all his hair, but judging from the long, white ponytail and the beard that could've rivaled a Viking's, I guess he wanted to hold on to all that hair for as long as he could.

Although he welcomed all of us into his very humble abode, we could tell that he was uncertain about our reason for being there, as any reasonable person would be. As he analyzed the multitude of ethnicities now seated in his living room, as well as how old we looked, he quickly started to speak in broken English that was understandable enough, with James translating the bits of Spanish that trickled in.

"Whatever you kids have for sale, I don't want it!" Señor de Guzmán said respectfully but forcefully.

"We are not selling anything, sir—"

"Are you the new cleaners, then?"

"No, sir, we are not here to clean anything, either," James said politely.

"Hmm, ah yes, yes! Then you all must be from the Castillo. Why didn't you say so? That is quite rude of you, quite rude, indeed!"

"Yes, we apologize, but we were trying to tell you that," James translated.

We now understood what the kind woman meant about being *patient*.

Straightening his beard hair by tugging on it, Gástonio asked, "So, what brings you to my home, and how did you find me? I don't think I want you all here anymore," Gástonio replied gruffly.

"Sir, we mean you no harm. We found you by asking around; we were looking for someone who used to work for the Zaragozas for more information about them," James translated for us.

"Ha! No harm, you say? Anything associated with that family and their Castillo brings us great harm! No one has come to see us asking about the Zaragozas. Well, not since that young man came barging in here asking similar questions. What was his name again? Jorge? But that was many moons ago. . . ."

Us? Jorge? *I thought.* Who is he referring to? Who is Jorge?

Despite desperately wanting to pick his brain about all the things he was rambling about, we had to resist the urge to follow up on this other person he was referring to, as well as who this Jorge person was. It became clear that we were going to have to be *much more patient* than we originally thought.

We asked if he had ever worked for the Zaragozas, and if so, what did he did for them. Realizing that this probably came off quite rude for a man that we just met and who invited us into his home, I apologized for my abruptness. I told him that importance necessitated such brevity.

"Never apologize for being direct! These people, they speak from multiple heads, multiple tongues, never quite clear in what and who they're talking about; it drove us mad!" Gástonio said, repeatedly standing up and sitting back down in a green leather chair that looked more like an artifact than a still-in-use piece of furniture.

Gástonio's comments caught me completely off guard, as I'm sure it did for my friends. We were growing increasingly troubled about what he was saying and what he was going to say.

After he spoke, we all looked at each other apprehensively, silent, and stone-faced. Well, almost all of us, that is. . . . Paul couldn't help himself and was smirking almost the entire time Gástonio was speaking. A pinch on the arm by Sarah did the trick.

After his short monologue, Gástonio sat there, looking at all of us, his once dilated eyes now carefully scrutinizing us, for God knows what. He stroked his fleecy white beard once more, took a puff from his pipe that looked like something borrowed off of Gandalf the Grey, and said that he knew what we were here about. "Yes, I have worked for the Zaragozas. I was a personal assistant of sorts to them, but something tells me you already knew that, so what do you really want to ask?"

"Well, sir, what do you mean by being a *personal assistant* to them? To who exactly?"

"To who, you ask? No, to *what* is what you really mean. "Arturo Zaragoza was more than just a man—"

"Arturo Zaragoza? Sir, we are not familiar with him; who is he?" James asked in full Spanish. Gástonio then went on rambling incoherently, first in Spanish, then a mixture of Spanish and English, then into some unknown language that sounded unlike anything we had ever heard before. Gástonio jolted up from his seat like he was struck by Zeus himself.

"No, no, no! I can't, not *again*! Please don't make me tell them. *They do not know what they face!"* Gástonio cried out.

We were all seriously startled, so much so that out of reflex, Tolu jumped out of his seat, as well. "*Oh shit*!" he yelled.

"Out, all of you! Out, now!" Gástonio barked at us. We

wasted no time, instantly standing up and scurrying out of his home, like roaches fleeing from the light.

"Jesus *fookin'* Christ, what was that about? I reckon if we left any later, he would've been bench-pressing our corpses!" Paul shouted out of earshot of Gástonio's home.

"Relax, Paul. How did you think that was going to play out? We investigate the most powerful people on the planet, follow up on some leads, and solve a mystery that has been ongoing for perhaps hundreds of years? It was never going to be that easy, and you all should've known that," Rafi stated, retying his hair into a neat bun.

"Yeah, okay, I know you're right, but fuckin' hell, did you see the arms on that old brute? That type of *strength* with that sort of *mind*? Dangerous stuff, innit?" Paul replied.

"Perhaps, but honestly, it is our fault. The lady told us to be patient with him, and we kind of blindsided him with all the rapid-fire questioning. He's an old man who's probably been through more than any of us could even imagine," Sarah said.

"You're right, Sarah. It's my fault. I thought that once we found Gástonio, everything would clear up instantly. We even received a warning but proceeded to pester him, anyway."

"Well, where do we go from here? I don't know about the lot of you, but dealing with a crazy prehistoric bodybuilder worked up quite the appetite. Shall we get some lunch?" Paul asked.

"Mate, first things first. He's not crazy. Dealing with some sort of cognitive degradation due to his advanced age, yes, but he's not crazy. I always hated that," Amir said sharply.

Ever the investigator, James pried further. "Always hated what, *mate*?" James said in a faux-British accent.

"Hated how carelessly people use the words crazy and schizophrenic. I hate how laymen use the terms to describe atypical behavior. Words have meanings, and medical conditions shouldn't be thrown around all willy-nilly," Amir said.

"Oh, come on, are all you northern folk wound up so tightly? I was just joking."

"Leeds isn't exactly the northernmost point in England, now, is it?"

"Enough from you two! Let's get back to the café, get some lunch, and go from there. Can we?" I interjected.

"Yes, please!" Sarah and Tolu added.

* * *

We got back to the café just as the afternoon soup was being prepared and got into discussing the events that had just transpired.

"Okay, I'll admit that was not what I expected, but we have to see him again," Rafi said.

"What do you mean *we* have to see him again? Are you crazy, err. . . . I mean, not thinking clearly?" James said as Amir scowled at him for his poor word choice.

"Rafi is right, James; you're giving up before we've even started," I said.

"Easy for you guys to say. You're not the ones speaking directly to an old man who has perhaps *lost his marbles* and can rip off your head as easily as squishing a grape!"

"You all need to seriously relax with all these insinuations about Gástonio acting out violently; there's no basis for it," Sarah chimed in.

"What say you, Tolu? You've been pretty quiet over there since your little outburst back there."

"No, no, I'm fine. I really just wasn't expecting all of this. But I agree; I think we should follow this out until the end. Let's just heed warnings better next time."

"You're absolutely correct. Now, shall we eat?" Rafi said.

Ordering for all of us in broken Spanish, James asked the server if we could have bowls of the fragrant soup she had just prepared. Continuing the excellent service we started to expect from the lady, she quickly went into the kitchen to grab the bowls required to enjoy her hearty broth.

Halfway into our meal, heads fully entrenched in our bowls, we felt the air of the outside wind gently caress the back of our heads as the front door flew open. Turning around to see who had entered but seeing no one, we turned around again to be in front of no other than Señor de Guzmán. Not entirely sure how we didn't hear his footsteps or sense his presence. It looked like he cleaned up a bit, too. His once long and wild hair had been washed and slicked back with pomade that smelled like honey. It was also applied to his beard, making it glisten like the first snow of winter.

"First things first, I must apologize to you kids. Sometimes we aren't ourselves, but it wasn't always this way. *'Us' used to be 'me.'* I'm sorry, please forgive me," Señor Gástonio de Guzmán said in almost full English. "I see that you have found Maria's restaurant. Surely it tastes as good as anything you've had at the Castillo?" He said with a mostly toothless smile.

Not sure if it was a rhetorical question or not, we just

nodded out of respect, but also because he was right. Maria's food was, indeed, just as good as anything we had prepared by the majordomo and his attentive staff.

Gástonio's present tone was more somber and measured compared to the erratic pattern in which he previously spoke. This was understandable, and I made a mental note to be especially patient this time around.

"May I join you all for lunch?"

"Please, sir, we would be delighted," James said.

Maria promptly brought out a bowl for Gástonio, as well, and he resumed where he previously left off: "We'll have to apologize once more, but our mind is not what it used to be. What were we discussing back at my home?"

"Arturo Zaragoza, sir," I blurted out.

Smack! "Ow! What was that for?" I mumbled as Sarah slapped my thigh underneath the table.

Patience, she slowly mouthed to me.

I put on a fake smile and rubbed my thigh to help alleviate the throbbing sting.

"Ah, right, '*Arturo the Great*.' He used to demand people to call him that, you know." Gástonio said, chuckling to himself.

"Who was he?" I asked.

"Well, Arturo Zaragoza was the founder of Zaragoza Enterprises, Inc., the predecessor of the Zaragoza Consulting Agency. He was its visionary, and I was his protégé."

We were all supremely mystified because, according to our lectures during orientation, Zaragoza Enterprises, Inc. restructured into the ZCA a hundred years ago, which meant Gástonio was considerably older than we previously imagined. Furthermore, we had no recollection of any *Arturo Zaragoza*.

"Are you kids cohorts of this year's ZNBS program?"

"Yes!" we all enthusiastically replied, glad that he had started to sound more lucid.

"Chosen because of your intelligence in each of your respective countries, no?"

"Yes," we said again.

"I see. The ironic thing about all of this is that we had a hand in creating the ZNBS all those years ago, so I am partly responsible for why you are here. But what it turned into was not what I wanted at all," Gástonio said as he sunk his head into his hands in remorseful shame.

"Oh, God, here we go again," Paul mumbled lowly, twirling his index finger in small circles beside his head: the universal gesture for crazy. For his gesticulating, Sarah served him her signature thigh slap, too, which I greatly enjoyed. I no longer had to be the only one dealing with the tingling agony from one of her slaps.

We all looked at each other for a moment, though no one spoke a word. The same question was on everyone's mind. What did Gástonio originally wish the ZNBS to be, and what was it currently. . . .?

"One final question. You all suspect that the Zaragozas are up to no good but can't exactly discern what their plans are?"

"Yes!" we exclaimed for the final time.

"Then you are the ZNBS recipients we've been waiting a long time for!" Gástonio said, his destitute body language instantaneously morphing into one that was more lively and optimistic.

Sitting up straight for the first time now, the glimmer in his eyes returned, and Señor de Guzmán said, "Let me explain. Our full name is Gástonio Luis de Guzmán. As I told you earlier, we worked for Arturo Zaragoza. In fact, he was like a father to us for many years. You kids don't know who he is because he hasn't been the patriarch of the Zaragoza family for over a century. That title now belongs to Arturo's great-grandson, a man I'm sure you all know well: Pierre-Antonio Zaragoza."

Captivated by Gástonio's vast knowledge of the Zaragozas, we sat and listened intently while he explained who he was and what he did for the family. He first went into the background of his and Arturo's relationship. As he explained it to us, Arturo did not have any legitimate children and became interested in the kids who lived in the towns near the Castillo, with Señor de Guzmán being the one he was most interested in.

Gástonio, as he preferred to be called, was always a hard worker and wanted to prove his durability to Arturo by carrying almost double the weight that the other kids his age could carry whenever the Zaragozas needed help around the Castillo. He told us that he did this to prove himself worthy of a life better than the one he was born into.

Eventually, Arturo caught wind of how hardworking Gástonio was and took pity on him, offering him a lowly job for the then Zaragoza Enterprises. He first started doing door-to-door deliveries for the company, gradually working his way up, eventually becoming aide-de-camp to Arturo himself, a job that Gástonio admitted filled him with immense pride when he realized how far he had come to be in this current position. However, he told us that he also became more and more skeptical of the true goals and ambitions of the Zaragozas as his responsibilities increased in the company.

He informed us that he started to notice strange occurrences at the Castillo, such as winged creatures, unlike anything he'd ever seen, flying around the Castillo at night, filling him with great trepidation.

Could they be the same beasts that the jeweler told us about? *I wondered.*

After weeks of continually seeing these creatures and other abnormal happenings around the Castillo, he finally collected enough courage to ask Arturo for an explanation for the things he witnessed. Señor de Guzmán told us that he'd never forget the day when he asked Arturo this question, referring to it as, *The Day of Two Firsts.*

The first day the true source of the Zaragoza wealth was revealed to him was also the first day that Señor de Guzmán realized he could no longer work for the Zaragozas without feeling conflicted with his own morals and beliefs.

Realizing that we were perhaps at the precipice of acquiring the information we desperately desired, we tried to get as comfortable as possible, giving us the best opportunity to actively listen to every word Señor de Guzmán was about to share.

"I remember the day like it was yesterday. Arturo called me into his private office—the highest tower in the Castillo, the office he didn't even let his wife and children enter—informing me that he was about to share something extremely important with me," Gástonio said, his voice now reverberating with a low, haunted whisper.

"He looked at me with a never-before-seen intensity. A part of me was hesitant to obtain the knowledge he was about to share, but being the young, susceptible, and impressionable boy I was, I succumbed and proceeded to follow him into the office," Gástonio paused momentarily, checking to see if we were still following him, and resumed again.

"'Gástonio,' he called out to me, 'do you know what transforms a mere family into a great dynasty?'

"'No sir, I do not,' I answered, and he told me that it was, in his own words, 'A sense of where your family has come from, how far you have come, but most importantly, how far you are willing to go . . . that's what. Though you may think the Zaragoza name carries a certain weight and respect automatically, this was not always the case. You see, my dear boy, our family origins are documented all the way back to the Dark Ages, but back then, we weren't the empire of a family you see before you. We were nothing but a family of peddlers and thieves who just happened to know the *right* people. I'm sure from your experience as a former lowly thief—before I gave you the opportunity of a lifetime, that is—that you understand what you get when you combine thieving and knowing the right people?'

"I was completely bewildered as to what he was talking about, but I did not want to lie to my mentor, so I humbly answered that I did not. Arturo then replied, 'You get an opportunity which, if you play your cards right, should lead to success.'

"Back then, I did not fully grasp what Arturo was telling me, but in time, I would come to understand exactly what he meant. . . .

"'You see, Gástonio, our family was penniless and worthless until our ancestors realized that if we stole certain things from certain people who had excess, anyway, we could amass a fortune. Not only monetary but also social fortune because as your reputation spreads, so does your admiration—in certain circles, at least. Eventually, all of the thieving allowed us to semi-legitimize our business. We eventually became something like importers/exporters progressing to where we are today as a company, mainly shipping vital commodities across the world.'"

Fully engrossed in the story, Paul abruptly interrupted Gástonio and interjected, "Oi! I thought that the Zaragozas were mainly a business consultancy firm?"

Unfazed by the shameless interruption, Gástonio, smiling with his eyes, looked over to Paul and calmly said, "Yes, boy, that is correct, but that is not the trade the family started with."

Growing collectively annoyed with Paul's infamous untimely interruptions, we all gave him the subtle but stern look *not to do it again!* Which he thankfully understood.

Gástonio resumed his story: "Though the other parts of his story roughly made sense to my young entrepreneurial brain at the time, what I did not understand was, who were these *right people to know* and what any of this had to do with the strange sights in and around the Castillo. I sensed Arturo going off on a tangent, so to refocus his story, I just came out and asked what I was so desperate to know: 'Who are these right people, sir?'

"While he was slightly irritated that I had interrupted him, he did answer my question. 'The people to whom I'm referring, my young Gástonio, aren't *people* in the way you understand the word. . . . They're beings of a different dimension. Our laws of science would not be able to classify them into anything conceptual. Gástonio, they are supernatural entities of another realm, another world intertwined with our own . . another world intertwined with that of our own . . . another world intertwined with that of our own. . . .'" Suddenly, Gástonio kept repeating himself like a broken record.

"Dios mío!" Maria, the shop's owner, cried out. "It's starting again, it's starting again; please, you all must escort him home, *ahora*!" Gástonio may have been old, but he was far from feeble, standing at around 5' 7" but remarkably carrying just as much muscle mass as—if not more than—my six-foot frame. Suffice it to say, Gástonio was not going to be an easy transport.

"Another world intertwined with that of our own . . . another world intertwined with that of our own . . ." he kept reiterating.

James and I then proceeded to stand up from the booth to get to the other side of the table to jointly carry Gástonio on our shoulders. Fortunately for us, he was still able to walk a little bit, helping us out tremendously.

"Another world intertwined with that of our own . . . another world intertwined with that of our own . . . another world intertwined with that of our own!" Gástonio repeated relentlessly throughout the entire village. We hurried as fast as our legs would take us to get him home,

arriving at his cottage sweaty and tired but glad that we finally made it.

James and I took him upstairs, got him out of his clothes, and tried to cool him down with some water. Gástonio's body was burning up, and we didn't know why. Still echoing those words, his cadence began to slow down. "Another world intertwined with that of our own . . . another world intertwined with that of our own . . . another . . ." Silent at last, Gástonio had fallen asleep, but it felt like we were back at square one.

Rejoining the gang downstairs, James and I were greeted with what could only be described by a palpable sense of dread that permeated throughout Gástonio's entire living room.

"Well, that went well," Paul stated without any humorous or sarcastic tone attached. Even he could not muster up his usual facetious propensity. Here we were with perhaps the only person who knew of the Zaragozas' true dealings, but we were now all in doubt whether his mind could've been lost ages ago.

"I'm sorry to say, guys, but how can we be sure to trust this man? I mean, no offense Amir, he may not be crazy, but he isn't exactly normal, either," Tolu said grimly.

"Yeah, I know you're right. It's pretty clear that despite his freakishly excellent physical health, his mental health is another story," Amir replied.

"So what you're really saying is that this old geezer could just be leading us on? Jerking us around?" Paul asked with fury.

"No, that's not what he said, and you know it. Regardless of his cognitive abilities, he could still be telling the truth; we can't just discredit him over his age. I mean, you were listening when he was recounting his early years as protégé to Arturo; did that sound like the ramblings of a senile old man?" Rafi barked at Paul, inching closer and closer to his face.

"And the part about fucking *supernatural entities?* That's as normal as a nice Sunday stroll through St James's Gardens, innit?"

"Alright, alright, that's enough arguing! A room full of

graduates several times over, and you all sound like freaking children. May I remind all of you, we're still in his home? Show a little bit of respect!" Sarah fumed. After her outburst, she corralled us all into the kitchen that was farther from the stairs to make sure that we didn't wake Gástonio.

"Sarah is right, guys. Rafi is, too, and believe it or not, so are you, Paul. Gástonio is our only solid contact in this whole investigation we got ourselves into. Yes, he may have lost his marbles before any of us were even born, but despite even that, he's not completely gone. When he first started to recount his time as Arturo's protégé, that became pretty clear, didn't it, Paul?" James said, trying to unite the different factions.

"Okay, yeah, I admit for something that happened such a long time ago, he did have remarkable clarity in regard to that," Paul said, his cheeks flushed with embarrassment.

"Amir, couldn't it be possible that he suffered traumatic abuse that could perhaps cause some disassociation and psychotic-like symptoms when it comes to the most traumatic of memories, justifying that seizure he had in the restaurant?"

"Yes, that would be possible," Amir said.

"Last but not least, Mr. Observant himself, Femi, what was the first thing that came to mind when we first came to Gástonio's house, and he answered the door?" James asked.

"I thought he looked like one of those mad scientists you always see in movies, in complete disregard of his outward appearance," I replied.

"And when we met at Maria's?" James added.

"He made an attempt to clean up his image, to look more presentable to us?" I said, not knowing if his question was rhetorical or not.

"Exactly! He made an effort. He was remorseful for kicking us out of his home because we probably brought up things he's been trying to repress for decades. To show his remorse, he trimmed his wild hair, rubbed some pomade into his beard, and met us there! Only freaking out when?"

"Only when he was getting deeper into the history of the Zaragozas, the source of their ancestral wealth . . ."

"And the *beings* that were responsible for their success," Tolu said, finishing James's sentence.

"Exactly, Tolu," James said.

Boy, was it a sight to see. Never have we seen James act in such a way. I don't know if some of the Spanish got lost in translation when he was relaying everything back to us, or if it was the shared faith between the two of them, but James was suddenly a firm believer that Gástonio was the key to figuring out the mystery of the Zaragozas. We stood there silently in awe of James's passionate plea for Señor de Guzmán because he was, indeed, correct. We couldn't give up on Gástonio. He . . . he hadn't given up on us. He didn't have to come to meet us in the restaurant; he didn't even have to tell us about his time working for Arturo Zaragoza, but he did, and he was clearly troubled. It didn't feel right in my gut to just let him wither away without trying to get to the bottom of what was ailing him. As selfish as it sounds, his health would be critical in finding out what we needed to know.

"Okay, okay, that was very nice, and you're right, we can't give up on him now, but where do we go from here?" Paul asked, scratching his flaxen head, literally.

"Well, the first thing we can do is help him out here. I say we clean up his home a bit and make some food for him when he wakes up. He'll be grateful for it, and when the time is right, I know he'll return the favor, I just know it," I said as I opened Gástonio's refrigerator to see what we could prepare for him.

About an hour later, we were finished tidying up Gástonio's home. In the process, we even found some bespoke metal engravings throughout his home, no doubt made by the same jeweler who had made our ZRC phoenix jewelry.

"Well, I feel like a better person now, but I think we should head back to the Castillo. It's getting late," Tolu said, fluffing up the pillows on Gástonio's couch for the seventh time.

"I'll catch up with you guys outside. I want to check up on Gástonio one more time," I said.

Heading into Gástonio's room, he was still sleeping soundly, but I noticed him shivering, from burning hot to colder than an arctic night. Gástonio's thermal regulation was completely whacked. Doing what I thought was best, I retrieved some more blankets out of his closet and placed them on him up to the neck, tucking them underneath his chin, just like my grandmother used to do for me. As I began to walk out, I heard a strange groaning noise that I couldn't pinpoint.

"Ughhhh." Not sure if what I heard was Gástonio or the heater, I looked around the room. *Nothing, still as a picture,* I thought and proceeded to walk out again.

"***Ughhhh***." There was no mistaking it this time. The noise was coming from Gástonio. I rushed to his bedside and leaned in.

"Jorge, Jorge, is that you?"

"No, sir, it's Femi. It's me, Femi."

"Please forgo your mission; it is impossible. Even with my strength, I failed. The Zaragozas and their plans for world domination cannot be stopped. You and your family are in grave danger; you do not understand the forces you are up against. . . . Promise me that you'll *abandon this folly*."

Gástonio rose up like a zombie erupting from the grave and grabbed my hand so tightly I thought I was going to depart without it. *"Promise me. . . ."* he said again before falling back to sleep, just as quickly as he had sat up.

As soon as I could confirm that he was sleeping, I left his room and home to join my friends outside and head back to the Castillo. *When would I tell the rest of the gang what Gástonio said, and how?*

* * *

The first thing we did once we arrived back in our quarters was to debrief one another on all that we just experienced. There was a tangible energy in the room that we could actually accomplish our goals, now more than ever after finding Señor de Guzmán. Here was living proof of someone who knew the unabridged version of the Zaragozas' vast fortune origin story, a person who had helped create the very scholarship we were in Spain for and had survived to recount his tales. Moreover, it provided the newly formed ZRC an ally who knew the insides of how the Zaragoza empire operated.

Although the ZCA did not technically exist back when he worked for the family, the original master plan of how

Zaragoza Enterprises would transform into the ZCA was all established during Gástonio's tenure working for Arturo, from the companies that the future ZCA would acquire to the conception of the ZNBS and the criteria for selecting the students.

One thing that became abundantly clear during our debriefing was, we would have to substantially increase the number of the ZRC if we were to pose any threat to the Zaragozas, especially if what Gástonio told me was true. In the same way that their scholarship was impeccably planned to select certain students from specific backgrounds, so would our coalition, standing toe-to-toe with the Zaragozas to take them down from the inside-out. . . .

But how? Who would we select? Who could be trusted? The first thing that we could all agree on is that no matter what, every potential member of the ZRC would've had to attended one of our Fireside Chats. Without attendance, scholarship recipients wouldn't even begin to grasp what we were trying to accomplish, though these criteria were barely adequate. Even if a recipient attended one of the chats, how could we know for sure where their loyalty stood? We needed to come up with a way to appeal to any potential ZRC member's heartstrings, not their logical mind. Any sensible person would realize that trying to take down a global empire is nearly impossible. Coupled with the fact that the very same empire could possibly fulfill all your dreams and desires would, at best, be foolhardy, and at worst, could mean our lives, so we took this mission deadly seriously.

However, if we could side-step that logical train of thought and appeal to more base emotions, we thought that with this in conjugation with whatever *gifts* would be endowed to us, we might be able to stand a chance.

This led us to create something we called *positive propaganda.* The messages broadcasted would obviously be biased in our favor, but they would mainly be truths relayed to us directly from Gástonio, as well as things that we discovered on our own. At what part, though, would I tell the ZRC the last words Gástonio imparted to me? That remained to be seen. The current task at hand was quite a difficult one, as was managing all of our communication to avoid alerting not only the Zaragozas but also duplicitous recipients who would report back to the Zaragozas what they were being told—or even worse, someone infiltrating our ranks as *double-agents.*

That whole evening, we brainstormed ways that we could produce this positive propaganda and screening materials required for future members. Identification of members was something that we thankfully didn't have to worry about since that issue resolved itself when we found the bespoke jewelry maker in Gástonio's small town. The next step, then, would be planning what event we would host to meet our potential recruits. Naturally, I suggested that we host one more Fireside Chat before the Second Trials started, but the rest of the ZRC had other ideas. To arrive at a solution once and for all, we discussed how we were going to do this over copious amounts of Catalonia's delicious red wine.

"Okay, okay, since we're trying to tailor to people who attended previous Fireside Chats, why don't we Occam's razor this bitch, and just host another one?" I asked.

"Mate, are you mad? Not only would that be stupid, but let's be honest—those things were just a way to vent about all the crazy shit that we've noticed during orientation. You remember how the Germans were always able to perfectly mimic Reverend Bert's hilarious Bavarian accent?" Paul said, almost heaving, trying to avoid spitting out wine.

"No, no, the best part of those chats were always when the architecture scholars made a comment about how useless a design of the Castillo was and how they could bring it up to 2040, instead of leaving it in 1540," James said, sipping his glass of merlot the slowest.

"Yeah, I think you and those architecture students are the only ones who share that sentiment," Amir said from the corner of the room.

"Okay, honestly, though, what were you guys thinking when you decided to come up with these chats in the first place? Because I thought you all were crazy talking that brazenly about the Zaragozas. Don't get me wrong; I agreed with everything you said, obviously, because I'm here. But it's clear that the ZNBS, not unlike any other *secret society,* keeps several things close to the chest because of pesky laws that could interfere with their plans, but to talk about it openly in their own home? Man, you guys had balls," Tolu slurred, shaming us all with his ability to down fermented grape juice.

Rafi and I looked at each other, then back to Tolu, each other once more, and back to Tolu again.

"Do you want to take this one, Rafi, or should I?" I said, unable to properly point to him due to the alcohol, so it probably looked like I was flailing my arms for help.

"Uh, yeah, sure. Well, for one, I thought they would just be a great way to vent about all of the strange shit occurring here, but the more chats we had, and the stranger shit that happened, the more I started to get a suspicion that there was more going on here. I wish I could explain it better, but it was just a hunch. As I started to talk it out to myself, it started to sound more and more plausible, then I told Femi about it, and he seemed to agree."

"You know, for me, Rafi, I did initially think you were crazy, but everything you said I had thought about before. Once those classes started to take a turn, I mean, it was basically textbook indoctrination: 'Get the future indoctrinated to believe in your ideologies,' 'Show them that they would be nothing without you,' 'Using their high and mighty position to mold you how to think.' It just all came off so slimy to me. But what really got me, similar to how you get those gift bags with all that paper wrapping to build anticipation for the actual gift, once I started to take off all the proverbial paper wrapping, I couldn't stop. Misery loves company, right? And I found you all, so cheers to misery!" I toasted.

"Cheers, cheers!" we all said, smashing our glasses together and indulging in the Rioja red, licking our lips to taste the velvety-smooth finish once more.

"What do you say, Sarah? Why did you keep attending the chats?" Rafi asked.

"Well, obviously because you *bråkmakere* were my flatmates."

"*What* did you just say?" Paul exclaimed, spitting out his wine.

"Ew, gross, man. And that's exactly why I'm in the corner. If there's anything I know more than medicine, it's Brits and alcohol," Amir said, smirking, twirling his wine glass in-between his index finger and thumb.

"Ha-ha, sorry, sometimes when I drink, I slip back into Norwegian, but I called you guys troublemakers. In all honesty, I first went to see what you guys were talking about. But the more I listened, the more I paid closer attention to what we were learning, and how it was being taught, my—how do you say—*bullshit detector* went off, and I became more curious."

Cleaning himself off, Paul continued this one-on-one with Sarah. "But really, what made you want to give up your dreams and possibly risk your life to take down perhaps the most powerful and well-connected people in the world?"

"Wow, such a thought-provoking question to ask while we're all drunk. Um, I can't say for sure. Call it some twisted sense of justice or call it just being twisted. We're all here because of our differences, the same differences that perhaps made us feel like outcasts where we're from, differences that I can vividly remember being ashamed about, wanting to do anything just to fit in. But as you get older, you come to appreciate those differences, even relish them sometimes because those are the qualities that make you who you are. Then here come people who initially made you feel appreciated for those differences, only to use them against you. The thought of that made me sick to my stomach. I told myself a long time ago that I worked way too hard in university and in graduate school to have anyone make me feel any less than who I am. I guess that was my reason." Sarah said eloquently.

"And the award for best speech goes to . . . drumroll, please . . . Sarah Øye!" Paul joked.

He was right, though—we weren't expecting it, but alcohol tends to bring out speeches like that. Then it came to me! "I love all you dorks and geeks so much. That's it," I said flatly.

"Mate, what are you on about now?" Paul replied.

"You said it yourself, Paulie-boy. You just said Sarah deserved to win an award for what she said. Why did she say it?!"

"Uh, because I asked—the same way I'm about to ask you if you took your antipsychotics this morning?"

"Ha-ha, Paul, the everyday funny man. Another good one, but no, Sarah said it because we're all freaking wasted! That's how we do it. We don't host another Fireside Chat; we pick a cold day and host a Fireside Drink! Do you all follow?"

"Sort of. You mean we get everyone drunk and see how they really feel about the Zaragozas?" James asked.

"Well, when you put it like that, yes, precisely! I'm sure there are more recipients that have deduced the same things we have. It's now just about getting them all in the same place," I said.

"What about those recipients who never attended a past Fireside Chat but had the same hunches, nonetheless?" Amir inquired.

"I second that," James added.

"Good point. So maybe we don't explicitly close it off just to those people. We let anyone that hears about it come, we start talking a little shite about the Zaragozas, we blame it on the ten bottles of wine we had, and no one is the wiser," Paul said.

"Wow, so we're really doing this, eh?" James asked.

"Seems so. Well, I'm just glad to be doing it with you all. Never have I met people so smart, yet so stupid. Let's hope whatever gifts the Zaragozas wish to impart, they also help in thwarting whatever plans they have for us."

"Ah-hem! speaking of plans they have for us, I have something to tell you all... you might wanna have your wine glasses close." I said, clearing my throat obnoxiously loud.

"Oh my, what is it Femi?" Sarah asked.

"Well, before we left Gástonio's, as you all know, I went back up just to make sure he was still sleeping."

"Fuckin' hell, mate, stop teasing, and come out with it," Paul said.

"Okay, okay, well, when I went into his room, Gástonio started to sleep-talk to me. I don't know if he had a dream or if he thought I was someone else because he kept calling me *Jorge*. Telling me, or Jorge, to give up our plans on stopping the Zaragozas because they're too powerful. But he said something that really stuck; he said that they had plans for *world domination* and that we don't understand the forces we're up against. . . . I know I should've told you all right after, but I didn't want to worry you."

The room fell silent for a few seconds that felt like years, apart from the occasional sound of someone swallowing their wine. *Better late than never, right?*

"So that means when he was freaking out that time, calling out for Jorge, he was actually referring to someone—someone who apparently tried to take down the Zaragozas, and most likely failed because here we are trying to do the same thing," Tolu said sardonically.

"Well, yeah, but he was alone—we're not," Rafi said sarcastically, finger-shooting at Tolu, the same way I previously did to him.

"We don't know that, Raphael. For all we know, he could've had an army," Sarah said.

"Fuck, I knew we should've asked who Jorge was. I'm sorry, guys," I said, apologizing.

"It's fine, Femi. Dealing with Gástonio was a lot already—especially since that was the last thing he said to you," Sarah said.

"Oi, oi, it's not fuckin' *fine*. We're literally risking our lives for this little endeavor, for what, world peace? I agreed to this whole thing, yeah, but once we start hiding things from each other, that's where I draw the line!" Paul shouted. He was right to be upset, and I didn't want to further provoke him, so I tried to reply as calmly as I could.

"I wasn't trying to hide anything from you all. I was just trying to choose the best time to come out with it, that's all."

"Let's all calm down. Femi, I understand why you didn't tell us when you joined us outside—especially considering your reaction the first time, Paul. But on the other hand, too, Femi, you have to realize that this is serious stuff. So whenever one of us comes across any pertinent information, it needs to be shared—especially between all of us," Amir said, trying to keep the peace.

"Oi, you're lucky I'm drunk, or I would've probably punched you already."

"Uh, I think you mean you're lucky I'm drunk because if you would've tried that, I would've taken that punching arm and used it to arm toss you onto your *arse, Judo-style*!" I teased Paul.

"So this is what guys are like when all that testosterone is flowing freely. Interesting . . ." Sarah quipped.

"Okay, okay, now that we're all lovey-dovey, back to this Final Fireside Chat/Drink, or whatever we want to call it. You all better not get drunk to the point where we can't discern potential friend from foe. We need to be alert even in our inebriation. We need to be able to see how the other recipients react to what we say and what they reply. For a castle filled with the best minds on the planet, our brains aren't going to be of much use in this task; we need to use our hearts. Any—and I mean *any*—sense that a recipient is *off, weird vibes, bad energy*, whatever you want to call it, we pull the plug on that person, and we don't mention anything if we see them around the castle again. And if they happen to bring it up, we play dumb, got it?" Rafi demanded.

We all nodded in agreement, so the only thing left to do was enjoy the rest of the opened wine bottles. The ZRC officially had a recruiting plan!

* * *

Being the newest members and also the ones who had the least contact with us initially, we charged Amir and Tolu with the responsibility of inviting those who they believed to have the most potential to support our cause. We purposefully arranged for the Fireside Drink to take place only a few days before the Second Trials. Hopefully, catching the recipients with their guards down, thus enabling more organic discussion about the Zaragozas.

Given the specific purpose of this chat, we did not want to just invite the entire general pool of recipients without any pre-evaluation. After positive propaganda brainstorming, we held a mini-meeting to discuss exactly who we would want to attend our impromptu soiree before the Second Trials. A name we collectively thought of was Alfred, a Swiss recipient and a psychopharmacology graduate student. He was inquisitive in a manner that was endearing enough not to be exasperating—partly the reason we collectively thought of him.

In addition, Rafi and Alfred were already close before we even met Rafi, so Alfred was already in the know of Rafi's detailed theory around the same time we were. Rafi only told me about Alfred a few weeks before the Fireside Chats, and the rest of the gang found out even later. Rafi and I used this to our advantage by keeping Alfred away from interacting with the main group. Our rationale was if we had one member of the ZRC who was never really seen with us but was aware of everything we were, it would grant him deniability if anything were to go awry.

Alfred was also quite eccentric, which would've resulted in two Pauls, something the ZRC definitely did not need! This worked in Alfred's favor, as well, since he preferred to be left alone with his own theories and research, but probably so he wouldn't have to feel ashamed for the out-loud monologues he loved to make whenever he made a new discovery. Alfred's primary task would be to conduct psychopharmacological research, if any was necessary, on the *gifts* we were to receive after the Second Trials.

We needed free and original thinkers, which paradoxically were in short supply in a mansion full of geniuses and prodigies. Don't get me wrong—my time spent at the Castillo was with some of the brightest minds on earth, but as many people fail to realize, there's more to intelligence than how well you can score on a certain test or how instinctively you can look at numbers. But unfortunately, in the world today, book smarts is often touted as the only measure of success and worth, failing to realize how vital social, emotional, and quite frankly, general intelligence is, in conjunction with natural curiosity.

It may have been a bit cynical, but I found it highly amusing that even when the fate of the world depended on some of the greatest minds on the planet, I still wasn't convinced that they would make the best choice for humanity. A story quite befitting for humans, even with our infinite ingenuity, our demise would still be self-inflicted. Thankfully, at least, we were not the only ones who thought this way.

Chapter 8: The Final Chat

As the dawn of our final chat was fast approaching, the fervor of its importance was felt by all. The first to raise doubt was Tolu.

"Are you all sure this will work?" he asked apprehensively. "What if someone snitches on us? We're all dead!"

"Just be cool, man," Rafi nonchalantly replied.

"Easy for you to say; this whole thing was partly your idea!" Tolu shot back.

"All of this fighting will get us nowhere. We collectively agreed on this plan, so now we just have to follow it to the best of our ability," Sarah interjected to stop the bickering.

"Sorry, you're right, Sarah. I . . . I just hope we know what we're doing, that's all," Tolu stammered, walking out of the room with his chin glued to his chest. Not wanting him to give in to despair, Amir and I quickly followed him into the corridor, hoping to assuage his apprehensions.

"Listen, dude, I know you're scared, but if this all works out, not only would we have a small army to take out the Zaragozas, we'll have powers, too!" Amir said, smiling. As the frown lines on Tolu's face slowly turned into a grin, I could tell Amir's humor attempt did not fall flat.

"Ha-ha, I know you're right, guys, but to be honest, what worries me most is my family back home in Nigeria. They're all counting on me to be successful, and I don't know what I would do if I failed them," he admitted, twiddling his thumbs.

"Listen, Tolu. What do you think would evoke the greatest change in the lives of your family—hell, to my extended family back in Nigeria, as well. The status-quo system that only allows us to view success through the lens of those that are all-powerful? Or to actually change the system so that the barriers of entry aren't so astronomical for the everyday person? By taking out the Zaragozas and the corrupt system that their business model thrives on, we stand a chance at bringing peace and prosperity—not only to Nigeria but the world," I pleaded, pressing his face with my hands.

"Ah, fuck it!" Tolu said, flashing me a reckless grin. "Let's just do it smart, then, and not muck it up!" he responded as the vibrancy returned to his eyes, and his voice became hearty again.

"That's my boy. Now let's get this alcohol flowing." Despite trying to curtail attendance by being selective of who we told about it, the turnout was similar to the previous Fireside Chats we hosted without screening criteria. In an attempt to verify that each person in attendance was, in fact, invited either by one of us or heard about the event through someone that was directly invited, we mingled around and acted like we were more inebriated than we actually were, asking recipients questions such as *Who invited you? What do you think of the Zaragozas?* and *What's your impression of the orientation so far?* If I'm honest, I'd like to think I had the best faux-drunk talking ability of all.

Most of the responses we got back were neutral—some people not entirely sure why orientation had been so *bizarre*, and a few who were downright cynical of what the Zaragozas were really up to. Unfortunately, though, there was a sizeable number of people who thought that orientation did, in fact, have ulterior motives but they did not want to stir anything up. Trying to penetrate further, we were now actively intermingling with the potential ZRC members to see what they truly believed in. "The whole lecture about demons and demonic possessions, eh? What was that about?" James asked Diego, one of the recipients from Argentina.

"Yeah, I can't really see what that had to do with anything. It's not like we're here to attend coursework—especially on things that aren't grounded in science, so I don't understand why they went over that blasphemy," Diego responded. Sensing not only a potential ZRC member but also another devout Catholic, James further pushed Diego into elaborating on his core philosophies.

"So, Diego, where exactly are you from in Argentina?"

"I'm not sure you would know it, but I'm from San Luis; it's literally in the middle of Argentina."

"I can't say that I do, and forgive me if I offend, but to me, you look like you might have Asian ancestry?" James asked.

"Ancestry? Ha-ha. The link is more direct than that. My father is Japanese, and his family first arrived in Argentina in the early twentieth century," Diego said gleefully.

"Wow, so interesting. I knew of the sizeable Japanese community in Brazil, but I didn't know that they also went to Argentina."

"Well, yeah, there's certainly more of us in Brazil, but there's also a sizeable Asian population in Argentina," Diego humbly replied. "James Lu, huh? I'm guessing you're Taiwanese yourself, but I believe I heard you speaking Spanish previously?" Diego asked James, inadvertently scratching his head in the process.

"Yes, I am Taiwanese, but I studied abroad in Honduras for a semester and picked up some Spanish," James mumbled.

"No, don't be ashamed! I've heard you speak to Rosario from Bolivia and was quite impressed," Diego said with a wry smile.

Now standing up straight instead of slouching, but still embarrassed by Diego's compliment, James said, "I thought I would be the only Spanish-speaking Asian, but color me surprised!"

"You and me both, brother," replied Diego. Getting back on track, Diego started to give his thoughts on our tenure at the Castillo. "This whole orientation thing has really had me questioning if I belong here or not. Don't get me wrong, of course; I realize that the Zaragozas have the ability to change my and my family's lives forever, but I can't shake the feeling that there's more going on than meets the eye. Something nefarious, and I'm not sure I want to be associated with such a thing. I was actually thinking of leaving once Pierre started mentioning NDAs, but I was more worried about what they would do if I quit. . . ."

"I know exactly what you mean, Diego, and guess what, I'm not the only one," James said leaning in closer to Diego.

"Oh, really? I was hoping so. I can't believe that freaky drink they had us consume, not even mentioning the fucking blood sacrifice and the mysterious Zaragoza zealots. It reminded me of those ayahuasca ceremonies that take place in the villages, but way creepier. What is this, a fucking

Stephen King book?" Diego said, his voice growing with Latin fury.

"Diego, I completely agree. We came here because we were awarded a scholarship, and now it seems like we're competing for God knows what while being indoctrinated; it's sick and an abuse of power, if you ask me," James said, matching Diego's tone.

"I agree wholeheartedly. I wish I could do something about it, to be honest, and just talk to more people this candidly," Diego said with a deep, remorseful sigh.

"It's actually funny you say that because there is something you can do about it," James replied with a sly grin. "A couple of my friends and I are starting a little group to talk about what's really going on in the Castillo and with the Zaragozas as a whole."

"A little group? That's not vague at all," Diego said sarcastically.

"Yeah, I know I'm being a tad secretive, but it's only out of safety. You'll have to trust me," James offered.

"Trust you? You're not even trusting me," Diego pointed out.

"I don't mean to be mistrustful, my friend, but for one, I've just met you. Two, we're not even completely sure what we're doing. And finally, three, if we were truly onto something, would we want to just share every bit of information with anyone willy-nilly? Especially considering how powerful the Zaragozas are?" James ended seriously.

"Fair enough, James, but I am intrigued to learn more about your *little group* if it turns out that the Zaragozas actually aren't what they seem. I'll never forgive myself for not doing anything to thwart their plans."

"I wholeheartedly agree with you, Diego, but you know what? We're going to be organizing a meeting that I want you to come to. We'll all be there, and if you like what we have to say, then we'll go from there. How does that sound?"

"Muy bien, mi amigo. Muchos gracias," Diego said with a quick smirk and a firm handshake.

"Oh, no, thank *you*, my friend. I'm just glad there are more like-minded people in this Castillo," James said.

When he finally regrouped with us, we could tell from James's accelerated rate of speech, his inability to stand still, continuously swaying side to side, that he couldn't wait to tell us everything he just experienced.

"Guys, guys, you won't believe it. I think I found a potential ZRC member!" he cried out, overcome by his immediate success.

"Not so loudly, mate. You want to let the whole mansion know what we're up to?" Paul snapped back.

"My apologies, but I just spoke to one of the recipients from Argentina, and believe it or not, he's Japanese Argentinian, which I didn't even know was a thing! The only thing I didn't like about him, though, is how chiseled his jaw was and how curly his hair was. Who does he think he is, a Japanese Argentinian Superman?"

"And what does that have to do with the ZRC, exactly?" replied Sarah.

"Which part?" James asked flatly.

"Both!"

"Well, nothing directly; I was just jealous that I was no longer the most attractive Asian guy here, but I thought it was cool that there's another Spanish-speaking guy who looks like me, that's all," James said.

"Well, if you take into account the fact that the indigenous people of the Americas originally came from Asia thousands of years ago from a land bridge that's now underwater, one could make the argument that a sizeable portion of the Spanish speakers in Latin America are *Asian,* too!" said Paul in an accent mocking BBC reporters, unable to even complete the sentence without laughing after every other word.

"Ah, just what we need, another Brit trying to teach history. What a surprise!" I joked. After poking fun at each other for a while, we finally got back on topic.

"Sorry, I digress. The point wasn't that he's another Spanish-speaking Asian guy; the point is that he wants to do something about the Zaragozas, as well," James said.

"Is that so? Exactly how did you come to this conclusion?" asked Paul in a more serious voice.

"Okay, first things first. Where is all of this hostility coming from?" James said, looking at Paul crookedly.

"Yeah, chill out, dude," Amir seconded.

Paul then said something along the lines of, "It's not that I don't believe you, James—I trust you with my life and I hope you know that. I just don't want to lose any more people that I care about. That's it. . . . I want to make sure that we're careful about everyone we let into this *thing* of ours."

"Yeah, Paul, I get that, I really do, but personal feelings aside, I really think we could have a remarkable ZRC member in Diego," James emphatically replied.

"Before I even mentioned anything, he pointed out how weird he thought everything was that has been going on and how his, just like my religion, goes against everything the Zaragozas might be up to. And if his faith is anything like mine, which I think is the case, he wants to get these bastards as much as I do."

"Well, I for one trust you, James," Amir said.

"Us, too," Sarah and I added.

"Well, guys, to avoid being bogged down about who we let in on ZRC stuff, I think we'll all just have to trust each other on any potential members and go from there," I suggested.

"But how exactly do we go about that?" Tolu asked.

"That's the easy part. We use this Fireside Soiree to meet more people. We each try to find one potential member, and tonight, we get all the recruits together, and we grill them like cheese to see where they truly stand!" Rafi said in an animated manner unlike we'd heard before.

Everything about Rafi's demeanor was understated, from the hands always in his pockets to his expressionless face. His low and soothing voice reassured everyone that this was, indeed, our best path forward, and if I'm being honest, was our *only* path.... The rest of the evening was spent on screening more applicants. and luckily since this event was my idea, I didn't have to take part in the process, allowing me to formulate a plan to recruit even more members while still enjoying the truly delicious wine we had at our disposal.

Rafi was the next person to bring in a potential recruit: Mikael from Armenia—not meeting the same way Diego and James did, but connecting, nonetheless. Rafi told me that he met Mikael while exiting the restroom as Mikael was entering. Holding the door open for Mikael as he left, he did not think anything of it, but Rafi did notice that Mikael's appearance was *interesting, to say the least*. According to Rafi, Mikael was wearing a striped rugby shirt that was purple and pink, matching his purple buzz-cut hair, and rose-pink sword-like earrings.

Mikael thanked him, and Rafi kindly replied with a casual, "No worries."

"Hey, wait! Aren't you the third American?" Mikael asked.

"Yeah, I guess you could say that," Rafi replied with an air of indignation. A blank stare, furrowed eyebrows, and tucked-in lips revealed Mikael's obvious confusion about the tone and wording of Rafi's answer.

Mikael followed up with, "I thought Femi and Grace were the only American students here?"

"Yes, apparently, the ZNBS made an exemption for the American recipients. I'm not sure why, and I'm not sure what it is to you, stranger," Rafi curtly replied.

"Forgive me if I'm wrong, but could it be because you're Native American?" Mikael asked, swinging his tongue.

Rolling his eyes and repeatedly tapping his foot, consciously or not, gave Mikael visual and tactile clues of Rafi's increasing annoyance.

Rafi replied, "*Perhaps*. What is it to you, anyway?"

"Well, believe it or not, but my doctoral thesis was on the parallels between the total annihilation of the Native Americans in the United States and the Armenian Genocide committed by the Turkish during and after the First World War," Mikael said.

"Is that so? And let me guess, you're Armenian, so you think that somehow the history of our people is the same?" Rafi asked pointedly. "Last time I checked, Armenia was still its own sovereign nation, and your culture was still intact. Can you say the same about my people, Mikael?" Rafi's voice went from his usual calm and mild-mannered tone to one that became forceful and enraged at the prospect of these distinct tragedies of human history being equated. Attempting to regain his self-composure, Rafi took a deep breath, repeated some meditation mantras, and returned his voice back to its usual controlled cadence.

"Hey, look, Mikael, I'm sure you mean well, and I apologize for reacting the way I did, but you have to understand something, as well: It becomes unbelievably tiring to constantly be told by others that although what happened to my people was horrific, it's still comparable to what other people have gone through. True or not, it's frustrating to constantly have to explain myself or my people each and every time someone wants to have a pity party. I'm not saying that's what you're trying to do, Mikael, and quite frankly, I don't know or care for whatever your reasons are for initiating the conversation, but this is where it ends," Rafi finally said, walking out of the bathroom fully.

His eyes facing downward and arms folded against his chest in an effort to perhaps comfort himself, Mikael looked dejected, and his body language surely reflected so. "Hey, man, I sincerely apologize for making you feel that way, and it was one hundred percent not my intention to do so," Mikael said regretfully. "All I was trying to do was establish some initial basis of familiarity, and I didn't mean to donwplay the impact of what you and your people had to face. I was just curious and excited because I've never actually met a Native American before, and allowing three recipients from the same country just fascinated me when only two recipients per country is one of the most stringent of all ZNBS guidelines," Mikael said, blushing.

"It's all good; it's my fault, too. I shouldn't have raged out in the manner that I did. It was rude and out of character.

You're right, there are similarities between what happened to our peoples—especially the fact that to this day, some people try to negate the impact of those genocides, while some even try to deny them altogether," Rafi responded with the glimmer in his eyes returning, reinforcing his sincerity with a soft smile.

"Let's try this again. Hi, nice to meet you. My name is Raphael; what's yours?" Rafi said, theatrically extending his hand.

Mikael responded in an equally comical tone, "Nice to make your acquaintance, Raphael!"

"You know what? It's weird that they allowed three of us, actually. It's something that Femi and I thought about, but not in detail. Do you have any thoughts on the matter?"

"Well, nothing conclusive, but it's interesting that for the rest of the world, only two people can be selected for a scholarship that is intended to support the brightest, yet most marginalized communities, yet for America, *and only America,* an extra recipient is allowed. It just seems like perhaps there's another angle to this scholarship that we aren't seeing, is all I'm suggesting," Mikael said. "Furthermore, since we're barred from speaking about the scholarship, or even the orientation process with outsiders, there's no way to confirm how long this exemption has been in place."

Mikael massaged his chin for a moment before carrying on. "I mean, think about it, what is America at its core? A nation full of immigrants, so why do the Zaragozas need all of these immigrants or children of immigrants for exactly, and why can't we talk about anything with *anyone?"*

Rubbing his face pensively, Rafi was pondering Mikael's words and realized that what he was saying could potentially align with his own theory and wanted to discover the full extent of Mikael's hypothesis concerning the scholarship and the Zaragozas as a whole.

"Can I ask you a question, Rafi?" Mikael asked.

"Go for it," Rafi responded.

"Well, initially, I found it very peculiar that there were three of you from America. Then, after all the weird classes, weird rituals, and just overall complete weirdness that's been happening here, it came to me to think that maybe there's more than meets the eye here. I just can't believe no one else is thinking this way or at least not talking about it, for a freaking mansion full of so-called scholars!"

"Well, it's funny you say that. What if I told you that you're not the only one who thought this way?" Rafi leaned in and said softly.

"What do you mean?" Mikael said, squinting his eyes as if the smaller his field of vision became, the clearer he would be able to think.

"What I'm saying is that I agree with you. I think there could be something more nefarious going on here, and let's just say I have my own theories about our purpose here," Rafi pointed out.

"What are you waiting for, then? Tell me," Mikael begged.

"Not yet. I'm not completely sure if I can trust you. It's not like what we're on about is playground talk. Speaking in this manner to the wrong people could have dire consequences, as I'm sure you could understand," Rafi said.

"Why, yes, of course, but I want you to know one thing about me: Wanton indoctrination paired with any form of coercion is not something I will tolerate from anyone," Mikael said firmly.

"Not even from a family worth trillions of dollars, a family that's actively offering you a chance to change not only your life but the lives of everyone you love and care for?" Rafi said, winking and nudging Mikael's arm.

"Not even for that. Injustice is injustice, and I'm sick and tired of people forgoing their morals and beliefs for a few dollars; that's a check I would *never* cash," Mikael said adamantly as he clenched his fist and struck it down forcefully on the bathroom dressing table.

"Well, then, sir, hang around for a while and come join a few like-minded friends of mine tonight, and we can talk more about this. How does that sound?" Rafi said.

"Wait, you mean you and your friends are going to do something about this atrocity?" Mikael asked.

"No, I didn't say that. I said that later I'll introduce you to some other people who might feel the same way you do, that's all," Rafi responded.

"Well, then, I guess that I'll see you later, Raphael!" Mikael said, smiling.

Sarah had a harder time connecting with anyone for reasons she never divulged to me, though I think it was just the amount of pressure associated with this chat that made the stakes much higher than the last chats. Sure, at all the previous chats, Sarah was quiet—that's her nature—but for some reason, this last Fireside party made her especially apprehensive about talking to anyone. I thought it was attributed to the same reasons Tolu and Paul previously hesitated in agreeing to host this last Fireside party and recruiting new members into the ZRC. There were fears of our plans being discovered by a potential interloper, or even the Zaragozas themselves, fears that were very much grounded in reality.

But no, the real reason Sarah was so withdrawn that day wouldn't be revealed to me until later. Nevertheless, there was something that caught her attention and the attention of several other hungry and drunk mid-to-late twenty-somethings: The fragrant aroma of various savory spices and vegetables such as green peas, lentils, and chilis had filled the air.

"Would you like one?" said a soft yet self-assured voice. Sarah turned around and was met with a girl she had never seen before. Adorned in gold jewelry, from the gold pin in her tumbling and lustrous black hair to the gold anklet around her left ankle that made her look like royalty. "Have you tried one before?" the young woman asked.

"I don't know what it is, but it smells heavenly," Sarah said with her eyes intensely transfixed on this strange, triangular pastry, then back to the stunning, caramel-skinned girl who was now smiling warmly at her.

"It's called a samosa; just try it." Doing as she was instructed, Sarah took the pastry from the platter the girl was carrying and took a large bite.

"Oooh! It's hot!" Sarah said as she tried to cool the samosa down by repeatedly inhaling and exhaling air from her mouth, blushing in embarrassment at her foolhardy attempt. "It's so hot but so good. Thank you, um, sorry, but I didn't get your name," Sarah said.

"Ha-ha, yeah, sorry. I should've warned you that it was hot, but your face was worth it! Suhani, my name is Suhani; what's yours?" She said with a smile.

"What a beautiful name. My name is Sarah. Nice to meet you, Suhani."

"Nice to meet you, too, Sarah," Suhani said graciously.

"It's so funny that you brought this because this is probably the fourth Fireside-related event we've had since orientation started, and it's the first time someone has thought to actually bring food!" Sarah said, laughing a little nervously.

"Oh, really? Well, I love to bake, so I figured that I might, as well," said Suhani. "I can't believe you haven't had one before. It's probably the most well-known pastry to come out of India. Where are you from?" Suhani inquired.

"Oh, well, I'm from Norway, and I don't travel much," Sarah said timidly. "I'm guessing you're from India, then?"

"That's correct! Northern India, in the Western Himalayas, to be exact."

"Wow, I've always wanted to go to the Himalayas; it must be cool to live so close by!" Sarah said as her eyes widened with excitement, opening up to the stranger.

"I guess it's like being from anywhere else, really; once you live there, you take everything for granted, but yes, it is very beautiful," Suhani said modestly. "If you can handle the cold, of course. But since you're Norwegian, I'm sure the cold is no problem for you at all!"

"Ha-ha, you would think so, but it still gets to me," Sarah said, twirling her hair at the coy remark. "I can't believe this is the first time I'm seeing you, but I'm sure I would've remembered . . . ?"

"Oh, is that so, and why would you have remembered?" Suhani pried.

A soft flush made Sarah stumble over her words. "Well, well . . . because you're very pretty," she blurted out in a panicked frenzy.

"You're just being kind. You're obviously very beautiful

yourself, but unlike you, I have seen *you* around," Suhani said, returning a warm smile to Sarah, filling her stomach with schoolgirl-like butterflies.

"Where have you seen me?" Sarah asked with a nervous smile.

"Just around the Castillo and always with those four guys," Suhani replied.

"Oh, yes, those are my friends and suitemates, Femi, Rafi, James, and Paul."

"You all must've gotten along pretty well initially to be so close now," Suhani said.

"Yeah, I guess you could say that," Sarah said, her face returning back to its normal complexion, although her hands were still twirling the ends of her hair.

"I wish I had connected that way with my suitemates, but no matter how hard I try, the only thing they focus on is being the best prototypical scholarship recipients they can be, if such a thing even exists!" Suhani said, swinging her fists in frustration.

"And how would you describe yourself, Suhani?" Sarah asked quickly and courteously, obscuring her true interest in the answer.

"Well, obviously, we're all very studious; otherwise, we wouldn't be here. So I was hoping to meet more open-minded individuals whose entire life didn't revolve around books! For example, I tried to talk to them about that whole thing with the cultists or whatever those guys were, and how we had to sign scrolls with our blood on them. . . . I'm sure that can't be legal, right?" Suhani asked.

Not knowing if Suhani was asking a rhetorical question or not, Sarah replied, "I'm not sure about the legality, but when it comes to ethics, that was definitely not cool."

"Like, who the fuck does that type of thing? This isn't the Middle Ages, and they just brushed it off like it was some sort of a *European aristocracy initiation thing*," Suhani said passionately.

"Yeah, you're right, but unfortunately, I think a lot of people here think the same way your suitemates do. It's the whole *don't bite the hand that feeds* mentality; in their defense, it's a very common human trait, no matter how educated you are," Sarah humbly replied.

"Yeah, I understand that, but at some point, doesn't your common-sense radar alert you that something could be amiss here?" Suhani pointed out. "But as the saying goes, 'common sense isn't all that common,' right? And maybe all the years of studying has a way of further diminishing that capability in some people!"

Both ladies laughed at this sentiment, agreeing wholeheartedly.

"But what about you, Sarah?" Suhani asked after their laughter had died down.

"What about me, what?" Sarah asked, rubbing the back of her neck, pondering the true intentions of Suhani's question.

"You know what I mean. I'm asking, what do you think of how orientation has been thus far?"

"Oh, yeah, well . . . things have definitely been bizarre, especially all the points you just brought up," Sarah said in a hushed tone.

"That's it? You don't have any other comments or observations thus far? I figured you for a smart and observant girl who would have more insightful comments to make on the matter," Suhani said.

"Okay, well, the thing is," Sarah gulped, "I think there could be something more sinister at play here, but there's no way to confirm it just yet. It's all accusations, but since you're so resolute on finding out more information, you should stick around after everyone leaves here today; I know some people who would like to hear exactly what you think."

"I knew you knew more than you were letting on!" Suhani exclaimed, jabbing Sarah's arm, unable to contain her excitement.

"Ssshhh, and ow! Not so loud. Just be there, okay?" Sarah said, placing her index finger on her pursed lips.

"Yeah, I'll be there, as long as you're there, Sarah," Suhani replied, not breaking eye contact with Sarah's honey-brown topaz eyes.

After James, Rafi, and Sarah had secured their potential recruits, Paul, Amir, and Tolu were next to follow suit. Amir found his potential recruit pretty easily since it was Kofi, the Ghanaian recipient, whom we all previously met the night I hosted the party and got shit-faced playing drinking games. To be honest, he wasn't that memorable, apart from being very polite and repeatedly asking questions about how to play the drinking games, and obviously those big brown eyes that made him look a bit owl-like.

Amir told us that he ran into Kofi not at our shindig but a few days beforehand. This was a point of contention for us since the main idea of hosting this final Fireside event was to recruit more members into the ZRC. However, an exemption was made for Kofi, considering he was someone we all knew and judged to be decent. Although, this wasn't enough for Rafi to consider his potential membership. Trying to appease Rafi's reluctance, Amir revealed that Kofi *roughly* knew what we were up to. This revelation came as a shock to all, but in accordance with the rule that stated, "If any core member of the ZRC had already vetted any potential candidates and deemed them to be suitable, then they would be able to join, as long as everything else was in order."

"Don't forget, guys, that's how Tolu and I joined the ZRC, as well, remember?" Amir had pointed out.

"Besides, this is someone we all know, too!" Amir said.

"Yeah, true, but when you say that he *roughly* knows what we are up to, what exactly does he know?" Rafi asked, his eyes laser-focused on Amir's shaky disposition.

"Well, what he knows is that we think that there's more than meets the eye here at the Castillo and that we're investigating it, that's all."

"Are you *sure?*" Rafi pressed.

"Yes, I promise!" Amir reassured.

"Okay, then, we'll place Kofi on the shortlist, as well, and then tonight, we'll be able to further vet all of these potential members. How does that sound?" I asked everyone.

No one verbally responded to my question, but their slow nodding heads was all the confirmation I needed to ensure we were still on the same page. I didn't admit it then, but I seconded Rafi's apprehension about Kofi, as well, but perhaps for more trivial reasons. Someone who holds up drinking games *and* is from Ghana is immediately questionable to me. There was no real animosity for Kofi on my part, but Nigeria and Ghana always have this friendly rivalry about whose food is best, and I occasionally indulged in this teasing, too.

When the time came for Tolu to find his recruit, we were at the time very skeptical of the motivation of his choice—all of us apart from Paul, anyway. This was because Tolu's choice was Daniela, the Brazilian recipient. It's not that we had anything against her—quite the contrary, in fact. But the thing was, it was basically universally agreed by all current members of the ZRC, and perhaps all ZNBS recipients in general, that Daniela was drop-dead gorgeous. Perhaps more interestingly, though, was that her beauty was *not* encapsulated by the traditional standards of European beauty that is often the global standard of the world. No, Daniela was different. Not in the stereotypical Latina archetype of beauty, either. Instead of luminous free-flowing black hair, Daniela sported a zebra-striped bobbed haircut that screamed non-conformity. Instead of pale skin and soft features, her skin tone was a warm brown that you could tell had been equitably sun-kissed, most analogous to the radiance of fine copper.

In regard to temperament, Daniela was also not the demure type. Where societal standards would've deemed it best if she were modest and reserved, Daniela was audacious and outspoken while still possessing a certain honesty in her brashness that was as attractive as it was admirable. Unsurprisingly, we guys swooned over her, but this time the ladies could relate, too! When it came to Daniela, there was barely any cattiness or sly remarks from other members of the female sex. Even when these comments were made, the positive energy that she effortlessly exuded often had the people who made those spiteful comments about how she dressed or looked feel moronic. Daniela's ultimate goal was the empowerment of all women, no matter their shape, size, or color.

How could you be mad at that? I often asked myself. However, this was all discovered after Tolu recruited her into the ZRC, and at the time, we believed it was his attempt to dazzle her with his vast knowledge of all things astrophysics. He always described to us in unnecessary detail how he was *scared shitless* to talk to her at the table where the samosas were placed, but *a message from the stars,* as he put it, told him to take action and approach Daniela at the table.

"Do you know what these are?" Tolu said, trying to mimic Paul's causal indifference.

"Hmm, I'm guessing that they're some sort of meat or vegetable-filled pastry from South Asia, often served as an appetizer?" Daniela said sarcastically.

The sarcasm didn't faze Tolu, though—how could it? He was too enamored with Daniela to even realize.

"Oh, really, yeah, I thought so, too, but what's it actually *callllledddd*" Tolu said, mesmerized.

Daniela let out a weird laugh/snort that made Tolu laugh, too, a laugh that would come to define one aspect of Daniela's quirkiness.

"I'm just kidding; I'm not sure what these are called, but they sure look tasty. Do you want to try one together?" Daniela said, smiling at Tolu, extending Suhani's samosa.

"I thought you would never ask; let's do it!" Tolu enthusiastically replied.

They then proceeded to take a bite into the lukewarm samosa simultaneously, not breaking eye contact with one another. "Mm-hmm, wow, I wasn't expecting so much savory flavor. That's very good. It sorta reminds me of a dish we have in Nigeria called a meat pie—same texture and consistency, though the spices in this are different."

"Ha-ha. It's seriously just called a *meat pie* back in Nigeria?

"Hey, hey! It's not my fault we were colonized by the

British!"

"Good point. Well, it reminds me of a triangular empanada!" Daniela said.

"I'm sorry, I was so transfixed with the food that I didn't even properly introduce myself. My name is Tolu Ademide."

"Nice to meet you, Tolu. My name is Daniela Gomes," the young woman said.

"Just to be truthful, I noticed you in the prehistoric ethics class we had to take and instantly thought you were so cool, so when I saw you at this table, I just had to talk to you," Tolu confessed.

Nervously trying to chew with her mouth closed to not appear totally uncouth, Daniela abruptly asked, "Well, why didn't you just talk to me, then?"

Not only did the question make Tolu a bit nervy, but the direct eye contact added to the effect, making Tolu stumble over his words like a grade-school boy timidly giving his first presentation. "W-w-well, umm . . ."

"Spit it out, dude!" Daniela quipped, smiling now with her pearl-white teeth sparkling freely. Though her comment had caught Tolu off guard, the manner in which she said it, while smiling, had a way of making Tolu feel more at ease, allowing him to finally speak coherently.

"I was just going to say that I was nervous!" Tolu said. "I'm not sure if you realize, but you're kind of intimidating to talk to!" Tolu admitted, blankly staring at his shoelaces.

"You really think so?" Daniela asked, no longer smiling.

"Well, in a way. . . . Most of us are pretty square and unassuming, whereas you have this otherworldly sense to you that is immediately noticed as soon as you enter any room. I just thought you wouldn't want to talk to someone like me, well . . . because . . . because you're so up there!" Tolu said, outstretching his arm as the sweat dripped down his shiny, bald head.

"Aw, that's really kind of you to say, but I didn't think of it that way. I'm just being myself, but if you think that's cool, then I appreciate it, I guess," Daniela said in a tone an octave lower than her normal speaking voice.

Sensing some discomfort from Daniela's body language when discussing her personality and outward appearance, Tolu tried to switch the conversation to another topic. Moving away from the samosa table, Daniela and Tolu were now sitting in front of the namesake fireplace.

"How are you enjoying orientation so far?" Tolu asked, his mouth still full of food.

"It's okay. I didn't expect it to place such importance on religion and ancient practices, but I guess it has been interesting, to say the least."

Tilting his head, Tolu pressed further, "In what way has it been *interesting*?"

"Well, you know, how else would we have learned about all those different beliefs and customs? It's not like the material that we covered during orientation is exactly taught in schools."

"Yeah, true, but what's the purpose of going over that type of material just to receive a scholarship?" Tolu asked. Growing fascinated with what Tolu had to say, she stood up from where she was sitting to get closer to Tolu, curious to see what else he thought.

"Well, when you frame it like that, yeah, it's not too applicable, but isn't the reason we're here in the first place because we are naturally gifted and curious students?" Daniela asked snappishly.

"Yes, true, but that doesn't mean it's not bizarre, that's all," Tolu replied firmly. "I see you are quite spirited, though. That's an admirable trait," Tolu said.

Taking her seat near Tolu at the fireplace again, Daniela responded, "Yeah, you can say that. I don't mean to be rude, but I had a pretty tough upbringing, and actually liking books and learning about anything that fascinated me wasn't exactly encouraged in the favelas of Rio de Janeiro, so I guess I had to develop a tough skin in order to survive. I didn't mean to make you uncomfortable in any way," Daniela apologized.

"No need to apologize. You are who you are, and you shouldn't be ashamed of it; it suits you." Tolu grinned, edging closer to Daniela.

"But now that you mention it, you know what was weird? That whole thing where Pierre gave that ominous speech about staying loyal to him and his family. What really did it for me, though, was when those creepy guys came out wearing those black robes and had us sign those fucking scrolls with our blood. What was that about?" Daniela said, finally admitting her apprehension.

Elated that he and Daniela finally had some common ground, Tolu eagerly responded, "Seriously, were they trying to depict a scene out of the History of Occultism lecture we had to take?"

"I'm not sure, but I think they definitely crossed the line with that. No matter how much we need this scholarship, It's not okay to give them our *fucking* blood! Who do they think they are? It definitely makes that NDA we had to sign make much more sense, which was another thing I wasn't okay with!" Daniela said thunderously.

Looking around to see if anyone was listening to their conversation, Tolu leaned into Daniela and whispered, "So, you actually signed the scrolls?"

"Unfortunately, yeah, I did—one of my biggest regrets. I wish I would've known beforehand to come up with something, anything to get out of that garbage. What about you?" Daniela asked.

"Over my dead body would I sign that piece of shit!" Tolu said colorfully.

Sparking the curiosity of Daniela's imagination, she started to brainstorm all the ways that Tolu could've avoided donating his blood to the Zaragozas.

"You used someone else's blood, then?"

"Nope!" Tolu said, smirking.

"You used ketchup to sign!"

"Wrong again!"

"Um, you used some sort of food coloring mixture?"

"Good guess, but I didn't do that, either!" Tolu chuckled, taking satisfaction in Daniela's state of confusion.

"Okay! Just come out with it. What did you do?" Daniela asked desperately.

"Well, I was fortunate enough to be friends with some people who also think what's going on here is a bit sketchy, so before we signed those documents, we used the blood of an injured bird."

"You guys killed a bird just to get out of signing those documents?" Daniela almost yelled. . . .

"*Ssssh!* Heavens, no. What kind of barbarian do you think I am?" Tolu said in a tone of exaggerated hurt. "The bird was already injured, and when we used its blood, it had already passed away," Tolu said.

"Whew. I was about to say, I was beginning to like you. You all are very lucky to end up in that position, though," Daniela remarked.

"Yeah, we were fortunate to get out of that bullshit initiation ceremony. It was almost as if the bird sacrificed his life for us."

"So, you're implying that the Zaragozas are up to no good, then?" Daniela inquired.

"You don't think so?" Tolu immediately replied. "The optics of everything just seems too weird to me. You're a smart girl; just think about it. You have a family worth trillions of dollars actively recruiting some of the smartest minds on the planet, but the icing on the cake is the fact that we're also the respective minorities in our countries. Yes, it helps us out tremendously, but it doesn't take knowing rocket science to see that the true benefit is theirs. Through us, the number of business connections they could make would be boundless. They would be the only major conglomerate in a lot of these local economies, producing even more wealth and power in the few places that they don't already have it."

Waiting just long enough to silently inform Tolu that she thought about what he just said, but not long enough for there to be an awkward silence, Daniela said only one word:

"Elaborate."

"You seriously don't follow?" Tolu asked. "Come closer; I don't want to be too loud. Okay . . . think about it: We're the ones that can contribute the most to their empire, while also being the ones most dependent on their fortune! It's genius, especially when you consider most of us come from collectivist countries in the first place. *'Don't stir the pot,' 'I am because we are,' 'If two people unite as one, their strength is powerful enough to cut metal'*—we've all heard countless proverbs like that growing up. They, of course, know that, too, and it makes it easier for them to indoctrinate us to follow their glory blindly," Tolu exclaimed in a frantic whisper.

"Jesus Christ, Tolu, you really think they're that diabolical?" Daniela looked aghast.

Now standing over Daniela and raising his voice, Tolu agitatedly asked, "Come on, Daniela. I thought you were the one that marched to the beat of your own drum? You don't think that orientation has been preparing us for something *extremely specific,* not only with the scrolls but the fascist-laden rhetoric that's been forced down our throats since we arrived?"

"Now you're the one who needs to *ssshh,* but I guess when you put it that way, there have been some aspects of orientation that can't be readily explained," Daniela admitted.

"Listen, I'm not trying to persuade you to do something that you don't want to," Tolu said. "You're obviously a very smart girl. I'm simply just trying to give you another perspective, a perspective that is shared by a few others and me, about what we think is happening in this place. It's your choice whether you believe it or not," Tolu said, before solemnly attempting to walk away.

"Wait, you said a few others believe in this, too?" Daniela hissed at him.

"Yes, I sure did, and if you don't mind, I would really like you to meet them. We're meeting tonight. Stick around here after everyone else leaves, and you'll meet the rest of our merry little gang," Tolu said with a sly wink, apparently learning something from Paul, after all.

* * *

As the non-ZRC affiliated stragglers began to leave, the rest of the gang and I started to brainstorm exactly how we wanted this impromptu ZRC *initiation* to go. The type of thing we thought of doing was to make it a grand ceremony (minus the blood donations, of course!). I knew that with ceremonies comes a certain aspect of inherent professionalism and solidarity. We also did not want to promote the belief that everything Zaragoza-related was evil and then turn to just and host something even remotely related to the structure of ZNBS orientation, ceremonies included.

We all agreed that doing so would come off as extremely hypocritical, yet we did need a way to formalize the process of officially joining the ZRC. Luckily, we still had the phoenix jewelry that would be used to officially represent a full member of the ZRC, but that was about all that we had.

Although we knew anything ceremony-related wouldn't come off so well, staying true to the core mission of the ZRC would be important to state, no matter how *preachy* it sounded, and initiation should be based on this principle. The plan was then for us to tell the new ZRC prospects about Rafi's theory, what we think is the primary reason for this scholarship, as well as what Gástonio shared with us. The big risk we were taking was informing everyone about our beliefs before we could officially trust them.

The only confidentiality assurance granted to us is that everyone in attendance was pre-screened by one of the founding members of the ZRC. We all wanted something more secure to ensure that no one would go on after this meeting and spill their guts to anyone who would lend them an ear, especially the Zaragozas. But this could not be guaranteed, so we proceeded, anyway. I was aware that we were taking a great risk but also possibly investing in an even greater reward.

As the evening went on and the last stragglers began to depart once the food and drink were either depleted or displaced, we rounded up our prospects and transitioned the meeting into the living quarters of our dormitory, ground zero of where this whole thing was conceptualized. It seemed only right for it to also be the place where we recruited and initiated more members.

The anticipation of what we had to say was practically palpable, leading me to postulate on what everyone was thinking based on their outward dispositions.

Mikael tried his hardest to remain unfazed by the gravity of this ordeal, sitting down quietly, crossing his legs, appearing as if he was cognizant of maintaining proper posture throughout (but knowing the emotional roller coaster that was Mikael, this was all a ruse). Nevertheless, what failed his artful attempt of coolness was the fact that although his legs were crossed, he could not stop shaking his feet or tapping his hand against his lap—no doubt an effort to keep himself grounded in the moment.

Next up came Diego, James's prospective new member. Reading his body language was a bit more difficult since he stood farther away from the rest of us, choosing to stand in the kitchen, while the rest of us were gathered in the living room. Though he was farther away, I could not help but notice his difficulty in deciding where to place his arms while he tried to stand stoically. He began with the classic folding of the arms which, according to what body language expert you ask, is an attempt to either close one off from others, or a way to self-soothe. Right arm over left, left over right, hands down to the side, and then in his pockets. Where he probably thought he was being cool by standing, all it showed to me was how anxious he truly was.

Suhani's body language was harder to read still—not due to distance, but because she was talking to Sarah until we made our introductory speeches. That is one quality that I always admired about her: Even under pressure, she remained calm and collected, despite whatever she concealed inside (Suhani and Sarah both shared that trait). The only point of nervousness I could remotely detect from her was the fact that she took a sip of water every time she finished a sentence. Though she was also eating the samosas that she brought to the Fireside Chat, so who knows if the water-drinking was to combat the flakiness of the pastry or if it was attributed to lingering anxiety.

Tomor, Paul's recruit, was by far the coolest of cucumbers, albeit in a different manner than Suhani. Where Suhani perhaps tried to hide her anxiety through talking, Tomor instead just remained silent unless he was directly addressed or was directly addressing someone. It wasn't a vow of false and untenable silence like Mikael, but rather, Tomor's silence had an authentic, military-like demeanor to it. His physical features perfectly complemented his mysterious personality, as well.

He had dark olive skin that accentuated his chiseled cheekbones, an effortlessly rugged five—o'clock shadow, and forest green eyes that looked like nature's perfect amalgamation of the sea-blue eyes of his father and the earth-brown eyes of his mother. Paul never really mentioned how he met Tomor, only saying that he met him when he was talking about almost joining the Royal Air Force to Amir when Tomor interrupted and introduced himself at a previous Fireside Chat.

From my brief conversations with him up until this point, I found out although he was Israeli-born, his mother had emigrated from Ethiopia, which I'm sure couldn't have been easy for anyone to bear due to the vast amount of discrimination half-white and non-white Israelis often face.

Kofi, on the other hand, well, his mannerisms were *interesting,* to say the least, at this ZRC meeting. It could've been attributed to perhaps something Kofi smoked or drank before he arrived, but he definitely didn't let the gravity of this meeting dampen his spirits, or at least he tried not to. Whether it was randomly coming to sit extremely close to others or sarcastically restating whatever had just been spoken, it was surprisingly effective in making everyone more comfortable, given the circumstances around why we were there and the topics being discussed.

I'm not certain if this was intentional on Kofi's part, or if he was actually just inebriated, high, or *both.* Nevertheless, his odd behavior helped to counter the overall serious tone of the meeting.

In the case of Daniela, she furtively sat in the corner of the living room, not talking to anyone, but apparently listening very attentively, according to her, at least. Curious to know what was bothering her after we addressed all the potential recruits, I tentatively approached her to inquire about her behavior. She wore a straight face and stared at me, which made me feel uncomfortable having her hazel-greenish eyes lasered in on me, but I was glad she was at least paying attention. Her apparent seriousness, coupled with her early doubts voiced to Tolu, made both of us worried that she may be having second thoughts about being here. How wrong I was.

Once I had finished gauging all of the potential recruits' demeanors, I thought that no one seemed uneasy enough for it to potentially be a concern to the rest of the ZRC members. Not wanting to do what I usually do and rush to a conclusion, I gathered the rest of the gang to ask their thoughts.

"Yeah, I think we can trust this lot. They may be a bit jumpy, but I don't smell any rats," Paul said.

"I think we should be careful about what we share with them," James said with a shifty look about him.

"And why do you say that?" I asked.

"Well, not because I don't trust any of them, which I'm not too sure I do yet, but just because the more they know early on, the more danger we put them in."

It was a valid point, so after he raised his concerns, we all agreed that we would initially only share Rafi's theory with them, gauge how they react to it, and then proceed into what Gástonio shared with us, if they react positively.

"Sarah, are you okay with all of this?" I somberly said.

"Too late to turn back now, right?" she calmly replied.

"Damn right," I smiled and winked at her, remembering her own hesitancy at our first discussion about the Zaragozas intention.

"Last but not least, Tolu, you still worried, or have we quelled your fears?" I turned to our newer friend.

"You know what, Femi, this is all going better than I

expected. I mean, damn, we actually have a little group here," Tolu said with a chuckle. "I think we can actually take these *baastads* down. I really do, oh!" he said with a thick Yoruba accent.

"Well, that settles it, then!" I couldn't describe how pleased I was. "Next up, I think Rafi should introduce himself and then proceed to explain his theory to them. Obviously, he won't be doing all the talking, but this was his brainchild, and we're all here because, in one way or another, we agreed with what he had to say," I said.

"Yeah, public speaking to rally morale isn't really my forte," Rafi said nonchalantly.

"Good thing we're not asking you to rally anyone's morale, but since you came up with the majority of the theory, I think it's only right that you make the introductions," said James, backing me up.

"Are we all in agreement that Rafi should start, then we all back him up with our specific thoughts? Yay or nay?"

"Yay, yay, yay, ***nay***, yay, yay, yay." There was a chorus of agreement from our *core group* (and one mocking nay from Rafi).

"Democracy prevails! Time to assume the position, Sir Raphael," I added irreverently. He wasn't pleased with the outcome, but being the good soldier that he was, he ultimately fell in line with the ruling and took his place standing in front of the room to recite his theory in detail.

Chapter 9: Addressing the Recruits

"Listen, as I just tried to tell my friends here, I'm not here to convince you in any sort of way."

I listened as Rafi outlined his hypothesis to the new potential members.

"You all are here literally because you're some of the brightest minds not only in your respective countries but also in the world. By coming up here and trying to get you to blindly believe what I am about to tell you would be a great insult to your collective intelligence, and I'm not sure about you guys—and girls—but I'm tired of people insulting my intelligence simply because of the way I look or dress. My theory—if you can even call it that—was made not only from what we've witnessed thus far at orientation, but also conceived from gathering all that I could, or lack thereof, about the Zaragozas themselves, their business dealings and, quite frankly, society as a whole.

"With that being said, it is my belief and now the belief of all of us standing here before you that the reason for us being here is not only to receive a scholarship because we are bright *minorities*. We believe the real intent is much more sinister than that. Speaking plainly, we believe that we ZNBS recipients are here to partake in voluntary indoctrination subjected to us by the Zaragozas for them to reach parts of the global population that they would not normally have access to, be it socially, geographically, or politically.

"Offering this scholarship, which would be a Godsend for any student, but especially to the most disadvantaged communities worldwide, serves two purposes: one that appears to be thoroughly altruistic in theory and practice; but the other, if you look just underneath the clean and crisp veneer of the Zaragozas, there lies perhaps the most diabolical scheme I've ever heard of. Direct access to most of the global population, those who weren't born privileged and affluent, by directly impacting its most scholarly, vocal, and able sub-population: *us*.

"You all may be thinking that this is ludicrous, absurd, and perhaps most of all, infeasible. For those of you thinking just that, I ask you: What is impractical for the world's richest family, as well as the world's most successful conglomerate, that has been that way for longer than any of us have been alive?

"If you're still on the fence, I then proceed to ask you, why have the Zaragozas gone through so much trouble hosting an orientation just to receive a scholarship? Why are we required to sign an NDA just to receive a scholarship? Why is it impossible to find anything about the scholarship before we arrived at the Castillo, as well as not being able to talk to any previous ZNBS cohorts or even know who the hell they are?

"And perhaps the most damning of all, why the *fuck* did we have to go through all of that weird ritualistic shit just to receive a scholarship?!" Rafi said vehemently. Whatever prior apprehensions Rafi had were now abolished, those previous apprehensions being transformed into vitriol and rage. His face seared as bulbous veins emerged from his neck all the way up to his head, and the end of almost every sentence was exaggerated with a thunderous banging of his fist on the poor nearby coffee table, emphasizing the syllables he roared, loosening his tied hair.

"I mean, come on. Signing a scroll with our blood, administered by what I could only imagine was some sort of ancient fanatic society, at best? If that wasn't the biggest clue that things aren't what they seem, I don't know what is. Needless to say, I'm fairly certain this isn't what any of us signed up for when we accepted this scholarship. I'm not even mentioning the classes that we had to take, having nothing to do with anything any of us studied, nothing academic, and barely applicable to any of us, outside of those overtly interested in theology or religious studies. Even if you did account for those scholars, what we covered was more closely aligned to the occult, taboo, and pagan beliefs than anything else!

"And when more traditional religions were brought up, it was at best, an afterthought, and at worst, constant rebuttals or criticisms. Of course, there's nothing wrong with being critical of the Abrahamic religions and the common philosophies they follow. Being critical is about objectively evaluating the pros and cons of a topic in order to expand your perspectives. The Zaragozas only focusing on the negative aspects of these philosophies feels more analogous to some sort of perverse manipulation," Rafi said, taking a deep breath to calm himself.

"Anyway, I've been doing a lot of talking without listening, so do you all have any questions, or should I continue?"

Looking into the audience of potential recruits, it was easy to see that they were all captivated with what Rafi was saying, allowing me to sigh in relief, knowing that if anything, at least they were all intrigued with Rafi's theory, or more accurately now, the ZRC's theory.

All eyes were intensely transfixed on Rafi, following his every movement, as he paced back and forth like they all had been given a field sobriety test. Instead of tracking a finger, they were tracking Rafi. No one raised any issue with the pacing of his speech, nonverbally letting Rafi know that his impassioned speech was not falling on deaf ears. As soon as he was getting ready to resume his oration, we thought it would be best to pull him aside to talk to him before he proceeded into our talks with Gástonio.

"How are you feeling, man? For someone who doesn't like to speak publicly, you're crushing it," I said, slapping his arm playfully.

"What are you talking about, Femi?" Rafi said,

"Take a look at their faces. Are those the faces of people who aren't convinced?" I said, turning him around to look at all our new companions. As he looked out into the living room from where we were standing in the kitchen, we saw Diego pensively rubbing the whiskers of his mustache down to his beard. Daniela was now sitting on the floor across from where she was previously sitting on the couch, legs crisscrossed with her eyes closed, in what looked like a deep meditative state. Presumably to reflect on the full impact of Rafi's words.

"Does that look like people who were not impacted by the

words that just came out of your mouth, you brilliant idiot?" I implored Rafi, now grabbing his arms. As Rafi looked at me, then again at the ZRC potential recruits, I could see a twinkle in his eyes, that maybe, just maybe, my words somehow penetrated his cerebral cortex, and perhaps he finally realized just how much he had impacted the recruits.

"Okay, guys, how do we proceed with telling them about the stuff Gástonio told us and told you, Femi? Should we even tell them? They just took in a whole lot all at once," Sarah spoke up to ask.

"That's a valid point. I don't want them to drink water from a fire hose. It's a delicate balance between giving them all the relevant information and informing them about all that we know thus far," Amir followed.

"Instead of asking amongst ourselves what we think is best, why don't we just go straight to the source and ask them directly if they would like to know more about this little theory of ours?" James said, rushing out of his bathroom to join us in the kitchen.

"Oi! I didn't hear the sink turn on, mate! Did you wash those disease-laden hands, or did you just dash out to run your gob?!" Paul said in his trademarked exaggerated Cockney accent, ensuing hysterical laughter from us, James included.

"Ha-ha, good one, but I was just in there to fix my hair—didn't think it was necessary to wash my hands, you cheeky limey!" James countered in faux spite. Laughter erupting from the kitchen made the recruits who were still sitting in the living room look up with puzzled faces, wondering what all the commotion could be about when we were discussing something so serious.

We all thought that Rafi had already said enough, and if anyone were to address the recruits again, he should be spared the burden.

Since I was primarily the reason why everyone was in this room and the entire situation to begin with, I felt it was only right that I should address them. Not taking the task lightly, my anxiety went through the roof, sprouting up like a pesky weed in a pristine garden.

What if they don't take me seriously?

What if my words can't articulate my thoughts clearly?

What if I have to use the washroom in the middle of my speech?

A wide range of disastrous hypothetical situations quickly flooded the ill-equipped dam that was my mind. Anxiety was something that I've always dealt with from my years in university to all the jobs I took post-graduation, but it felt as if nothing could prepare me for what I was dealing with now. The worst part was, anxiety has a way of compounding itself, adding more anxiety onto what was already felt, creating a feeling analogous to running a cross-country race in a parka.

Like a jaguar constrained in a tight enclosure, I paced back and forth, trying to ameliorate my worries, which helped a little but not completely. I went back to the gang to rid myself of the situation for which I had volunteered myself.

"Guys, are we even sure we want to bombard them with more information? I mean, Sarah and Amir have a point; maybe we are trying to make them drink from a fire hose. Perhaps we should just wait until tomorrow?" I asked sheepishly.

"Oh, no, you don't! If I had to speak, so do you, mister!" Rafi said, wagging his finger at me, like a mother scolding her child.

Making excuses for myself, I quickly replied, "I'm not necessarily trying to get out of making the speech, of course—I know I have to address them at some point—I'm just worried that perhaps doing so right now is a bit . . . well, a bit hasty."

"Ugh, sounds like a big, fat excuse to me, but I guess it was a lot," Rafi said with crossed arms, rolling his eyes, and focusing them back at me with a scornful look.

"I still have a feeling you're punking out, Femi," Tolu said, joining the conversation. "But to be fair, it was a lot they had to take in all at once. Hell, when I first heard all of this, it took me much longer to comprehend everything you all were telling me," Tolu added.

I tried to interject quickly to finally put the nail in the coffin and to give myself at least one more day to prepare and not look like an inept idiot to the recruits, who I genuinely wanted to win over. "So, it's settled, we just address them tomorrow?"

We all agreed—all of us except Rafi, of course. But I didn't blame him; I did just force him to tell his account of our theory without returning the favor, but if only they knew just how crippling the anxiety could sometimes be, I'm sure they would understand—at least that's what I told myself to justify my spineless actions. Besides, it was also getting late, so perhaps this was all for the best. Before the night was over and everyone went on their way, I did, however, have enough courage to muster up a quick speech before the recruits went back into their respective rooms.

"Hey, everyone. We can't thank you enough for agreeing to hear this story of ours, and we apologize if the content matter was heavier than what you expected. Now that you are aware of this theory, we hope you all will be cognizant and respectful of all that we risked arranging not only the Fireside Chats and the Fireside Drinks, but also everything Rafi just told you. All things considered, we hope it goes without saying that this should all remain confidential, even if you choose not to hear the rest of our theory."

"There's more?" Diego asked.

"Oh, yes, we're just getting started, but since it's late and we don't want to overwhelm you, we decided that it would be best to continue the rest tomorrow afternoon, assuming you all would like to hear it, of course," I said.

"I think I speak on behalf of all of us when we say that we absolutely want to hear out this theory in its entirety, am I right, guys and gals?" Mikael asked his fellow recruits. Their heads nodded up and down like a collection of bobbleheads, with Kofi's head bouncing faster and out of sync compared to his fellow recruits.

"Wow, I'm glad to see that you are all in agreement, then, as it would've been cumbersome to kill those of you who disagreed," I joked.

There was polite laughter but nothing hysterical. I guess I didn't possess that surgical ability to insert comedy into the times where it was most needed. Nevertheless, we had Paul and James for such occasions, anyway.

"Well, that's settled! We shall see you all tomorrow at 1 p.m. Thanks again to all of you for hearing us out and continuing to do so. Have a good night."

Just like that, they all left the room and granted me time to prepare what I had to say in the comfort of solitude, which was when I thought with the most clarity. Surprisingly, though, Amir and Tolu decided to stay the night and help me plan out my speech if need be. I told them that wouldn't be necessary, but they stayed the night, anyway. Although I thought I got away with dodging my speech scot-free, my friends weren't going to let me off that easily.

"Mate, we all know why you decided to wait a day before telling the lot of them what Gástonio told us," Paul said in a disappointed tone, cupping the back of my neck with his hand. "If what we believe about the Zaragozas is even remotely true, they'll surely capitalize on any and all weaknesses like that and use it to destroy us," Paul added in a low and serious tone, removing all traces of the superfluous manner in which he usually spoke.

"Yeah, I know, buddy; it's just that I didn't want to make a fool of myself right after that brilliant speech Rafi just gave."

Wasting no time after uttering my last word, Paul tore into me: "You believe in this cause, no?"

"Yeah, I do."

"You believe in what Gástonio told us, no?"

"Of course I do," I said unequivocally.

"AND you believe that what we're doing is fair and just, NO?"

"*Yes*, I do. I really do!"

"Then if you truly believe in all those things, just let the truth speak for itself; don't worry so much about how it comes out. No one here is stupid. That earnestness will speak for itself!"

It was this ability that I admired most about Paul. One second, he would be all shits and giggles, and in an instant, he would transform into this sage orator, wise beyond his years. His simple yet poignant questioning was what I needed to rile myself up and to leave the persistent anxiety at the door, at least momentarily. I thanked him, hugged him, and wished him goodnight, for I had to sleep myself; tomorrow was an important day.

* * *

The next morning, I woke up with a vigor of spirit I haven't felt in quite some time. I told myself that if I couldn't come up with a captivating way of inspiring belief in myself and the ZRC, I didn't deserve to be addressing the recruits. Tearing up the draft I had haphazardly prepared the previous night, I told myself that I was going to deliver this speech without preparing it beforehand. I was going to purposefully make myself uncomfortable and *shoot from the hip*.

The morning started like any other morning, groggily stumbling from my bed into the en suite bathroom, vaguely remembering the dream I had just had. The normalness of the morning had a way of subverting the gravity of what was to come in just a few hours, but times of great change are always shortly after the most humdrum and inane moments. As 1 p.m. drew nearer and nearer, I was overcome with a feeling of tranquility that even my compatriots sensed.

"So, you're all cool and composed now but couldn't speak yesterday, eh?" Tolu teased.

"Yes," I said flatly.

"What caused the sudden change, Femz?" Sarah asked, overhearing our conversation from across the room.

"Doctors don't recommend a good night's sleep for no

reason!" I answered in the most braggadocious tone that I could emulate. Sensing annoyance in my good-natured arrogance, I toned it down a bit, but not before uttering one more cliché, telling them that the *truth really did set me free!*

Knowing my personality, Sarah, James, and Tolu were just happy that my spirits were renewed right before I had to deliver one of the most important speeches of my life. The moment was finally here, a full twenty minutes before the time I told the recruits to arrive. They were already present in our living room, coffees in hand, and outfitted in oversized comfortable clothing or, in other words, ready for a long speech. *I forgot these were the type of people to never miss an 8 a.m. lab*. Thankfully, I rose to the occasion, or at least, I like to think I did; hindsight is always twenty-twenty, right?

"First of all, I would like to thank each of you for agreeing to hear us out, attending the numerous Fireside Chats, and listening to Rafi speak about what we think is going on here," I started.

"So, thanks to you, Mikael, Diego, Suhani, Tomor, Kofi, and Daniela. Seriously, I mean it. Rafi told you all yesterday why we think the ZNBS could be a covert indoctrination ploy for the Zaragozas to spread their influence into regions where they don't exert as much dominance through us, the ZNBS recipients.

"The thing is, we actually lied about some things. . . ." I admitted. "Before you all get your knickers in a bunch, the part that we lied about wasn't the indoctrination plot, but rather the part where I said, *we think*, because, in actuality, we know for a fact that this is what they're doing. . . ."

Their faces dropped faster than a Japanese bullet train. The anticipation and excitement that once painted their faces were replaced by the deepest shade of blue.

"Before any of you interrupt with incessant questioning, let me explain to you how we know that our theory is, indeed, correct. You see, we actually met up with a certain someone who has key insight into the Zaragozas' operations, or more accurately, *had* key insights. No doubt the question you all are now asking yourself is, *How does this person have this insight?* So let me address that first. The person that I am referring to was a mentee of Arturo Zaragoza. If that name doesn't mean anything to you, that makes sense. That's because he died when Queen Elizabeth II was still a princess. You see, Arturo was the great-grandfather of Pierre and Julie."

The previous look of dread on the faces of the potential recruits was swapped with astonishment and wide-open eyes, dropped shoulders, and eyebrows full of confusion, tension, and perhaps, intrigue. Their bewildered faces discouraged me a bit from continuing, but at least I could tell they were paying attention. . . . I continued, anyway.

"How we met this mentee is not of your concern at this moment, but his information was consistent with things that we already knew, and he was also able to fill in the blanks for things that we weren't quite sure of.

"I don't want to keep you all here for too long, so I'll get straight to the point for why the Zaragoza family has become the de facto most powerful family in the world, and how I know if we don't stop them, no one will....

"Their family was once nothing but thieves and bandits, but one of their ancestors realized that if he stole certain things from certain people, they could elevate their position in life. They couldn't do this alone, though, and their luck finally changed upon that ancestor meeting a person or thing that granted them all the success they could wish for. I say person or thing because that part is a bit more confusing to explain.

"As it was relayed to us, the person the Zaragozas' ancestor made a deal with wasn't a person at all but a *supernatural entity*. Yes, trust me, I know how ridiculous it sounds, but another thing that was relayed to us that might make it a little less ridiculous is that the last person who tried to investigate these claims is, well—"

"He's missing. That's what Femi is trying to say," Rafi rushed in and finished the sentence for me.

"The final warning that was relayed to us was that the Zaragozas' plan is indeed a plan for world domination, and it was clearly stated that we would be putting ourselves in grave danger if we tried to stop them."

I paused for a moment to assess the crowd of recruits, and Kofi started to break out in what could only be described as hysterical laughter.

"Do you guys even realize what's at stake here and the danger we're putting ourselves in if even a smidgen of this stuff is correct?! Supernatural entities? A clear warning that we would be in danger if we pursued this? We're here to receive a scholarship and get on with our very bright professional lives. Do you all have a death wish?!" Kofi said, now visibly agitated.

"Obviously, we are aware of that and had many conversations about that before we brought you all here, and we will continue to have those conversations accordingly. But I ask you, if the Zaragozas annually risk their secret coming out every year by hosting this scholarship and grant us these alleged abilities, who really has the most to lose if we actually worked together to bring them down? We would possess not only strength in numbers but also a strength of mind.

"That collective brainpower would be like nothing they have ever seen, and if we were actually granted *gifts,* what better way would there be than to use it against them!" I said, feeling the gravity of each word amplifying in importance and weight immediately after speaking it.

"But why? What possessed you all to pursue such a dangerous plan? For what glory?" Daniela countered.

"I'll take this answer, Femz. What possesses us to pursue this, you ask, Daniela?" Rafi answered. "Why would we put ourselves in danger purposefully? Let me ask you: Why did you accept this scholarship? Why did you sign those scrolls with your own blood? A chance at a better life for you and your family? Okay, fine, a noble answer, and an answer that is probably true for the rest of us, too. Now I ask, though: What are you willing to risk for that dream to come true? What are you willing to give up to guarantee that your family and friends would be okay even if you no longer roamed the earth?"

"Obviously everything. Family is the most important thing to me," Daniela responded.

"Me, too, and we all feel that way. That's why we're doing what we're doing; that's why we're attempting to bring down the Zaragozas, not because of any attempt at glory or proving something. We all want peaceful and fruitful lives. We would risk our lives to achieve that, so when a family is using our bodies . . . and our minds to achieve whatever twisted sense of *unity* they're longing for, we would in turn use whatever advantages they think they have going for them, against them. Ensuring *true* peace and prosperity for all peoples, no matter their advantages or privilege," Rafi said triumphantly.

"It's true, Daniela. It may seem like the Zaragozas are doing us a favor by offering this scholarship, but it is we who are really doing them the ultimate favor. Not only will it be people who look like us that will be the first to perish in a Zaragoza-controlled world, but it'll also be directly the fault of us ZNBS recipients granting them that initial access to our people." I said.

"If I can chime in for a second . . . I, for one, understand this sentiment quite intimately. Yes, I was a soldier, but the ethos of any soldier should be words that everyone abides by: If you're not willing to fight for peace, you'll die in subjection," Tomor eloquently stated.

"But we're scholars, not soldiers!" Kofi barked.

"We may not be soldiers, Kofi, but we've been fighting our whole lives—discrimination, prejudices, injustices, you name it. I'm sure each of us experienced it, but now because of our scholastic achievements, we have a chance to do something greater than the sum of our parts, we have the chance of combatting perhaps the *head of the snake.* How often do you think a chance like this comes around? I hate to use a platitude but it really is true. If you're not willing to stand up for something, you'll fall for anything," I said proudly. Clapping silently to himself, I could tell Tomor appreciated my conviction as well.

"Look, we know we're putting you all in grave danger, but you weren't picked by accident; we chose each of you because we knew that if we worked together, we had a chance of ridding the world of this great evil, but only if we truly stood together, '*E pluribus unum,*'" I quoted. "Out of many, one. So, I ask you all now, after hearing what Rafi and I had to say, coupled with everything we've discussed at previous Fireside Chats, are you all sure that this is the path you wish to embark on? This will be the last chance to back out."

"Okay, okay, we get it. Very inspirational and heart-warming, but the second you start espousing that American patriotic bullshit, I'm out," Mikael said sharply, rolling his eyes, flashing the purple-colored make-up he had on his eyelids.

"Oh, you definitely don't have to worry about that—not my style. I'll be the first person to tell you how flawed America is. But it's hard to deny that the ideals America was founded on were just in principle, *only if they were strictly adhered to and didn't apply only to a subset of its population, but I digress.*" I said under my breathe.

Luckily for us, we didn't have to wait too long to find out what we're made of because the Second Trials started the next day. Mikael and I talked more after our meeting about the current state of American politics and the glaring signs of empire collapse before both heading to bed. We had to get ready for tomorrow, a day we've all been waiting for.

No one raised any concerns or objections, and the recruits were officially made full members of the ZRC—not like we could afford to turn down anyone, anyway, but of course, this was not something the recruits had to know. The occasion, although significant in the grand scheme of the ZRC, was not necessarily momentous.

Nevertheless, I was filled with great pride and optimism. Not prideful of my abilities as an orator or as a salesman, but rather proud that despite the odds, there will always exist people who are willing to fight for what's right and just.

Likewise, the feeling of optimism wasn't because I especially fancied our chances to topple the Zaragozas' visible and invisible empires. It was quite the opposite, in fact. What I was optimistic about was the latent fervor of the room that felt like we could move mountains. I was optimistic about the fact that even if our rag-tag coalition were smacked, crushed, and defeated, there would always be opposition to malevolent forces that refuse to stand idly by as chaos descends upon the spines of everyday people.

Chapter 10: The Second Trials

The morning of the Second Trials began like any other, except our room was much more occupied than usual. The newest members of the ZRC slept over after we celebrated their induction the night before. Not sure when we would have the next chance to do so, we celebrated in the only way we knew how: with an abundant amount of food and drink. I can't remember at what precise time it happened, but around midday, the voice of Pierre Zaragoza rang out sharply from the Castillo's intercom.

"Attention, all ZNBS recipients: As you all know, today begins the last part of ZNBS orientation and the final portion of the trial process. We are proud of everything you have accomplished thus far, and we know you all will go on to accomplish bigger and better things within the Zaragoza extended family. However—*make no mistake!*—the Second Trials will be the most difficult thing any of you have ever experienced, and you will be better for it. The purpose of the Second Trials is to test your ability to thrive in uncomfortable situations, the art of remaining couth in threatening and uncertain situations.

"But most of all, the Second Trials will require the use of your special abilities to achieve what is required. Successful completion of the Second Trials will also mean completion of the ZNBS orientation. Afterward, you all will be sent back to your respective countries as proud ZNBS recipients, fully funded scholars, and post-docs of any program you have started or wish to complete.

"Most importantly, completion of the Second Trials means you will be full members of the Zaragoza family, which comes with a generous universal basic income for life—our little way of thanking you for all you have done and for all you will do for our esteemed family.

"That being said, not all of you will survive, and if this possibility alarms any one of you, you will have a chance to leave the Castillo and the ZNBS program. Granted, it would be without the benefits ensured by us, and *your memory of certain aspects of orientation will be modified.*

"One last thing: Your abilities at first may be unknown to you. You are all individuals who know yourselves better than we possibly could, and at the right time, at the right place, your abilities will make themselves known to you, and you will finally witness the greatness that has lain dormant for far too long.

"In a few hours, each of you will receive an email detailing what you have to accomplish in the name of the Zaragozas, and in three weeks, you must have completed your task assigned to you. If not, you will be forced to vacate the ZNBS, return home, and *your memory of certain aspects of orientation will be modified.*" Pierre repeated again ominously.

"If you wish to attend, there will be lunch provided for you in the courtyard after this message is completed. Note:

The social nature of this lunch may result in awareness of the abilities that have been granted to each of you. Our advice is not to be alarmed, but instead, be cognizant of the way you will feel, understand the difference between how you feel now and how you will feel after. Becoming intimately aware of these differences will allow your powers to manifest fully, as well as granting you complete control over these abilities, turning them on and off without a moment's hesitation. The lunch is not mandatory, and no penalties will be associated with non-attendance, though attendance is highly encouraged.

"And last but not least, co-completion of the Second Trials is permissible as long as it does not hinder the completion of your own trials. After all, as I have told you on multiple occasions, we are now all family, and family is the most important tenet of our philosophy.

"Julie and I personally wish you all the best in completion of the Second Trials. We hope you all survive the ordeal. . . ."

As Pierre's voice began to fade, the gravity of the Second Trials was firmly settling in. Those few minutes immediately after his speech felt like a lifetime, waiting for the email that would define the next few weeks of our lives. If we were not all together, my anxiety would've easily been bursting at the seams, but being around those I cared for always had a sort of therapeutic effect on me. I can still remember it like it just happened, the *pinging* sound of Mikael's phone going off while he was in the kitchen looking for salty snacks.

We all looked toward him as he looked back at us. The room fell quiet but not silent as the nonverbal communication ran rampant. I was the closest to his phone, so naturally, I approached it to see what the notification was—not before looking at Mikael for visual confirmation that I could look at his phone, which he granted with a quick and firm nod. But as soon as I extended my arm to check his phone, *ping, ping, ping, ping . . .*

Like clockwork, Rafi's, James's, Diego's, and Sarah's phones went off in rapid succession, the anticipation in the room now soaring to new heights.

Why have some of us received a message and some of us have not? *was the only thought spiraling in my mind.*

Could it be that the Zaragozas were sending out specific tasks to be completed by subsets of us? If that's the case, do they already know those that they want post-Second Trials? But if they already know the recipients they want to survive, why would they let us work in teams? Surely, it's possible for a person who they wanted to survive to team up with a person that wasn't meant to survive. What do they do in those situations?

Feeling like I was slowly traversing down the rabbit hole of random negative thoughts that come along with the reoccurring generalized anxiety disorder, I tried my best to utilize all the self-cognitive behavioral therapy I was taught to alleviate my current condition—granted, with only limited success.

Only a few minutes had gone by until we all received an email sent to us from the same email address from which we initially received our ZNBS award confirmation email. When I received that first email, I can distinctly remember thinking all my problems would become memories, whereas now, opening this email gave me the complete opposite feeling—a feeling of fright and despair, a feeling that all my problems were, in fact, just starting.

Surprisingly, all of our messages were rather similar. We had to retrieve certain items for the Zaragozas and either keep them until told otherwise or relay them to someone else. I didn't make the connection at first, but looking back on it, the Second Trials, in a way, had eerie similarities to how the Zaragozas first gained their familial prominence, operating as common thieves and peddlers. Was it a coincidence or an elaborate ploy the Zaragozas hatched for comedic effect, or better yet, some way of continuing a perverse *familial tradition*? No matter the reason, we had a task in front of us, and completing it successfully was the only way to get closer to our goals.

Making things even more interesting, we were all sent dossiers containing more information, such as an approximate location for the items, or *family heirlooms,* as the Zaragozas called them. We racked our brains, wondering if this, too, was on purpose, but there was no telling if other ZNBS recipients received a similar task, so we headed to the courtyard to gain some insight into what our counterparts were tasked to complete. The excellently prepared *pa amb tomàquet* coupled with a dizzying array of tapas and sangria didn't hurt, either.

The courtyard was charmingly decorated, with the flags of every nation that we recipients hailed from combined into a collage draped over the outdoor space we were now in. The sun radiating over the flags created a nice ambiance, as the reflection of the flags onto us made the outdoor area look like it was illuminated by rainbow-colored lights. By chance, I ran into Keito, the Osaka-born Japanese recipient who previously helped me activate the Castillo's PA system to announce my party. It had been a while since I last saw him, so the usual pleasantries were exchanged first before we got into the meat of the conversation.

"Second Trials, eh?" Keito said with raised eyebrows. I knew exactly what he meant.

"This orientation keeps getting more and more interesting, doesn't it?" I said, trying to break the ice. Small talk was always awkward for me, an awkwardness that I think Keito sensed, too, because he asked if something was occupying my mind.

"I'm glad you asked. There is something, actually. What were you tasked to do for the Second Trials?" I asked Keito.

"Well, I'm not sure if I fully comprehend what is being asked of me, but my task was to retrieve a document from a prominent Japanese minister visiting Brussels. How about you?" my friend said with apparent confusion painted all over his body.

"I was tasked with retrieving a vase from some former ZCA employee here in Spain," I replied.

"Jeez, that's not a lot to go on; best of luck with that. I'm sure you'll find it easily," Keito reassured.

Though I'm sure his response was genuine, as his tone was upbeat and encouraging, I couldn't help but notice his hands were placed in his pockets the entire duration of our conversation. His eye contact was, at best, inconsistent, relaying to me that the confidence he had in my success was perhaps... not so certain.

"Thanks. I appreciate the sentiment. I wish you the best of luck with your task, as well," I politely replied.

"We all have these new powers to help us though, right? How cool is that?" he asked, shifting the conversation away from the daunting task that was ahead of us. I didn't mind;

the next thing I wanted to discuss was our *special abilities,* anyway.

"What do you think our powers would be like, anyway? Like, the ability to fly, super strength or speed, invisibility, teleportation, et cetera?!"

Chuckling at my tone and the increased rate of speed at which I delivered my sentence, Keito replied, "I am not sure if they would be the superpowers of comic book heroes, but I definitely wouldn't mind running at the speed of light myself! In all seriousness, though, I doubt they would be powers similar to fictional superheroes, but I guess you can never truly know until they are activated. . . ." Keito finished before he headed to the refreshments table for an icy glass of sangria.

We initially came to the courtyard to see if any of our abilities would be *pre-activated,* per Pierre's comment. But all I was experiencing was fatigue from all of the schmoozing and dreary conversations about esoteric research that I didn't even understand or care to know of. Reminiscing endlessly on what Pierre had talked about, one part of it kept replaying itself over and over again in my mind:

"Your abilities at first will be unknown to you. You are all individuals who know yourselves better than we possibly could, and at the right time, at the right place, your abilities will make themselves known to you, and you will finally witness the greatness that has lain dormant for far too long."

That got me to think about what our powers could be once they were fully manifested. If we could roughly surmise our abilities before completing the Second Trials, we would place ourselves in a much better position to complete them successfully. I thought it would be safe to assume that our own abilities will be derived from our traits, personality, specific aptitudes, or a combination of all those factors.

Not wanting to have these thoughts in a vacuum, I located the rest of the ZRC to see what they thought about my hypothesis. Naturally, the first person I sought out was Rafi. True to his nature, I found Rafi in a section of the courtyard that was unoccupied, near an almond tree that I had never noticed before. It's not that I regularly observed every tree that I came across, but for the fact that it was such a beautiful tree with radiant pink and white blossoms, I thought it would've been more salient in such a frequently visited place.

Nevertheless, I approached Rafi, tiptoeing to not disturb the deep meditative state he appeared to be in. *"Rafiiii,"* I whispered. "Earth to Raphael, it's *me*, Femi," I said.

My comedic efforts barely broke through the steadfastness that was his concentration. Slowly extending out his arm and bringing his outstretched index finger to his mouth, or in other words, not so subtlety telling me to *shut the fuck up*. I heeded his gesture and sat beside him, ruminating how to best deliver what I had to tell him.

After a few minutes went by, he sprang up like a tightly coiled cobra suddenly striking its captors. "What's up, Femi? Sorry, I was just meditating on the tasks we have before us," he said rather nonchalantly, in true Rafi nature.

"No worries. I actually wanted to speak to you on just that, *the tasks we have before us,* or more specifically, the special abilities that are supposed to aid in that endeavor," I admitted.

"Yeah, what about them?" Rafi quickly replied, jogging in place.

"Well, I was just thinking: What if our special abilities

are derived from our own unique talents and aptitudes? Especially when you take into account what Pierre said about how we know ourselves better than anyone else, and how at the right place, right time *yadda yadda yah* . . . our abilities will present themselves to us?"

After tilting his head from left to right, right to left repeatedly and saying, "Hmm, hmm," a few times, I could tell that his interest was finally piqued.

"That's an interesting point and highly likely at that. You very well could be right; I don't take Pierre to be a person to choose his words merely on a whim, and I would hypothesize the same thing," my dear friend said.

"So, where do we go from here?" I asked Rafi.

"I believe the best thing we can do is to first see if everyone else agrees with us and, if they do, proceed in trying to get our powers to reveal themselves in some way."

Rafi's words instantly gave me an idea. "Well, wasn't the point of this impromptu lunch an effort to let us know what our powers could be? By that logic, our powers have already *been* activated; we just have to figure out a way to actually discover what they are. I say we get the gang back together somewhere and try to figure out exactly what we're capable of," I said.

"Let me get this straight: You want to replicate what was supposed to happen here in the courtyard privately, just between us ZRC members?" Rafi inquired.

"That's exactly what I want to do, Rafi-boy. Additionally, it would probably even be best if we did this in the presence of Gástonio since he could probably help us out, too," I said, coming up with the idea on the spot.

In full agreement, we both ventured into the main portion

of the courtyard to find the rest of our friends. Finding the rest of the ZRC was easy enough, as they were all near the refreshment table (*those drunks*) talking to Professor Hayes, who taught abnormal psychology back in the early days of our orientation.

Dr. Hayes was an interesting man and one of the few lecturers all of the recipients got along well with, mainly due to his dark yet brilliant sense of humor. Though the topic of psychopaths vs. sociopaths seemed highly stimulating, Rafi and I gestured out of Dr. Hayes's eyesight that they should hurry the conversation along, as we had important matters to discuss. Once they were done talking, we all met back up in the de facto ZRC HQ of our dormitory's living room.

"Ladies and gentlemen, Rafi and I have an idea," I led with. "Instead of chitchatting around with the other recipients in the courtyard, why don't we liaise on our own to find out what our abilities are? We also thought it might be best to talk once more with Gástonio to see if he had any advice for us for the next stage of our journey. You know, since we have these dormant powers and all. Lastly, it'll also allow us to go to his town again to meet the jeweler and have the new members adorned with the ZRC phoe—"

"Yeah, but didn't we buy five extra pieces precisely for this?" Sarah interrupted before I could finish my sentence.

"Yeah, true, but I thought since we'll be there, anyway, it wouldn't hurt, and the new members getting their phoenix pieces directly from the man himself could be a nice touch," I answered.

"Yeah, okay, sure," Sarah said in an unconvinced manner.

After consensus was reached, we headed back to the room for a brief discussion about how tomorrow would play out, as well as getting to know each other a little better, now that we were all on the same page. Back in the comfort of our own abode, we were more able to talk freely about the day and how we would proceed.

"So, this Gástonio Luis de Guzmán fellow was a protégé of Pierre and Julie-Marie's great-grandfather, you say?" Daniela asked.

"Yes, that is correct," Tolu responded.

"Making him easily over a hundred years old?" Suhani said, her furrowed eyebrows easily revealing her disbelief.

"That is correct, as well," Amir echoed.

"And you all trust him?" Tomor said.

"With our lives," James retorted seriously.

"Well, I guess it's settled, then?" Kofi assumed.

"No, not necessarily. We are now all equals in our little coalition, so if any one of you doesn't feel comfortable with something, you should air that grievance out," Paul said.

"Well, I'm not sure if this Gástonio guy is legit, but if you all trust and confide in him, then I will go along with that," Mikael followed, his voice ranging in pitch. He was constantly playing with his long earrings as he talked, revealing a sense of unsureness.

"Like James said, we trust Gástonio and wouldn't put you in any dangerous position we wouldn't put our own selves in," I assured them.

Rafi spoke up: "Mikael, let me take this time to apologize for my behavior in our first encounter. When I first met you, I wasn't sure what your angle was when you kept badgering me about my background, but I now know that you were just trying to find a way to relate to a stranger. I appreciate the effort; that's also one of the reasons why I recommended recruiting you, as well," Rafi stated.

For a person who was all about meditation and self-awareness, Rafi played his cards pretty close to his chest, and openly admitting something like that wasn't common, so we could all tell this was something that was coming from the heart. It was also interesting that Rafi stated this because when Mikael was the topic of discussion, we always found it fascinating how he had this capacity to make you feel at ease, no matter the conversation, as if he were actively pulling strings in the background of every interaction you had with him—not in a nefarious sense, but in a way to make all involved parties as comfortable as possible. We all, in a sense, possessed this ability, too. But with Mikael, it felt as if the effort came naturally, not forced, but not entirely attributed to his natural demeanor, either. This was something he had worked at.

This was the perfect segue into what I wanted to do, anyway: gain more insight into the beliefs, goals, and personal histories of each ZRC member—especially the newer ones, so that we could have at least an inkling of the type of abilities that we might have been granted. Since we were already talking about Mikael, it was only natural for us to start with him.

"What drives you, Mikael? What made you apply for the ZNBS?" I inquired.

"What made me? I'm sure it was the same thing for all of you: a chance to actually make a difference in the lives of those I care for and for others. A chance to be something other than the flamboyant gay Armenian," Mikael stated after a moment's thought. "Specifically, though, as you all know, most of my family on my father's side were murdered in the Armenian genocide, which some people deny to this day. What I wanted to do was to bring awareness to this cause—not only for my people, but for others, as well, who have gone through grave injustices like that; not to constantly remind people of the past, but to inform them that it could happen again and *will* happen again, if the precursors of such vile acts continue to exist.

"You all have told me in the past that I exude a certain energy that makes you feel comfortable around me, which I appreciate, but thinking about it now, I guess that's where it comes from. My core belief that to truly understand how these things happened, and still happen, you have to get down to the core emotional components of what makes people, *people*, which I try to do in every interaction I have.

"How about you, James? I don't think I've ever heard your personal motivations and beliefs," Mikael asked.

"Well, there's not that much to me, I guess. I've always been pretty studious, but my work ethic originally came from trying to learn different languages," James replied. "Ever since I was sipping apple juice and taking daily naps, I've always been fascinated with languages. How something that we take for granted can be so powerful; it was always my goal to learn as many languages as possible."

"Why, though?" Mikael probed a little deeper. "What did you want to gain from acquiring that knowledge?"

"Well, believe it or not, our goals are actually quite similar. I became enamored with speaking numerous languages because I craved that connection with people, all people. I watched a lot of foreign TV shows when I was a kid growing up in Taiwan and was always so amazed by how differently other languages sounded. I wanted that, I needed it: the ability to speak to strangers in their own tongue. I wholeheartedly agree with the statement that we are all more similar than different, but one factor that obscures the similarities between us is language," James said passionately.

"Wow, you truly believe that, huh?" Paul said in a mocking, though non-offensive tone.

"Yes, I truly do. I know there are many ways to be able to connect with someone, but in my opinion, language offers the most direct path," James answered as he sat back down, perhaps feeling a bit deflated from Paul's snarky comment.

"It's interesting that you and Mikael have similar motivations, yet go about it in a different way, James, because I think that my motivations are similar, as well. Albeit, I think I go about it more fundamentally," Diego said, replying to James with his hand raised as if he were back in primary school.

"Oh yeah? Then why don't you share with the class?" Paul remarked, this time getting a few laughs out of us, Diego included.

"Well, since you asked, *Paul*, music is my thing. Growing up, I've played everything from the flute to the bass."

"The class wants to know which bass?" Paul said sardonically.

"Both!" Diego quickly snapped back. "Music to me was almost something mystical, in the sense that the right song could elicit so much happiness, yet in a different set and setting, that same song could bring out feelings of sadness and longing for someone or something.

"For example, think about a song that is—or was—you and your significant other's favorite. What are the feelings associated with that song?" Diego asked. "Elation, warmth, connection? Now think of that same song after you and your partner have split up. I'm sure the emotions evoked when you hear that song, and even similar ones, are antonyms of the adjectives first used. Anyway, to make a long story short, the ability that music, or sound in general, provides is powerful if used correctly, which in a way, goes back to Mikael's and James's point about understanding people through emotions and language, different branches of the same tree, I guess."

"How about you ladies?" I asked.

"Well, I guess I can go first," said Sarah softly. "Like some of you, I've always been an introvert, but not because I don't like engaging with people. It's just that I prefer the company of a select group of friends rather than having countless acquaintances. When I was younger, I tried to be the popular girl who was friends with everyone, but one thing I found out about that approach is that people will use you for their own purposes and goals.

"I guess that was partly my fault, though, because I tended to always be that friend who would be there any time someone needed me, but the more people realized that, the more they would take advantage of me."

"Can you give an example of this maltreatment that you experienced?" Kofi asked.

"Uh, sure. One that readily comes to mind is, in high school, I was one of the only students who drove. Not because I wanted to, but because where we lived dictated that I drove to school or walk for an hour in the freezing cold each day just to get there.

"Anyway, I soon became everyone's driver, so much so that when *friends* called me, the first thing that came out of their mouths, wasn't 'How are you doing?' or 'How did your day go?' but rather, *'Where are you?'* and *'Can you pick me up?'"* Sarah said with a brooding look on her face.

"I guess what I'm trying to say is, sometimes I stretched myself too thin just to please others, which only made me feel lonelier. Don't get me wrong, though—all of my friends weren't this way, and with them, the favors were always returned organically, and they made me feel cherished, which only makes me want to be an even greater friend in return," Sarah concluded.

"So, it was the appreciation that you weren't receiving that upset you?" I asked out of genuine curiosity.

"Yes. I would do anything for the ones I loved and cared for. All I need is to know that what I do is valued and not in vain."

"I see. I was also like that in a similar sense, but mainly because I was just the class clown who made everyone laugh to take attention away from me, in a weird paradoxical kind of way," I said.

"Let me guess, you were either fat, ugly, had braces, or some combination of the aforementioned?" Paul said, cracking his signature wry smile.

Though it initially stung, I laughed it off and agreed with Paul because he was, indeed, correct. If the fat dorky kid can make you laugh, then mean-spirited kids have a way of forgetting he's the fat dorky kid, as long as you supply them a steady stream of laughs. I didn't counter back at Paul because even if he didn't realize it, he was actively using the same defense mechanisms that I employed back in primary school; I knew the pain he tried to hide in his comedy, but I was damn close to calling him out at that moment.

"What about you, Suhani? What's your driving force in

this thing we call life?" Rafi asked, locking eye contact with her from across the room. She looked back at him, smiling, her legs crossed, and leaned back into her chair. Suhani remained silent for a few seconds and then responded.

"Hmm, let me think. Well, I am the middle child and a girl, so that pretty much sums up my existence from ages one to eighteen, before I left for uni," she said.

"What do you mean?" Mikael politely interjected.

"Well, my eldest sibling is my brother, then follows my sister, me, then my younger brother. I'm not sure if it's the same in your family, but growing up, my elder brother was always allowed to do whatever he wanted. *Staying out late? No problem! Not coming home? Make sure you eat! New girlfriend? I didn't like the old one, anyway!* In my parents' eyes, he could do no wrong; whereas my elder sister had it harder, with every move she made being constantly scrutinized by my traditional Indian parents. On the other hand, since I was two years younger than her, and three years older than my younger brother, I always managed to slip just underneath the radar of my parents.

"Either they were too busy pampering my brothers or scolding my sister, my presence was more of an afterthought, which gave me more 'freedom,' in a sense, than my other siblings," Suhani said as she prefaced the word *freedom* in air quotations.

"What do you mean by 'freedom'?" I asked, mimicking her gesture.

"What I mean is, obviously, I didn't have more freedom than my elder brother, or even my younger brother when I was his age, but what I was afforded more than any of my siblings was autonomy.

"For example, my sister and I were never too *girly* and were always more interested in sports and games than dresses and dolls. But for the reasons I just laid out, when my sister wanted to pursue a career as a professional footballer, my parents dismissed her. They said sports was a field reserved only for men and recommended she become a pediatrician or a nurse if she couldn't make it all the way through medical school because these were adequate jobs for a woman.

"However, I've always been fascinated by mechatronics engineering, stemming from my love of Japanese anime, which led me to the ZNBS, but when I initially brought this up to my parents, they were too preoccupied, wondering why my elder brother came home drunk that night, to even hear that I had already gained admittance to one of the best engineering schools in America and was leaving the following week.

"Don't get me wrong, though—I've used this to my advantage to do the things that I know my sister could only dream about; plus, it allowed me to gain a better sense of who I was much earlier than I perhaps would have if I'd received more scrutiny from my parents.

"I feel like I've been rambling on, though; I'm sure you've all grown tired of hearing me speak."

On the contrary, this and perhaps a few other times before were the only times Suhani spoke this candidly about her past. That's another trait that Suhani and Sarah shared: They rarely enjoyed talking about themselves and always thought they were bothering us when they did. But in those times when they did share the more personal aspects of their past, we were all engrossed by the depth as well as the seamless storytelling abilities they both possessed. I always found their unrelenting modesty highly endearing. It didn't hurt that they were also very smart, very capable, and very beautiful women (but this was not the time to be thinking with my genitals).

I always hated in school when the teacher used to call on the student who appeared the most disinterested. Back then, I thought, *Can't they tell that my overt attempt at avoiding eye contact and efforts to make my body smaller were non-verbal ways of saying,* leave me the fuck alone*?*

However, advanced age allowed me to realize a few things about this seemingly innocuous behavior. First off, yes, avoiding all forms of contact is usually a way to silently communicate that you do not want to partake in the current activity. Though this seems an obvious form of social occlusion, it can also mean an entirely contrasting thing when a person actually has a lot to say about the matter, but for whatever reason, attempts to hide the fact in quasi-disinterest—which is what Tomor was doing during our get-together.

Whereas most of us were sitting together in the living room of my dorm, Tomor made what seemed like an obvious attempt to keep himself away from us. I'm not sure if anyone else caught onto this behavior, but it was the only thing I could think about while Suhani was speaking.

Is he that disinterested in learning about the backgrounds of everyone else?

Was the looming threat of the Zaragozas finally getting to him?

Is he just so hungry that the only thing he could think of was his next meal?

Many questions spun around my mind, as they usually

do, so as soon as Suhani finished speaking, I asked if Tomor would like to take the floor. He attempted to politely decline the invitation by waving both his head and one hand side to side, just at the right tempo to indicate his unwillingness to engage, not slow enough to gain a stranger's attention, yet not fast enough to appear frantic.

Through my gentle yet firm nudging, the rest of the gang eventually caught onto his withdrawn behavior and assisted me in goading him to speak. Our efforts eventually paid off, and he took the floor.

"You are all really something else, but fine, I'll speak," Tomor said in exasperation. "As you all know, I used to be a special forces operator for the Israeli Army. What you don't know is what drove me to reach such great heights in the first place. I guess the motivation to prove myself came at a pretty early age. I was one of the few bi-ethnic kids growing up, and I would always get teased for it by the full-Israeli kids, only for the full-Ethiopian kids to treat me as an outsider, as well. They would say that I wasn't as smart, funny, hardworking, or whatever adjective used to make a person feel unworthy. Having this mentality as a kid does two things. First, it puts a massive chip on your shoulder, which drives you to accomplish things you didn't think you could, but it also does another thing.

"Deep down, it makes you gradually withdraw yourself from a society that doesn't fully accept your existence as worthy. So, I did what I'm sure a lot of kids who feel the same way do: I got the most badass job to prove my existence, my value. Military service is mandatory in Israel, so I knew that distinction wouldn't necessarily set me apart. That's when I decided to become a special forces officer with a specialty in strategically complex and hostile negotiation situations.

"What started as a means to get back at all those people who doubted my ability turned into a career that I excelled so well at; the color of my skin was no longer a burden, but rather, a service ribbon. Not because my skin color was earned but because of all the achievements I received, despite all the racism and bigotry I had to endure.

"Anyway, I can't tell you what I think my special power would be since I've been so well trained to adapt in every type of situation. Sorry for being a party pooper." Tomor shrugged.

Paul interrupted first (as was his style): "All interesting stuff, but was that before or after you decided you wanted to become a microbiology-slash-genetics professor?" he said.

"Believe it or not, I wanted to become a microbiologist before I went into the army," Tomor said shyly. "I know for most young boys, the action-packed career of a secret soldier sounds way more exciting than learning about the building blocks of life, but to me, understanding the world at the scale of microbiology was my way to fundamentally understand why people who didn't even know me, despised me.

"I thought if I could teach them that despite all our differences, we're all composed of the same things, it would allow them to see me just as another Israeli—no different than their brother or sister, just painted in a different shade."

"And how did that turn out for ya, mate?" Paul asked in an irreverent tone.

"Well, I ended up thinking that becoming a special forces commando was the quicker path to acceptance!" Tomor said laughing, playfully putting Paul in a headlock.

I couldn't tell if Tomor took Paul's comment as a joke,

but after he grabbed Paul, I could see that even a stoic professional killer has a softer side.

"Wait, you didn't finish. What about the microbiology career? How did that go? Did you just give up on that dream once you realized the army was a quicker path to acceptance?" Daniela asked astutely.

"No, not necessarily. I still earned my bachelor's degree in microbiology, and I'm using the ZNBS to fund my Ph.D. in genetics, so really that dream was just placed on hold, but it remained a dream, nonetheless."

Tomor talking about his past looked like it resonated especially well with Kofi, who appeared as if he was holding back significant emotions when Tomor was speaking. For example, when Tomor was talking about how he was picked on in school, Kofi's orb-like brown eyes looked like tears were just starting to form, but his effort holding them back made it look like the tears were too heavy to fall from his face and instead, remained in his eyes like a rain cloud that was going to come roaring down at any time. I'm not sure if anyone else realized the impact Tomor's words were having on Kofi, and anytime I attempted to make eye contact with him, he would dip his head low, actively avoiding eye contact with me.

After Tomor was finished, I stood up, walked toward Kofi, and placed my hand onto the middle of his back, rubbing it slowly, trying to comfort him through whatever he was feeling. This overt act of thoughtfulness intrigued the others, wondering why I was doing this. Explaining everything that I witnessed from Kofi as Tomor was speaking would've taken more explanation than I cared to give, but I didn't need to; Kofi did the explaining for me.

"Sorry, guys. You are all probably wondering what the hell is wrong with me, but hearing Tomor recount those stories just brought back some memories that I tried to forget. I also got bullied extensively, but not because my skin color differed from those of my peers. Instead, they found other things to berate me about.

"I was never particularly as athletic or as handsome as some of my counterparts, and that was made clear almost every day of my early life. They would question if I was even black, ask if I was gay, as well as the customary beatings they would give me because I appeared too effeminate in their eyes.

"I just wasn't as into football and girls as they were, but that didn't make me any less of a boy or a man, but back then, it felt like if I didn't have their positive affirmation, the world was going to crash down on me.

"I was always good in school, too, which only fanned the flames of detestation even more. My only respite was that I loved to draw and would make drawings of different natural landscapes and portraits for everyone in the community.

"If someone wasn't into landscapes or portraits, I would draw whatever they wanted, which would give me a bit of breathing room from their onslaught. My drawings were so intricate, that even the staunchest art haters became converts as my paintings transported them to lands both near and far, weaving in designs I knew they would enjoy to truly encapsulate them into my work.

"The more I matured, the more my drawings did, as well, which led to me double-majoring in architecture and art history as my career aspirations were always to become an architect of modern home designs while using those homes as a gallery to display the local landscapes that inspired the home: *an artistic circle of life*, I thought of it as.

"That's why I accepted the ZNBS in the first place: to fund my escape from the world I so desperately wanted to get out of, and in the process, inspire others in similar circumstances to do the same. . . . I went off on a tangent, sorry; I'm not sure how that would translate into an exciting superpower, but that's all I have." Kofi said flatly.

Even though Kofi was granted one of the most prestigious scholarships known to man, I could still sense lingering trepidation and low self-esteem that originated from his childhood. Another thing I picked up on was that his past was no longer a crutch for him but operated in a way to keep him grounded and provide a steady supply of intrinsic motivation. Kofi never forgot where he came from or what he had achieved. But even with all of that, he was never satisfied, detested mediocrity, and always pushed himself to be better in any way he could.

Kofi's past wasn't a unique one, though, as similar minds often have similar origin stories, and Tolu, a few hundred miles away in Nigeria, could also relate. Tolu told us that he didn't have to face the incessant bullying that Kofi faced. Instead, he had to fight for his existence on a more fundamental level. Tolu had already told us a few times before that he basically grew up as an orphan, even though he could only vaguely remember his parents. According to him, his father passed away due to lymphoma before he was seven, and he lost his mother to a car accident when he was twelve. From then on, he had been living with either extended family members or friends of the family, not fully settling into any home or place before he had to pack up and move again.

"As most of you—if not all of you—know, I got separated from my birth parents at an early age, and it's been my baby sister and me ever since. I try not to delve into it too much because it brings me great sadness whenever I bring it up. But despite having some family members and friends take us in when our parents passed, all of those experiences weren't equal, nor were they all conducive to a safe familial structure.

"For example, the first family we stayed with when my parents passed was my father's older brother, my paternal uncle. At first, he and his family were really caring and took my sister and me in shortly after my mother passed away.

"Things were alright at first. We weren't especially close to our uncle when my parents were still alive, but we still knew who he and his family were and had even frequented their house a couple of times for Christmas.

"Though *being familiar* doesn't equate to *being a family,* and that's something I realized early on. They never said it explicitly, but there was always an air of, *you should be grateful that we took you two in,* you know?

"I'm not sure if you all know what I mean when people only perform kind acts because they believe it's something they *should* do, not something they necessarily *want* to do, and disingenuous acts like that were especially clear to us kids at the time. Long story short, we left their home, which I'm sure my uncle loved, despite disguising his delight as detest.

"After that ordeal, we then moved in with my mother's family and stayed with her younger sister and her husband. Living with my maternal aunt was, overall, a more amicable situation. But our aunt had her own kids to take care of, who were even younger than us, requiring more attention, which made my sister and me hesitant to stay with her for as long as we wanted to, though she never said anything about it.

"So I did what I thought was best: I moved out to lessen the burden on my aunt in taking care of my little sister and cousins. There were times when I didn't even have a roof over my head to sleep under, but no matter what, I knew I had to succeed in putting myself in a position to take care of my sister and me, no matter what.

"Fortunately, I always excelled in school, so when I figured out that chemistry and math were topics that came easily for me, it became a no-brainer that my way out of poverty would most likely be a career in chemical engineering."

I stopped to interrupt Tolu for a second. "Wait, you're a chemical engineer? Why is this the first time I'm hearing this?" I asked, genuinely confused.

"Well, yes, chemical engineering has always come easily for me, but that doesn't mean I enjoy it. . . . What I really wish I could do is follow my passion for writing poetry."

Tolu's revelation came as a shock to us since we knew him as the uber-serious ZNBS recipient, who just had a peculiar taste for fine Islay Whiskey and all things Canada. What we didn't know was that he was also a remarkably talented poet. Thinking back on our first full ZRC gathering, I'm not sure why I was so surprised initially because I've heard so many stories of immigrants and first-generation citizens telling countless tales of how they had to put their true dreams on the back burner to have a chance of a financially stable life in careers that are more traditionally associated with success, such as becoming a doctor, engineer, or lawyer.

Funnily enough, this is the exact sentiment that I received as a child, but for some reason, when the same story was retold with a different character and a different occupation—

Tolu the poet, in this case—the trope more readily associated with me. I took this as having a highly refined theory of mind ability, mentally patted myself on the back, and moved on.

"So after all of that, what do you think your special ability would manifest itself into?" I asked Tolu.

Slouching over in his chair while covering his mouth with his hand, Tolu took a few seconds to think about his answer before speaking. "I'm not exactly sure, to be honest, but all I could say is, I'm probably more accustomed to being comfortable in situations that would make others, let's just say, uneasy. . . ."

I thought, *Well, that could manifest itself into anything,* but that wasn't my top concern. I still wanted to know about the rest of our members.

The amount of synergistic energy flowing in the room that night felt dreamlike. Here we were, fourteen previous strangers from fourteen different backgrounds, yet when talking about our pasts, despite all the differences we had, a common thread of shared beliefs, motivations, and experiences brought us all together so effortlessly that where one recipient's origin story ended, another's could start.

For example, the common thread between James's and Diego's stories was *sound,* or with Sarah and Suhani both having this *je ne sais quoi* ability to be both understated yet abundantly impactful at the same time. Tomor's, Kofi's, and Tolu's early adversity in life molded them into the resilient men they were today, but the uncanny commonalities did not end there.

Next up was Daniela, whose background growing up in the favelas of Rio de Janeiro also made her the indomitable spirit that stood, or *sat,* before us.

"Yeah, it will probably come as no surprise to you that growing up in Rio comes with a certain set of challenges that makes any person especially cognizant of their surroundings," Daniela began. "Tolu, all I could think about in your situation was how similar it was to mine, even though we hail from different continents—"

"Well, your ancestors came from my continent, so maybe not that different, after all!" Tolu joked.

"Yes, but unlike you, I had both of my parents around, even though they weren't *all there,* to put it kindly," said Daniela. "When I say they weren't all there, even though they were around, what I mean is that my father was a detective for the local police department, but injuries sustained from a failed drug bust left him paralyzed and wheelchair-bound. As far as my mother goes, if she wasn't taking care of my little brother, who has special needs, she was trying to sell custom trinkets out of our home, which never brought much money. I'm not entirely sure to what extent growing up in that environment does to the psyche of a young girl, but for me, it made me acutely aware of my surroundings and the energies that different people and places have with them."

"You're losing me; I want to understand, but I don't," Kofi said. "What do you mean by different energies for people and places?"

It looked like Daniela especially piqued Kofi's interest because those enormous eyes of his lit up like Times Square on New Year's Eve. He even moved his chair closer in her direction after he asked his question as if every word Daniela was about to speak was gold, the year was 1848, and he had just arrived in San Francisco.

"Well, take for example my father: When I was younger,

and before the accident happened, I could remember how spirited he was, probably stemming from his standing in the community and how he felt about himself. He was a person that everyone could rely on without asking for anything in return. All he wanted was to know he had a positive influence on someone's day.

"However, after the accident, you could sense, well, *I* could sense that he no longer thought life was worth living. Although I knew he was still the same person inside, and that vigor still burned somewhere, even if he forgot this. But once the realization of his disability kicked in, he became a candle that burns especially bright when the wax is nearly depleted. You can remember just how bright it previously was, but once it's out, it's out. . . .

"But unlike that candle, my father's spark at times reignited as bright as it did before his accident, only for the flame to die out again. As his daughter, who thought he could do anything, watching him constantly relive that experience was a sadness I wouldn't wish on anyone.

"It didn't stop there, though. Eventually, I developed the sense to instinctively know if a person was up to no good or if they were about to be. Along those same lines, if many people who were up to no good congregated around an area, then that place would be filled with their energy, as well, giving me *más vibrações*, or bad vibes, saving me from a lot of potential negative encounters. So, yeah, that's what I mean." Daniela shrugged.

"I get that, and some may even call it intuition. I also believe that everything in this world has different energies associated with them, and knowing what energy a specific thing radiates provides insight most don't possess," Rafi said, supporting

Daniela's sentiment wholeheartedly.

"You're probably right, Rafi," Daniela endearingly replied, accentuated with a sincere smile. "With that being said, I apologize if I sometimes come off as brash or mean. Some say I have resting bitch face, but it comes from having a highly refined bullshit detector! My face just naturally weeds out those who I have no time for, but I'm not sure what sort of *gift* these experiences would translate into."

"Well, I, for one, don't mind that face of yours at all," Tolu slyly quipped.

"Okayyy, let's get back on track," I said, looking squarely at Tolu. I understood that for some of us, this was the first time we had all met others so similar in many regards, especially in the opposite sex, so I wanted to keep everything and *everyone* focused on the task at hand and not each other! What stood out from Daniela's story for me was this idea of different energies for people and places. Throughout high school, college, and even grad school, there were always those people who I couldn't be around for too long without feeling drained mentally and physically. She was onto something with this belief, whether or not it could be verified empirically. All I know is, if this theory of energies were true, everyone in the room that night was certainly on the same wavelength.

After discussing more common elements that were brought up in all of our stories, we serendipitously remembered Rafi had not yet gone. I almost want to say that this was something done by design on Rafi's part, but I did not want to assume and just gave him the benefit of the doubt since I had not gone yet, either—not because I did not want to participate, but because I feared that I did not know myself well enough to deduce what my ability would manifest itself as. Anyhow, I asked if Rafi would like to go first.

"Hey, buddy, could you help me grab something from the kitchen?" I suggested, kicking the side of Rafi's boot with my own. He turned his head and looked at me confusingly, not knowing what I was talking about, but taking the cue, nonetheless. As I sat up and walked toward the kitchen, Rafi followed closely behind.

"What was that all about, Femi?" Rafi looked at me with a wondering frown.

"I didn't want to put you on the spot in front of the other members, but I wanted to know if you wanted to go before or after I did."

"Um, I haven't really given it much thought, but I don't mind going next," he said.

It was settled then. Rafi would present his *origin story* of where he believes his powers would come from. We walked back into the living room, the eyes of every member closely following our every step until we reclaimed our seats.

"Where did you two go?" Sarah asked first.

"Femi just needed some help with something, and we started talking about something else," Rafi replied.

"Would you like to share with the class?" Sarah giggled.

"Sure, I don't mind. We were just discussing what we thought our powers would be and where they would come from," Rafi told Sarah honestly. "I was trying to think of a way to eloquently and succinctly tell you all my background and to surmise what my powers would be, but I don't know where to start.

"Yes, my upbringing was arduous, and my mere existence meant a life of hardship, but that's the life many Indigenous

Americans have to face, so I didn't really consider that having any influence on whatever *super ability* I may have.

"One thing that may play a part, though, is that ever since I was young, I would meditate for guidance any time I faced a difficult decision to make.

"There were even times where I wouldn't speak to anyone for hours if it was an especially challenging thing I was going through. The most interesting thing was, I was never specifically taught how to meditate by my parents or any elder. It just instinctively came to me as a means to reach clarity without having to involve anyone or anything else. That's why I can't readily think of what my powers could be."

"Maybe you should *meditate* on that answer, then, so we have a clue of what to expect?" Paul sarcastically said to Rafi, which was returned with a cold stare and a thin crescent smile.

Amongst all the chatter about whatever Rafi's ability could or couldn't be, an awkward silence soon blanketed the room. Though the silence would not last for too long, as it was interrupted by Amir, who had barely spoken a word until now. "You know, guys, I don't really know what my superpower would be, either."

We all now directed our attention to Amir. He was sitting in the corner of the room, rubbing down his impeccably shaped eyebrows with his fingers and occasionally re-parting his hair with a comb he always had near, a scene that could've come out of a movie. Here we were, trying to figure something out, then the only person who hasn't been actively participating in the conversation suddenly starts to speak.

Moreover, for further dramatic effect, that one person who hadn't been speaking is also sitting in the corner of the room on a rocking chair, of all things, self-grooming. "Similarly to Rafi here, I can't surmise how my special ability would manifest itself, either," Amir said. "Unlike some of you, for the most part, my upbringing wasn't too difficult, so I don't feel like I developed any special way to see the world; nor have I developed any special resiliency mechanisms to manage any difficult situations that I found myself in. Yes, my parents were immigrants to the UK, just like many of your parents were, but they were already solidly middle-class when I was born. Obviously, yeah, by being a brown kid in predominantly white spaces, I experienced some racism—not anything other children of immigrants didn't experience, though.

"That's why, for the life of me, I couldn't tell you what I think my powers could be, either," Amir confessed.

After a brief pause from replies, I interjected, "Listen, you all. I'm not saying, nor do I think anyone else suggests, that our powers can only manifest after extremely traumatic things," I was eager to point out. "My background is similar to yours, too, Amir. I didn't necessarily have the same experiences that our other members have had, but I still have an inkling of what my powers could be.

"It's not necessarily the situations you've lived through, but how *you* believe you would react in a situation based on your personality dispositions that will determine what powers we gain, I think. . . . The fact of the matter is that although we are all minorities in our respective nations, our situations and experiences are not equivalent." My statement was greeted with warm nods and pleasing smiles, which reassured me that we were still on the same page, despite our different upbringings.

"I apologize for my tangential detour, but as far as powers go, the only thing that readily comes to mind is that I've always had what is now referred to as a *vivid imagination*. My family would often find me locked in my room, silently clanking or smashing various action figures and stuffed animals together as if they were engaged in a battle royale! Little did they know, though, in my mind, the figurines became larger than life and engaged in all sorts of adventures full of mystery and suspense.

"After a while, they began to leave me alone and let me engage in one of my favorite pastimes—what you might call daydreaming, I suppose.

"Similarly, that fascination of the world you have as a child never seemed to escape me—especially when it came to historical topics. For example, how the land we live on today was shaped by the past, how atmospheric elemental compositions caused vast differences in the animals that exist," I said.

"Evolution, I guess," I continued, "but going from where we are today to where we started from. These were all things that impacted me profoundly and many times, sent my sense of imagination to run rampant with various possibilities, worlds where our rules of physics no longer applied. The ideas humored me, and the science humbled me—all reasons I chose to study paleontology.

"If my powers would come from anywhere, it would come from these two aspects, which I believe mainly define who I am," I told my ZRC family sincerely.

"Well, I guess I'm the odd man out," Paul said as he sprang out of his seat, arms outstretched, always the showman. He effortlessly directed the attention onto himself once again.

"Oi, what can I say? I'm an open book to you all at this point, and I'm sure you all have an idea of what you think my abilities could be. The ability to talk someone to death? The power to fire laser beam projectiles from my gob? The truth is, I don't know what my ability would be, either. I can sit here and tell you once again about my childhood and how I was raised, but being completely candid, my story isn't that much different from you all.

"Yes, I've experienced the loss of a close friend, and yes, I've experienced prejudice, too, and yes, my parents weren't perfect. Add that up, and what do you get? No offense, but it would probably be something similar to what you lot have already described—and yet I find it unlikely that our powers would be that identical. That's why I truly have no idea what my abilities could be. We done traveling down memory lane, yet?" Paul said sourly.

Chapter 11: The Zaragoza Directive

That was the end of that. Some of us had opinions on what or where our special abilities might come from and others had told stories of what specifically drives them. Some of us still had no idea at all. Regardless of where any of us had landed on the issue, we still knew more than what we had before we started, and that was all that mattered. The next step was to go back to Gástonio's village to meet both him and the craftsman jeweler.

All of the talk about special powers and growing up made James crave a meal he always enjoyed as a kid. French toast made with heavily buttered brioche bread with a side of crinkle-cut sweet potato fries. Initially making fun of him for naming something so oddly specific, the way he went on about the dish also made us crave the airiness of the bread, perfectly paired with the taste and texture of powdered sugar sprinkled on top, immediately conjuring memories of youthful vitality—especially around the holiday time.

Arranging for the delicious yet slightly weird brunch combination was bread and butter (pun intended) for the eternally professional majordomo, who made quick work of our request.

Stomachs full and questions primed, we left after brunch for Gástonio's village.

* * *

We arrived quicker than we did last time. The anticipation and weariness of venturing into a small village in a foreign country were now replaced with familiarity and refuge. Within the small community, news of our interactions with locals such as the coffee shop owner, the jeweler, and various other townspeople must've left a positive impression because we were greeted with warm smiles and welcomes making us feel instantly at ease. To them, we were the only foreigners from the Castillo who took the time to converse with them and also support their local economy. To us, though, they were a means to an end, despite how genuinely respectful and cordial we always maintained to be.

That was one thing that always charmed me: Despite all of our overt differences, we were all just humans in the end, who reacted the same way to respectfulness and appreciation. If anything could be summed up as the core tenet of the ZRC, I think it had to be that. It was the common human element shared between all, no matter our ethnicity or beliefs, that permeated throughout all of our interactions as species. It's the joy that comes with treating others the way you wished to be treated—often the first thing we are taught, and the first thing forgotten.

After being treated to a charming impromptu tapas meal

arranged for us by the locals, we made our way toward the jeweler's stand in the market square. Before we were even in the vicinity of his arts and crafts stand, his boisterous voice rang out, "*¡Bienvenidos, mis adorables hijos!*"

This was easy enough to understand with the level of Spanish we all now possessed, but for safe measure, we gently shoved James in front to resume his obligatory translating duties.

"Greetings again, Señor Craftsman," James said respectfully to the old man. I found this hilarious because, despite all the time we'd spent in this village, we still did not know the name of the man who crafted all the ZRC jewelry that we were decorated in. This humorous and ironic fact did not fall short on James, who promptly asked the genial old man what his name was.

"Señor, forgive us, but despite our visiting your stand previously and adoring the phoenix pieces you made for us, we still did not get your name," James said.

"Ha! I wondered why you just addressed me as Señor *Craftsman*, but my name is Tiago Pascal Morales . . . but since you are now my friends, you can call me Jaime," James translated for us.

Admittedly, after he told us what Tiago just said in Spanish, we looked amongst ourselves with blank stares and scrambled brains. *How in the world do you go from Tiago to Jaime?* we thought.

After James and *Jaime* conversed some more, we found out that Diego, or Diogo in Portuguese, were actually Iberian cognates of the name Jaime. Adding even another layer to the etymological version of *Inception* we were now engaged in, we came to find out that James, Tiago, and Diego all had different versions of the same name! You really do learn something every day, it turns out—even when you are engaged in upsetting a diabolical worldwide domination plot by the world's wealthiest family!

After the small talk ceased between Jaime and James, we got into the real reason why we were there in the first place.

"*Mi amigo,* my friends and I are here because we now need six more pieces of the phoenix jewelry that you provided for us," James said.

"If my memory serves me right, you all left with many pieces back then. Are you sure you need more pieces?"

The sincerity of Señor Morales really stuck out for me. Here was a businessman inquiring if we actually wanted to contribute to his fledgling business given the enormity of our previous contribution. *This type of honesty is exactly what's missing in the world today,* I thought.

"Yes, Señor, we are absolutely certain that we would like to purchase six more pieces, if this is okay," James said in perfect Spanish, now strangely embellished with Jaime's own accent.

. . .

"Well, you will be pleased to know that I have actually been working on some new phoenix pieces because something told me you would be back looking for more bespoke pieces," Señor Morales said to us.

He produced two new necklace designs, two new rings, and two new bracelets, all as impeccably crafted as our first order. Daniela and Suhani took the rings, while Tolu and Kofi took the necklaces, leaving Mikael and Tomor with the bracelets. After we thanked Tiago profusely for once again providing us with his fine goods, we departed for Gástonio's.

However, there was one question housed in our collective

consciousness that I couldn't wait to ask: "How the fuck did your Spanish get so good, so fast, James?" I said, pulling his shirt back so that I was asking directly in his ear as he walked in front of me.

"What?!" he answered back on loose footing, regaining his balance from my forceful tug.

"You heard him. Your Spanish was always just good enough to get by and be understood by native-born Spanish speakers, but just now, you spoke perfect Spanish with even a tinge of a local accent!" Diego exclaimed, raising his voice a few decibels after every word spoken.

James looked at us like we were the ones speaking a foreign language! "I'm not sure. The words just came to me as easily as they come to me now, speaking to you in English."

"And the accent?" Diego pushed.

"The accent? I didn't notice any accent change." James shrugged, confused himself.

We were now more puzzled than ever before—so much so that we stopped walking to Gástonio's house until we all understood what was going on.

"How long have you been practicing your Spanish since the last time we were here?" Sarah asked him.

"Not at all, to be honest," James responded.

"That doesn't make any sense. As a native Spanish speaker myself, that amount of improvement so quickly is *¡muy imposible!"* Diego stressed.

We all gawked at James, actively trying to comprehend how he could gain these skills in such a short amount of time.

"Well, what are you are looking at me for?" James burst out. "I seriously don't know where it came from; it just came out!"

"This could only mean one thing, then: It has to be your *gift*. It must have something to do with vastly improving the languages you're able to speak to the proficiency of a native-born speaker," Rafi said.

"Yeah, you could be right. . . ." James stated. From the low tone of his voice and the unsteady pacing of his words, it seemed like there was still something that he was not telling us.

"Out with it, man; you know more than you're letting on," Paul accurately pointed out.

"Okay, okay, you're right. When Tiago was speaking to me, not everything he was saying was in Spanish . . . I think," James said cautiously like he was scared of how we might react.

"What do you mean?" Daniela pressed.

"Well, I think some things he said were in Catalan, and I may or may not have responded in Catalan . . . or was it in Spanish? I'm not entirely sure. When we were speaking, it just kind of felt like we had this connection where I could even feel his words and accent influencing the way I responded. I really do wish I could explain it better. Sorry, guys."

* * *

This revelation came as a shock to us but also justified the time we spent trying to figure out what our powers could be. We didn't want to waste any more time and pushed on towards Gástonio's house. As soon as we were to arrive, we made it a priority to tell Gástonio about our potential superpowers and the extent of James's newfound ability.

Given the warm and awfully gracious welcome we received, all things considered, we didn't expect anything different from Gástonio, as long as we remained patient.

Out of the entire village, Gástonio was the happiest to see us, and the feeling was reciprocated. "Ah, you have come back! This fills my heart with happiness. Even an old man like me can still have frequent visitors; how lucky I must be!" Señor de Guzmán said gleefully, with James translating for us, his accent now mirroring Gástonio's distinct accent.

As James translated, I couldn't help but notice how Gástonio looked at him—as if he saw a family member or old friend returned from the grave. Señor de Guzmán's pupils began to rapidly dilate from extremely wide to very small, soaking in every visual cue he could extract.

"*It has awoken. . . .*" Gástonio mumbled in broken English.

"What has?!" we asked in unison.

"It has been awoken," he slowly repeated.

"Señor, what has awoken?" I probed.

Gástonio looked at James, at all of us, then back to James, grinning widely, all of his missing teeth in full display. He began to speak a language that sounded foreign to us—all of us except James, that is.

"What bloody language is coming out of his bloody gob?!" Paul wailed.

"A language that was spoken prior to the Latinization of Columbia, or South America, for that matter," Diego slowly replied.

Shortly after, Gástonio then switched to German, which I, at least, recognized but still had no capacity for its comprehension—something that did not bother James as he replied, even matching the Spanish accent Gástonio had when speaking the foreign languages.

Switching back into broken English, Gástonio's message was short: "This boy has a very special ability. He can speak and perhaps even write in any language known to man. I am not sure as to the limit of his power, but if his has been activated, you, too, will soon find out what yours shall be. . . ."

Although we each had a litany of questions to ask the hearty old man, time was not something that was on our side.

"Señor, yes, we know that our powers have been activated, but we aren't sure what they are," James told Gástonio. "We have already received instructions on what to do for the Second Trials, but we hoped you had some advice for us before we set out on our missions," James said.

Perhaps Señor de Guzmán didn't hear us, or perhaps he was so fixated on what he was thinking about that it simply went in one ear and out the other. Regardless of his reasoning, he completely ignored James's question and instead asked one of his own: "Well, do you all know what the Zaragozas have planned for their next big directive?" Gástonio asked as his jovial demeanor transformed into a more serious one.

We all looked at each other with mystified faces, internally thinking, *What directive?*

"We don't know what you mean by a *directive*, but we do know that they are up to something big," Sarah replied.

"Well, every couple of years, there is a Zaragoza Directive; it could either be ZNBS-related or something specific to the business side of their conglomerate. No matter what it is, it's always a huge multi-year plan that ends with a significant restructuring of their organization," Gástonio pointed out.

"For example, the main Zaragoza Directive back when I worked for the family was establishing the ZNBS and what Arturo wanted to get out of your predecessors and their respective countries. . . .

"I digress; I believe you asked me something before I got sidetracked. . . . Ah yes, now I remember, since you are inquiring about advice . . ." Gástonio stopped mid-sentence to take a seat and relight his pipe, chuckling as he spoke.

"He-he. The only advice we can impart on you younglings is to trust your intuition, trust your instincts. We appreciate you visiting us for guidance and wisdom, but the fact is, you are already far wiser than we ever were at your age. The answer to each of your questions lies within. Trust yourselves, trust in one another, and every answer will be revealed to you. We see that you have grown in number since you first visited. This is good, very good, for we sense a resolution in all of you that is steadfast and unwavering. This will serve you well if taking down the Zaragozas is your true desire because it will take many, and it will not be easy.

"When it comes to the Second Trials and your abilities, the original goal of these trials was to weed out anyone who doesn't have the ruthlessness and the ingenuity the Zaragozas possessed. And when we say 'weed out,' we don't mean if you don't make it, you just go home. You already know far too much for the Zaragozas to tolerate if you do not complete your trials fully and successfully. . . .

"They will not hesitate to put you in harm's way, nor would they lose any sleep if you died. The tragic reality of the twenty-first century is that human lives are expendable, a fact that is especially true for the Zaragozas, even if you do possess some of the greatest minds on earth.

"Again, remember, trust in yourself, trust in each other, and most importantly, *trust your instincts*. They are evolutionally time-tested and proven. Go now, waste no more time. You all must do what we could not. You must bring down the Zaragozas before the global power they possess becomes insurmountable. We must rest now, but something tells us that we shall see each other again."

Each word that Gástonio spoke felt like daggers piercing us, deeply and profoundly. Unlike daggers, though, his words did not draw blood but rather, conviction. The conviction that we had what it takes to complete the task we set out for ourselves, and if we did not, then we would probably die trying. The salience of Gástonio's words was not lost on us.

As he fell asleep after speaking, we placed a blanket over him and set out with renewed focus. If a man who has been alive for more than a century tells you that you can accomplish something historical, those are odds that we would take any day, and with that said, we headed back to the Castillo to formulate our plan to retrieve the Zaragozas' heirlooms.

"What was he talking about with all that *we* stuff back there?" Mikael asked as we left Gástonio's house.

"It's a long story," Rafi simply replied.

"A long story I'm sure you will eventually share with us, right?" Suhani added.

"If you're good, perhaps," Sarah teased.

Chapter 12: Retrieval

By the time we arrived back at the Castillo, it was already in the wee hours of the morning. Too tired to do any coherent thinking, we headed straight to bed the ZRC way, or in other words, everyone came back to our room, and we slept anywhere free space was available.

It was as if we already had this unofficial routine any time we did anything together. We would get back late to the Castillo, all sleep in the living room, wake up, and conjure up a marvelous breakfast, talk for a while, and then get back to business. For some reason, every time, it occurred just like that. I would revel in the amazement that it turned out like this *again*, but that surprise was always a pleasant one.

After our previous discussion about what our *special gifts* could be, we decided that it would probably be best to look over what we were tasked to do again for the Second Trials with fresh eyes. I was up first, forgetting exactly where we had to go for our benefactors, we all checked our emails for a quick reminder.

I was tasked to retrieve a vase that was gifted to a former Zaragoza Consulting Agency middle-manager who was axed upon having an affair with a subordinate and getting caught literally with his pants down on company CCTV! I had no idea why the Zaragozas would want to get involved directly—or indirectly, I guess, since I was the one tasked to retrieve it. Nevertheless, I didn't ask too many questions, and we quickly got to work brainstorming how we would get the vase back.

Since we all had a task to complete and they could be anywhere on the continent, we decided to work together and accompany each other when the items were geographically close. The closest to mine was Rafi's Second Trial task: retrieving a whole car the Zaragozas gave to the mayor of a nearby town.

One thing became pretty clear after reviewing what Rafi and I were tasked to do: What we would be doing for the Zaragozas wouldn't be exactly legal, but in and around Spain, they were practically the law, anyway.

Being the former special forces officer that he was, Tomor took point on planning how we would retrieve each Zaragoza heirloom. "Okay, since none of us apart from James knows what we're capable of, I say for these first two operations, we do them all together. Everyone takes up a specific role; not only will it help us shed light on what our special gifts could be, but it'll also help you to be exposed to inherent danger, making you all sharper in the process," Tomor pointed out coolly.

I'd never heard Tomor speak in this manner. It was exciting to see a new part of him that was integral to his personality but not needed for any situation that we previously found ourselves in, until now. Not to anyone's surprise, though, he quickly and effortlessly took command of both the planning and execution of all operations or *ops,* as he liked to say.

As ZNBS recipients completing our Second Trials, resources weren't an issue. If the Zaragozas were good for anything, it was for this: crossing out another thing that we didn't have to worry about. The plan to retrieve the vase was relatively straightforward.

With the Spanish-speaking abilities of James and Diego to help me pass with some conversational Spanish, I would portray myself as a fellow disgruntled ex-employee of the Zaragozas' and tell him that the vase was actually stolen from me before the ZCA stole it and gave it to him. Yes, I know what you all are thinking: My cover story wasn't too solid. But I also wanted to test if my imagination had anything to do with my eventual gifts, and this was the safest way to do so since, worst-case scenario, I could claim to be either crazy, distraught, or just confused from my recent *firing*.

Rafi's plan was a tad more involved, as it had to be; he was stealing the mayor's most prized car and no amount of confusion would be able to justify such an undertaking! Tomor then thought that Rafi should portray himself as a rare car collector and offer to pay top dollar for the vehicle, while the rest of us would serve as his car collection crew, coming along to inspect the vehicle for assurance.

To be honest, I was expecting Tomor's plans to have more *sophistication,* for lack of a better word. But the biggest challenge we faced would be balancing between airtight strategy versus leaving room for improvisation to allow our natural abilities to be showcased if they were applicable. The Trials were meant to be completed using our abilities; we had to admit the Zaragozas were correct in doing so. Little did they know, however, their desired abilities of ours would lead to their eventual demise. . . .

With no time to waste, we contacted our old friend, the majordomo, whose name we finally found out was Francis. He must've preferred us to the other recipients because he quickly arranged for a car to be used at our disposal. The town that we had to visit wasn't too far away from the Castillo, and I was aching to get behind the wheel again.

As if Señor Francis instinctively knew our plans, the cars that he chose for us fit the bill of being an authentic team of classic car collectors. Señor Francis outfitted us with a pair of impeccably restored first-generation Mercedes-Benz G-Wagens painted in a void-like matte-black color that almost appeared purple at certain angles, an excellent shade to physically represent the hollow essence the Zaragozas embodied: a family obsessed with the influence and authority that comes from being a prominent family, but in reality, is actually devoid of any light or brilliance.

* * *

Packing for what we thought should only take three days, we set off in subdued style. We arrived in the town of the ex-employee and mayor just a few minutes before the sunset allowing us to witness one of the most beautiful we'd ever seen in Spain. The next morning, we arrived at the home of Javier Estrada, the mayor of the town. Rafi walked up to the front door, cleared his throat, and knocked three concise times, loud enough to be heard but not loud enough to startle him.

"Hola, Mr. Estrada, my name is Elliot Stormsson, and my team and I are following up on the purchasing of the 1965 Jaguar E-Type gifted to you by the Zaragoza family," Rafi said, beginning the sentence in severely broken Spanish, resulting in Javier being barely able to understand him, despite our impromptu lessons from Diego and James.

But as soon as he realized Javier was perfectly capable of understanding the English words he spoke after every other Spanish word, Rafi repeated himself in full English, naturally coming off more authoritative and surer of himself, despite telling a complete lie. The weight of his words must've been enough because shortly after, we were all in Javier's home.

Conversing on surface-level things initially proved to me that Javier was probably a nice enough guy, but we were here on a mission, and even if his disposition was friendly, we had a job to complete. Once the pleasantries were out of the way, Mayor Estrada started to ask more substantive questions about how we got in contact with his people and how we knew about the car and its connection with the Zaragozas.

This was the perfect opportunity to test my special gifts theory.

You may be asking yourself why we would try to retrieve the car before the vase, which would've been probably much easier, and why we would attempt such a brazen attempt of deceit. Well, to me and Tomor, and how we initially conveyed it to the rest of the ZRC, if the tasks undertaken at the Second Trials could potentially result in death, as it has done in the past, according to Gástonio, we had no choice but to metaphorically and literally *go big or go home!* With home representing the potential nothingness from which we were born, and return to after death.

Obviously, we decided to go big and listen to the advice of our unofficial mentor and advisor, Gástonio, and followed our intuition. It was like Rafi read my mind or something because he stopped talking right when I was preparing to interrupt him, as I wanted an opportunity to respond to Javier's insistent questioning.

"Mr. Estrada, my client here, Mr. Stormsson, is a very busy man. We know you're running for reelection in a town that is quickly becoming restless with your policies. So, instead of pestering my client about how we came in contact with you, I suggest you arrange the car to be delivered back to the Zaragozas' Castillo at once!"

Mayor Estrada's face and body language proved that he did not fully understand the current situation in which he had found himself. Repeatedly scratching his face, long pauses before replying, and general uneasiness in his shifty eyes told us he could not readily discern if what I was saying to him was true or not.

The very fact that he was cognitively deliberating on whether he should release his Brilliant Silver 1965 Jaguar E-Type, described by Mr. Ferrari himself as, "The most beautiful car ever designed," filled me with optimism. I thought, *A man in possession of such a fine vehicle, even considering turning it away on a whim, surely is a man influenced by some outside force. . .*

We could tell that he was actually mulling this over, the actual *mayor* of the town we were in! Making matters even worse for him, to reach his house, you had to first pass a police outpost that only allows credible guests to visit the mayor due to ongoing political unrest incidences. However, convincing the patrol group stationed outside his house was an even easier task since the twin pairs of matching G-Wagens storming into the driveway played up the debonair yet imposing businessmen image we sought to achieve rather convincingly. Perhaps it was attributed to good luck, or how intimidating bombastic self-righteousness can be—no matter the reasoning, what I did next amazed even me.

Annoyed at how long it was taking to convince Mayor Estrada, I got up to stop his pacing, firmly grabbed him by his shirt collar, gave him a good shake or two, and yelled straight into his face, "If the car is not delivered to the Zaragozas' Castillo by the end of the week, your political career is as good as over!"

As liberating as it felt to scream into the face of a morally questionable elected official, what worried me most was (a) how natural it felt and (b) the perverse thought of seeing how far I could take this. . . .

Therefore, when Rafi told me the next morning that he had a dream where he saw the successful delivery of the Jag back to the Zaragozas, a general weariness wrapped over my body like a wool blanket, from a sensation of frozen extremities to a sunken feeling in my gut.

Was I really responsible for this? Can my words actually change outcomes? These were all things that I thought of after taking Mayor Estrada's car from his own house. Nevertheless, this feeling was quickly replaced with a rising tide of excitement since I took Rafi's dream as a good omen and the first ZRC completion of the Second Trials.

Once the initial feelings wore off, I realized that we had not yet made any contact with the disgruntled former ZCA employee. With only one more day remaining in the town, this was something I wanted to handle personally. Although the plan was to complete every retrieval together as a team, I wanted more certainty in relation to what I could do before we retrieved any more heirlooms. It required me to be a bit dishonest to my friends, which I hated but it had to be done.

Nightfall came, and I made an excuse to visit the ex-employee on my own.

"Where are you headed?" Sarah asked me.

"I'm just going for a walk," I mumbled underneath my breath.

With Sarah seeming to accept my lie and not questioning me further, I stepped out and headed toward the man's house. Clenching my fist as hard as I could, I banged on the stranger's door with the force and self-importance of a vengeful police officer. Hearing faint footsteps become louder as someone approached the door, I stepped back and waited for the door to swing open. The door opened, but I could not see anyone until a small voice rang out. "*Hola?*"

I looked down to see a little boy with a bowl-shaped haircut, his eyes full of wonder at who could be visiting so late and knocking so loudly. I knelt to be at eye level with the young boy and asked him for his father. I must admit, seeing him answer the door made me feel uneasy about what I was about to do, and I instantly regretted banging on the man's door in such a ferocious manner. I couldn't let that bother me now, though; *I had a mission to accomplish, and thoughts like these would only cloud my judgment,* I reminded myself.

A few moments later, the boy's father came limping to the door, his leg bandaged for some unknown reason as his cherry-red face gave away his surprise and, perhaps, apprehension.

"Can I help you, sir?" The man's voice reminded me of a

Spanish teacher I had in high school, further complicating my ability to be completely objective in the situation. I soon realized that the asshole routine I previously pulled with the mayor was not going to work this time and I had to change my strategy fast if I was going to retrieve the vase.

Frozen in indecision, I came up with a story claiming to be the ZCA secretary who arranged for the vase's delivery to him and that it was actually a mistake. The father was obviously confused about my backstory.

"Why would someone come now for something that has been in my possession for so long? And why would you come at this hour?"

All fair questions, but after going back and forth for a while, the man eventually went back into his home to retrieve the vase for me, and he did it with a smile. Was this an instance of me using supposed powers to bend the man's will to do my bidding, or was it just attributed to the man's obvious good nature, or more likely yet, a combination of both?

Despite my best intentions, my mission didn't bring me any closer to confirming my abilities, and I probably just scared a young boy before he went to bed. *Great job, Femi.*

Feeling shitty for my actions, I offered to replace his vase with another one. The man humbly denied the request, and asked if I would like some tea, which I declined. I apologized for disturbing him and thanked him again for making the retrieval process easy.

I always thought I was smoother than I actually am, so when I returned to the hotel and saw everyone in the hallway as soon as I walked in, I knew they had figured out where I was coming from.

"Well, how did it go?" was the question that came up most

often after they barraged me with inquiries.

"Can you really just alter reality by thinking about it?"

"Does it work on us, too?"

"Enough!" I called out in exasperation.

"I don't know what my power is. Maybe I can, maybe I can't alter reality, but even if I could, I shouldn't be the one playing God in people's lives—even if it is for the better. No one man should possess such power," I erupted, slamming my hotel door shut in the process.

I felt bad that I'd lashed out at the people who meant the most to me, and I felt bad about the things I did in this town. Most of all, I was terrified that even if I did have the power to alter reality, did I also possess the responsibility to handle such a power, or would I crumble as most do under the weight of amazing power?

All of these questions mattered not if this actually wasn't my ability, so despite all the planning and executing, I still didn't know if the heirlooms retrieved were due to any powers I had or just dumb luck.

* * *

The next morning was a bit awkward. I woke up approximately twenty minutes before we had to check out but saw no one in the hotel room. I proceeded to wash up and eat like we normally had for the past few days, but this time I did it all alone. Confused about where everyone was, I stepped outside to see that they were already packed and ready to depart for the Castillo. I sighed at the potentially awkward four-hour ride back, dreading having to apologize for the night before, but I hopped into the SUV sitting shotgun this time around while Rafi drove us back.

"I'm sorry everyone; I promise there's a method to the mad—" I tried to say.

"There's no excuse for what you pulled!" Suhani yelled from the seat directly behind mine, slapping the back of my headrest.

Stunned but not surprised by her reaction, I waited patiently for her to finish before I said my piece. "I understand all of that," I said in my usual annoyed voice, but in this instance, I knew that she was right; they all were.

"I thought we were all in this together. We complete all of the Second Trials together. That's what you said!" Suhani shouted continuing to lay into me.

Suhani wasn't one to often criticize, but nothing she said was wrong. Adding insult to injury, she also had a way of saying things that really drove the point home, containing the most vital aspect of telling someone off, making the person being told off—in this case, me—feel shittier than a dog eating forbidden food.

Trying to plead my case one more time, I stressed, "I only did it to be sure what my abilities would manifest themselves as! I didn't want to put any of you in trouble; nor did I want any interference from any of your abilities being co-activated."

Chapter 13: Portugal

Nothing I could say would convince them. I realized that and made my peace with it. I had to; we were almost at the Castillo and had to move on with the next set of heirloom retrievals.

Back in Sarah's, James's, Paul's, and my room—or, more aptly, the ZRC headquarters—we all agreed that we should next proceed to what Mikael and James were tasked to retrieve since they were both based in Portugal.

Logistics for getting everyone to Portugal was a nightmare, so we decided that from now on, missions would only comprise of two ZRC members, whose locations were closest to each other. This was the first time we had to depart from Spain for an heirloom, which naturally upped the stakes. Our transportation and accommodation would be provided, but everything else would be left to us.

Mikael's heirloom for retrieval was a rare Spanish coin from the time of Pierre's and Julie's infamous ancestor, Rodrigo Zaragoza, and James was tasked to retrieve a sword that was last seen with a retired Portuguese naval officer who had done business with the Zaragozas in the past.

The only details that we had to go on for both items were an address and a name. Everything else would have to be devised by Tomor. We had to rely on our eventual abilities to take care of anything he couldn't account for.

Since we'd left the previous town earlier than we'd originally planned, for better or worse, thanks to me, we had the afternoon and the night to think about what the plan would be when they got to Portugal. Fortunately, the retired Captain Joao Alves was last seen in the Alcântara district of the capital, Lisbon, while the coin was last seen in a pawn shop not far away in the Alfama district.

None of us had ever been to Portugal before, so the language barrier was a terrifying concern of mine, for all of five minutes, until I remembered that we had our own resident omnilingual in James! The flight to Portugal was a measly one hour, allowing for them to land feeling refreshed.

With no time to waste, Mikael and James arrived at their hotel, not far from the ancient São Jorge Castle, dropped off their bags, and set out to find the pawnshop. They decided beforehand that it would be best to pursue the coin first since it was closer to their hotel and since this would be the first time James would be testing out his ability in a new place speaking a new language.

The cover story for retrieving the coin was a bit brazen in its scope. Tomor's previous plan was cavalier, at best, and at worst, downright dangerous, but he insisted that the plans should be as simple as possible for them to casually claim plausible deniability in case something went wrong. Nevertheless, he was the professional, and we followed his orders.

To retrieve the coin, Mikael and James posed as pre-World

War Spanish treasure collectors/restorers and were looking to collect the sword and coin for a museum that would be opening soon in Madrid. This plan amused me because James—and especially Mikael—didn't look the treasure-collector type but more like starving artists! From James's free-flowing licorice locks to Mikael's scruffy, colored hair, coupled with his affinity for wearing various eccentric accessories, such as gemstone rings and chain-like bracelets.

Going a step further, Mikael also had several earrings and piercings that would immediately make him stand out in the characteristically reserved setting of a museum. This wasn't even the most entertaining aspect of their backstory because Mikael was to also play a mute, while James obviously did all the speaking. The hilarious part wasn't that Mikael was a mute, but rather that he could stay quiet for any prolonged period, even if he didn't understand the language being spoken!

At half-past noon, wasting little time, James and Mikael found the pawnshop where the coin was last seen. From their vantage point, the store looked empty, apart from a single clerk working at the desk. James and Mikael descended from where they were and entered the shop.

"Good evening, my friend! My colleague and I are esteemed historians looking for the rarest pre-war Spanish artifacts, and it has come to our attention that you are in possession of a rare Spanish doubloon," James stated in an overly exaggerated well-to-do Spanish-accented Portuguese.

The store clerk, who was also the owner, looked bewildered, but not doubtful of who James and Mikael said they were, which gave them the confidence to continue their fictitious backstories. James even went into a full spiel about how the coin was linked to an infamous Spanish pirate that sailed around the Caribbean. However, what happened next was pivotal in the successful retrieval of the Spanish doubloon. After about five minutes of James trying to convince the store owner to release the coin to him, Mikael pulled James outside to tell him that he knew how to get the coin.

"What's going on, man? I was in the zone back there; we were getting so close!" James stated in an ecstatic and rapid way, nearly out of breath from speaking so much, while at the same time, brushing his hair from his face to tie into a ponytail reminiscent of Rafi.

"I just had this overwhelming feeling come over me, and when it passed, the answer came to me as to how we could convince this guy to give us the coin," Mikael replied in an equally rushed manner, careful not to let the store owner hear him.

"Are you saying that this could be your ability being activated?" James asked, scratching his head, perplexed by Mikael's strange and abrupt behavior.

"All I'm saying is that I *sensed* that the only way to retrieve the coin from the man would be to tell him that the coin is cursed, so that's what you need to convey to him!"

"And what *I'm* asking is where this is coming from because I'm going to need more than a hunch to say something so outrageous," James replied to Mikael.

Not knowing whether to tell James if his hunch was attributed to his potential powers or not, Mikael did the only thing he could do and just told James the truth: "Look, buddy, I know what you want me to say, and I'm not going to say it because I won't lie to you. I'm not sure of the *origins* of my hunch. I just know that this is what we have to do, what *you* have to do, Mr. Portuguese-speaker," Mikael teased.

With that said, both men walked back into the store laughing, shaking hands, and patting each other on the back. Even if they did have these powers, a little acting still went a long way, and the image of two gentlemen from the scholastic profession of Spanish artifact-collecting, stepping outside to arbitrate and reach an agreement, resonated greatly.

"*Senhor,* I did not want to bring this up, and I already apologize for doing so, but there is something that you must know about this coin if you intend to hold onto it," James stated in perfect Portuguese, trying to look as dejected as he could, per Mikael's recent instruction. It must've worked because the man's face until this moment was resolute in his defiance to sell the coin. But as soon as James mentioned a curse, the man's complexion went from light brown to indigo. The store owner's face betrayed his best attempts of remaining steadfast, and like the final impact of a bulldozer demolishing an old building, the pawnshop owner crumbled immediately and gave the coin to James and Mikael, stating that he wanted nothing to do with cursed objects!

Next up was Mikael's task to retrieve the sword from the retired naval officer. According to him, whereas the Alfama district was more historical, the Alcântara looked trendier to him and more closely resembled a place where he could live.

Tracking down the retired captain proved more difficult than they initially thought. Despite Mr. Alves being well-known in these parts, that cult of personality made his current whereabouts difficult to come across, especially since some of his mystique was attributed to how fleeting his appearances were. The retired Captain Joao Alves was renowned not only because he was the son of the most acclaimed admiral to come out of the Alcântara district, but the younger Alves also had a storied military career, which carried on to his business acumen, eventually gaining the attention of the ZCA and how he originally came into contact with the sword we were tasked to retrieve.

The sword was going to be the most difficult item to retrieve thus far due to its inherent value, once belonging to a high-ranking officer from the First Carlist War and because of who it currently belonged to. After hours of talking to locals in order to track down Joao, one man informed James and Mikael they had heard Joao was at the Lisbon Cathedral back in the Alfama District, not too far from where they were originally.

Hailing a taxi cab, the two quickly rushed back to the labyrinth-like streets of the Alfama District to catch Joao before he left.

Serendipitously, as Mikael and James stepped out of the decrepit excuse for a vehicle, Joao was also walking out of the cathedral in a 16th-century, pirate-like, swash-buckling costume. Here was a man who apparently defined even his attire by his past profession.

"Captain Alves, Captain Alves!" James called out, trying to catch his attention before he caused them to go on another wild goose chase.

"Do I know you?" Joao slid down his Italian designer sunglasses and asked.

"You don't yet, but you soon will. My name is Thiago Lopes, and my partner and I are something of historians/antique collectors. It has come to our attention that you might have a sword that we are very interested in," James said, one foot still in the cab.

As soon as they mentioned the sword, Joao's body language immediately relayed to them, *Leave me the fuck alone, or else. . . .* His arms that were once free-flowing and used to add emphasis to his words were now crossed over his chest, only uncrossing to accentuate the swear words that flowed like water toward James and Mikael.

I guess what they say about sailors is accurate, I thought when James recounted this story back to me! His face and eyes that were at first neutral and curious had evolved into almost a menacing glare that made Mikael and James feel uneasy, to say the least.

Yes, we all were required to retrieve various valuables, all with inherent danger, but Mikael and James were now dealing with a retired combat veteran trained to spot all sorts of deception. According to Mikael, the only reason they were even able to talk to him was that James's Portuguese accent was so similar to that of Joao's; it made him feel at ease talking to *Thiago*.

"What sword are you referring to? I am a military man; I own all sorts of swords and things of the like," Joao said with an air of superiority.

Sensing that retired Captain Alves was attempting to strong-arm them into submission, James became even more direct with Joao.

"Stop playing with us—the sword from the First Carlist War, *Joao*," James said, leaving out the pleasantries by respectfully addressing him as *captain*.

If Joao was tense and apprehensive before, after James mentioned which sword he was specifically referring to, Joao became stiffer than a plank. "How do you know of that sword? Who sent you?" Joao demanded.

However, James and Mikael made sure not to cower in his presence, denying him any sign of dominance. "It doesn't matter who sent us. I told you that sword does not belong to you, and if you do not return it to us, the proper authorities will be informed!" James said forcefully.

Though it was the right tactic to use with this kind of person, at this moment, it backfired because as soon as James mentioned the authorities, Joao, being who he is, used his influence to alert some nearby police officers and inform them that James and Mikael were *disturbing his peace* and should be apprehended at once! The rookie officers looked at each other, dumbfounded, not knowing the exact law that was being broken by talking to Joao, but knowing who he was in society, they begrudgingly agreed and took James and Mikael away.

As the officers drove off, Joao was heard in the distance, "And you two can tell the Zaragozas that they will never see that sword again. I don't care if they control Spain. This is my country; this is Portugal!"

James simply smiled at Joao from the rear window and mouthed, "We'll be back. . . ."

With that said, James and Mikael were taken away to the local police station to await questioning. Once they arrived at the station, the police didn't spare a single second before they began to grill the two.

"What are you two here for? What did you want with Captain Joao Alves? Why doesn't this one speak?"

The questions came to them rapid-fire style, but exuding new levels of confidence, James would not despair and answered every question thoughtfully and succinctly. "We work for a museum and were asking Captain Alves if he would like to donate one of his prized possessions for the sake of it being preserved and admired by the public, in safety!" James had returned tartly. "My partner here does not speak because he is not Portuguese but is an expert at identifying genuine items."

The officers quickly abandoned the Mikael line of inquiry because they wanted to know more about the museum now. Sensing they were running out of time and that the sword was in jeopardy of not being retrieved, James and Mikael had to think of a way to get out of the police station, and fast, if they were to get back on Joao's trail.

"We're not getting anywhere with this James. I have an idea," Mikael whispered to James in English. Fortunately, or perhaps it was an aspect of James's abilities, the officers did not speak English, allowing Mikael to talk to James relatively freely.

"I hate to say it, but the only way we're going to get out of here on time is for us to blackmail these officers," Mikael murmured.

Right on cue, the officers stepped out of the interrogation room to look for an officer who spoke English. Unknowingly to them, though, this allowed Mikael and James to speak even more freely and bought them time to come up with an escape plan. "And how do you suggest we blackmail them?" James asked in exasperation.

"It's happening again, the feeling that's telling me how we should proceed with this. Just trust me again, like in the pawnshop," Mikael coolly replied with a sly grin.

"Listen, the younger officer is hiding something, something that could ruin his career, and the older officer knows of this, too, and is keeping it a secret from their superiors because he could be implicated, as well. We'll use this against them. . . ."

"But what exactly are they hiding?" James asked.

"I'm not sure, but I say we start with this and see what we can fish out from them," Mikael said, and James agreed with him. After all, he had no choice but to do so; they did not have any other plan. James said he was as scared as he'd ever been, but why wouldn't he be? They were preparing to blackmail police officers in a foreign country!

"So, how do you suppose we do this?" James sighed as he asked.

"Well, the specifics are still hazy, but what I do know is that the two officers are involved in a racketeering ring—exactly what fraudulent activities I'm not sure of, but with your superb acting abilities in conjunction with the language stuff, I'm sure this would be child's play for you," Mikael said to James with a sardonic smile.

"How the fuck can you be so calm while we are sitting in a fucking Portuguese police interrogation room?" James complained.

"Because I know everything will be okay if you just follow my lead!" Mikael barked back at James. "Okay, I hear them coming. Look alive and remember, play it up!"

"Do I even have a choice?" James said, now laughing uncontrollably—not because he was happy, but because he was about to do something completely ludicrous.

"If you don't start telling me the truth about why you two are here, I promise you'll regret it. Do you have something to say to me now?" the older cop shouted at James while shoving him in the chest.

After a few more minutes of expletives thrown at the two of them, with no response from either James or Mikael, the two officers grew increasingly agitated, first trying to do the whole *good cop, bad cop* act. They quickly abandoned that strategy once they realized that James and Mikael wouldn't roll over so easily, reverting back into their natural roles of *two crooked cops.*

"Alright, we let the two of you have your fun; now it's time for you to release us—that's if you two value your jobs, at least," James slyly said, leaning back in his seat, hands crossed behind his head. This sent a shock wave to the officers' bravado and brought them back down to earth.

"W-w-well, well, what do you mean?" the younger officer said, fainthearted and stumbling over every other word.

"You know exactly what I'm talking about, and I'm sure the chief of police wouldn't be pleased once he caught wind of what you and your overweight and underpaid *amigo* have been up to in your spare time. . . . You see, we aren't actually museum curators but have been, in fact, sent by the Zaragozas. I trust I don't have to mention who the single largest Spanish benefactors in Portugal are?"

Although he could not understand what was being spoken, Mikael knew that James was doing exactly as he instructed and couldn't help but smile, psyching out the officers even more.

"Okay, okay, let's not be hasty. What do you two want?" the older officer said, his once thunderous voice now reduced to librarian-like levels.

"We need the address of Captain Joao Alves, and we need it now!" James demanded in perfect Portuguese.

"*My friend,* this is an unreasonable request. Senhor Alves

and his father are well-respected in this community and, and—" the younger officer started to say, clearly already shaken.

"And if you don't give us his address, he will still be highly respected, and you two will be in jail alongside those you've arrested," James said, finishing the crooked cop's sentence for him.

"You know what? Something also tells me that not only will you give me his address, you'll also do something else for us!" James said, channeling his inner Taiwanese loan shark.

"You'll order a small raid and retrieve a specific sword for us, and upon successful completion, you and your partner will be handsomely rewarded, and you'll never see us again."

Though Mikael had no clue what James was talking about with the officers, the changing dynamics of the conversation grew readily apparent. The previous submissiveness of James's interactions with the cops quickly transformed to that of a hardened mafioso, with James making and changing demands as he saw fit.

Soon after, it was discovered that Joao wasn't the perfect admiral's son, either, and was in fact, currently under federal investigation, so a search of his house wouldn't exactly come as a surprise. The only surprise would be if the local cops had enough balls to actually go through with the raid without federal support, given his family's local prominence. But even despite that status, the slightest mentioning of Zaragoza retribution was enough to get the ball rolling in the ZRC's favor—using the status of *ZNBS recipients* to threaten the iron hand of the Zaragozas coming down on anyone who opposed us, all while trying to take down the Zaragozas themselves.

How meta, I thought.

Mikael's planned manipulation and James's language and acting abilities were successful. The police had agreed to their plan, and Mikael and James were released from custody, a *cake-eating* situation, in the words of Mikael.

After relaying to their superiors that an imminent raid was needed on Joao's property based off of bogus information (something I'm sure they had no problem doing), the raid was approved to be completed the next morning at the crack of dawn. Mikael and James were promised their sword, and the Lisbon police were promised that the Zaragozas would continue to fund their police department and Portugal as a whole.

Sticking to their word, the sword was retrieved, and now James and Mikael had both the sword and the coin safely in their possession and were ready to come back to Spain. Just like that, the ZRC were well on our way to successfully completing the Second Trials and moving forward with the plan to topple the Zaragozas, as the abilities we were granted were on the verge of being understood. But James still wasn't satisfied; although they were wildly successful with their Portuguese mission, the only thing on his mind was the extent of Mikael's powers. Mikael's *instincts,* in combination with James's omnilingualism, had been the reason they'd successfully retrieved the sword and coin. But whereas James's gifts were clearly defined and established, the same couldn't be said about Mikael's. . . .

With both heirlooms in hand and having one day to spare in the Portuguese capital, James decided it was time to decisively know what Mikael's special ability was. From the interactions they'd had so far, it was obvious that

Mikael's abilities revolved around knowing what people were thinking, but how? Was he reading their minds? Could he pick up non-verbal cues that no one else could see? James was tired of guessing and wanted concise answers. Just past 8 p.m. on their last day, James decided to do just that.

"Mikael, I'm sure you know this already, but it's time we found out exactly what your special gift is." Mikael was dreading having this conversation. He knew as much as James did and wasn't even as confident about his own abilities.

"How do you plan on finding out?" Mikael asked, nervously scratching his head repeatedly.

"Well, so far, you've been able to tell what people have been thinking or feeling, so you must be able to interpret emotions on some level, right?" James offered.

"Maybe, but I can't articulate it clearly. I can pick up on whatever someone is feeling. I can sense their fears, and sometimes even their temperaments, but it doesn't just stop there; it's almost as if . . . as if I can feel what they feel, which helps me act and plan accordingly," Mikael said apprehensively.

"Well, then that settles it. The only way we'll conclusively know what you're fully capable of is for you to try it on me," James suggested. "I'll try to put myself in a mood and you'll have to tell me how I'm feeling. To really see how far it can go, I'll first go into the other room to see if you can sense my feelings even behind solid objects. I'll continue to get closer to you until you correctly guess what I'm feeling. How does that sound?" James said with utmost seriousness.

"Doesn't sound like I have much of a choice in this situation, but sure, I'll try it. When do you want to start?" Mikael asked.

James excitedly replied, *"Now!"* and pranced into the bathroom to begin the experiment. "So like I just said, I'll stay in here, and you'll have to tell me what I'm feeling!" he shouted.

It wasn't exactly the most scientific experiment, but their powers weren't necessarily grounded in science, either, or at least any science readily understood. . . . For this first test, James wanted to make things easy for Mikael and decided to start with simple yet strong emotions to see how specific Mikael could get.

"Okay, okay, I'm picking up on something, but I'm not sure what it is. Oh, wait, hold on, it's starting to become clearer . . . whoa, this is something I haven't sensed before." James could hear Mikael sniffling from the other side of the door.

"You okay there, buddy?" James asked.

"Yeah, I'm fine. It's just that I didn't know you felt that deeply," Mikael said in a softer voice, barely audible through the door.

"I take it that you know what I'm thinking about, or better yet, what I'm feeling?" James said.

"Yes, I can, but it doesn't just stop there. I'm feeling it now, too. Your heart is yearning for someone you were once very close to—dare I say it, yearning for someone that you fell deeply in love with. Wait, wait, there's more. This isn't the first time you've been in love, either, but this is surely the purest love you've ever felt.

"The only thing is, you two have recently been separated—not by choice, but rather, circumstances. She's always on your mind, but you know there is nothing you can do about it.

"From spending every waking minute together to being on

separate continents, you miss her dearly. Fuck, now *I* miss her dearly, too" Mikael ended, wiping away a tear from his cheek. "Who is she, if I may ask?"

Opening the door to speak to Mikael face-to-face, James confirmed everything Mikael sensed.

"I met her when I did a study abroad program in Vancouver back in my undergraduate studies. I never met anyone like her. Literally, the moment I laid eyes on her, I knew she was special.

"From that first date we had at her favorite wine bar, almost every day that year was spent together. It was something I've never felt before—a person who just understood me, without having to say a word, and when she did speak, we were often finishing each other's sentences," James said with a twinkle in his eye.

"Up until that point, the significance of the word *soulmate* had no meaning to me, but after I met her, soulmate was the only word that adequately conveyed how intensely the love I felt for her was. I'm sorry, I didn't mean to make this conversation all about me. The point of today was to find out the extent of your powers, not the extent of my broken heart," James said, wiping away the tears that now flowed freely.

"Anyway, what did you mean when you said that you missed her, too?" James asked, sniffling the nasal congestion away.

"Well, I think I finally understand the extent of my gifts—well, beginning to understand it, at least. When you were thinking about her, I could feel just how much you loved her. I also sensed why you loved her so much—how you previously felt that you would not meet anyone like her until you did, how comfortable you two were with each other as if you were tailor-made for one another, the type of love that many people dream about, but rarely attain. I felt exactly as you felt. I missed her just as you missed her."

Mikael continued, "Now I understand how I was able to interpret what the pawnbroker and those seedy police officers were feeling and what they were thinking. I wasn't exactly reading their minds, but I didn't have to. Their emotions were clearer to me than the words you're speaking to me now. I knew exactly how to manipulate them based on what they were feeling, not what they were saying. . . .

"So that settles it, then, your power is some sort of emotional manipulation?" James inquired.

"I'm not saying I have all the answers, but based on what I do know, then yes, it can be safe to assume that I have the ability to interpret and replicate the emotions, moods, and temperaments of others without any sort of communication," Mikael considered. "I wouldn't call it *manipulation* per se, more *sensing. . . .*"

"Sensing with the ability to manipulate is more apt, wouldn't you say?" James quipped.

"Your words, not mine," Mikael said, grinning sharply.

"Well, I would call this trip a success, no?" James asked Mikael. "If you call getting arrested by the Lisbon police, being threatened by the hands of a trust-funded, spoiled retired naval officer a success, then yes, we couldn't have asked for anything more! Jokes aside, yes, it was a success, and I'm glad you were right here with me the whole time!"

"I'll take a success in any fashion it presents itself, so what do you say you dye those ebony-colored locks blond and sport a buzz-cut like me?" Mikael asked.

"I'll just take whatever success we had and leave my hair alone, thank you!" James replied as he ran his fingers through his wavy hair.

After having a debriefing on their newfound powers and the heirlooms retrieved, Mikael and James were finally ready to leave Portugal and couldn't wait to return to the Castillo.

But they weren't out of the woods yet.

* * *

Upon landing back in Spain, Mikael couldn't help but notice a mysterious black sedan that was seemingly following them.

"I think we spoke too soon about all that success back in Portugal," Mikael gulped, constantly checking over his shoulder.

"What do you mean? What are you looking at?" James asked.

"Well, don't turn around now, but ever since we landed, that black car has been following us. . . ."

"Wait, is that why you wanted to walk all the way to the other terminal?"

"Yes, exactly. I wanted to see if it was going to follow us," Mikael responded, trying to avoid eye contact with the mysterious sedan.

"What do we do, then, Mr. Emotions?" James asked nervously, trying to keep up with Mikael's pace.

"First things first. Instead of driving back ourselves, let's call a cab, see if they follow us with an uninvolved third party." Mikael and James then went to hail the first taxi they saw, departing the airport hastily.

"Is he still following us?" James asked.

"I can't tell. I think we're in the clear."

Or so they thought. Whoever was behind the wheel of the shadowy car had ample experience doing this because they stayed back just long enough for the two of them to think they were in the clear.

"What the fuck? He's still there, and he's gaining fast. Who the fuck are these people, anyway?" James panicked.

"Lo siento amigos, pero esto es muy peligroso. Tengo que parar," *the cabbie said.*

"What did he say? . . . James! What the fuck did he say?" Mikael pleaded to James.

"He said he's sorry, but it's too dangerous, and he has to stop!"

"He has to *whattt?!*"

In the blink of an eye, the taxi driver pulled over to the side of the road, opened the door, and let Mikael and James out as the mysterious black car accelerated hard and braked just as rapidly, stopping a few feet behind the two. Exiting from the car were two men dressed all in black. They were both well-dressed, each of them wearing suits, but their ample facial hair, among other things, made it hard to ascertain their allegiances—too well-dressed to be from around where they were, but too scruffy to be associated with the Zaragozas. The two men approached Mikael and James, with the taxi driver now long gone, only leaving behind a trail of Martian-colored dust. . . .

"Do you know who we are?" the shorter and stockier goon asked in broken English.

"No, but we can assure you, we're not the people you're

looking for," Mikael said.

"Our boss said to speak in English, so your flamboyant friend could understand, too. *Capitão Alves sends his regards."*

The moment the hired thugs finished their sentence, utter dread took over Mikael and James as they froze in fear on the side of the road, contemplating that this could be the end of their lives. However, there wasn't much time to think as the taller bearded thug drew first blood.

Smack! was the sound that erupted from the swing the taller thug took, connecting his fist to Mikael's nose in thunderous fashion. Not one to miss out on the action, the short and fat thug let out a maniacal laugh and joined in on the action, tackling James onto the dusty road in order to dish out his own ground-and-pound.

The two thugs repeatedly struck James and Mikael with their hands, feet, and anything nearby they found. The pair was now defenseless on the ground and taking substantial damage from the heavy blows the brutes indifferently inflicted upon them.

"Is that all you got? I've taken harsher beatings on the playground," Mikael muttered, trying to laugh in between spitting out globs of blood.

"Ah, we have a fighter in this one, Marco," the shorter goon said to the taller one.

"Oh, that's fine. Stand him up and let's see how many blows he can take to the stomach before choking on his words," Marco said.

The goons were as brutal as they were true to their word. They stood Mikael up, Marco the taller goon holding him, as the shorter one continuously punched Mikael in the gut as hard as he could, making sure each blow had full force from swinging his hips, heavily loading up on the punches. *Whack, whack, whack!*

"Gilberto, that's enough; he's unconscious already. *Gilberto, stop*. There are cars coming!" Marco shouted at his partner-in-crime.

"Wait, let me remind him that only women wear earrings," Gilberto said. Holding Mikael's throat with one hand in order to tear out his disco-ball earring with the other. The excruciating pain from the earring tearing his earlobe in two sent a shock wave through Mikael's body that was enough to help him regain consciousness.

"We have to leave, *NOW!*" Marco shouted to Gilberto.

The two men sped off as quickly as they had come, the dust flailing in the wind, the current condition of Mikael and James the only traces of their menacing rampage.

"*¡ Ayudanos! ¡Ayudanos por favor!*" James said, crying out for help from the cars passing by as he held his rib cage.

Fortuitously for Mikael and James, one of the oncoming cars was carrying a medical team that had just returned from Spain on a relief mission in Algeria. The team did what they could for both men, paying especially close attention to Mikael, who was flickering in and out of consciousness.

"Please, just get us back to the Zaragoza Castillo," James begged. The team agreed, nursed their injuries, and set off.

Though he was badly beaten, Mikael still used the opportunity to make jokes in between his moments of consciousness. "I guess we shouldn't have been so cavalier about messing with the captain, huh?" Mikael chuckled, coughing out more blood.

"Dude, you're insane. I can't believe you taunted them in the process," James replied, wiping away the blood from

Mikael's badly bruised head.

"Ahh, that was funny, huh? I was serious, though; I have taken worse beatings even from those who claimed they *loved me*."

"Jesus, you're a crazy guy, Mikael."

"I know, I know. . . ."

"You two shouldn't be talking so much; rest up. We have a long way to go," the chief of the medical team said while driving.

So the two did just that and rested until they got back to the Castillo.

By the time they arrived, the gang and I were already preparing dinner, the finest of Andalusian cuisine, to welcome Mikael and James, awaiting tales of their Portuguese adventures. However, when we first laid eyes on the two, my stomach sunk down to my feet at their condition.

Daniela was the first to actually be able to say something coherent, and when she did, it was just repeating the words *what the fuck* in Brazilian Portuguese.

"They did say that the Second Trials would be dangerous, right?" Mikael joked as James carried him back into our room.

"This is it, guys. We're way out of our league now," Kofi said, his bright eyes dancing around in their sockets.

"Oi, shut up, mate. Grab a towel and make yourself useful," Paul replied.

A man of few words, Rafi sprang into action, relieving James of holding Mikael up so that he could rest, as well. I followed his cue and started to make the couch more comfortable for the two of them. Surprising all of us, Mikael was still in good spirits. "Don't worry, it looks worse than it actually is," he casually said.

"Well, as you guys can see, the Zaragozas clearly have a lot of people out there who don't like them," James said as Amir carefully attended to his wounds.

"Yeah, no doubt, and shit definitely just got real," I said.

"So where do we go from here?" Sarah asked.

"What do you mean? We go retrieve the rest of the heirlooms and take down those bastards," Suhani said unwaveringly.

"You guys are crazy. Can't you see what Zaragozas' enemies can do? Imagine what they can do themselves once they figure out what we're planning behind their backs, in their home. No less!" Kofi cried out.

"Mate, close your legs; your vagina is showing," Paul barked at Kofi.

"Real funny. You may think this is a game, but I don't." Kofi shot back.

"If you believe I think this is a game, then you don't know who the fuck I am, nor what I've been through, you *Muppet*!" Paul said, millimeters from Kofi's face.

"That's enough from you two. We'll take care of the boys. Finish this dinner, and we'll talk more about this another time. Emotions are running too high right now to discuss anything clearly. Let's let cooler heads prevail," Sarah said.

She was right, and although James and Mikael were battered and beaten, they were not broken and even managed to have the strength to recount their Portuguese adventures.

Although it was a lovely dinner-time story to listen to (all things considered), while they were gone, we, too, were busy formulating the best way to go about retrieving the next set of heirlooms.

* * *

The next morning, we did talk about it, but contrary to what Kofi would have wanted us to do, we doubled-down on our goals with Diego and Sarah itching to go next and, as no one really put up any arguments against the notion, it was settled that the next heirlooms retrieved would be the ones tasked to them. By being in real danger, the stakes of this were not lost on anyone. We were putting ourselves in danger's path intentionally, and for the sake of what? Well, for the sake of everyone we loved and cared for back at home, but now we had to learn how to defend ourselves, and Tomor, for one, couldn't wait to teach us some basic self-defense.

So that morning, after we debriefed about Mikael and James's trip to Lisbon, Tomor had us report to the courtyard for training. Tomor was a good friend but an even better instructor. His instructions were always clear and concise as he taught us the basics of Krav Maga, the martial arts developed specifically for the Israel Defense Services.

"Now, like every other martial art developed, the best thing to do in a confrontation is to avoid it, but as we know, that's not always possible. So to account for that, Krav Maga was originally designed to finish a fight as quickly as possible, which often means as aggressively as possible," Tomor said as he marched back and forth in front of us, now standing in a neat and orderly line, shoulder to shoulder with each other.

Tomor showed us a myriad of different techniques, common variations, and other attacks we could do based on our body types and physical limitations. The girls took to it faster than any of the guys did. Perhaps by trying to *out-macho* each other, our egos got in the way, and before we knew it, all three of them had us on our asses, using their lower center of gravity to their advantage.

It wasn't completely fair, though, as Sarah and Daniela had previous experience in Brazilian jiu-jitsu, and Suhani could probably knockout any one of us anytime she felt like it.

After going over the areas of the body that are particularly vulnerable such as the eyes, throat, groin, and liver, Tomor decided to give us a much-needed break.

I was always eternally grateful to have an actual super-secret soldier on our side. That day was one of the best reminders of what we could actually accomplish with the non-supernatural abilities we were *gifted*. We practiced a little more, each of us trying to be better than the other until we all felt like Mikael and James looked. We spent the rest of the day and night picking Tomor's brain about different tactical strategies and martial arts techniques until it was time to sleep and send Diego and Sarah off on their Second Trials tasks the next day.

Diego was tasked to retrieve a guitar that was originally made from the trees near the Zaragoza Castillo, and Sarah was not even tasked to retrieve a thing, but a person.

When we first reviewed all the things we were told to get and noticed that it was a person for Sarah, we thought that it was strange but didn't scrutinize it any further. However, now that we had retrieved some of the heirlooms already, it became even more bizarre that the Zaragozas would have Sarah return a person to them, but still classify it as an *heirloom*.

The traditional definition of an heirloom is a valuable *object* that has belonged to a family for generations. That definition obviously explained the first part of our task, but were the Zaragozas so high and mighty that they considered even a human life a mere *object*?

Whatever the case might be, that still didn't explain the second part of that definition. How could a human belong to a family for generations? The answer to this question and more were just a few hours away.

Diego and Sarah were headed to the city that was perhaps most historically associated with tyranny and humans viewing themselves so superior to others that they decided to conquer most of the known world and provide themselves external validation of their superiority! It was official; Diego and Sarah were headed to the capital of the United Kingdom: London.

Even as they stepped down into the land where the red double-decker buses roam free, not much was known about the guitar that Diego was tasked to retrieve, apart from its origins near the Castillo, which made it easy to hypothesize its value to the Zaragozas. Diego was also a musician who breathed music in and exhaled excellence, so it was no surprise that he was tasked to acquire the guitar, even though no one had an idea about what his abilities could manifest themselves as. His acoustic renditions of Pink Floyd classics at the Fireside Chats became a thing of legend.

Sarah, on the other hand, had even less of a clue of her potential powers or the meaning of her heirloom being a person, or Yessica Garcia, to be exact.

The only thing that we knew about Yessica was that she was a Spanish national, now living in London, and she had past affiliations to the Zaragozas, who now wished for her to return. Diego's guitar proved to be more difficult than first imagined once they found out that the guitar was now in the possession of not only a lord but the lord that also happened to be a patron of the Royal Society of Musicians.

Unfortunately, Tomor was not available to assist Diego and Sarah with a plan to retrieve their items, so they had to rely primarily on improvisation.

Chapter 14: London Calling

Diego and Sarah made the decision to retrieve the guitar first, mainly because Diego, at least, had a solid connection to the heirloom he would be returning, making it easier to come up with a cover story to persuade Lord Stephen Barrington. Once the guitar was secure, Diego and Sarah would work together in locating and retrieving Yessica since more unknowns existed for her.

What they could find out about Lord Barrington was both encouraging and distressing at the same time. Though he was a classically trained guitarist who appreciated all forms of string music, he was also known to have *never* lost nor sold a guitar. Furthermore, while he was known to be jovial and good-spirited, he was also known to be vengeful and cold-blooded to those who opposed or defied him. Which of the lord's many personality traits would greet Diego when he made contact raced like a hamster on a wheel in Diego's mind as he tried to formulate his own plan. Above all, Diego knew that for his mission to be a success, he had to be authentic, and it had to be about the music, always. Both Yessica and Lord Barrington were primarily seen in the well-to-do West

London area, which made the jobs of Diego and Sarah a bit easier since they only had to focus on a single area as opposed to the sprawling metropolis that is Greater London.

Tomor arranged their accommodations to be strategically placed in the middle of where both their targets had been seen. After a few days of silence, Diego received word from a ZCA subsidiary in London that Lord Barrington would be visiting the London Palladium to show support for an upcoming concert. This was Diego's opportunity to make initial contact with Lord Barrington, and he was not going to let the chance go idly by.

Arriving at the theater one hour before the lord was scheduled to arrive, Diego wanted to get there early to scout out the theater to look for potential places to intercept the lord. But he also came early just to relish the fact that he was in London for the first time and was attending a free production of the Royal Society of Musicians, at that!

Diego also knew that if he had any powers, it would be related to his primary love for music. So, by attending a musical production while under the pressure of trying to retrieve the heirloom tasked to him, Diego ingeniously thought so much stimulation would cause his sensory experiences to be heightened and perhaps cause his abilities to reveal themselves earlier. He was right, albeit he did not immediately realize it. Ballad after ballad, Diego said, "The music started to sound different…." Not because of any strange rhythmic structure, lyrics, or arrangement, but because he began to *feel* the energy waves each song generated, coursing through his veins like blood. Not only that, but he could also feel the mood the musician was in when the song was being performed. The way Diego first described it to us, we thought he was going bonkers!

At our wit's end, we decided to ask our undercover ZRC member, Alfred, who had a background in neuroscience, what he thought about the matter. According to Alfred, it sounded like Diego was referring to synesthesia. But Diego said he was not merely seeing sounds as colors but seeing and feeling them as living entities capable of changing and altering moods and evoking certain feelings. The energy waves of classical music were felt as forceful yet graceful waves on the open sea. Electronic music had an ability to disrupt, but if he listened closely, the ability to aid focus, and jazz music had the most mixed effects of all. Having hybrid-like qualities of being forceful and direct, just as classical music did, but also the ability to be disorienting.

Almost an hour into the performance Diego had become completely mesmerized by the experience, describing it as *orgasmic*. As he sunk deeper and deeper into his seat, he could feel the music starting to affect him differently. Not only could he recognize every note being played, see the mood evoked by the tones, feel the waves they generated, but now he felt as if he could replicate the song's essence, *exactly*.

More specifically, he found that he could absorb and mimic the feelings evoked by the music he had just heard, first by humming their tones and melodies. Initially, Diego found himself overwhelmed by this strange phenomenon. The complex and atypical rhythmic patterns of math-rock left him dazed and confused, not knowing if he was alright. But as he quietly hummed Chopin's Raindrop" prelude, he found himself to be comforted by its melodic repetitions, putting his mind completely at ease, reorienting him on his goals.

Diego wasn't satisfied with just being able to change his

moods by making different sounds. He wanted to find out how far his abilities could go; he wanted to see if he could affect others with the same feelings, if he could interpret and manipulate their feelings through music. At first, he did not know how to go about this. Would he hum classic show tunes to make people dance? Or would he recite rap lyrics to inspire confidence and optimism to the worn and oppressed? The possibilities were endless, but the time to complete the Second Trials was not.

Not long into Diego's internal decision-making process, everyone in the audience had begun to stand and clap for no apparent reason. The song that was previously playing had since ended, and the stage was still being set up for the next performer. But before Diego could scan the room to figure out what all the commotion was about, he saw an older gentleman emerge from the stage's curtains. The abrupt applause confused Diego as the man did not appear exemplary in any manner. The man was solidly average in both appearance and build, apart from questionably high cheekbones and a soul patch that was sixty years too late. However, before he took his seat on the stage, he was announced as *the* Lord Stephen Barrington, and a single classical guitar was promptly brought out for him, resting on a velvet pillow. Although this guitar was not the one that Diego was there to retrieve, it was beautiful, nonetheless.

As Diego watched Lord Barrington assume the classical guitarist stance and begin to play, he immediately acknowledged that the previous praise for the lord was merited.

He played the guitar with impeccable grace and accuracy that appeared almost like he wasn't even trying but rather doing something as mundane as walking or talking. But

Lord Barrington really *was* talking, just not with his words. Every note was perfectly fretted without hesitation. His fingers were like heat-seeking missiles, hitting their targets each and every time. Diego was at a loss for words, and his mission had just become much harder and easier at the same time—easier since Diego no longer had to feign interest to appeal to Lord Barrington's gentler side because he was now genuinely interested in the man and the music behind him. Conversations no longer had to be about theory and history because he had just been serenaded with the Lord's actual arrangements, ripe for discussion.

Nevertheless, Diego knew that a musician of Lord Barrington's caliber would not easily part with a guitar of such significance. If Diego's mission were to be successful, he would need outside help of the mystical variety!

Lord Barrington's performance lasted for about thirty minutes. Afterward, a small crowd gathered around him to ask various questions about his playing and inspiration, as well as the customary groveling routine journalists loved to do whenever in the presence of the so-called *elite*. It was around this time that Sarah joined Diego in the theater, eager to help him in any way she could.

"Did you get a chance to hear him play?" Sarah asked.

"Yeah, I did," Diego replied coolly.

"Good luck getting that guitar from him now," Sarah joked.

Not wanting to cause a big commotion, Diego waited until all the slowpokes had departed before he dared to approach Lord Barrington.

"Sir, I have never heard anyone playing like that in all my years," Diego congratulated the man honestly.

"Well, fortunately for you, you still have many years to

reach my ripe old age, my good young friend," Lord Stephen Barrington cheekily replied. "Are you a musician yourself?"

"Yes, sir. I consider myself a musician and appreciator of all things musically related, *especially the craftsmanship of fine instruments*."

Diego's answer made Lord Barrington's head tilt to the side as he muttered a low *huh* sound. Perhaps wondering why and how this strange foreign young man in London had the audacity to seek out this non-publicized concert and was now talking about his love of fine musical instruments to the man who probably owned the most valuable guitars in all of England!

Or maybe Lord Barrington just didn't understand Diego's answer. Diego told us that he didn't know why Lord Barrington reacted in such a way to his answer but carried on regardless.

"I've heard that you are a collector of exquisite musical instruments yourself, sir. Is that true?"

Not one to waste any opportunity to relish in himself, Lord Barrington took the bait. "Well, yes, my dear boy! I've been collecting fine musical instruments since you were just learning how to sight-read." Lord Barrington pretentiously laughed out loud, slapping Diego on the shoulder.

I can't wait to see what those pearly whites look like once that guitar is in my possession, you pompous prick, *Diego had thought.*

Lord Barrington's egotism just motivated Diego to retrieve the Spanish guitar even faster.

"Although you surely have been playing and collecting instruments since I was just a boy, that doesn't necessarily mean you are at or even near my musicianship level," Diego said with a soft grin, accentuated with a wink and a shoulder-slap of his own.

Lord Barrington's face quickly grew red at the overt, yet restrained slight. According to Diego, Stephen did everything in his power not to give in to his anger, to do or say something brash, but the veins in his head began to bulge, and his once thinly veiled condescending attitude started to crack through its polished veneer. Diego knew exactly the type of person Lord Barrington was and how to push his buttons.

Although Stephen Barrington was undoubtedly a skilled musician, everything he could lay claim to was attributed to his family's immense wealth and the top schools and training that came along with it. People like Lord Barrington, must have known deep down that without their carefully curated upbringing, they would not be where they were, causing deeply rooted cognitive dissonance, and that would be Diego's way in.

"Whilst this was entertaining, I really must go now, but if you're half the musician you espouse yourself to be, then I cordially invite you to participate in a *small concert* I'm organizing for the other members of parliament that are patrons to this society. Surely a musician of your caliber wouldn't miss a chance to participate. Then we can all be amazed by the skills you claim to possess," Lord Barrington patronizingly said, starting to walk out of the venue.

"I humbly accept the offer, sir, but my talents don't come for free. Why don't we make it more interesting and raise the stakes?" Diego offered instead with a rakish smile.

"And what exactly do you propose?" Lord Barrington turned back one step before exiting the venue hall.

"The Spanish guitar you have. If I generate more of an applause then you, it's mine; if you do, then I will get you an instrument that is of greater or equal value, no questions asked," Diego had said with utmost seriousness.

From the Lord's reaction, you would've thought that Diego was a first-rate comedian, Sarah said, watching the two from the stands. Lord Barrington erupted in hysterical laughter, hands on his knees and all.

"How could you *possibly* retrieve an instrument of equal or *greater* value for me? Don't you know who I am, boy?" Lord Barrington said. His increasing arrogance only fueled Diego to respond in an even more insolent manner, realizing that the extremely egotistical Lord Barrington wouldn't be able to contend with this type of behavior forever and would do anything to one-up Diego and save face.

"You're not the only one with benefactors," Diego ominously said, which didn't make it hard for Lord Barrington to surmise who his benefactors were, taking into account what Diego wanted.

Once Lord Barrington made the connection, he snappishly left the hall, but not before stating, "The Zaragozas will never have that guitar!"

The chase was on, and Diego had put his plan in motion. The next step was now to find out how his potential gifts would aid him in this task. He had an idea of what he could do, but he didn't need an idea, he needed results, so using the only person he could, he asked Sarah if she could be his proverbial guinea pig.

"What are you going to do to me? What do you think your powers are, exactly?" Sarah had asked.

"It's just a theory, but I think I can manipulate sound to

replicate anything that I've heard, but I also think I can replicate and project the emotions that the sounds produce," Diego had explained.

"Can it be any sound, or does it have to be musical?" Sarah astutely asked.

"I'm not completely sure. All I know is, when I was at the concert, I knew every note that was being played, and I felt like I could play it just like I had heard it. Not only that," Diego continued, "but each sound made me feel something different—not in the sense that you *feel* something after you've heard a piece of music that touched you on a deeper level . . . it actually felt like the music was transmitting something tangible. The only thing is, obviously, feelings and moods aren't tangible, but it felt like they were. That's not even the strangest part, but just hear me out before you say anything!" Diego carried on excitedly. "It also felt to me like I could transfer that feeling onto someone else," Diego said reverentially.

"What? But *how*?" Sarah pressed.

"I don't know, but that's why you're here, Sarah," Diego said.

"When you said that you thought the music felt tangible, what did you mean, exactly?" Sarah sought an answer and was not going to give up until one satisfied her.

"Well, if you insist, it almost felt like two separate entities—different but the same," Diego replied.

By the way Sarah had told this part, I knew that it was clear she was extremely annoyed at Diego because it seemed like he was talking in Jedi Master-like riddles on purpose, but from speaking to Diego, I think that he was simply at a loss for words when he attempted to describe what was going on with him. I, for one, could relate....

"What I mean by two different entities, different but the same, is that on one hand, I can feel the emotions that music brings, and as it flows through me, I can *literally* feel the force of the sound wave being contained within me. I think with practice, I'll be able to release that energy onto someone else, like propagate it onto another medium. But it's not just the sound itself, it's everything that is encompassed within that sound," Diego said, trying his best to explain. "On the other hand, that very same sound wave, at times, feels like it can be modified in any way I want," he said in a slightly more numinous tone.

"Meaning?" Sarah said, looking up briefly before placing her face back into the palms of her hands out of frustration.

"Meaning I think that I can intensify, distort, strengthen, speed up or slow down sound waves, and if that's true, I think I would be able to use these sound waves as physical force. Or as something else entirely," Diego said.

"And you figured all this out just by hearing a few songs at a concert?" Sarah said, raising her eyebrow.

"Well, yes, that's where you come in, so I can conclusively figure out what my abilities are! I have an idea; just hear me out. I'm going to play a few songs and describe how they make me feel, and then I'll try to see if I can make you feel the same way," Diego offered.

"After that, I'll then test out the second theory and see if I actually *can* use the physical properties of sound waves to concentrate and direct it!"

"Whatever you do, just be careful, okay, Diego?" Sarah said cautiously.

"Aren't I always?" Diego slyly responded.

What they did next, although important, was also very funny to me. Diego and Sarah started to listen to music to see if Diego could get Sarah to receive the messages he was sending.

Diego's ability ended up very powerful once he learned how to master it, but every time I think of their London adventure, it makes me chuckle. In my head, Diego was this angsty teenager who was desperate to be understood and tried his best to relay his feelings to Sarah via music. That's not exactly the way it happened, but I like to think it did; plus, it always annoyed Diego anytime I told him what I thought, which just made me laugh even more. His eyebrows were especially thick, so anytime I could get them furrowed at me in annoyance, it always brought a smile—making *the bushy twins do the tango,* I always thought.

Getting back to Diego and Sarah's Second Trial, Diego started off with easy, upbeat, and happy songs. While the song would play, he would listen intensely, with his eyes closed, trying to focus on every aspect of the song: its timbre, tonal qualities, and arrangement. He dissected each song like a careful musical surgeon. The better he knew its composition, the better he could relay his feelings onto Sarah. The process wasn't so smooth in the beginning, but after a while, Sarah began to notice her emotions varying wildly from song to song, sometimes even in the same melody, as Diego held her hand.

"What are you doing to me?" Sarah looked up, confused. "My mood, my thoughts, my emotions, I feel them there. They're mine, b-b-but, they aren't fully mine." Sarah received no reply from Diego. He was too preoccupied with fine-tuning the messages he was expressing to Sarah phonically.

"Let's take it up a level, shall we?" Diego was thoroughly enjoying himself at the moment; he had never felt anything like it. Here he was, a lifelong musician who strived to perfect his craft so that his audience could feel the messages he was trying to send, and now he could seemingly do so at will without having to even play an instrument!

Although disoriented about what was going on, Sarah was a good sport about the whole ordeal until Diego really started to test the boundaries of what he was capable of.

"What if I take a happy song for you and twist it to make you feel something different?" Diego said impatiently.

"I'm not sure about tha—" Sarah had started to say. Before she could finish her sentence, Sarah told me that Diego suddenly put on one of her favorite childhood Norwegian songs and manipulated it so that the song now evoked feelings of disgust for Sarah.

"Why the fuck would you do that!?" Sarah yelled loudly, letting go and slapping Diego's hand away.

"You know what this song means to me; now I can't stand it!" Sarah said, enraged, throwing various hotel items at Diego in the process. Diego said it was the angriest he had ever seen her, and I could hardly remember Sarah ever raising her voice above conversational levels.

Diego had apologized profusely for the blunder, although I'm sure he knew exactly what he was doing. Sarah eventually came around and forgave him as she often does, but if that day had taught us anything, it was that our powers were growing more powerful, and we had to be careful about using them on each other.

After taking a break for a moment to cool down, Diego popped the question: "Well, now that you know what I meant when I said I could manipulate the emotions evoked by songs, it's time to test that other theory of using sound waves as concentrated forces," Diego said, gently nudging Sarah's shoulder with his own.

"After that little stunt of yours, do you really think I'll let you do anything else to me, asshole?!" Sarah's tone was adamant and resolute, but Diego couldn't help himself, regardless. His mouth formed the shape to pronounce an *o*, and an almost inaudible sound gently pushed Sarah back onto her bed.

"Whoa! That was weird but kind of cool," Sarah exclaimed, visibly startled as the goosebumps on her pale arms became clearer than a cloudless sky.

"I strengthened a sound wave to push you back down on the bed." Diego was overjoyed.

"How did you know you could do that?" Sarah looked at him in wonder.

"Well, it's like I said: I just instinctively felt like I had the ability to do so." Diego grinned.

"Do it again!" Sarah said, now excited and curious, also wanting to figure out the extent of Diego's newfound abilities. Though she wasn't fond of how Diego manipulated her favorite song, using sound waves as a weapon could prove very useful, and this fact was not lost, even on her.

"By having this ability, you do know what it means, right?" Sarah asked.

"No, but I'm sure you'll tell me!" Diego replied gleefully.

"It means that now we know at least one of us can defend and protect each other directly!" Sarah congratulated him.

Diego agreed, but now that his powers piqued the interest of both of them, they set out to figure out how strongly he could project these sound waves.

Though they both retold the story differently afterward, they could agree that it started when they visited an abandoned factory they had previously discovered while visiting the outskirts of East London. Initially, Diego started off using inaudible sounds to push small objects around, such as old bottles and scrap metal across the large room. As Diego's confidence grew, so did his desire to see if he could move the old rusted and very heavy machinery that was deserted decades ago.

"Stand behind me, Sarah," Diego said as he took a deep breath and concentrated for a bit before letting out a thunderous clap. Old workstations long cemented to the ground shook and rattled a bit, like withering trees during a storm, but after a few more claps, ***BOOM!*** They shimmied free out of their nuts-and-bolts restraints, freely flying across the room at momentous speeds, with some machinery even flying out the window at the end of the hall.

The impact was so great that the shock wave caused debris to fly everywhere and resulted in an oblong piece of metal ricocheting against a rusted, metal-clad wall, knocking Diego out cold.

"Diego, *Diego!* Can you hear me?" Sarah appealed to Diego's unconscious body, cupping his head to lift it up from the ground, only to find her palms drenched in his blood.

"Please, please wake up!" she begged his silent body, but it was all to no avail. Diego's body remained there . . . motionless.

Still holding him in her arms, Sarah closed her eyes and focused on Diego's injuries, not letting go of him, not even for a second. Not knowing what to do or who to call, she just crouched there, holding onto his head. Crying and pleading, she began to feel a gradual heat that her hands were mysteriously generating as the gash behind Diego's head seemingly started to shrink in her palms. Perplexed as to what was going on but not knowing what else to do, Sarah concentrated even harder. "Wake up, please. Just wake up, Diego," she repeated over and over.

Several minutes later, Diego let out a forceful exhale and jolted up from Sarah's arms.

"What happened?" he said groggily. "One second, I was moving metal with my mouth and hands, and out of nowhere, everything went black."

"You mean that you don't remember? Your sound waves were growing stronger and stronger, and before I knew it, you started to move all of that old heavy machinery when the shock waves they were generating sent something flying toward you and hit you like a freight train! Blood was everywhere! You were bleeding from your head, and I didn't know what to do," Sarah said, still trembling.

Yes, she was a naturally pale girl from Oslo, but the face that Diego looked into once he awoke was the palest he had ever seen, like she was completely devoid of any blood in her body.

"If I was bleeding so badly, where did it all go? My head feels fine," Diego whispered.

"I did something to you while I was holding you. . . . I don't know what it was, but my hands got really hot, and before I knew what was going on, you sprang up, like those morning boners you and Paul are always talking about!" Sarah laughed, cried, then laughed again.

Diego laughed, too, as they regained their composure, but

the air was still thick with unasked questions.

It was late, and they were tired, so they returned to their hotel room and decided that was enough adventure for one day. The ride back was quiet, each one not knowing what to say, nor did they want to mention moving things without touching them and stopping a potential new world order that was based on oligarchist principles in the back of some stranger's black cab.

As soon as they stepped foot into their hotel room, Diego came right out and addressed the awkwardness. "Sarah, are you a healer? Did you heal me with your hands?"

"No! I mean, I'm not sure, *maybe*?" Sarah said, shrugging off his question timidly.

"You're always trying to make everyone as comfortable as possible, often neglecting your own needs and wants, so the ability to heal others would make perfect sense to me!" Diego had pointed out.

"I guess you're right, but why now? I'm not ready. . . ." Sarah said, shaking her head.

"I wasn't, either, but if this is your ability, you know what we have to do next. We have to be absolutely certain."

"Well, what do you suggest, Diego?" Sarah asked before looking up to see that her friend had apparently disappeared. "Diego? Diego, my God, what are you up to now?"

"Relax, I'm right here," Diego said, returning to the living room, now brandishing a chef's knife and looking at Sarah with his signature crooked smile. "You're going to have to heal me again. . . ." The second he finished his sentence, Diego took an underhanded grip of the blade so that the sharp side was pointing toward him and dragged it against his forearm in one swift motion, immediately collapsing to the ground in a loud thud, with his arms and legs spread out akimbo-style.

"Oh my God, oh my God, Diego, what's wrong with you? What have you done? You idiot, you idiot, you *fucking idiot*!" Sarah agonized.

When she retold the story to me, her account naturally contained more f-bombs, which was always a sign indicating that Sarah was starting to lose her mile-long patience.

Without thinking, she ran to him, knelt beside him as she grasped her hands around his slashed forearm. Diego later recounted that he was in and out of consciousness, and the only thing that he could think about was how his arm, bleeding profusely, resembled a Chicago-style deep dish pizza! Admittedly, I found this hilarious and thought it was so indicative of Diego's personality. As his arm was actively bleeding out due to an injury he caused to himself, the only thing he could think about was pizza. Classic Diego: part musician, part scholar, all crazy.

As Sarah clamped down on his arm with all her might, she noticed that, unlike the last time, nothing was happening. Diego was losing blood fast, and he was no longer regaining consciousness. To make matters worse, he was starting to lose the color in his face.

"Why isn't this fucking working!?" Sarah yelled, not knowing what to do or how she had done it previously.

In that moment of complete despair, Sarah was at peace for a split-second, realizing that his fate could be out of her hands, that this was something out of her control. It was in that same instance of hopelessness that Sarah removed her hands from Diego's forearms to find that the open wound was now gone, completely healed. It took about ten minutes for Diego to wake up after his wound was healed. It could've taken even less time, but Diego said he was in the most pleasant dream he ever had where he was in the middle of a guitar solo at Wembley Stadium and just wanted it to play out for a little longer.

"If I ever heal you, try to wake up as soon as you can, buttface, or better yet, how about you stop slicing yourself up like a fucking potato!" Sarah said, laughing as her tears of despondency turned into tears of jubilation.

"I'm sorry, Sarah, but you and I both knew that this was the only way to see how far your powers go, and from the way my arm looked ten minutes ago, it appears they go quite far!" Diego congratulated.

Despite their many trials and tribulations that day, when it was finally over, Diego realized he could manipulate not only music but sound itself, and Sarah had figured out that she had the power of induced healing.

* * *

The next day was Lord Barrington's sponsored concert, and Diego had a guitar to retrieve. But how would he do so? He contemplated doing it with a show of force, as he easily could've done; he could create sonic shock waves, for Christ's sake!

But for Diego, and for all of us for that matter, we were researchers, not brutes. Everything that we had achieved thus far was done with only one muscle: the brain. Finally, Diego arrived at the idea, inspired by internet troll culture no less.

*What is the best way to get back at a self-righteous asshole? Confront and insult their intelligence right in front of them without them even realizing what's going on—**play the player**, so to speak!* Diego thought, remembering a video of the world's most elite food critics trying out what they believed to be first-class gourmet burgers when in actuality, they were just fast-food burgers dressed up on ornamented plates. Instead of fooling critics into thinking they were eating burgers made with sea salt plucked out from Poseidon's own personal collection, he was going to fool well-to-do lords and ministers into thinking that a very average piece that he composed for his dying dog was a masterpiece that should've been debuted at Royal Albert Hall!

In theory, the plan sounded quite easy, but the real test would come from the execution. Although Diego had successfully manipulated how Sarah responded to her favorite song, he had never done so for a piece of music that wasn't already recorded—nor had he done it in front of hundreds of professional musicians, composers, and producers. For Diego, though, this is what excited him most. How awesome would that be to fool everyone and make off with that guitar like a bandit-ninja? I think if there were a singular aspect that made our dormant powers more readily available, it was this: confidence, and Diego had it in spades.

The beginning of the song that was dedicated to Veritas, Diego's late Pit bull/Siberian husky mix, or *pitsky* as he aptly referred to this amalgamation. The first minute of his arrangement consisted entirely of dissonant chords, which, if you don't know what that sounds like, just know it isn't pleasant if not played melodically, which Diego had no interest in doing.

Only when he saw the faces of all the bloated aristocrats in their fine evening gowns and three-piece suits start to clench and distort their faces in obvious disgust did he decide to *turn it on.*

There was one quick check to make before he did: How was Lord Barrington reacting?

Diego momentarily looked up to see Lord Stephen in his private booth, laughing in his typical hysterical way, face pink from being unable to control his giddiness for Diego's incoherent musical piece. However, this was still not enough for Diego, for he wanted Lord Barrington not only to eat his words but to choke on them, too!

Several minutes later, Diego looked up again to see how relieved and pleased Lord Barrington was with Diego's (apparently disastrous) performance, congratulating himself and the other cronies who had accompanied him. Wanting to savor the moment even more, Lord Barrington had now even ordered several bottles of an overpriced cognac to rinse down the bowl of shrimp and lobster that he previously ordered. While he enjoyed the *apparent* disaster that was unfolding before his eyes, gorging on jumbo shrimp drenched in cocktail sauce, Diego knew that it was time.

Amazingly, the music on his guitar started to sound more harmonious as he began to use chords that belonged to the same scale with beautifully arpeggiated notes to accent each chord's specific tonal qualities. The faces of the audience members and especially Lord Barrington's entourage dropped faster than a skydiver at terminal velocity, as they became absolutely enamored with the affair their ears were having with Diego's music.

Unsurprisingly, the inverse relationship continued as the audience members grew more and more attached to the music, even applauding at Diego's pauses. Lord Barrington's hasty ending of his feast conveyed its nonverbal message perfectly: He had lost his appetite!

Once Diego's ballad was complete, there wasn't a dry eye in the theater as Diego put the cherry on top of his performance by even including a backstory to his piece, part factual/part fictitious.

"For those of you who don't know, that piece was a dedication to my dear dog, *Veritas,* who gave me the best twenty-two years that a dog can. No one can replace a friend like that, but thanks to Lord Stephen Barrington, the most humble patron of this event, he'll give me something slightly less meaningful than my dog, but meaningful, nonetheless. Thank you again, Lord Barrington."

Pouring more salt into his self-imposed wound, Lord Barrington even promised to hand the guitar over to Diego in front of his colleagues if his performance had the impact that it just did. Unable to renege, especially in the presence of his esteemed peers, Lord Barrington had no choice but to live up to his word and hand the guitar over to Diego. After all, the game of politics heavily revolves around saving face, and that's exactly what Lord Barrington had to do if he wanted his reputation to remain intact. But the most ironic thing was, even for his obvious detestation of Diego, Lord Barrington probably did, in fact, enjoy Diego's "Ode to Veritas"! Had he enjoyed it merely out of peer pressure, or had Diego's handiwork also affect Lord Barrington? Diego didn't know, nor did it matter. The guitar was secure, and his powers were revealed.

Sarah and Diego couldn't depart London just yet, though. Sarah still had to find Yessica. Luckily, with the help of some local ZCA private detectives, finding her wasn't too difficult, and her humdrum schedule made it even more so. While Diego was busy planning how to retrieve the guitar, Sarah was also contemplating how to make contact with Yessica. Deception had never really been her thing, and I don't think she could be remotely manipulative even if she tried, so I was especially curious to hear how she got Yessica to return to Spain with her. The good thing was that Sarah was now aware of her healing gifts. Although she didn't know how they would help her at the time, unlike Mikael's, Diego's, or even James's, Sarah's abilities didn't lend themselves well to taking advantage of other people. Indeed, it was quite the opposite, actually.

After noticing that Yessica went to a specific café every other day, Sarah decided that intercepting Yessica at her favorite coffee shop would be the best way to make contact, so she did just that. Like clockwork, Yessica arrived at the artisan coffee shop at quarter past ten, took her seat in the corner closest to the Wi-Fi router, and ordered her beloved iced chai latte. Coincidentally, a chai latte was also Sarah's preferred caffeinated beverage of choice, so this opened her up to a natural conversation.

"No way. I love the iced chai lattes from here, too!" Sarah said to Yessica.

"Yeah, they have a way of making them here that I haven't been able to find anywhere else," Yessica replied warmly.

Sarah couldn't readily explain it, but she felt a connection with her from the moment she started talking to Yessica, which made her want to prolong the conversation.

"You're not from around here, are you?" Sarah asked Yessica.

"No, I'm not. I guess the accent kind of gave it away!"

Both women laughed.

"It sure did! Sounds Spanish to me."

"You're absolutely correct. How did you know?" Yessica asked, smiling and now visibly blushing. They talked about surface-level things for a while, which I knew, similar to me, was a bane for Sarah to contend with, so if she did this without frustration, she must've gotten along quite well with Yessica. Even when Sarah initially mentioned Yessica, I could see that her impact on Sarah wasn't one of insignificance, and there were probably things that Sarah intentionally left out of the story. According to Sarah, it took a while for Yessica to realize Sarah wasn't a native English-speaker, either.

"I've been trying to figure it out, but I'm not sure where your accent is from. I don't think I've ever heard it before," Yessica said.

"Yeah, I get that a lot, and it makes sense that it isn't too common because we Norwegians can do a pretty good *English* accent!" Sarah giggled.

"Oh, Norway! I don't think I've ever met a Norwegian before," Yessica said in a tone a decibel louder than her speaking voice, which got the attention of the people sitting at the booth next to them.

Giggling and smiling, Sarah put her finger to her lips to jokingly gesture to Yessica to keep it down.

Yessica smiled back. "I don't think I want to, señorita," Yessica said, holding her face in her hands.

Making Sarah blush and smile a bit more, feeling what she could only describe as butterflies from talking to Yessica, she immediately came out with her reasoning for being there before things became too friendly.

"So, I have to tell you something, Yessica. Please just try to understand," Sarah said seriously but warmly as the signs of previous cheerfulness retreated back into the laugh lines on her cheeks.

"What is it?" Yessica had anxiously responded.

"I was sent by the Zaragozas to bring you back to Spain. For what reason, I'm not sure. . . ."

"Wow, you're definitely the most upfront ZNBS recipient thus far. I'll give you that," Yessica said, quickly gathering her belongings from the table.

"Wait, you mean there were others who tried to bring you back to the Zaragozas?" Sarah asked, wide-eyed in astonishment.

"Of course there were. Let me guess: You're currently in the Second Trials portion of orientation, right?" Yessica said with slight tiredness.

"Yes, you're right. . . ." Sarah responded guiltily.

"Well, good luck with that," Yessica said in passing, speed-walking out of the café.

"Wait! Yessica, please, I need to tell you something. I'm not like the other recipients you've met so far. Please, just let me prove it!" Sarah pleaded.

From the look on Yessica's face, and her tone immediately after the Zaragozas were mentioned, Sarah could tell that whatever reason Yessica left Spain, the Zaragozas must've been responsible. Though not a part of the plan, Sarah was going to have to get creative if she wanted to be successful in her Second Trials ordeal.

"I don't even know why I'm doing this, but you give me a

different feeling than the others, so I'll hear you out," Yessica said and handed Sarah a coffee-stained napkin that had her Chelsea address on it. "Be there, and I'll hear you out, one final time."

After speaking her piece, Yessica left the café, and Sarah had one more chance to convince Yessica to return to Spain.

Returning to the hotel to get ready for her meeting with Yessica, Sarah confided in Diego to help her accomplish her task. "What do I do? What do I tell her? Here we are, trying to take down the Zaragozas, and here I am trying to force someone against their will to return to them. I don't know what to do," Sarah said, misty-eyed.

"I certainly don't envy your situation—especially since your powers don't lend themselves well to this situation," Diego said bluntly.

"I don't understand. I thought our powers and the tasks that we are responsible for are tailor-made so that they could help us in completing the Second Trials?" Sarah said as her tears dried up and she began to critically evaluate her situation from a new perspective.

"That's a good point. That's what they specifically told us: Our *gifts* would assist us in the completion of the Second Trials," Diego acknowledged. "So, there must be some aspect of your abilities that hasn't revealed itself to you yet, and I can bet it'll be that aspect of your powers that will help you succeed in convincing Yessica to return to Spain!"

"That's a lovely theory, Diego, but I have to meet with her in an hour, and I have no idea what that 'aspect' could be," Sarah responded, her hopes dwindling once again.

"The only advice I can give to you after my whole ordeal with Lord Barrington is to trust your instincts, Sarah.

They've gotten you this far," Diego said, still brimming with confidence from his own recent success.

"I guess you're right," Sarah said half-smilingly.

With their discussion over, Sarah was off to Kings Cross Station and then the London Overground to meet with Yessica for the final time.

Arriving twenty minutes early, Yessica was surprised not only to see Sarah arriving but bearing gifts. In her left hand was a gift basket with two bottles of Spanish wine, chocolates, and an assorted cheese platter. Sarah told me that despite Yessica's best efforts of maintaining a cold, piercing stare combined with her emotionally neutral to slightly negative facial expressions, the gifts had softened her up considerably.

Before getting into any of the nitty-gritty details, Sarah and Yessica shared a few glasses of wine and continued their conversation from the coffee shop. Unbeknownst to them at the time, they both shared a love of Brazilian jiu-jitsu that was exposed rather serendipitously, from Sarah briefly choking on a chocolate croissant that they shared earlier.

After more than an hour and a half of random conversation, Yessica finally asked, "Why should I return to Spain and the Zaragozas after all that they did to me? They took my family away from me—my father, my brother—and when that wasn't enough, they even took my mother's life. Why should I ever return to those malicious and manipulative people or that dreadful country that they control in all but name?"

"For one reason, and one reason alone, Yessica: *to help us take them down*," Sarah said.

Overwhelmed and speechless, Yessica dropped the piece of goat's cheese that she was about to place in her mouth, which caused her to try to retrieve it midair, only leading her to knock over her wine glass, spilling red wine all over her cream-colored Persian rug. Without hesitation, Sarah went into the kitchen to retrieve some paper towels to clean the mess.

"Thanks, Sarah. You didn't have to clean up after me, but did I hear you correctly? You want to *take down the Zaragozas*?"

"Correct. Well, partly correct; *we* want to take down the Zaragozas, and correct me if I'm wrong, but it sounds like you do, too," Sarah said, scooting closer to Yessica.

The utter shock of the situation was enough to bring Yessica to tears. Here she was, being approached by yet another ZNBS recipient, but this was the first time someone wanted to take down the Zaragozas instead of work for them. Sarah wasn't sure if Yessica's tears were tears of joy or of sadness. Regardless of the reasoning, Yessica's current emotional state was that of vulnerability lining up perfectly with Sarah's specialty of comforting those around her. For almost twenty minutes, Yessica sobbed in Sarah's arms, recounting the years of physical and emotional abuse done to her by the Zaragozas.

Regaining her poise, Yessica apologized, "I'm sorry, but for some reason, all of those emotions that I've been repressing for the past five years just erupted. It's a strange feeling, but it feels right being vulnerable with you. I'm sorry. I promise I'm not a crazy person who just cries on people all night long," Yessica said, simultaneously chuckling and wiping away the tears from her face.

"It's okay. I'm glad you feel that way," Sarah said into Yessica's ear, still holding her in her arms.

"So, what is all this talk about you stopping the Zaragozas? You're the first ZNBS recipient I've heard say that," Yessica said, taking Sarah's confession more seriously now.

"Well, it's true. I'm not sure what all you know about them and their dealings, but from your reactions earlier in the coffee shop and just now, I think it's safe to assume, there's no love lost between you and them, either. But for us, we acutely realize the global risks the Zaragozas present, and that's not even mentioning the darker stuff they're involved in."

"You don't have to sugarcoat things with me, Sarah. I'm well aware of the Zaragozas, their dealings, and even their relationship with the supernatural—one of the many reasons I left Spain," Yessica said, as a shadow crossed over her face.

Sarah was stunned to hear this revelation. This was the first time that any of us were aware of other people who knew the Zaragozas' well-kept secrets, immediately justifying why the Zaragozas were so hell-bent on having Yessica close by again.

"So, what can you do?" Yessica asked.

"U-u-uhh, I can do a lot of things. What do you mean?" Sarah answered evasively.

"When I said I know what the Zaragozas are up to and that you're not the first ZNBS recipient I've met, I meant it," Yessica quipped, taking a quick swig from her wine glass. Sarah was taken by surprise and stuttered over her words, trying to get a coherent sentence out.

"I— I can help people, I mean, *heal* people. I can heal people."

"A healer? Well, that's a first. What can you heal?" Yessica looked amazed.

"Well, cuts, gashes, and abrasions. Other than that, I'm not sure; I kind of just found out about my abilities recently," Sarah humbly replied.

"Well, your presence for some reason is reassuring, and I don't remember the last time I broke down like that, so you're definitely having an effect on me—although positive or negative, that remains to be seen," Yessica smiled, pouring another glass of merlot.

"Well, why don't you come back to Spain with me, so we can find out exactly what effect you think I'm having on you?" Sarah replied in playful jest. I couldn't tell if she was matching the lighthearted tone that Yessica was speaking in or if there was anything deeper to her words; that was something I had to find out later.

* * *

The next morning, Diego awoke to just himself in the hotel room, as Sarah had slept over at Yessica's flat, a fact that she just happened to gloss over when she recounted this story to me. Diego didn't ask any questions, either, because they were tasked with two things once they arrived in London: retrieving Lord Barrington's guitar and bringing Yessica back to Spain. Both were completed, and Diego, Sarah, and now Yessica were on their way back to Spain.

Their arrival was welcomed by all of us. Even though they were only gone for a few days longer than James and Mikael, that's how it always was anytime someone went off on separate missions. We had become so close in a matter of months, anyone's absence was sorely missed by all.

Fearing for Yessica's safety within the Castillo, Sarah stayed with Yessica for a few nights at a nearby hotel until further notice. Since she was Spanish, I thought it would be easy for her to reintegrate back into her country of origin, but I guess the Zaragozas had taken so much from her that even her home didn't feel like home anymore.

Yessica had already stated that they took her father, brother, and her mother's life. Did that mean her father and brother were still out there somewhere? And if they were, would they also be considered Zaragoza 'heirlooms'? So many questions, and despite how much we all wanted to help Yessica due to her proximity to Sarah, we had to press on to complete the Second Trials. However, before the next group was off for their Second Trials tasks, some of us got an email from none other than Pierre Zaragoza himself. . . .

Chapter 15: The Tallest Tower

Tolu, Daniela, and Kofi all received the email with the subject only reading: *Highly Important (do not share).* We pondered what it could be, but there was no time to think. They had to report to the Castillo's tallest tower immediately—the very same tower that housed the office Gástonio previously told us belonged to Arturo Zaragoza many years ago.

We had no clue what their meeting would be about, but we knew one thing: If it was going to be taking place in Pierre's private office, no good could possibly come out of it. Tolu was the first one scheduled to report to Pierre's office, and to say he was nervous would've been the understatement of the year.

"Guys, what do I do? I'm not a good liar; if he asks me anything about the ZRC, I obviously won't spill the beans, but I'm worried. He'll be able to tell that I'm hiding something."

"Mate, it's easy. Don't even think about it that way. Just have in your mind that you lot are especially awesome, and he just wants to thank you for accepting the ZNBS!" Paul said.

"Easy for you to say, Paul; you aren't the one being summoned," Tolu gloomily replied, his face longer than a surfboard.

"I, for one, am not worried. I've dealt with assholes like Pierre all my life in Brazil. Whether it be the white Brazilians, who tried to boss around everyone who was darker than them, or even some *morenos,* who could pass as white, thinking that they were holier than thou,"

Daniela said.

"Moreno? Then what would you be? Because you're pretty fair yourself," Tolu said, confused.

"It's confusing, yeah, I know, but with the demographics of a country like Brazil, classifying *race* would never be easy. To put it simply, being p*ardo* or m*oreno,* like most Brazilians say, is a racial classification in Brazil when your ancestry is a hodgepodge, but, yes, I would be considered a m*oreno,* as well," Daniela said.

If Tolu looked nervous, then Kofi's disposition could only be described as on the verge of a breakdown. It wasn't as much what he was saying; rather, it was what *wasn't* said that worried me most. The entire time we discussed what their meeting could be about, what *his* meeting could be about, Kofi sat there silently, clenching his knees in his hands, rocking back and forth.

"Mate, you alright? You look like you could vomit at any time," Amir asked, wondering if he should retrieve his medical kit.

"I'm fine, just thinking," Kofi said, his huge eyes a quarter of their ordinary size.

"I have to get there soon, guys; I'll let you know how it goes," Tolu said.

Once he said that, Tolu was off, leaving our room, not to return until half an hour later.

Inauspiciously, the anticipation, or more accurately, the dread of meeting with Pierre was only exasperated by Pierre's office being so difficult to locate. Yes, it was easy to see his office from outside; it was the tallest tower! But from inside, the Castillo's halls could best be described as a maze designed by a masochist in the middle of an LSD trip: hallways that seemingly ended nowhere, doors and windows that opened up to nothing, and this did not even include the several scissor-like stairways that put you right back from where you came from. Almost late for his meeting, Tolu ended up going to the majordomo to ask for directions. We all at least knew where the kitchen was!

"Majordomo, Francis, please, I need your help," Tolu asked the tall, slender man.

"Ah, I recognize you. You're one of Femi's friends. How can I help you, young sir?" Señor Francis asked cheerfully.

"I have a meeting at Pierre's office in five minutes, but I don't know how to get there," Tolu said quickly and out of breath.

"No problem at all. Follow me. I know a secret entrance. Many years ago, when my father was the majordomo to Pierre's father, he showed me all the secret passages within this Castillo. I reckon I know it even better than the Zaragozas themselves," majordomo Francis replied with an almost ear-to-ear smile, making him look like the Grinch.

After a series of twisting turns and hidden doors, the final staircase was in front of Tolu.

"Just up these stairs and Señor Zaragoza's office will be the only door. Good luck, my young friend," Francis said, shaking Tolu's sweat-drenched hand.

"How could I ever repay you for your deeds, sir?" Tolu asked.

"Something tells me you and your friends will think of something." The tall old man smiled, patted Tolu on the back, and departed, leaving Tolu on his own.

This was it. This was going to be the first time any of us had direct access to Pierre Zaragoza, the man, the myth, the *monster*.

"*Hellloooo*?" Tolu cried out, slightly leaning into the door to knock on it. Unaware due to his ball of nerves, he didn't hear the door creak open, causing Tolu to stumble forward briefly.

"Yessss, come in, young Tolu, yesss, come in, indeed!" a wraithlike voice echoed out—not seen, just heard. "Do you know why I called you into my private office?" Pierre's low and gravelly voice reverberated around the timber-clad room.

"No, sir, I do not," Tolu said, spinning around in circles, not knowing where to orient himself, nor where the source of Pierre's menacing voice was coming from.

"Well, as you know, my family and I have been offering the ZNBS since the end of World War II. It was our charity to the rest of the world, our way of *giving back to humanity*."

"Yes, sir, I understand," Tolu mumbled.

"Ha-ha-ha! Grand!" Pierre's laugh boomed, reverberating throughout the wooden room. Tolu couldn't see any speakers in the room, which appeared frozen in time, not even containing a laptop.

"If you understand, then you also understand that our scholarship has changed the lives of many from your continent, but you, Tolu, have the chance to rival their success if you listen closely, very closely," Pierre said seriously.

"H-h-how do you mean, sir?" Tolu stuttered.

"I'm aware that you are in my Castillo to use my scholarship to further fund your Ph.D. in chemical engineering. Is this correct?"

"Yes, sir."

"To use that degree to help improve the lives of your compatriots back home in Nigeria, correct?"

"Yes, sir, that is also correct."

"Well, Tolu, my dear boy, you will accomplish your dreams because I deem it so, but what if I told you that you need not stop there? Tolu, I want to groom you and some other cohorts of this year's ZNBS to rise above the petty squabbles and self-admiring nature of academia. In my vision, you shall become the Minister of Transport or its equivalent back home in Nigeria. Approximately one year after holding this position, you will then become the President of Nigeria, the youngest to ever hold that position. How does that sound, son?"

"Wow, sir, I don't . . . well, I don't know what to say. . . ." Tolu said in shock.

"Ha-ha-ha, well, that's the easy part, my dear boy. Just say, *yes*," Pierre replied, his voice ranging wildly from his boisterous laugh to the deadpan way he finished the sentence.

"Of course, sir, but how? How do you have the power to make such a thing so?"

"Oh, my dear boy, that's the *easiest* part. We Zaragozas have been installing cohorts like you in key positions in governments for as long as the scholarship has been hosted! The hard part is up to you. You must still *survive* the Second

Trials. Once you do that, the rest will be up to me."

"And what would you have me do as president, sir?" Tolu astutely asked.

"Your eagerness pleases me greatly, my dear boy. Don't worry about that just yet. With that being said, our meeting is now complete."

"Hello? Hello, sir? I don't understand," Tolu called out, but all that was returned was the echoing of his own voice. Pierre Zaragoza was gone—or was he ever really there...?

* * *

When Tolu came back into our room, it was as if he had seen the devil himself. His usual dark chocolate-colored skin looked more like a shade of gray upon his return.

"Mate, you don't look so good," Paul said, stating the very obvious.

"Sit down. I'll get you a glass of water," Mikael said.

After downing the whole glass in one gulp, Tolu was finally ready to speak. "He offered me the role of Minister of Transport once we complete the Second Trials. After a year, he said he would make me the President of Nigeria—"

"*He said what*?!" Rafi interrupted, spitting out the orange juice he was about to swallow.

"Yeah, my thoughts exactly," Tolu said, his face sinking down into his knees.

"This has to confirm it, then. The ZNBS, without question, has to be an indoctrination ploy. He's installing us as puppet leaders of our own countries in order to bleed us dry. Surely any of you still on the fence must realize this."

"And what's exactly wrong with that!? If Tolu became the President of Nigeria, don't you think it would be run better than the way it is now?" Kofi replied adamantly.

"Are you fucking serious?" Rafi said bluntly.

"*Yes,* hear me out. Even if the Zaragozas are up to no good, even if they do want to *control us,* I'm sure a Zaragoza-controlled country run by one of us will be a hell of a lot more effective than any of the despots we currently have in Africa. Guys, I know it sounds crazy, but maybe that's what the ZRC is meant to be: just a way to keep the Zaragozas honest. It doesn't necessarily mean we have to *take them down.* We could just work with them instead, push them to be better people. I don't know. Maybe we think about it, anyway. I'm up next to meet Pierre. See you guys soon," Kofi said just before leaving our room to meet with Pierre Zaragoza.

"It's official. I don't trust that guy," Paul said, his voice devoid of its typical whimsical-like qualities.

"I never thought that I would say it, but I'm with Paul on this one. If we're not careful, that guy could get us discovered, or even worse, *killed.* Work with the Zaragozas and try to push them to be better? Where have we heard that before, Femi?" Raphael asked me.

"The Democratic Party of the United States," I laconically replied.

"Ding-ding-ding, exactly."

"Wait, what are you Americans on about now?" Mikael asked.

"Should I take this one, or will you, Rafi?" I inquired of my compatriot.

"You do the honors, Femi." So I did and explained what Rafi meant.

"You see, the Democratic Party in the United States was once the party of people like Franklin D. Roosevelt, the very same man who hosted the original Fireside Chats. FDR, unlike his contemporary party-members who decided to give up on the interests of the working men and women, made this his priority. However, in the year 2040, and for as long as I can remember, the party has represented the wishes of the ruling class ever since, occasionally appealing to the cultural aspects of their former base to placate them whenever an uprising was looming.

"Indeed, they are now just a shell of those progressive policies that brought America out of the worst financial disaster the world (up until that point) had seen, though FDR wasn't perfect by any stretch of the imagination. The twenty-first century version of the party quickly abandoned those progressive ideals as soon as the country recovered from the war to pander to the corporate elite who lined their pockets. In return, the politicians further stifled real systemic change at every opportunity to appeal to their capitalist overlords, who found the status-quo to be just fine. America has become sort of a game of let's divide the country based on identity politics, show them how stupid they are, and see how long we can fuck up the country, until the Greek root word of democracy was re-discovered, and the *people* revolted for real change.

"Now, here comes the analogy: Whereas the opposing Republican Party told you where they stood on multiple issues, the Democratic Party liked to say one thing and do another, similar to how the Zaragozas would have us act, without question."

"The analogy doesn't end there, though," Rafi added. "The Democratic Party were always admirers of the easy cultural wins.

"Gay marriage? Sure, that's easy enough while getting rich off of companies that still opposed such declarations.

"Racial Equality? Definitely! We'll wear Kente cloth and raise our fists in solidarity with our black and brown brothers while still not doing anything substantive to address the systemic racial inequality that has plagued our nation since its inception.

"Overpriced medication? Americans shouldn't overpay for prescriptions while they own stocks in numerous pharmaceutical companies that price-gouged the cost of drugs like it was going out of style, and don't even get me started with universal healthcare. . . .

"That's what Femi and I meant, and unfortunately, that's what it seems Kofi would want of the ZRC, as well."

"Jesus, I had no idea things were that dire up there," Diego said.

"Trust me, we can go on for days with many more examples," Rafi replied, retying his hair.

"So what do we do about the Kofi situation, though?" Daniela asked.

"I say we let it play out; we see where his allegiances fall. We can't just give up on him like that. Maybe he's just scared," Sarah emphasized. And she was right—up to a point, at least. "Obviously, I wouldn't want to give up on Kofi, either, but I, for one, and Rafi, I'm sure, have been surrounded by these people extensively back home, and even if he made those comments out of fear, it was still something that comes from within him."

"That's a big chance we're taking. Not only with risking the ZRC being discovered but also our lives. I hope you all don't forget that," Suhani said resolutely.

"I agree. We need to watch Kofi closely. Hey, that rhymed!" Paul joked, his normal tone returning.

"Right, so we proceed with caution and need to be especially careful with what is said around him. Agreed?" All of us eventually agreed, even if it took Sarah a bit longer to see things from our perspective.

Wondering where Kofi was since it had already been about forty-five minutes since he left, he texted us a few minutes later to say that he got tired after the meeting and decided to return to his own dorm. *Jesus, this guy isn't making it easy to trust him,* I thought, but it's not like I was going to travel across the Castillo just to drag him out of his dorm. We let him be for now because Daniela was up next to meet Pierre.

It seemed like Daniela had the shortest meeting of all, coming back just twenty-five minutes later.

"Well, it looks like you didn't have any trouble finding his office, then?" Tolu joked.

"Yeah, I'm not a stupid engineer like you. We architects actually notice things like written signs!"

"Yeah, but I'm not the one who can read Spanish, either, am I?"

"Enough from you two, bickering like an old married couple. What did Pierre say?" I begged, itching to know what we were up against.

"Sorry. Yeah, he said mainly the same things. It was weird, too, because he wasn't actually in the room, but his voice seemed like it was coming from everywhere and nowhere at the same time."

"You see, I told you guys!" Tolu effused.

"What else did he say?" Rafi asked.

"He knew of my father somehow. He knew that he was a police officer who cared very deeply about his community. He kept referring to my father like he knew him; it made me sick hearing that vile man refer to my father like that!" Daniela said, intermittently wiping the tears away from her face. "That wasn't all, though; he offered me the position of Minister of Regional Development for three years before *installing* me as the President of Brazil."

"Ha, so you have to be minister for two whole years more than me before you reach my level as head of state, eh?" Tolu joked.

I'm glad he found humor in the situation because I was worried for a moment that he would crack under pressure, similar to how Kofi had.

"So funny, Tolu, but I told him I'll *think* about it," Daniela said.

"You told Pierre Zaragoza, the richest man on the planet *by a lot*, that you'll *think about it?!* Wow, the balls you have must be so big, they can't even be seen!" Paul quipped. "How did he take it?"

"Well, he let out this weird kind of laughter because I'm sure he wasn't expecting such an answer. People like that are so used to being surrounded by yes-men that he probably forgot how to take a refusal. Hell, he was probably never even taught how to lose properly because he just said, 'We'll see about that' before the room went silent, so I left."

"Wow, you go, girl!" Suhani exclaimed.

"These guys think they're the ones calling the shots. Oh,

how little they know," Sarah added.

I'm just glad these ferocious ladies are on our side, *I thought.*

"Okay, but what about the next set of trials? Are we all good on that front?" Mikael asked with impeccable timing.

"Any words from you, Tomor?" I asked.

"Yes, it's still a go. Suhani, Paul, and I shall be next," Tomor neatly replied.

"That's all? Nothing to say about the meeting with Pierre and Kofi?" I followed.

"What more can be said? We proceed with caution and do our best not to spook him. It's that simple."

Ever the man of few words, Tomor was right. If we started to act weird now, it would be a dead giveaway that we were onto Kofi, so we laid low and proceeded onward with the Second Trials. We still had to survive them first. . . .

Chapter 16: City of Love

Next up to go on their quests were Suhani and Paul, and I must admit, I was super jealous because they were off to Paris!

Even though I knew they were only there for business and not pleasure, the city always had a special place in my heart. When I was in college, I had an uncle who lived in Paris, so I visited the city quite often in my early twenties, from celebrating my twenty-second birthday on the Seine with random Parisians and some kids from the Banlieue to exploring the Catacombs beneath the city. Despite desperately wanting to indulge in my wanderlust and take a break from all the Zaragoza treasure-hunting, this was no time for those kinds of thoughts.

Suhani was tasked to retrieve a brooch stolen by the French from the Spanish way back in 1640 during the Franco-Spanish War. What always amazed me about lost heirlooms that are several centuries old was how people kept track of their location throughout the years. Was there a website or an app that only the *elite* had access to that just pinged the location of all these antique items so that everyone always knew where they were at all times?

Furthermore, they're just material items, and often times the actual value of these items was mainly sentimental. But still, *aristocrats* would risk life and limb to have them returned, so I guess sentimental value carried more weight than monetary value, right?

Although Paul was going to Paris with Suhani, his tasks were not based in Paris but in the city of Strasbourg, the French city that I always thought was in Germany, known for its magically festive Christmas shops. Paul was tasked with one of the most audacious missions of all. He was not tasked to retrieve an heirloom but to change a European Parliament member's mind on a political matter. *Surely things the Zaragozas would routinely have us do after the completion of the Second Trials!* I thought.

I guess Paul just had a head start, but given his oral abilities, I wasn't surprised! Concerned about leaving Paul up to his own devices in Strasbourg, Tomor accompanied him, as well, since his Second Trials task was located in the nearby German city of Stuttgart. Tomor probably had the coolest mission of all, in my opinion, tasked to retrieve several Spanish artifacts stolen by the Nazis during World War II.

Having had a few hours to talk about our Second Trials progress after discussing Pierre's impromptu meetings, our spirits were renewed, as was our morale—especially when we discussed those of us who already had their powers revealed. Here we were, a group of random international scholarship recipients taking down the most powerful people on the planet. While the task was daunting, many of us came from existences that were daunting just to stay alive, but we had still prevailed. That's the mentality we tried to maintain throughout our whole ordeal to keep us grounded.

Spending so much time chatting, the morning dew was soon replaced by the intensity of the high-noon Spanish sun, and Suhani, Paul, and Tomor had a flight to catch. Touching down in Paris just before sunset allowed the three of them to catch the beautiful but often forgotten migration of the sun, bidding *adieu* to our part of the world, off to illuminate another. As nightfall blanketed the French capital, Suhani, Paul, and Tomor began planning their courageous heists.

Since Suhani and Paul weren't adamant about what their abilities were just yet, Tomor devised a plan that would allow them to at least get close to the items they were ordered to retrieve, hoping the severity of the situation would cause them to rise to the occasion and bring out their abilities as they'd done in the past. All we had to go on with Suhani was what she told us about her youth and how independent and unassuming she was, which we presumed would manifest as some sort of illusion ability. For Paul, it was quite obvious that his abilities would be related to his gift of gab but in what way was still uncertain. No matter how it would present itself, Tomor's cover for Paul would involve putting him in the spotlight so he could do what came naturally to him: *talk!*

First things first, they had to conduct reconnaissance to see exactly what they were up against. The current owners of the brooch Suhani had to recover were similar to the Zaragozas, though not with the same scope of influence. The esteemed Deschamps family had origins that could be traced back to French Basque Country but had moved to the French capital in the early 19th century. In unusual old-money European fashion, they displayed their wealth in an overly ostentatious manner. From being chauffeured around in the swankiest automobiles Germany had to offer, to being decorated only in the latest Italian and French fashions from head to toe, these were the sort of people not to care what the cost of anything was, severely hindering their ability to appraise real value.

The plan thus became to take the brooch and replace it with an identical counterfeit. Tomor concluded that they wouldn't even be able to tell the difference, and we all concurred. Suhani would present herself as an heiress to an Indian jewelry company in order to gain access into their Neuilly-sur-Seine home. Welcoming a foreign jewelry magnate would surely be right up their alley. We knew that flaunting extreme wealth to foreign elites was amongst the favorite pastimes of the rich worldwide, and the Deschamps family was no different.

Comparing the number of trailing zeros associated with their bank accounts was only part of the fun; the best was saved for last. For many Europeans and especially the French, money wasn't the only thing that maintained their *elevated status*. It was also the perception of being from a superior culture, and educating the *less refined cultures and ethnicities*, wealthy or not, was just another part of the job.

The whole family reeked of The White Man's Burden complex. Little did they know, we were well aware of the blind spots that this sort of mentality perpetuates, and we were poised to capitalize on this by targeting the matriarch of the family, Marguerite Deschamps.

Marguerite had a semi-successful jewelry company of her own that, you guessed it, specialized in *fine pieces of the Orient*. This is what influenced Tomor's cover story for Suhani in the first place. Fortunately for us, we were allowed a healthy stipend for all Second Trials retrieval missions, so we spared no expense in making Suhani look the part.

Through some clever internet tricks that Tomor learned in his cyber warfare training, in just under two hours, he already had a jewelry website up and running, rave reviews and all, which displayed Suhani modeling all of her bespoke and exquisite jewelry pieces. No prices were listed on any items, a key sign that alerted the rich and well-to-do that this was a website where if you had to ask for the price, you probably couldn't afford it, anyway—a small gesture that made a huge impact on their psyche. Needless to say, the message of Suhani being a rich twenty-something heiress was received loud and clear, and Madame Deschamps couldn't wait to meet with Suhani at her *maison*.

As expected, the Deschamps home was decorated in all sorts of gaudy gold furniture that would make any nouveau-riche family proud. For an *old*-money family, the Deschamps decorated as if gold was sacred, and their home was its preeminent vault. For what it's worth, though, at least the gold-speckled walls and ceilings were real, or appeared to be.

From what was relayed to me by the three of them, the gang wasn't sure if Suhani would get another chance to visit Marguerite's home, so during their first encounter, Suhani had the counterfeit brooch on hand. To justify entering Marguerite's private jewelry room, Suhani's cover would be that she was in Paris looking for specific European time-period jewelry pieces to purchase for a limited European-only sale at her company. In return, the same offer would be extended to Marguerite to visit Suhani in India if she also required any specific Asian time-period jewelry. The cover was airtight, and Suhani was a natural.

"I hear you have a lovely Spanish brooch from the Franco-Spanish War of the 1600s?" Suhani had politely asked.

"*Oui,* it is one of our most valuable possessions that has been in our family for generations," Mrs. Deschamps purred proudly in her thick Parisian accent.

"If you don't mind, I would love to see it in person," Suhani commented.

Suhani could tell that Mrs. Deschamps was reluctant to show the brooch, especially since it was to be shown the next day at a jewelry exhibition in Paris. Mrs. Deschamps then proceeded to escort Suhani down two sets of winding spiral stairs, finally leading her to a large and imposing French-style door made of solid steel. As Marguerite opened the door, it was like the pearly gates of heaven themselves had opened. An immediate and almost blinding light of shimmering gold, silver, and platinum engulfed Suhani, causing her to let out a low but audible gasp.

"Ah, don't worry, my dear, you're not the first to have that reaction," Mrs. Deschamps boastfully claimed, flashing a crooked smile in the process.

Turned off by her snarky remark, Suhani casually replied, "I was just surprised there weren't more gemstones, that's all," which visibly annoyed Mrs. Deschamps, who clenched down on her teeth as she proceeded to show Suhani another quarter of her jewelry warehouse.

After discussing at length where the exhibition was, and when the brooch would be showcased, it became increasingly clear that the retrieval of the brooch would have to be at the exhibition instead. For one, Mrs. Deschamps loomed over Suhani's shoulder the whole time she was in the jewelry room, not giving her a chance to stealthily replace the brooch with the imitation. Secondly, from the way Marguerite had described the exhibition, there would be a few minutes delay between when the brooch would be brought out and when it would be showcased. This was Suhani's opportunity to not only return the brooch to Spain but also to find out exactly what she was capable of.

It was approximately seven in the evening when Suhani returned to the hotel to inform Tomor and Paul about all that happened at the Deschamps' lofty residence.

"Well, come out with it. How did it go?" Paul asked ecstatically as Suhani opened the door, his face just inches from hers.

"*It went,*" Suhani replied, less than energetically.

"What happened over there?" Paul now said in a more restrained tone.

"I saw the brooch and a lot of other things in Mrs. Deschamps's jewelry fort, but she was on me like a coat the whole time!" Suhani grumbled.

"What about your powers—any insight into that?" Tomor chimed in, sitting across the room, taking sporadic sips from his coffee mug.

"*Nada,*" Suhani replied, now lying face-first on her bed, clenching her pillow. "I felt so uncomfortable in that stuffy old house with that stuffy old lady that perhaps it's better that the brooch will be at the exhibition. One more minute in there, and I would've passed out from breathing that overly perfumed air!"

"With the brooch being in a public place, too, it'll be easier to replace it without raising any suspicions," Tomor offered. "Also, if we have anything to learn from how the others found out about their abilities, for the most part, it was in situations such as these," Tomor said with the enthusiasm of a gravedigger.

"You know, the biggest thing I'm worried about is not replacing the brooch with ours," Suhani muttered. "I know you, Tomor, and your plans are usually excellent, but what I am worried about is in the event of retrieving the brooch, I still don't find out what my powers truly are," Suhani said despondently, stuffing her face into her hotel pillow once more.

"Hey, Suhani, listen: I don't know what your power will reveal itself as, but I do know that stressing out is a sure way to delay its activation. I know it's a stressful time, but if an Israeli commando and an international man of mystery can't help ease your mind, nothing will!" Paul said as he threw the pillows off the couch at Suhani.

Laughing at his perpetual silliness, there was a method to Paul's madness. He managed to help Suhani assuage her apprehensions, which helped her get a good night's sleep.

* * *

The next morning, however, they had to come up with a plan to get the brooch once and for all. While Paul and Suhani slept, Tomor was busy digitally digging for everything he could find for the logistics of the exhibition. Fortunately—or skillfully, I should say—he managed to find an encrypted document shared with all the employees of the venue on the logistics of the exhibition, including where and when the brooch would be at all times. It was there he found out that from 12:30–1:00 p.m., the brooch would be in a tent alongside other Spanish treasures before being transferred to the main hall for all to admire. This would be Suhani's only chance to retrieve the real brooch and replace it with the copy. The only hindrance was, each tent was guarded by an armed security officer. How would she get past an armed guard? What sort of cover would be required to gain entry? These were just some of the questions that were going on in Tomor's head.

Unlike me though, Tomor wasn't one to let his nerves get the best of him. Tomor relied on his breathing exercises learnt from his training to calm his anxiety, allowing him to think effectively.

Regaining his calm, Tomor thought it would be best for Suhani to continue her cover as a jewelry heiress. If the situation occurred where Suhani was attempting to enter the private and secure tent-room, she could just blame it on ignorance or attribute it to the language barrier.

Even if the cover worked, though, it would only justify being at the tent's entrance, not actually entering it, Tomor had to admit to himself. The only way for Suhani to replace the brooch would be to get past the security guard altogether. To work around this, Tomor incorporated Paul into the plan, being the smooth talker he was. If Suhani got into any dicey encounters, perhaps Paul's persuasion in addition to Suhani's unassuming yet steadfast nature would be enough to get them out of any sticky situation.

These strategies were purposefully risky for their abilities to shine through just when we needed them, or at least for us to have an idea of what our powers could be. But in Suhani's case, danger had already been built into the situation.

Suhani and Paul woke up to the inviting aroma of freshly processed arabica beans being poured into mugs, just as room service knocked at the door. The smell of French pastries quickly seeped into the room, as well, filling the air with fragrances that would make any Parisian proud.

"Aww, you prepared all of this for me? You shouldn't have," Suhani said, smiling, simultaneously fixing her lion-like bedhead.

"Well, you know, you're not the only one here, miss!" Paul said, playfully throwing a couch pillow at Suhani.

"It's for the both of you," Tomor groaned. "Now stop squabbling and join me here for breakfast," Tomor said with a forced grin.

Tomor told us later that he had thought if this were to be their last happy moment in Paris, at least they could enjoy a hearty breakfast, just like they did in the Castillo.

"You two come join me at the table. There are some things I want to discuss with you," Tomor insisted.

As soon as Suhani and Paul had joined Tomor in the dining room, he got straight to it.

"I don't know how to put this lightly, Suhani, but your mission will probably be the most dangerous yet." He paused, making sure Suhani didn't have any questions. She continued to look at him motionlessly, acknowledging that she was giving him her full and undivided attention.

"Anytime I plan these things out, I always try to minimize the potential risks you all may face. But this time, the variable that is the armed security guard gives my strategies a lot less room for error and puts a lot of responsibility on you. That's why I suggest you and Paul complete this mission together.

At least with the two of you, ignorance is a more believable claim to be made.

"You'll continue your role as a wealthy yet aloof heiress, and Paul here will be your bodyguard," Tomor outlined. "I know it's not what the original plan was, but I don't want you to take any unnecessary risks with an item so valuable that it has to be guarded by armed security," Tomor said.

Not breaking eye contact with Tomor, arms folded over one another, Suhani succinctly replied, "*No way!*"

"What do you mean, *no way?*" Tomor asked, flabbergasted both by Suhani's answer and delivery.

"I appreciate the concern for my safety, I truly do, but I do this alone."

"There's no shame in having help, Suhani. That's why we're all in this together," Paul said.

Suhani, however, could not be swayed. "*Again*, I thank you both for having my back, but like I said, this is something I can do alone. I know I can," she said resolutely.

Tomor and Paul later told me that they'd never seen Suhani like this before. It wasn't like they did not know Suhani was strong-willed and independent, but even that didn't prepare them for how she appeared to them now. That was the thing I admired about her most. Always in that in jovial and aloof state, Suhani was so self-assured that it practically oozed out of her. Her aloofness almost served as a mechanism for those around her to let their guard down, while she completely dissected who you were as a person, informing her on how to interact with you. For lack of a better metaphor, Suhani, to me, had the Zen attributes of Yoda or those other grandmaster-types that you see in old samurai movies, with the abilities to back it up.

Her self-confidence was sky-high, yet she was also humble, so it never came off as braggadocious, but more as an understated but ever-present serenity about her.

"That settles it, then; the woman has spoken. But if things go south, I'll still be at the exhibition if you need me," Paul said, respecting Suhani's decision.

"That I can agree to, you silly excuse for a man!" Suhani said, giggling.

"Then it's settled; tomorrow we'll report to the exhibition at 11:30 a.m. to get a feel of things. While you two are out and about, I'll try to find somewhere that I can safely watch over you, *just in case*." Tomor was relieved that they had at least reached some sort of agreement, even if it wasn't his original plan.

Finishing their *Croque Monsieurs* and gulping down their now lukewarm lattes, the three of them set out for the Paris Nord Villepinte Exhibition Centre.

* * *

The exhibition was more crowded than any one of them could've anticipated. Not only was it an exhibition showing off European jewelry throughout the centuries, there were also a few select pieces from Africa, North and South America, and even Oceania. Such a crowded space made it easier to blend in for Suhani, but it also made it harder for Tomor to keep watch. A few minutes before Suhani was due to approach the private tent, Tomor checked in to make sure everyone was still, as he put it, *frosty*.

"Frosty? Did I just hear you correctly? No, I'm not frosty; it's quite warm today!" Paul said.

"Frosty is just another word for being alert Paul—even I knew that!" Suhani replied, covertly pressing her earpiece against her ear.

"Okay, thanks for clearing that up for him, Suhani, but you two try to focus. What's the sit-rep? I mean, what's the situational report?" Tomor sighed from his end of the microphone.

"Well, I'm about two hundred yards away, and I can see Suhani approaching the tent," Paul said.

"Suhani, what about you? How are you feeling?" Tomor asked.

"I feel surprisingly good. I'm calmer than I thought I would be, so I guess that's good."

"That is good. I'm glad to hear that, but stay focused. Any insight on your abilities yet?" Tomor asked.

"No, but I have an idea. . . ." Suhani was saying before she was abruptly cut off.

"Is that so? What is it? Hello? Hello? Suhani, come in. Paul, do you still have eyes on Suhani?" Tomor said, panicking, repeatedly removing his earpiece to tap on it, just in case it was malfunctioning.

"Tomor! I'm sorry, I don't have eyes on Suhani. She, w-w-well . . . she just vanished!" Paul said stutteringly.

"Well, regain visuals on her, now!" *Tomor screamed into the earpiece.*

Paul approached the security guard at the tent where the brooch was. In his best attempt at French, he asked, *"Excusez-moi, monsieur, je cherche ma femme, vous l'avez vue?"*

The puzzled look on the security guard's face said a

thousand words that could all be simplified to just one: *What?*

"I speak English. Now, tell me again, please," the guard said, looking increasingly annoyed.

Trying to regain his breath after running around searching for Suhani, Paul recovered his composure and asked again in English, "I am looking for my wife; have you seen her? She's about yea high, long, black hair, with honey-colored skin?"

"I'm sorry, sir, I have not, but now I must ask you to leave," the guard stated firmly.

"Please, monsieur, you must have; she was just around here not too long ago," Paul pleaded.

"I have not, and this is the last time that I'll repeat myself, *Englishman*," the guard said sourly, gesturing toward the clip securing his handgun.

"Oi, okay, okay, I get the message, tough guy; you just stay there and keep looking pretty, you Muppet," Paul said, walking away. In case of situations such as these, the three of them agreed to rendezvous at a café not far from the exhibition to regroup and restrategize, so Paul and Tomor met there, obviously with no Suhani in sight.

"What exactly happened there, Paul?" Tomor demanded, slamming his fists on the table so hard that the salt and pepper shakers on the table went flying.

"I— I don't know. It all happened so fast. One second she was there, and before I knew it, she was gone. I'm really sorry, Tomor," Paul said, sounding understandably shocked.

"It doesn't make any sense. You were positioned perfectly to see her every step!" Tomor said through gritted teeth.

"I understand what you're saying, and I'm trying to get you to understand what *I'm* saying. *She just freaking vanished into thin air, mate. I swear it!* But what about you? I thought you had eyes on the both of us," Paul asserted.

"I did, but you had a better angle. I figured in the eventuality that I did lose sight of her, you would be able to see where she went!" Tomor objected.

"Well, I didn't, but we're not going to get anywhere by screaming at each other," Paul said.

Less than a minute after speaking, Paul's phone began to ring. It was Suhani. "Where are you guys? I'm on my way back to the hotel already."

"Who was it, Paul? *Paul*, I asked, who was it?" Tomor repeated. Paul continued to stare at Tomor, his phone still up to his ear, his hand frozen in disbelief.

"You won't believe it, but it was Suhani . . . and she's on her way back to the hotel!" At this point, Paul said it looked like he was staring into a mirror because Tomor now had the same expression as he did, a mile-long stare and a wide-open mouth, both seemingly paralyzed from bewilderment. A few more seconds of this ensued until Paul asked the server if he could have his *île flottante* to go as they hailed a cab back to the hotel.

The car ride back to the hotel was mainly a silent one and for different reasons. Paul was preoccupied admiring the French Gothic architecture that was historical Paris, especially in awe of the resolute stone façade of the Notre-Dame de Paris and how it's sturdy, robust-looking façade contrasted with its main wheel-like rose window that softened the ancient cathedral.

"Is it me, or does that window look like it can be used as a teleportation device? I mean, seriously, I can get lost in those spirals!" Paul said, his eyes glued on the grand cathedral.

"Yeah, I'm sure it's just you." Tomor shrugged.

Tomor was busy theorizing in his head how Suhani could've managed to take the original brooch, replace it, and take off back to the hotel without being noticed at all by either himself or Paul. Once the cab pulled into their boutique Parisian hotel, the two men dashed inside like they were being pursued by panthers.

Making their way down the hall to where their room was, both Tomor and Paul were overtaken by the aroma of warm raclette cheese and potatoes. Briefly transfixed by the smell, they were surprised to see that the classic Franco-Swiss pairing was coming out from their room. Suhani had ordered it and was enjoying a plate accompanied by a glass of Pinot Noir, with two plates set out for Tomor and Paul.

"Oi, what in the bloody hell happened, Suhani?" Paul exclaimed.

"I took the brooch, replaced it with ours, and didn't want to take any chances, so I left the expo," Suhani said nonchalantly, simultaneously handing Tomor and Paul a plate of food. Suhani's care-free behavior was both equally impressive and worrying for Tomor.

"Suhani, that wasn't the plan, though," Tomor said.

"I know it wasn't, but aren't you always the one instructing us to *improvise* if we sense that something is awry?" Suhani questioned.

"I guess that is correct," Tomor grunted. "But—But . . . how did you do it?"

"With my powers, I suppose," Suhani said, twisting her legs and twiddling her fingers.

"Care to elaborate?" Paul said, mouth full of food, with a piece of charcuterie still dangling, like those inflatable car dealership things.

"Well, the only explanation that I can offer you two is that somehow *my powers were activated, I guess*, and it helped me escape." Suhani shrugged it off like it was no big deal.

"Yeah, we figured, Sue, but how?" Paul mumbled and then gulped, finally swallowing his food.

"Okay, I'll try to walk you guys through it. While I was getting ready to approach the tent, I got really nervous—the most nervous I've ever been, actually, to the point where I couldn't even take a step. To help myself calm down, I thought of all the other times I felt like this and how I always persevered. I thought about how much I struggled that first year at Carnegie Mellon, but I got through it. I thought about how hard it was to stay true to myself back in India, despite living in an environment that constantly told me to be someone else, but I got through that, as well.

"So, when I was only steps away from that tent, I reminded myself of how capable and worthy I was and got through that, as well!" Suhani beamed proudly.

"That's all lovely and sweet—really inspiring, too—but what happened when you got to the tent, woman?" Paul said, leaning back into his chair, flailing his arms.

"Ever the stickler for details, aren't you?" Suhani said, smirking. "Well, I was trying to build up my nerve, but if you must know, once I thought of all the things that I've already accomplished in my twenty-four years of living, I suddenly felt extremely at ease and light, almost like I was floating, and just walked straight into the tent.

"I couldn't believe it, but I was standing right in front of that security guard, and he didn't move, *like he couldn't even see me*. To test this theory out, I even did a few jumping jacks right in his face, and he didn't move one inch! He started to move around the tent, though, as if he sensed something . . . that made me nervous."

"*And* what happened after you got nervous?" Paul interrupted, standing on his chair instead of sitting on it.

"I believe she was getting to that part, but what are you standing for?" Tomor asked.

"It helps me think!"

"Ooookay, Paul, but yeah, when I started to feel nervous, I repressed the nervous feeling and tried some of those mantras I always hear Rafi and Femi using. Before you interrupt, Paul, *yes, they worked*."

"I'm glad you were able to think so quickly on your feet, Suhani, but what you did was dangerous and stupid," Tomor said bluntly.

"Yeah, I realize that now, but once I was confident that he couldn't see me, I did what I had to do with the brooches and took the next bus back to the hotel. Have you seen the Pompidou Centre, though? For a city that looks so medieval, that thing looks like it was designed by steampunk aliens on shrooms."

"Nice try on changing the subject, but Tomor isn't as stupid as he looks," Paul said before taking a quick chug of his dark purple wine.

"So, you can become invisible?" Tomor finally asked after silently enjoying his meal.

"I don't know if it can actually be called invisibility, but I definitely couldn't be seen, if that's what you're asking," Suhani answered.

Wiping his mouth with the hotel-provided napkin and taking one sip of his wine before standing, Tomor said, "Well, there's only one way to find out. You have to replicate what you did then, now."

"My thoughts exactly!" Suhani enthusiastically replied. "I have an idea. As you both know, there's only one way into the bathroom and one way out. Before you say anything, yes, there is a window, but it's far too small for anyone to climb out of, correct?"

"Yes, yep," Tomor and Paul replied, respectively.

"Great, so I'll go in there now, and ten seconds later, I want you two to come in there and see if you can see me. How does that sound?" Tomor and Paul silently nodded, and Suhani departed for the bathroom, concentrating on not being seen, just like she did earlier.

Paul and Tomor waited a few seconds and then proceeded to follow her into the bathroom. Amazed, she was nowhere to be found.

"Suhani, Suhani?" they called out, exiting the bathroom and looking around in the main quarters to see if she'd snuck out somehow. After thoroughly searching the room three times, they gave up and sat back down where they were before she went into the bathroom. A second after they took their seats, they shot back up at breakneck speed, wondering what was crawling up their necks. It wasn't an insect at all, but Suhani slowly dragging her fingers along their necks from behind.

"Surprise, gentlemen!"

Even the ever-cool Tomor lost his composure and fell onto the floor after the incident. "How the *fuck* did you do that?"

"Well, I guess I can become invisible!" Suhani said, breaking out into uncontrollable laughter. "You two reacted as if you saw the devil himself!" Suhani said, holding her stomach to alleviate the discomfort all the laughing was causing.

"But how did you do it, though?" Tomor asked, recovering

his cool.

"I told you guys already; I just concentrated on not being seen, and I wasn't! You two were cracking me up, looking in that tiny closet as if I could even fit in there!" Suhani giggled.

"Wow, that's really amazing! I can't believe you can become invisible. That's huge for us," Paul said.

"It really could change our whole process on how we take down the Zaragozas," Tomor added.

"Well, come on, spill the beans."

"Spill the what?" Suhani asked.

"Oi, you know, the beans! What does it feel like when you go, you know . . . *ghost*?!" Paul asked, standing on his chair once again.

"Well, it feels pretty much the same, but I do feel a tingling, buzzing sensation when it's active. The best way I can describe it is when you have that first alcoholic drink of the night; you feel the effects of the alcohol but aren't completely overwhelmed by it," Suhani said.

"And you can even interact with things while you're invisible; that's amazing!" Paul said excitedly, barely able to control his excitement.

"Yeah, it is quite the feeling," Suhani admitted.

With the brooch now secured, the three of them spent the rest of the late afternoon enjoying more wine and cheese. Suhani played a few more tricks on Tomor and Paul. They got ready to depart for Strasbourg the next day, for Tomor and Paul still had work to do in the evening.

"You know, Paul, back at the Castillo, you never really shared anything about yourself that you think could lead to your abilities," Suhani said.

"Yeah, that's because I'm an open book. You all know that

it will probably have something to do with my gob!" Paul laughed.

"Yeah, but the only things we really know about your background is what others have told us. Granted, you've seen some things people shouldn't have to see, but it would still be nice hearing it from you," Suhani continued.

Ceasing to make eye contact and closing off his body language, Paul was visibly uncomfortable with this unforeseen line of questioning directed at him, but Suhani was correct. Indeed, Rafi, Sarah, James, and I all knew about Paul's past, but he seldomly shared his story with anyone outside of us, and when he did, he always glossed over the more horrible bits and summarized instead. For the amazing orator that he was, Paul did not like talking about himself, and the few times he did, his tone was always remarkably different.

His laid-back and carefree demeanor rapidly morphed into one that was deeply reflective and stoic any time the conversation was focused on him. I wished to be a fly on that Parisian hotel's wall because hearing Paul talk when he wasn't clowning around was always a sight to behold, but unfortunately for me, all I had to go on was what Tomor and Suhani told me.

"There's nothing important about me that you don't already know, Suhani," Paul said snappishly.

"Well, I beg to differ," Tomor chimed in. "For one, why did you apply to the ZNBS in the first place?"

Taking a prolonged deep breath, Paul finally succumbed to the incessant questioning levied onto him. "I applied to the ZNBS to get out of England. I always knew I wasn't as clever as some of the other kids, but I could see things that they couldn't see, which led me to say things that they couldn't say.

"One thing led to another, and before I knew it, I was going to these debates, winning even against seasoned debaters. It all started, though, when I got noticed by some professor from Oxford, and he was the one who encouraged me to apply," Paul said in a low, modest tone.

"Wait, so when was this—before or after university studies?" Tomor pondered.

"Neither, it was during. I was studying English at King's College but later switched to law, once visiting Professor Lloyd noticed me."

"Why is this the first time we're hearing about this, Paul? I had no idea you had a law degree!" Suhani exclaimed.

"Well, no one outside of my roommates asked, but I didn't want to say, either," Paul said.

"I knew a lot of people like you back in my time in the army, Paul," Tomor interjected. "Guys and girls so afraid of their potential that they preferred to just dawdle in the background while life passed them by."

"Oi, well, I guess I just prefer to lead from the back, innit?" Paul muttered underneath his breath.

"So, what were you going to use the ZNBS scholarship for?" Suhani inquired.

"Well, I was going to apply it for law school at Columbia," Paul appeared shy at the suggestion that he could go to such a prestigious university.

"You were going to go all the way to America for law school? It's not even your country," Tomor said.

"Well, if you know what happened to me, neither was England—*not anymore, at least*," Paul said somberly. "Look, guys, I appreciate the concern you two have for me, I really do.

But let's recover these blimey heirlooms for these assholes, take 'em down, and then we can crack into just how fucked my childhood was whilst holding hands, singing songs, and all that crap—how does that sound?" Paul said in a mocking, high-pitched tone.

"He's right. We are here on a mission; best stay on track until we're done. What do you know about this politician you have to convince, anyway, Paul?" Tomor asked.

"Well, apparently, he has been a thorn in the Zaragozas' side for a while, and he's single-handedly the reason why the Zaragozas haven't penetrated the shipping industry in Northern and Eastern Europe.

"It only took a few minutes of research to find out that he's pretty much the most well-known anti-trust politician in the European Parliament," Paul said sagely.

"And what do you have to convince him about, specifically?" Tomor asked.

"Well, the dossier just says that I have to get him to agree to allow the Zaragozas to buy some old shipping ports in Norway, Turkey, and Romania."

"This will be a mission in which we have to take extreme caution, then. We don't even know what your powers are," Tomor pointed out.

"Ah, I'm sure I'll get this done in no time, then we can go get your precious artifacts from those sodding Nazi descendants. What time do we leave for Strasbourg, anyway?" Paul asked.

"We leave in two hours. Should get to Strasbourg in the early morning, and then the next day, I've arranged for you to intercept this politician before he heads to a parliament meeting."

"*Thanks, Dad,*" Paul said sarcastically.

Having Tomor around always streamlined whatever plans we had, and I was a bit jealous that I didn't have him for my mission.

Chapter 17: Notre-Dame de Strasbourg

Once they touched down in Strasbourg, the gang went for the customary walk around the city center, which they claimed was even more beautiful than they had imagined; Tomor even preferred it to Paris for a number of reasons, but mainly for its charming cobbled roads that looked like they hadn't been restored since France had a monarch.

Strasbourg's architecture had hints of Bavarian charm, but the French *joie de vivre* still reigned supreme. French balconies and German timber-framed houses coalesced perfectly in neat and tidy rows that reminded Tomor of the regimented life he previously had.

After walking around the city for a bit, the group thought it was best to head back to their hotel near the Cathedral of Notre-Dame to recharge and get ready for the next day. However, while Tomor and Suhani were busy counting sheep, Paul was conducting a more thorough investigation on Sébastien de Ile, the politician he had been sent there to sway.

Rudimentary research confirmed Paul's previous suspicions. Sébastien was a stand-up guy, championing the rights of the exploited by limiting the market share the Zaragozas had in the shipping industry. Despite desperately wanting to aid in Sébastien's efforts, Paul knew that to hit the ZCA and the Zaragozas as a whole where it hurt, he had to bite the proverbial bullet and do as he was instructed . . . for now.

* * *

The next morning, Paul set out alone to trail Monsieur de Ile. Sébastien was a man who ardently stuck to his routines, making it easy for him to track.

"Monsieur de Ile, excuse me, monsieur de Ile!" Paul approached the slender but athletically built man.

"Yes, do I know you?" The politician asked in a polite, but standoffish tone.

"Do you mind if I take this seat next to you?" Paul asked Sébastien, impersonating a newscaster's *proper* received pronunciation accent.

"And who might you be, my English friend?" Sébastien asked.

"I could be your best friend or your worst bloody nightmare," Paul said, accenting with his trademark debonair smile.

"If you truly know who I am, then you know that idle threats won't have an effect on me, so you can either tell me who you are and what you want, or you can leave so I can enjoy my breakfast in peace," Sébastien said, stirring the granola in his strawberry parfait.

"Listen, Sébastien, I'm going to try something different here and actually be honest with you," Paul said seriously.

Silently nodding, Paul had Sébastien's undivided attention. "I work for the Zaragozas. . . ."

The moment Sébastien heard the name *Zaragoza,* he stood up in defiance, forgoing his breakfast, and ready to leave his favorite restaurant at the very mentioning of the malevolent family.

"Wait, wait, hear me out!" Paul instructed. "I work for the Zaragozas informally; well, they awarded me the ZNBS. . . ."

"Save your breath. I'm well aware of what you ZNBS recipients do for the Zaragozas—lobby for them so that your wildest dreams can come true, no?" Sébastien said.

"Well, yes, sort of, but that's not the reason I'm here! Well, it's kind of the reason. *Listen,* just hear me out, okay?" Paul said, growing frustrated with Sébastien's interruptions. "Like I said, I work for them, but I probably loathe them just as much as you do, if not more. I want to bring them to their knees for all the chaos they've caused from their greed."

Sébastien fell silent again, lazily waving his hand at Paul to gesture for him to continue.

"I know you have plans to introduce legislation to severely curb the amount of influence the ZCA has in the shipping industry, correct?" Paul said, taking a bite out of de Ile's muffin.

"Yes. I, a few other parliament members, and some international lawmakers have been looking into this, but I am spearheading the cause. Why?" Sébastien asked.

"Well, I need you to pause on that legislation, mate."

Slamming his utensils on the table, Sébastien exploded. "I

will do no such thing; this is my life's work. If the Zaragozas' claim on Europe goes unchecked, who knows what global repercussions we'll face? They already control more than seventy percent of the entire European shipping industry, close to forty-five percent worldwide, and that's not even including the various other monopolies they possess!"

"Oi, calm down. I understand your sentiment more than you know. Their influence in my hometown caused mass unemployment, and what little commerce remained after they took over was primarily attributed to their subsidiaries," Paul said, grabbing Sébastien's arm, pulling him back down.

"Now, imagine what they did to your town happening to every town and city in Europe, hell, in the world, because that's what you're asking me to allow," Sébastien replied, his face growing as red as the strawberries in his yogurt bowl.

"Trust me, Monsieur de Ile, there's a method to the madness, I promise—"Paul began.

"Madness is still madness, and I'll have no part in it," Sébastien interrupted again.

"Oi, you bloody will," Paul said in a low and guttural tone that strangely subdued Sébastien's fervor.

"What exactly is your angle . . . uh, what's your name?" the boyishly handsome politician asked.

"My name is Paul."

"Okay, Paul, now it's your turn to tell me what you're trying to do here."

"It's quite simple. I'm sure you're a European history buff—isn't that one of the requirements for your kind of position, anyway?"

"Not really a requirement, but yes, I am broadly familiar with the history of this continent," Sébastien gruffly replied.

"So then, you know the story of Operation Valkyrie, correct?" Paul inquired.

"Of course I am familiar with the plan to assassinate Hitler by his very own army. . . . Oh, wait, I see. . . ." Sébastien raised his eyebrows at the younger man.

"You're smarter than you look, Seb," Paul said mockingly.

"And you're even more stupid than I originally thought if that's what you're planning to do to the Zaragozas. There's no way that you, or whoever you've managed to convince, will ever do anything remotely close to the ambitious plan that was Operation Valkyrie," Sébastien said with an air of pretentiousness.

"Well, I guess that we will have to just agree to disagree, *monsieur.* It matters not what you think we can or cannot do, but what you will do is hold out on advancing legislation until I or someone on my behalf instructs you otherwise. Is that clear, mate?" Paul ordered.

Only telling me what he saw in Sébastien's eyes that day, Paul immediately knew that his abilities were activated. "How did you know?" I asked Paul.

"I just did; the second after I asked if it was clear, it was as if Sébastien was instantaneously hypnotized, and his eyes for a second looked like they rolled back into his head, then returned to their normal positions, although slightly glazed over. And in a monotone, almost Frankenstein-like manner, he repeated and confirmed everything I said to him," Paul later recounted to me.

"I will wait to advance the legislation regarding the increasingly monopolistic nature of the Zaragoza influence in Europe and abroad until I hear otherwise from you or someone on your behalf, sir," the politician repeated verbatim, completely under Paul's sway.

"As he finished his sentence, he took the last bite from his parfait, thanked me for showing him reason, smiled, exchanged contact information, shook my hand, and left—that's it!"

I couldn't believe what Paul was telling me. He basically just compelled a European Parliament member to do his bidding just by commanding it. Paul's abilities would change everything for us, the ZRC, but most importantly, for ordinary citizens tired of tyranny.

Brimming with so much excitement that he was barely able to walk correctly, Paul skipped all the way back to the hotel, almost bursting at the seams to relay to Suhani and Tomor what he had just accomplished.

"Oi! Suhani, Tomor, I come bearing gifts! Crème-filled *Mille-feuilles* and *chocolat éclairs* for you, Suhani, fresh off the streets of Strasbourg, France!" Paul said in an overly exaggerated French accent.

"What are you so giddy about?" Suhani asked, rubbing sleep residue out of her eyes.

"Oh, well, nothing, really. I just convinced Sébastien to hold off on introducing that legislation until I told him to do so!" Paul said, very happy, indeed.

"And how did you manage that, Paul?" Tomor chimed in.

"I just told him, and he agreed,*" Paul said coolly.*

"You just *told* him, and he gave up his life's work investigation into the Zaragozas just because a Brit that he's never met *told* him to do so?" Tomor asked, visibly annoyed with Paul's pompousness.

"Well, I guess it was more like I *compelled* him to do so."

The irritation that was just in Tomor's voice was now

replaced with intrigue: "You *compelled* him to do so?"

"Yes, and it felt damn good, too, like strangely, tickling-good!"

"Are you saying what I think you're saying?" Tomor asked.

"Yes, and if they're what I think they are, the Zaragozas have no chance!" Paul said, punching the air enthusiastically.

"What did it feel like when you used them?" Tomor said.

"You know that feeling when you're swindling someone, and you have them eating out of the palm of your hand?" Paul said.

"I can't say I'm familiar with that exact feeling, but yes, I do know what it feels like to convince someone who didn't previously share your sentiment," Tomor frowned.

"Yes, that! But times a thousand! Your words that were perhaps said in a joking manner suddenly become resolute, more than just mere suggestions. And here's the kicker—well, at least from my encounter with Sébastien: I felt that when I told him to stop investigating the Zaragozas, there was a bit of resistance from him, but the more I repeated it, and the firmer I became—like a fatigued fighter gradually diminishing throughout the fight—I could feel his will losing steam. And when I felt that he was on his last legs, I went in for the kill and compelled him to do my bidding, and then I bought breakfast for the lot of you!"

"Sounds like you really enjoyed yourself, Paul. Just don't lose sight of what we're doing this for and become the sort of sleazebag we're trying to stop with your newfound powers," Tomor warned.

"Well, let's see it in action!" Suhani said cheerfully, easing the tension-filled room.

"You actually want me to try it on one of you?" Paul asked.

"Yes, exactly. Try it on me, for example. C*ompel* me to do something, *me* lord," Suhani said in a mocking British accent.

"Well, if you insist." Paul walked over to where Suhani was standing, looked deep into her amber eyes, and said, "Suhani, go the Cathedral and retrieve a crucifix for me."

"No!" Suhani proudly snapped back.

"Off!" Paul shouted out weirdly. Amused at Suhani's and Tomor's blank stares and obvious confusion, Paul then yelled, *"On!"* And proceeded to repeat himself, "I said, Suhani retrieve a crucifix for me from the Cathedral, AT ONCE!"

Instantly, Suhani's eyes began to glaze over, and it even appeared that her irises were spinning counterclockwise. "Right away, Paul."

Suhani immediately left the hotel room and came back fifteen minutes later with a crucifix in hand.

"Whoa, why do I have this?" she asked upon her return.

"You don't remember, do you?" Paul asked, unable to stop smirking. Like a police lieutenant observing through double-sided glass, Tomor stood there silently, watching without comment.

"I *compelled* you to get this crucifix for me from the Cathedral," Paul said as pleased as a Saturday cartoon villain.

"I remember you asking me, and I remember saying no, but then it gets kind of hazy, and before I know it, I'm in the Cathedral Notre-Dame de Strasbourg donating money for a crucifix!" Suhani said, her voice trembling with shock.

"Fascinating. Just by telling someone to do so, you can bend them to your will, and it seems like it's something you can turn off and on, like a switch, yes?" Tomor asked.

"Exactly, and like I said with M. de Ile, the harder they try to resist, the harder I can push," Paul said.

"Okay, now do it on me," Tomor said.

"Um, but don't you think that's enough for one day, Tomor? You've already seen it firsthand." Paul winced.

"True, but I haven't *felt* it firsthand, so try it on me . . . now." Tomor was insistent, and Paul reluctantly obliged.

"Okay, if you say so. . . ." He took a deep breath. "Tomor, admit to me now your deepest fear."

"You can't be serious, right? Is that what you're going to ask? Something else, please!" Tomor's voice had raised a notch.

"If you want to know if my power is for real, it's going to have to be tested—meaning I'm going to have to get you to do something you don't want to do, army-boy," Paul said, rubbing the back of his neck apprehensively.

Tomor was naturally a guy who kept his cards close to his chest, but for all his battle-hardened experience, he was still a human with anxieties, hopes, and fears.

"I don't want to do it, either, but you know we must," Paul said.

"Yes, I know. Okay, do your thing then, I guess," Tomor said as he physically braced himself, taking a wide stance and clenching his fists.

"You know I'm not going to punch you in the stomach, right?" Paul joked.

"Just get on with it, Paulie."

"As you wish, Tomor; tell me your deepest fear."

Tomor flinched a bit, seemingly trying to resist Paul's magic words.

"I said to reveal to me the secrets you try so desperately hard to hide," Paul repeated louder.

"I don't want to be a disappointment to my parents," Tomor

began hesitantly.

"That's not the whole truth, and you know it!"

"I don't want people to think I'm not worthy," Tomor mumbled again.

"Tomor, stop resisting and tell me now!" *Paul bellowed.*

And in a moment, just like Suhani previously and Sébastien before her, Tomor's eyes began their dance. "I don't want people to think I'm less worthy or any less capable due to my mixed heritage. . . .

"My Ethiopian friends always berate me for not being *African enough,* while my Israeli friends always ask me why I didn't go into medicine to be more like my acclaimed Ashkenazi father. It's . . . it's just debilitating," Tomor confessed.

Never had he appeared more vulnerable but also free. Tomor was quite literally fighting a war on two fronts, the war that he was trained for and the war that was his identity in his homeland. Unlike Suhani, though, Tomor remembered exactly what he said while he was under the influence of Paul's remarkable ability.

"I'm sorry, guys; I wish I never asked to test you," Paul said sheepishly.

Neither Paul nor Suhani had ever seen Tomor like this before, nor could they even imagine that he could've felt in such a way. Here was the tough-as-nails former commando who trained with Navy SEALs and the British SAS but still battled with things that are seemingly negated through accolades, promotions, and other things we tell ourselves will make us feel *whole*.

Fortunately for Tomor, though, he was surrounded by people who only had his best interests at heart. Rather than put him down, or let him revel in his despondency, they did what any fellow member of the ZRC would: They reminded him of who he is and what he has accomplished—not through his career but with his character.

"Tomor, buddy, *brother*, are you even serious? Not only are you the most badass genius I've ever met, but you're also the nicest bloke around!" Paul said emphatically. "No matter what color you are, you're a hero in the eyes of so many, and I know for a fact that your parents are prouder of you than you could even imagine," Paul praised.

"For the first time, he's right, Tomor; not only have you made your country safer, but your achievements both on the battlefield and in the classroom are just reflections of who you are as a person—a good, caring, and decent person. Don't let others tell you your worth," Suhani said smilingly.

"Thanks, you two. I'm glad that I accompanied you here. To think that I thought my being here was to assist you two on your missions, but you have helped me more than I could ever imagine," Tomor said.

"Don't go getting all sentimental on us now, army-boy," Paul joked.

"You know, I can't believe it. If you had told me two months ago that being awarded this scholarship was going to change my life, I wouldn't've believed you. Now, if you were to've told me then that the very same scholarship would also be the reason why we've been traveling all over the continent, stealing and recovering things, while trying to take down a family with ties to the supernatural—who in turn granted us with powers out of comic books—I would've probably laughed in your face, but here we are!" Tomor said, visibly tipsy from the strong wheat ales he had been drinking all evening.

The three of them were in good spirits; how could they not be? Suhani and Paul had already secured their heirlooms and figured out what their abilities were. I mean, for God's sake, Suhani could turn invisible, Paul could *compel* anybody to do anything, and Tomor was a master strategist! All that was left was for them to travel to Stuttgart the next day and recover various paintings, among other things, stolen by the people who wanted to destroy Tomor's religion and its followers. We were, quite literally, kickin' ass and takin' names from people who had gotten away with far too much for far too long!

* * *

Since Stuttgart wasn't too far away, Suhani, Paul, and Tomor could sleep in a little longer than usual, given there was no flight to catch. Preferring to lay low, the gang rented a car and decided to drive to Stuttgart instead.

"What do you know about the artifacts you're supposed to retrieve, Tomor?" Suhani pondered.

"All the dossier said was that it was last seen at a museum that closed down a few years ago. I looked up who currently owned the museum but found out it was purchased by a company that became defunct last year," Tomor responded.

"Oi, so we're back at square one, then, innit?" Paul had groaned.

"No, not necessarily; I managed to find two names that kept reappearing every time I tried to dig deeper into who owned the company that owned the museum. It took me down a very deep rabbit hole, but the guys' names are Johann Schwartz and Franz Kappes, two disgraced former German soldiers turned mercenaries-for-hire that I actually heard about during my time in the service," Tomor said.

"How do two mercenaries end up owning a museum, anyway?" Suhani asked.

"When that museum is your way of laundering money, peddling, and selling stolen goods, I would assume," Tomor answered gruffly.

"What was the consensus on these two guys back when you were still active duty?" Paul asked.

"One word: *scum*."

"I guess that settles it, then, lad and lassie; we take these artifacts back and tell these cunts off, then!" Paul cried out.

"No, you two have been put in enough danger already. I'm taking point on this one." Tomor was adamant.

"Uh, military lingo again, Tomor? Suhani said."

"Sorry, Sue. I meant I'm doing this one alone."

"Says the man with no powers. I could just talk these guys into giving us the artifacts, while Suhani could literally just take them and walk away!" Paul insisted.

"No can do, Paul—this mission is mine." Tomor wasn't one to argue with; plus, this was his Second Trial task. If he wanted to do it solo, then that was his choice and his choice alone.

Chapter 18: Waffenbrüder

Excited to finally be in the home country of her favorite automobile makers, Porsche and Mercedes-Benz, Suhani was surprised to see that Stuttgart was a land covered in verdant lush vineyards and not totally made out of tarmac. After arriving in Germany, the gang quickly found a hotel not far from Johann's last known address. For a man whose job revolved around order and structure, Johann's home was dilapidated beyond belief. So much so, police tape was used to discourage anyone from trying to take shelter in the rubble.

"Jesus *fookin'* Christ, it looks like a tornado took this place out for breakfast, lunch, and dinner!" Paul exclaimed.

"Or someone really wanted to cover their tracks and leave no trace. I'm going inside to take a closer look," Tomor said.

Tomor's suspicion was correct. After they left the house, they soon discovered that the home's current condition was the result of arson. Tomor theorized that Johann set fire to his own home probably to thwart the Zaragozas' search for him, *or anyone else that was after him*. Johann was good, but Tomor was better.

"Hey, you two, come look at this," Tomor called out to Paul and Suhani. Rummaging through the charred ashes, now on his knees, Tomor found a scorched but still legible matchbox of a bar not too far from where they were.

"Der betrunkene Fisch."

"What does it say?" Suhani asked.

"My German is pretty rusty, but I think it reads, The Drunken Fish. I say we go check it out. The address is written on here, too," Tomor said.

"Man, I sure wish James was with us now," Paul bemoaned.

"We don't need him; he's already done his part. Time for us to do ours!" Tomor said.

* * *

The bar was only fifteen minutes away from Johann's former home, so the three of them wasted no time getting there. Finding the bar was easy enough; however, getting the information they required would be more difficult. The Drunken Fish was not a regular bar but, in fact, a bar that catered to a specific type of clientele: the ruthless, ex-military type. This mission was really turning into a solo job for Tomor, quite organically. Could the Zaragozas have known specifically what path retrieving these lost artifacts would take Tomor down? Are they that omniscient to know exactly which ZNBS recipient would be best to retrieve each heirloom, or was it purely a coincidence? Questions my mind struggled to answer, but even if they did have all this foresight, we wouldn't let it deter us. *We couldn't let it deter us.*

Fitting the bill perfectly, Tomor had no issues gaining patronage at the bar. Somehow these military-types just instinctively knew who was one of them and who wasn't. Suhani and Paul thus decided to stay in the car instead, while Tomor worked his magic.

"Barkeep, what do you have to drink?" Tomor asked.

"Anything you require, sir," the barkeeper politely responded.

"Anything? Is that so? Okay, I'll take a double shot of Tubi 60," Tomor said.

"*Ahh, an Israeli.* I haven't had your kind around here in quite a while. Coming right up, my Semitic friend," the barkeeper said, chuckling to himself.

Downing the shot in a blink of an eye, Tomor proceeded to question the barkeep about the mercenaries he was looking for, hoping to at least get a clue of who Johann Schwartz and Franz Kappes really were. "I'm looking for someone. You might know him; his house burned down not too far from here. . . ."

"*Ja, Ja,* I know of whom you speak: Johann. He used to be a regular here," the barkeep said in a thick but intelligible Bavarian accent.

"*Used to be*? What happened to him?" Tomor asked.

"He and his buddy—a taller guy with a scar on his cheek, ex-military, too—were known to regularly partake in high-stakes poker matches. Rumor has it, they entered a game too rich for their blood. They lost and tried to escape without paying. The only thing about playing high-stakes poker with ex-commandos is, well . . . they're all ex-commandos, and if you run, they will find you at all costs. Long story short,

Johann's debtor didn't find him, so they burned his house down as a warning to pay up before worse things happened to him," the barkeep said gravely.

Intrigued and spotting an opportunity to kill two birds with one stone, Tomor indulged the barkeep's loose lips. Tomor bought a round of shots for the barkeep and himself to keep him talking. "Tell me more about these debtors. Do you know them?"

"Know them and know them well for that matter!" said the barkeep, who was now gratuitously pouring drinks for Tomor and himself.

"Real nasty guys who *allegedly* committed atrocities throughout Eastern Europe and South America—acts so foul that they were court-martialed. But the story goes, their wanton violence wasn't unsanctioned and was actually ordered by someone who had the type of sway that gets you out of trouble like that.

"Needless to say, they are really dangerous guys, and believe it or not, one of their creditors is actually sitting right over there!" The barkeep pointed behind Tomor to a rugged older man who appeared to be in his mid-40s, slouched back in a booth.

Physically, he was intimidating, standing a hair under 6' 5", his shoulders as wide as he was tall. The ex-commando's hair was long and unkempt, just like his beard, both sprinkled with specks of gray that contrasted heavily with his jet-black hair and steel blue eyes.

"You've been very helpful, barkeep. Take this." Tomor handed him 100 euros, which the barkeep was more than happy to accept.

"I didn't get your name, Israeli," the barkeep said, raising his shot glass to him.

"I know. . . ."

Taking a final shot of the Tubi, Tomor made his way toward Johann's creditor, sitting alone in his booth. "You look thirsty, friend. What are you having?" Tomor said to the burly stranger.

The mysterious man looked Tomor up and down repeatedly, burped, and then finally spoke, breaking the awkward silence. "*Israeli, eh*? I know that accent from anywhere. You're a long way from home, buddy," the stranger said in a German accent not immediately familiar to Tomor.

"Indeed I am, so let me buy you a drink, and I'll tell you why I'm so far away."

The stranger nodded, and Tomor returned to the talkative barkeep and purchased two pints of his finest pale ales.

"A German might be offended that you returned with ales instead of lagers." The man winked at Tomor.

Tomor gave a short chuckle. "Well, it doesn't seem like you're too offended."

"I'm not, but then again, I'm not German; I'm Swiss!" the man said, and cheersed Paul.

"That explains the accent," Tomor said. The two men clashed glasses and took a generous gulp out of their golden brews.

"So, what brings you here, Israeli? You guys were always the shrewd, *snipe 'em from afar* type." The creditor squinted toward Tomor, wiping the froth from his beard.

"I hear we are looking for the same man, a man who can't pay his debts, a man who is fleeing like a dirty rat," Tomor said resolutely.

"Ahh, yes, then we are looking for the same man. What is

your business with him?" the Swiss stranger asked.

"Just like you, he has something that belongs to me."

"And what does this have to do with me?" the man asked, now sitting up straight.

"If you find him and his rat-buddy that I'm sure you're well aware of, I'll pay you and whoever you're working with the debts owed to you and then some," Tomor offered, knowing that the Zaragozas' accounts could easily cover the tab.

"And why would a man be concerned with the debts of a rat?" the Swiss mercenary snarled.

"Because that rat has things that I need," Tomor replied just as brusquely.

"Well, then, I hope your wallet is ready to pay up because my colleague is closing in on him and his acquaintance as we speak. I'll be receiving a call informing me about the location of our mutual friend, after which I'll call a helo to pick me up, take me to him, get my money, and kill him—or just kill him since you have now offered me that money!" the Swiss stranger said, smiling and pressing down the tips of his mustache into his beard. "But before all of that, drink with me and tell me what Johann is to you."

When Tomor first told me his story, all I could think about was how many men you had to kill before it became as casual as making a sandwich, how many men you had to kill before you could just nonchalantly threaten to kill another while laughing and adjusting your facial hair. Could Tomor talk so nonchalantly about murder, too? He probably could, but happily for me, he was a friend and not a foe. Ordering another round of beers, Tomor finally acknowledged the Swiss man's question.

"Just as he is to you, he has something that isn't his," Tomor admitted to the Swiss mercenary.

"That's all I need to know, then. For some reason, I like you, and I'm not usually so trusting, but you don't seem like a man who would turn on his word."

"You're right, my friend," Tomor said as they cheersed once more, taking another mouthful from their chilled glasses.

"Did you ever serve in Dagestan, say, three to five years ago? the Swiss man inquired. "I heard stories of a black Israeli who was quite the young Spec-Ops officer."

"Perhaps I did," Tomor replied with a cheeky smile.

"Ahh, then that is the reason I feel like I can trust you—quite the reputation you have earned for yourself! Entering a house full of hostiles armed to the teeth and disarming them without a shot fired. Very impressive!" The man smiled, his second glass already nearing empty.

"You seem to know a lot about me, yet I don't even know your name," Tomor smirked.

"Ah, I must've left my manners back in Switzerland. Apologies. My name is Klaus, and yours?"

"My name is Tomor."

"Tomor, eh? Isn't that the name of the Albanian Zeus?" Klaus said.

"It is. Tomor is the name of the Albanian father of gods and humans. It was also my grandfather's name, whom I was named after." Tomor had been impressed by this man's knowledge.

"So, tell me, Tomor, grandson of Tomor, if I catch—sorry, *when* I catch—Johann and his buddy, how soon could I expect my payment?" Klaus said, returning to business.

"Right after I get what I'm looking for and however long banks take to accept transfers here," Tomor promised.

"Fifty thousand euros is a lot of money, Tomor namesake of Tomor," Klaus said in a deep and menacing but slightly comical way.

"I understand, Klaus, but it's a price I would gladly pay to retrieve what I need."

"One second, please, I have to take this." Klaus winked. "*Hallo, yes? Right now? Cornered? I'm on my way.*" Klaus said into his earpiece, ending the call with the press of a finger. "Your good fortune has followed you from Dagestan; let's hope your wallet will, too, because I just received word that Johann and his friend have been found, and my men are surrounding them. A helicopter will be here shortly to take us to them. Shall we order one more round of drinks?" Klaus said, grinning ear to ear, his black mustache once again outfitted with a golden finish.

"If you are having one, then so will I," Tomor responded.

The two men enjoyed one final pint together before the sound of the incoming helicopter made it impossible to talk at conversational levels.

"Tomor, Tomor, are you there? What in the bloody hell is that?" Paul said.

Unable to hear Paul or himself, Tomor stepped into the bathroom in order to hear more clearly. "Paul, Paul, you there? Anyway, I met someone who is taking me to Johann and possibly Franz. I'll be going quiet for a few hours, but don't worry about me. Once I'm done and have recovered the artifacts, I'll meet you guys back at the hotel. Tomor, out."

"What did he say?" Suhani asked Paul, slapping the back of his car seat to get his attention.

"He really wants to do this one alone. He met some other ex-special forces bloke who's also tracking Johann, and they are going somewhere in that helicopter to go find him!" Paul said, trying to shout over the helicopter's whirring blades.

"I hope he's not overcompensating for his lack of—well, you know—powers like ours." Suhani sighed.

"He's the most capable of us all; with or without superpowers, he'll be fine," Paul reassured.

"The helicopter is outside. Time to go, Israeli!"

Klaus and Tomor reported to the roof of the bar, which obviously also had a helipad. They greeted the pilot—who, as it turned out, had also been in Dagestan, and who greeted Tomor warmly now—and swiftly departed.

"So, where do your men have Johann pinned down, anyway?" Tomor asked.

"Rats do as rats do—flee as far as they can go and as fast as they can. We found them shacked up in an abandoned mountain cabin near the border between the German and Austrian Alps," Klaus shouted over the helicopter's mechanical roar.

"Klaus, I have to ask you: The other man that Johann is with, do you know if he is Franz Kappes?" Tomor asked, showing Klaus a picture of Franz for confirmation.

"This man you show me has no facial hair. The man that's with Johann now has a sparse beard. I'm not sure if he's your guy, but if he's not, I'll help you find him, too, no charge!" Klaus assured.

"You're awfully kind to me, Klaus; if you're hitting on me, um, I'm flattered, but I . . ."

"Ha-ha-ha, so you really don't remember, eh?"

Scratching his head, puzzled, Tomor replied, "Remember what, exactly?"

"In Dagestan, we were stationed with the Germans when we got ambushed, and one of ours got captured—our medic, actually," Klaus said.

"Wait, are you talking about *Heinrich?*" Tomor asked shockingly.

"Yes! The one hostage that was in that house you raided, that was our medic, *our Heinrich*. When he got back to where we were camped, he couldn't stop raving about you—an Israeli Superman he called you, the way you disarmed and took those guys out. They had a treasure trove of information on them that we used to break up their syndicate, and Heinrich went on to save many more lives because of you.

"Since that day, my squad and I always told ourselves, if we ever had the chance to actually meet you, we would be forever indebted to you!" Klaus confessed.

"Wow, I had no idea. I used to talk to Heinrich from time to time, but a year or two ago, I lost contact with him and couldn't find him anywhere."

Suddenly, Klaus removed his headset and placed it in his lap.

"What's wrong, Klaus," Tomor asked, placing his hand on Klaus's back.

"You didn't hear back from Heinrich because he passed away. Too bad you weren't there to save him that time, eh?" Klaus said, flashing his misty blue eyes at Tomor, doing his best to hold back incoming tears. "You know what, Tomor? Forget about the payment. I get Johann, and you get what you need from him, and I'll take you back to your friends. No amount of money can bring Heinrich back, but I'm grateful that you allowed us to spend more time with him before he passed."

According to Tomor, he went in to shake Klaus's hand

after his kind gesture, but Klaus instead grabbed his hand and went in for a bear hug. Honestly, that was one thing about the military I greatly admired—the brotherhood built on mutual sacrifices, the band of people risking their lives together.

Even if you didn't serve the same country, the sacrifices were always the same, and going through that forges a bond deeper than blood, a bond that can never be broken. Only if we could recognize that no matter our backgrounds or what we sound like, there is something intrinsic to humanity that promotes peace, love, and mutual understanding—although we as a species often get distracted by things that aren't so important in the grand scheme of it all.

Tomor and Klaus, as well as most people who have served, understood this deeply and were better for it.

"We're almost there. Look alive!"

Shortly afterward, the men landed on a patch of fresh snow, still fluffy and powdery. A few yards north of where the helicopter landed, a ramshackle but still structurally sound cabin came into view.

"This is it. My men are in there with those *Rattenmänner*!" the Swiss mercenary bellowed.

Upon entering the derelict cabin, Tomor found Johann and Franz cowering in a broken and bloody mess. As Klaus and his men continued to extort information out of Johann and Franz in their *hands-on* kind of way, Tomor continued alone farther into the cabin, looking for the artifacts he was tasked to retrieve.

At first glance, the cabin appeared to be mainly empty. However, walking around the back entrance, Tomor noticed a discolored wooden plank that made a hollow thump every time he walked over it. Pulling the floorboards apart, he found a ladder that went down to God knows where.

"*Klaus!*" Tomor yelled. "Get over here. You're going to want to see this!"

Klaus rushed over to where Tomor was, laughing like a madman. He called his other companions over so they could take a look, too.

"Hans, Ulrich, get over here and bring a bag . . . a big bag!" Klaus shouted just before his two subordinates came at once, and the four of them descended down to the damp and dark sub-level floor.

"Oh my God," Tomor cried out.

"It can't be real!" Klaus followed. It was as if the men walked into a literal dragon's den: jewels, paintings, gold coins, you name it, Johann and Franz were sitting on priceless valuables as far as the eye could see. It must've taken them well over a decade of thieving to amass a wealth of this magnitude.

Sitting nicely in a corner all by themselves were the artifacts Tomor came for: small Spanish trinkets, paintings, and jewelry from before World War II, all adorned in various precious metals, such as emerald, ruby, and sapphire.

"This is what I'm here for, brother, and as I see it, the rest of it now belongs to you and your men," Tomor said, elated, all the men now congratulating each other and patting themselves on the backs. "What will you do with all this treasure?" Tomor asked Klaus.

"You know what, Tomor? Heinrich still has a family that needs to be taken care of. I'll take heed of that first, and then I'll make sure the rest of the treasures are put to good use . . . in my bank account, that is!" Klaus snickered.

"And Johann and Franz?" Tomor asked.

"Oh, don't worry about those two—"

BANG, BANG! The sound of two .45 rounds rang out in quick succession, sending a shock wave from above.

"I guess that's your answer," Klaus said with a whimsical smile, running his hands through his cookies-n-cream colored hair. "Listen, Tomor. Tell the pilots where you need to go. My men and I will take it from here. And don't be a stranger, okay? You and I are war brothers—*waffenbrüders*—for life."

Tomor respectfully nodded, gave Klaus a *manly* hug, shook the hands of his men for the final time, went back to the helicopter, and departed back to the Stuttgart hotel.

* * *

Arriving just past nightfall, Paul and Suhani greeted Tomor with open arms. "Don't scare us like that again, Tomor!" Suhani said, slapping Tomor's arm.

"I'm sorry, you two, but I didn't want to put you in any danger, *especially* given the type of people I was liaising with," Tomor said sarcastically.

"That's all fine and dandy, mate, but remember, we aren't so useless, either," Paul replied.

By the time Tomor had finished getting Suhani and Paul up to speed on everything that took place with Klaus, Johann, and Franz, the sun was already beginning to rise, which was a good indicator that it was time to head to bed.

* * *

When they woke up, they traveled around Stuttgart for a while, taking in the picturesque city. More importantly, at least to Suhani, they visited the Porsche museum since Suhani was an admirer of their early, air-cooled engines. She only admitted it to me much later, but she told me that for a second in that museum, she wondered when she would be able to afford a Porsche. I just hoped she wouldn't betray the ZRC for a mid-engine German sports car. I know I probably would!

After leaving the museum, their flight back to Spain was soon approaching, so they took the opportunity to finally indulge in the clichéd German staples of bratwursts and schnitzels coupled with pints of the local lager, and departed for their flight back to Spain.

Chapter 19: The Capital

"You guys have been gone for so long!" I immediately exclaimed as they entered from the Castillo's courtyard entrance.

My friends caught all of us up on their powers and travels while we listened with great intrigue and delight to their harrowing adventures. All of us except Amir and Kofi, that is, for their adventures were soon to begin, and it turned out that they were reluctant to leave.

"Okay, gals and gents, what if, just what if, one of us actually *didn't* have any powers?" Amir faux-rhetorically asked.

"*Dude!*" Daniela yelled in her quirky but lovely Brazilian accent. "Why you keep hinting about these powers? Is there something you want to tell us?"

"I just don't want to be the odd man out, is all. From hearing all of your stories, it just seems that even before your powers had been activated, you all still had a sense of where they could come from," Amir said, his face long with concern. "But I have nothing, nada, zilch!" he fretted.

"Brother, you don't know that. Plus, tell you what: I'll go with you since our locations aren't too far from each other," Kofi said.

"Would you really?" Amir asked, the despair in his voice replaced with a certain optimism.

"Yes, I promise. You're going to Madrid, no?" Kofi said.

"Indeed, I am!" Amir jovially responded.

"What do you even have to get? I completely forgot," Kofi asked.

"Definitely one of the more random things that we've been tasked to retrieve; the dossier just said, *an old book*." Amir shrugged. "And to make matters worse, the person who was last seen with it has been declared deceased, and all I could find was a name of a *possible* relative."

"That's not a lot of information to go on, but you're a charming British doctor. I'm sure you'll be able to get anything you want," Kofi said sardonically.

"Regardless of you two going together or not, just please be careful and watch each other's back," I warned.

"What about you, Kofi? What do you have to retrieve?" Amir asked.

"Hmm, I think it was a key of some sort?" Kofi scratched his chin. "Let me just make sure, okay? One second." As soon as Kofi said *one second,* though, we all busted out in laughter because we knew his *one second* actually meant we had enough time to run a 10K, have a gourmet three-course dinner, as well as time for spirits afterward.

It was Kofi who had the last laugh, though, because for the first time, it actually didn't take him an eternity to retrieve the dossier since the email he received wasn't as detailed.

"Okay, so it looks like I am to collect a *vault* key."

"But a vault key to what?" Rafi, Sarah, and I said at the same time.

"Jinx!"

"Double-jinx!"

"Okay, okay, that's enough of that, but seriously, that's all it says?" I asked Kofi.

"Yep, that's all it says. I wonder what that vault key opens," he responded.

"I say that if we ever have a chance, we ask Pierre—or you, Femi, could ask Julie-Marie about it," Sarah jested.

My skin tone is a few shades too brown for it to be noticed, but underneath all the melanocytes, I was beaming brighter than Rudolph's nose, thinking, *What if I could stop the ZCA while potentially being with Julie?* No, I quickly snapped out of that foolish thought and focused.

"When will you two take off?" I asked quickly, just in case they recognized my embarrassed look.

"Probably tomorrow—the day is pretty much already gone," Amir said.

"So, what shall we do for the rest of the evening?" I asked my ZRC family.

"Oi, mate, is that really a question?" Paul said. "I tell you what we do—we fool around with our powers, and I compel you to double-backhand slap yourself." Instantly and without my control, my arms flew up, and just as he said, my left hand whacked the right side of my cheek as my right hand slapped the left side of my cheek with thunderous speed.

"Ouch, man, not cool!" I said to Paul, though he could barely hear me. In fact, I could barely hear myself think over his animated laugh.

"Okay, okay, do you guys want to see something cool?" Diego muttered in a low tone.

"Why are you whispering, man?" James asked.

"So you all can hear this!" Diego clapped his hands together and emitted a large sound wave that blew open all the doors and windows of the courtyard, almost breaking them off their hinges!

"Jesus Christ! That's what you can do?" Suhani said, wide-eyed.

"Oh, it doesn't even stop there. I can produce much stronger waves, depending on how much I choose to amplify each one," Diego said with his signature cocky smirk painted on his face.

"Yeah, but can you converse with people in their natural tongue, though?" James countered.

I couldn't believe my eyes. Here we all were using our powers for *fun*. If you told me that this scholarship would've led to this, I couldn't have even imagined it in all my wildest of dreams, yet here we were.

"What do you say, Mikael? I'll show you mine if you show me yours," Suhani said.

"I'd rather not. It's not exactly something that I would want to use on you all."

"No, I'm seriously asking you to. I used to love pizza until I saw an example of a fast-food pizza that got decayed and moldy; that forever made the sight and smell of that delicious triangle seem like the things nightmares are made of!" Suhani giggled.

"So, if I'm getting this right, you want me to make you love pizza again?" Mikael rolled his eyes.

"Exactly. Isn't your power emotional manipulation?" Suhani asked, genuinely confused by his less-than-eager disposition.

"Yeah, it is, fine." Mikael eyed Suhani for what felt like a lifetime, not blinking once. Moments after the intense stare-down, he casually said, "All done, you now love pizza again."

And like clockwork, Suhani was on the phone with the majordomo, Francis, ordering two large boxes of *quattro formaggi* pizza, settling the future debate of what we would be having for dinner, as well as displaying just how powerful Mikael's emotional manipulation ability truly was. The night continued on like this, having pizza and playing around with our powers.

Though not everyone took part. I, for one, certainly did not. I still didn't know the extent of my powers, but one thing that I did know was when Paul compelled me to slap myself, for a brief moment, I thought of Paul dying an excruciating death, for even having the audacity to *compel* me against my will. To think I could possibly manipulate reality to erase his powers or erase his most annoying traits away flattered my ego momentarily, but I couldn't give in to such thoughts.

Obviously, it's Paul that we're talking about here, so that thought was quickly brushed off. But the fact is, *I still had the thought,* and from my encounter with Mayor Estrada, I had to make sure my thoughts didn't become my words, and my words didn't become my actions. . . . It was fun watching the gang testing their powers and all they were capable of doing—especially Suhani, who became more of a prankster with her powers. Some of us, though, didn't have that luxury.

Rafi, Mikael, and I had serious repercussions if we tried playing around with our powers, and no one was ready for that—not even us. With Rafi perhaps having abilities to see into the future, Mikael being able to manipulate anyone's emotions— in a more direct manner than Diego—and me, who still didn't know the full extent of what else my thoughts or words could do, it was just safer for some of us to see what our powers could do only when we actually needed them. . . .

* * *

Before we even woke up the next morning, Amir and Kofi had already departed for the capital city.

"Didn't want to bother you all. We decided to get to Madrid as early as possible. See you guys soon." As I read their letter, I thought, *Gee, why doesn't anyone write letters anymore? Such a simple task to do, but also one of the most endearing, as well.* I gave them a call to wish them luck, as the rest of us still at the Castillo had some research to conduct on the Zaragozas' future ZCA business objectives.

* * *

"Mate, are you sure we're going the right way? The last address of that relative is down this way," Amir and Kofi bickered.

"Bro, I'm trying to tell you, it's not a right, but a left. I thought doctors were supposed to be smart?"

"And I thought architects knew how to read instructions!" Amir countered.

"When we asked that old woman if she knew of someone named *Benavidez*, she said she knew of a Sophia Benavidez, who lived in that lavender house on the *left!*" Kofi shouted, exasperated.

"Okay, okay, you got it, big man; we'll follow your lead," Amir said. Turns out, Kofi was correct and Sophia Benavidez did live in the lavender house, but that was about the last normal thing associated with Mrs. Sophia Benavidez, the last living relative of Roberto Benavidez, the mysterious book's previous owner.

According to Kofi and Amir, the house was worn down, but the elegance and charm of its previous life still lingered in the dull but once vibrant exterior color of the home, which made it that much more alluring to see what it looked like on the inside.

As the two of them approached closer to the door, they were surprised to see that it was already slightly open.

"Come in, my dears," a sweet, low, elderly voice rang out. "I'm just over here," the voice said again as Amir and Kofi continued deeper into the home, wiping away the cobwebs and snaking themselves out of the way of old and oversized furniture as they followed the frail voice. They finally found the source of the voice, a feeble old lady, her silver hair pinned out of her sharply defined face, sitting alone in a large library that looked like its catalog was printed when paper was first invented. The smell of old paper overwhelmed the room, but the graceful elderly woman's presence somehow soothed them, making them feel at ease.

"Ah, you've brought a friend. That hasn't occurred in quite a while.... I've been expecting you," the woman said, sitting in a green leather chair, her back still turned away from them.

"Are you Sophia Benavidez, ma'am?" Amir asked politely.

"And formal, too. How delightful!" Sophia said. "Yes, my

name is Sophia Benavidez, and you must be Amir Abdelaziz, and your friend's name is, hmm, ahh, right, Kofi Mintai," Sophia said, spinning around in her chair to face the two of them. Sophia had hair that was long, flowy, and white, which Kofi said most resembled the way Elves were portrayed in Peter Jackson's *The Lord of the Rings,* but she kept it tied, understandably to keep it out of her aging eyes.

Similar to those Elves, as well, there was a profound sense that Sophia possessed great wisdom. Although now adorned with wrinkles, her face did not betray her beauty that was still evident, which was only enhanced by her grace and charm.

"H-how— How did you know our names?" Amir asked, breaking out in a cold sweat.

"Because I've been expecting you, my young friend," Sophia said smilingly, exposing her still porcelain-white teeth. "You're after my grandfather's book, are you not?" she said, slowly extending her arm out and then pointing to the top of a bookcase to what looked like the oldest and largest book in her sizeable library.

"Yes, I am here for a book, ma'am, but I am not sure what book or what for!" Amir confessed.

"So, they have told you nothing?"

"Wh-wh-who?" Amir asked, shaking in fear. Despite all the abnormal events that took place in the Castillo, Amir and Kofi had never felt anything like what they were feeling now.

"The Zaragozas, silly. I know they sent you to retrieve this book, but they haven't told you why, or even why they need it?" Sophia inquired.

"No, ma'am, it doesn't quite work out like that; they tell us to retrieve these items. And that is all," Amir said.

"But surely you know that you're not like the others, right?"

Sophia questioned, squinting particularly close at Amir. "I'm sorry. All these years of solitude, and I've forgotten my manners—would you two like any tea?"

"Yes, ma'am, I'll have some," Kofi said politely.

"Me, too, please." Amir nodded. Sophia stood up gingerly, put on a mint green cardigan that was on her chair, and left for the kitchen to prepare some tea. According to Amir, the way she moved seemed like she no longer possessed nor desired any earthly possessions. Her movements were slow yet deliberate, and her footsteps made the faintest of sounds when she walked, almost as if she was gliding across the floor.

After returning from the kitchen with three mugs of herbal tea, they sat down and conversed.

"You don't know how happy it makes me that I was able to meet you, Amir," Sophia said. Puzzling Amir and Kofi in the process. "Your path is very important, so I'm glad that I'll be able to hopefully impart some wisdom to you. The path that you and your friends are undertaking is more important than you could ever realize, and your part in this is *extremely* crucial…."

"I don't understand, Señora Benavidez," Amir said. "All of my friends are starting to have their abilities revealed to them, and I'm still clueless about everything. They all seem so sure of themselves and roughly can guess what their powers would and could be—all except for me."

"In due time, it will all reveal itself to you. There is one among you who knows what your path will be, for his path will forever be intertwined with yours—until it isn't, that is," the older woman said cryptically.

"What's in the book?" Amir asked, leaning forward in his chair, facing Sophia.

"That book contains all the information you seek, the answers to the questions you have, and the questions you have not yet thought of, written by those who came before you. I'm sorry. You two must forgive me, but I have grown terribly tired. I must rest now."

"But, ma'am, how am I supposed to return the book to the Zaragozas if I need it for myself?" Amir pleaded.

"Ah, now that is a question I can answer. This is the book you need, and here is an exact replica; they may look identical, but this one is riddled with gibberish. But don't worry, even the Zaragozas will be fooled by the replica—trust me, *their kind always is*." Sophia brought out a book that looked exactly like the one she pointed at for Amir to take, with the same leather-like hardcover and purple spine.

"Don't think I've forgotten about you, either, Kofi. Your role is also important, but for different reasons," Sophia said, turning toward Kofi, whose attention was directed at the vast array of books. "Your power will be *key* to unlocking the secrets from the past, which is why you were assigned to retrieve the vault key, but your actions could lead you down a path… a path you never anticipated," Sophia said, her tone transitioning from joking to quite stern. Amir and especially Kofi didn't know how to react, and let out nervous laughter in response.

"I know you two are wondering where that key is, given the sparse information you currently possess. As a gift to you two, I'll tell you where that key is located. Its retrieval will be up to you."

"I would appreciate that very much, miss," Kofi replied.

"You're very welcome. The key you seek is currently in the possession of the Bank of Spain," Sophia said.

"The Bank of Spain? It'll be impossible to get through that type of security," Kofi said under his breath.

"My hearing is better than it looks. Don't worry, young Kofi; you haven't had the easiest of childhoods, yet you've overcome some things that people couldn't even imagine. But still, you doubt your capabilities. Will you let this minor hiccup stop you from becoming who you were meant to be?" Sophia said, softly placing one hand on Kofi's shoulder.

"Now, I must rest, but I wish you two the best of luck in your endeavors. For now, you and your friends remain our only hope."

"Only hope for what, Miss Sophia? Only hope for wha—" Kofi started to say eagerly, as Amir interrupted him.

"Give it a rest brother. She's already sleeping."

Amir and Kofi took the mugs the three of them shared, went into the kitchen to wash them off, and left Mrs. Benavidez's home.

"Wait. Before we leave, I just have to do one more thing," Amir told Kofi. He went back into the library where Sophia was sleeping soundly, pulled a blanket over her, and gave her a soft kiss on the forehead before he saw himself out.

"What did you do?" Kofi asked when Amir rejoined him outside.

"I just wanted to make sure she was warm, that's all," Amir said.

When I asked Amir why he kissed her on her forehead much later, he said that she reminded him of his own grandmother, and *it just felt like the right thing to do.* I understood the sentiment, admired his bedside manner, and didn't ask anything else.

"The Bank of Spain, she said, right? I hope we're granted a

miracle to pull this off. Tomor didn't even prepare a plan for us," Kofi said worryingly.

"Don't sweat it, man; we have our abilities, and most importantly, we have each other." Amir smiled.

"And exactly where is all this newfound confidence coming from, *Mr. I don't Know What My Powers Are,"* Kofi teased.

"Mate, you know what? I couldn't tell you myself, but I just have this overall sense of peace after talking with Sophia." Amir shrugged.

"So you understood everything she was saying? But she was talking in riddles, bro. All that stuff about my *path?* How did she even know who we were?" Kofi sulked.

"So, out of all the weird stuff that's happened to us in these past few months, you're still surprised that some people may have more insight into this thing than we do?" Amir said, shaking his head.

"I mean, when you say it like that, it sounds silly. But I guess you're right," Kofi said.

"Look at it this way, bro: We made it this far, correct?"

"Correct."

"So, since our brains have gotten us this far, maybe it's time for us to start relying more on our intuition if we want to be successful in accomplishing this daring plan. With that being said, though, what did your gut tell you about Sophia?" Amir asked.

"My gut told me that she was an ally, someone to be trusted," Kofi replied.

"So did mine, so now let's get on and get this sodding key!"

Before planning to take the key, Amir and Kofi first decided to scope out the bank to get an idea of how frequently the security shifts changed and how often the bank's vault doors were opened.

Two days of reconnaissance gave the two enough insight to know that the vault was usually opened one time per day, but that was only if a high-profile member did not use the vault that day. However, if a high-profile member *did* request to use the vault for whatever reason, their wish would be granted. That would be their sole opportunity to retrieve the key.

"Mate, are you absolutely sure you want to do this without knowing exactly what your powers are?" Amir asked Kofi.

"*Now* that's *the Amir I remember*, but yeah, I'm sure; that little speech you just gave me really did boost my confidence. After all, how hard could this be after growing up on the mean streets of Accra? I'm sure I can steal a key from the Bank of Spain!" Kofi cheered.

"Yeah, mate, about that: When you were talking back at the Castillo about how rough you had it growing up, you said you used to distract the people who bullied you so that they would leave you alone, right? The old sleight of hand trick, yeah?" Amir said with a smirk.

"Yes, I guess you could say that. Why do you ask?"

"Well, if that worked for you then, maybe it could work for you now."

"Are you saying what I think you're saying? Wow, you English guys sure are crazy!" Kofi said, laughing wildly.

"That's exactly what I'm saying, mate. Just pretend to be someone you aren't. What's the worst that can happen? So far, what we've learned from the others is that what we think our abilities could be usually turns out to be what they are, so go into that bank tomorrow and Jedi mind-trick the fuck out of those guards!" Amir exclaimed.

"Wow, so it's true; you really have lost your marbles. But you know what? You're right! We have the Zaragozas in our corner *for now at least,* so if worse comes to worst, they'll know what I'm doing here is for them, I guess?" Kofi shook his head ruefully.

"So, do we have a plan?" Amir said, jumping up and down, shaking Kofi as he did.

"Yes, I'll do it. Just calm down!" Kofi said dizzily.

It was settled. Kofi would then attempt to *Jedi mind-trick the fuck out* of the bank's personnel and fool them long enough to retrieve the key and head back to the Castillo.

One trick Kofi had up his sleeve back when he was growing up in Ghana was the colorful language usually associated with African stories to back up his outlandish tales. But for a tale of this magnitude, he had to up the ante. If he couldn't use his first language, he'd use aspects of the culture instead. Consequently, he thought the perfect picture to paint would be to portray himself as some sort of foreign dignitary, wishing to retrieve an item from his safety deposit box. For that to be successful, though, he needed to look the part. In short, he needed the works—similar to how Rafi and I used the intimidating image of twin Mercedes-Benz trucks to convey the image we set out for ourselves as astute international businessmen.

"For this to work, I need traditional Ghanaian clothes and all, an entourage, and a fancy car should help, too," Kofi instructed.

"Good thing we have the richest people in Spain at our disposal. Do you remember the personal Zaragoza concierge number they gave us if we ever needed anything?" Amir asked.

"No, but Femi and Rafi will have it; I'll get it from them!" Kofi said, and being the wonderful friend I am, I happily texted them the number, and Kofi and Amir were well on their way to being successful in their Second Trials duties.

* * *

At a little past eight in the evening, Kofi's car and clothes were delivered to their sunny Madrid hotel with a panoramic view of the medieval Plaza Mayor. The entourage was scheduled to arrive at the bank shortly before Kofi and Amir did the next day.

This was it; it was time to see if Amir's idea would work. That morning, though, Kofi was a ball of nerves. "I don't think I can do this, Amir, I really don't," he said.

"I thought you would say that. That's why as soon as you were done with the concierge service, I called them right back and requested all of this," Amir said with a cheeky smile.

"Requested what, exactly?" Kofi gulped.

"Follow me. . . ." Amir teased. Kofi followed Amir to the next room over, which Amir unexpectedly had the room key for.

"We didn't have enough space in ours, so I asked if I could put all of this into this room's bigger fridge instead." Amir opened the double doors of the refrigerator, exposing what Kofi said looked like every type of alcohol known to man.

"As a doctor, I know I shouldn't be recommending something like this, but in this instance, I think some liquid courage could serve you well, my friend," Amir said with a reckless grin.

Kofi was still speechless, gawking at all of the alcohol that was gleaming at him in all of its flammable glory.

"You do love me." Kofi said, grinning at Amir.

"I do, so let's toast to the future success of your mission and enjoy this champagne!"

About seven or eight toasts later, the timid Kofi morphed into the version that was full of confidence and self-assurance.

"My friend, I have a . . ." *BELCH.* " . . . key to get!" Kofi said, slapping Amir's back forcefully. "Help me get these clothes on, will ya?"

"Wow, I've never seen such ornate colors and patterns," Amir said in awe.

"It's called Kente cloth, and it's these designs that people usually just blanket with the vague term *African-style,* but the real stuff is Ghanaian!" Kofi said proudly.

"Clothes make the man, I guess, because you look sharper than a razor, mate."

"That's *Senator* Mate to you," Kofi said jokingly.

"How do you feel?" Amir asked.

"Like I'm ready to get this key and take these motherfuckers down!" Kofi said, twirling in his new clothes.

"That's the spirit," Amir replied as they made their way downstairs and into the limousine they had requested.

According to Amir, Kofi spent the whole car ride going over some lines, over and over again. Even piss-drunk, Kofi was ever the perfectionist. Unfortunately for him, though, before he knew it, they had arrived at the bank, and it was now or never for him to see what he was made of.

"You got this, bruv; it's just like the stories you used to tell growing up—no different, no different," Amir chanted, as Kofi stayed silent in his seat for a few moments.

Amir's words of encouragement did not fall on deaf ears; Kofi was more than ready.

The driver followed instructions to the letter by parking right in front of the bank, purposefully drawing attention, especially when a black man was seen getting out of a limousine in front of the most prominent bank in Spain. Staying as cool as an ice cube, Kofi reveled in the attention he was now drawing, making sure that every step out of the limousine was as deliberate as it was stylish.

Accenting his fine traditional clothes, Kofi also wore sunglasses which, according to Amir, not only made him look like a superstar but also concealed how drunk he was. If phase one of Kofi's plan was to make a big scene outside the bank, then phase two was to replicate that inside the bank, as well.

Kofi then proceeded to snap his fingers in quick succession, prompting the entourage, who arrived in a second limousine, to swing open the bank's heavy doors, which Amir said even caused some patrons to gasp at the occasion. It wasn't long before the whole charade caught the attention of the bank's short and portly manager, who looked like he could also double as the bank's vault!

"Welcome, Señor. How may I be of service?"

"The senator does not speak, but you can address me," Amir said, doing his best to contain his laughter, as Kofi stood stoically behind him.

"Very well, then, does your client—um, I mean the senator have an account here?" the manager asked.

"You will show me the vault containing my security deposit

box at once," Kofi abruptly answered for himself, making his accent stronger than usual.

"Yes, sir, right at once, but first, I will still need some identification," the round and diminutive manager asked timidly.

"Ha-ha-ha-ha!" Kofi laughed, which prompted the entire entourage to laugh, as well, while the manager stood there, visibly puzzled. "You fool, if you do not show me the vault this instant, not only will I pull out the millions of euros I have placed in this account, but I will also tell my friends at the African Union that their hundreds of millions of euros would be better kept elsewhere!" Kofi boomed.

"That won't be necessary, sir," the manager mumbled, pulling out a handkerchief to wipe his now repulsively sweaty forehead.

Not waiting for the manager to retrieve his keys, Kofi walked right up to the vault and stood in front of it, repeatedly tapping his foot. He tapped and tapped and tapped . . . until the tapping became rhythmic, almost trance-like. Amir couldn't believe his eyes, but the tapping had sent the entire bank staff into some sort of stupor, the plump manager included. Kofi continued to tap, leading the bank staff to start swaying their heads in unison to the tapping beat of Kofi's foot.

"Do you see what you're doing?" Amir asked, running up to Kofi, meeting him where he stood in front of the vault. Kofi did not respond, only looking at Amir expressionlessly, and then looking away.

Tap . . . tap . . . *tap.*

"Mr. Manager, doesn't this remind you of the time you opened that vault so I could reclaim my possessions?" Kofi asked in a low, monotonous voice.

"Yes, it does, and I'll be opening that vault now once more," the manager repeated back.

"Good man, good man."

The manager slowly approached the vault, fumbling with the keys in his hands, his eyes still looking like they were under the control of another.

"Right this way, sir," the manager muttered, still swaying his head to the sound of Kofi's tapping, which now switched to snapping as he followed the manager into the vault.

"What were you looking for again, sir?" the manager said in a hazy voice.

"Look into my eyes. You know what I'm here for," Kofi said, raising his sunglasses up, still snapping rhythmically.

"But of course, the key..." the manager whispered.

"Yes, the key . . ." Kofi replied, smiling. The manager then proceeded deeper into the vault, reaching what appeared to be a wall but was actually a secret door, leading to a spiraling staircase.

"We keep the most valuable items here, sir."

Kofi nodded, continuing to smile, continuing to snap. . . .

"Here it is, sir." The manager was now on his knees, hauling out a safety deposit box that looked like it was as old as the bank itself, riddled with cobwebs and dust. He held it outstretched in his hands, opened it only halfway to make sure the key was still there, which it was, and handed it over to Kofi before walking back up the stairs and out of the vault.

Kofi's snaps became more and more intermittent, as it became abundantly clear that whatever the taps and subsequent snaps were doing had a powerful effect on the psyche of the entire bank staff and its security.

"You all have been fantastic, and I will be happy to leave my money with such an esteemed bank," Kofi said, proceeding to walk out of the bank, key in hand.

But the farther Kofi and Amir ventured out of the bank, the closer the bank staff were to breaking out of their trance. And when Kofi and Amir walked out of the bank, Kofi's power ceased to work.

"*Pararlo, Pararlo!*" the obese manager screamed at the top of his lungs, waddling like a penguin toward the door after Kofi and Amir.

"What is he screaming?" Amir panicked.

"I don't know, but run—those guards are armed!" Kofi slurred, still drunker than a sailor.

"Kofi, keep up! You're slowing down!"

"I can't help it! These clothes are slowing me down."

Bang . . . bang, BANG, BANG!

"Kofi, what was that sound? Kofi?"

Amir turned back to see where his partner was. Turning around, Amir's stomach sunk into the ground. Kofi had been shot twice and now lied motionless outside of the bank.

"**NO**!" Amir screamed, rushing back to grab Kofi, slinging him over his shoulder, and running back to their limousine.

bang . . . BANG . . . BANG!

As soon as the driver opened the door to let Kofi and Amir back in, he sped off instinctively toward the nearest hospital.

"Driver, please, no! We can't head to the hospital now. Take us back to the Castillo at once!" Amir demanded.

"But, Señor, your friend is badly injured. He'll die if he doesn't receive medical attention immediately," the driver said.

"I'm the bloody medical attention! Now, do you have a

first aid kit?" Amir said, trying to maintain his composure.

"Yes, of course. There should be two of them underneath the middle seat."

"Perfect, *muchos gracias.* How long until we arrive at the Castillo?"

"My friend, that drive is at least an hour and a half from here. He'll never make it," the driver warned pessimistically.

"You worry about getting us to the Castillo in under an hour, and I'll worry about if he makes it, okay? Amir snapped." He then proceeded to retrieve the first aid kits the driver told him about as Kofi laid there lifeless in a pool of his own blood.

"Where was he hit?" the inquisitive driver asked.

"Two shots pierced him in the shoulder, closer to the chest than I would have liked." Amir quivered. "I have to concentrate now. Please just drive!"

Amir first tried to stop Kofi's bleeding by applying pressure with his palms firmly placed on Kofi's shoulder. Afterward, Amir used some gauze to help seal the wound, finally improvising an effective tourniquet that kept sustained pressure on Kofi's gunshot wounds. Kofi was unconscious but stable, and Amir breathed a quick sigh of relief as the driver sped through the Spanish countryside.

* * *

Before they got to the Castillo, Amir had already called us several times, so we were all aware of Kofi's current condition, which made every minute that they were on their way back gut-wrenching.

Amir and Kofi arrived at the Castillo just before dinner-time, but this was not a time to be thinking of meat roasts and potatoes. One of ours was shot, and badly. Sarah was the first to greet them, as she should've been. She wasted no time in getting into the limousine, attempting to use her power to save Kofi's dwindling life. Eager to see Sarah's *magic hands* in action once again, Diego lurked over her shoulder like a seductive devil, watching her every move closely and without comment.

This time, though, Sarah fully knew what to expect and did not let her nerves get the best of her at the sight of once black but now red-stained leather seats.

"Remove all the dressing, as well as that tourniquet," Sarah ordered Amir.

"You got it," Amir replied quickly. Although here was a doctor taking medical orders from a biochemist, but Amir wasn't the one with the ability to heal—*not supernaturally, at least*.

Sarah placed her outstretched hands onto Kofi's shoulders closing her eyes to concentrate, just as she had done with Diego back in London. Amir and Diego watched as the gaping holes on Kofi's shoulders began to shrink and shrink and shrink. Diego was amazed to finally witness what Sarah did to him; Amir was just astonished by the whole situation and Sarah prayed intensely, hoping that her abilities would shine through like they had in the past. This went on for a few more minutes until the warm orange glow Sarah's hands were emitting gradually faded away.

"I'm done. He needs to rest now. You two should take him back upstairs," Sarah said.

Amir and Diego did as Sarah instructed and took him up to our room. Never has the boisterous room that was our dorm, the ZRC headquarters, been so quiet. The danger of what we had gotten ourselves into was the clearest it had ever been.

"No one says anything about this until Kofi is recovered. Agreed?" Rafi said.

"Agreed," we all answered. This wasn't the mood for discussions, anyway.

After about an hour, Kofi's eyes opened, but they weren't the big, warm, and inviting orbs that we associated with Kofi. Instead, they now perched low, in disdain.

What could be troubling him? *I thought.* Well, if I got shot, I probably wouldn't be so happy, either,.

"I told you guys . . . I told you that this little game of ours is stupid and will get one of us killed. Now I've shown you. I've shown you all. . . ." Kofi said in a weak and sickly voice, coughing intermittently.

"This isn't the time for that, brother," I said solemnly.

"Then when is, Femi? When one of us is actually *dead*?" Kofi barked back at me.

"Let it go, dude. Just let it go," Mikael said to me.

He was right; this was no time to play the moral high ground, so we just tolerated Kofi's condemnation of the ZRC until he fell asleep again.

"Well, if he needed another reason to hate what we're doing, we just gave it to him, gift wrapped and all," Paul said.

He was right; we'd worried about Kofi's allegiances previously, but now, who knew how he would feel about the ZRC after this ordeal. . . .

"It all happened so fast. One second he was tapping and

snapping the entire bank staff to his will, the next, we're running out of the most famous bank in Madrid, dodging gunshots," Amir said woefully.

"The important thing is, you retrieved the book and the key," Rafi said stoically.

"The *important thing?* Come on, man, the guy got shot, for Christ's sake; give him a break," Daniela shot back.

* * *

After waking up for the second time, Kofi was in a slightly better mood and even joined us for dinner.

"I hate to break the ice like this, but how did it go? What can you guys do?" I asked in a respectful tone, careful not to ruffle any feathers.

"Well, I can hypnotize people with noises, I guess, and Amir over here has a girlfriend older than my grandmother," Kofi said sarcastically, blowing on his mushroom soup to cool it.

Ah, he's joking. That's a good sign, right? *I thought.*

"*Hypnosis*?" Paul blurted out, with the food still in his mouth.

"Well, if you can hypnotize, what went wrong?" Sarah asked.

"Well, that's what I think, at least, and in the bank, it felt like it was working fine. I guess my concentration wavered for a second once we were close to the exit, and that second was all it took before it happened," Kofi said.

We didn't want to push him any further, and no further questions were asked after Kofi and Amir had recounted their Madrid adventure.

With Diego being able to manipulate sound; Kofi being able to fool people into believing what isn't real; Sarah having the ability to heal seemingly anything; Raphael potentially having visions of the future; James having the power to converse with anyone; Mikael's insight into others' emotions; and Amir's inexplicable connection with a strange elderly Spanish woman telling him of his supposed destiny, we began to feel like we could take on the whole world, albeit with more precaution.

I still didn't know how my abilities fit into this equation. Was my ability fooling people into believing illusions, as well, or was it something else entirely?

"Amir, so you said this old lady knew exactly who you were, and she gave you this book that isn't even written in any known language?" I asked.

"Here, let me take a look at it," James interjected. "Hmm, I can't make it out, either. Are you sure she didn't say anything else?" James pressed.

"Not really, but the strange thing is, this book looks familiar, but I don't know why," Amir said in confusion.

"What say you, Rafi? Have you had any *visions* as of late?" Amir asked.

"Nada, I'm sorry," Rafi replied, viciously cutting the carrots on his plate.

"If we ever see Gástonio again, I say we ask him about this Sophia lady and see what he says. Apart from that, let's enjoy this dinner, and then tomorrow starts the final week of the Second Trials, leaving only you two to retrieve your assigned heirlooms," I said, pointing to Tolu and Daniela with my fork.

"Where are you two going again? Somewhere in Scandinavia, right?" I asked them.

"We're off to Sweden," Tolu said impassively.

Daniela seconded Tolu's very apparent disinterest.

"Oi! And by the looks of it, it seems like the two of you can hardly wait!" Paul said sardonically.

"Guys, I'm from Nigeria. What the hell am I going to do when I freeze my ass off in Sweden?" Tolu grumbled.

"Well, what about me? Brazil isn't known for its winter wonderland, either, you know," Daniela said.

"Take it from me, guys, the cold is something you get used to. You just learn to live with it," Sarah said, relishing in their discomfort.

"What are you guys even retrieving?" Tomor asked.

"I was told to obtain a notebook that once belonged to a conquistador who apparently traveled to Sweden but never returned," Tolu said.

"And I was tasked to retrieve a locket that belonged to his wife. The dossier says the two *should* be in the same place," Daniela added.

"Ah, the ole two-for-one deal, innit?" Paul winked.

"What are you two looking forward to the most? And remember, if you lie to me, I'll be able to tell!" Mikael said half-jokingly.

"Although the cold doesn't agree with me, I do enjoy the beauty of the snow," Daniela answered.

"And you, Tolu?" Mikael asked, smirking the entire time, his hands hugging his face in delight.

"I'd rather not say, but I'm guessing you already know," Tolu grumbled.

"Oh, I definitely do, and it seems like your dream will finally come true!"

The rest of us weren't immediately privy to what Mikael was referring to, but as soon as Mikael glanced at me with that *look* and that not-so-sly wink he gave me, I immediately knew what he meant. Tolu would finally be getting that alone time with Daniela that he so desperately wanted.

"Time to hit the hay; the love birds have an early flight tomorrow," Mikael teased.

Chapter 20: Venice of the North

The next morning, I was awoken to what sounded like a bungled burglary in progress.

"What's going on out there?" *I shouted.*

"Sorry, I'm packing," Daniela yelled back from the living room. "Sarah, what should I pack? I've never traveled to such a cold place before!" Daniela asked.

"Only the warmest clothes you brought," Sarah said.

"And also clothes that are easy to breathe in!" Suhani chimed in.

"Droga! Looks like I didn't bring anything like that," Daniela said.

"Don't worry about it. Tell you what: You can take the winter coat I brought, and once you get there, you can buy another and just return mine when you get back. How does that sound?"

"Muito obrigado, *Sarah!"*

HONK! HONK! That was the sound of the car waiting outside to take them on their Scandinavian adventure.

"Dani, we're going to be late!" Tolu yelled as he waited patiently in the car.

"I'm coming, relax!" Daniela shouted back, all while I was trying to get some sleep.

Their arguing did make me laugh, though. It reminded me of my own parents—my dad yelling from the car as my mom hurried to check for last-minute items that were often forgotten, only for my dad to realize that he was the one who forgot something.

"Okay, I'm ready. Let's go!" It was Tolu and Daniela's first time in Stockholm and needless to say, I was jealous.

When they recounted their adventures in the Venice of the North, it sounded like paradise to a person like me who doesn't mind the Arctic winds of Northern Europe and the ingenuity of the tools and gadgets that climate often calls for. Moreover, I longed to visit the eclectic art gallery that was the Stockholm Metro.

Nevertheless, Daniela and Tolu eventually got over the weather once they were encapsulated in the beauty of the city.

"What do we know of our Spanish conquistador, anyway?" Daniela asked Tolu, who was still shuffling along, trying to get his luggage into the hotel room.

"It says that his mission here back in the sixteenth century was to learn novel Scandinavian sailing techniques to show the Spanish, but he defected from the Spanish Empire and remained here until his death," Tolu said before asking, "What does your dossier say about his wife and this locket you're supposed to find?"

"It says that the locket holds something very valuable within," Daniela answered.

"Where should we start our search, then?"

"My dossier also said that he had a boat-building workshop

by the docks," Daniela said.

"I see that in mine, too. I guess that'll be a good start," Tolu replied.

They both agreed and set off.

From the sound of things, Tolu and Daniela didn't waste any time retrieving the heirlooms. Not that I could blame them, though—the Second Trials deadline was fast approaching.

"Hey, Tolu, before we go, what did Mikael mean at dinner the other day?" Daniela asked.

Stumbling over his words, Tolu struggled to get a coherent message out. "Huh? What did you say?"

"You heard me loud and clear, boy. Why did he say that your dream would come true?" Daniela said, scowling at Tolu.

"Oh! He only said that because he knew I couldn't wait to leave Spain and go on a new adventure," Tolu rushed to say, trying to avoid the conversation behind nervous and sporadic laughter.

"Okay, well, if you're going to lie, you should know that I can tell your heart is racing faster than usual, and you are starting to sweat, even though we're in freezing Sweden!"

Tolu was stunned that Daniela knew how fast his heart was beating, despite being fully clothed, and how she noticed the one drop of sweat on his forehead that he didn't even notice himself until it trickled into his eye.

"How, how can you tell?" Tolu asked in disbelief.

"Because I didn't need to retrieve this heirloom before my abilities became obvious…."

"So, you're telling me that you already know what your abilities are? How? When?"

"I became aware of it when the others were out and about, traveling the world, collecting those *coisas,*" Daniela said.

"*Coisa?*" Tolu interrupted.

"Sorry, Portuguese for *things.* I don't like calling them heirlooms because, from the way I see it, the things they want us to retrieve never belonged to them in the first place," Daniela said tartly.

"You're right, but what exactly do your powers do?" Tolu insisted.

"I can see things that others can't. When you were just blatantly lying to me, I could see your heart beating quicker the same way that I could see that drop of sweat falling down your face."

"Why didn't you tell me or anyone else?"

"Because I wanted to be sure of it; plus, I was practicing." Daniela giggled.

"Practicing?" Tolu asked, scratching his scarce facial hair.

"Well, yes, practicing, in order to see different things: to see in a different spectrum of light, or how to adjust to the night. I started practicing by walking through the Castillo in pitch blackness of the night, while everyone was still sleeping, seeing through walls, seeing farther away, and noticing when people were telling the truth versus a lie." Daniela grinned. "Now, are you finally going to tell me what Mikael meant?"

"Okay, look, Daniela, I like you. . . . I like you *a lot,*" Tolu said bluntly.

"Did you just recruit me into this thing so you could be with me, and what, try to *sleep* with me?!" Daniela fumed.

"No, it was nothing like that! I asked if you would want to be a part of the ZRC because I thought you were smart, capable, and as perceptive as they come," Tolu insisted. "I swear that I put my feelings aside when I initially asked." Tolu appealed on his knees.

"Okay, okay, I believe you. Your heart is racing again but not because you're lying this time. It's just that, for us girls, sometimes it's hard to tell whether or not a guy is all nice and friendly just because . . . or because he wants something from us in return. Plus, you're too nice of a guy to be that slimy, right?" Daniela joked, regaining her cool.

"Yes, exactly. I'm too nice to pull that type of stuff! But you do know that nice guys could be just as slimy as the assholes, right?" Tolu teased.

"Don't play around! In all honesty, I'm flattered Tolu, but please, let's just focus on the task at hand. If we can survive this thing, we can talk about the other stuff later," Daniela said with an encouraging smile.

Tolu agreed, and the two of them carried on to find the former shop of Miguel Alonso. That required the two of them to head to the Stadsgården region of Stockholm, where the larger ships visiting Sweden usually dock.

All the blue and gray dancing with each other—from the sky, to the sea, and ships—made Daniela feel seasick without even touching the water. "Let's find this workshop and quickly before I faint," Daniela said.

Miguel's Age of Discovery shop was easy enough to spot since it was the one that looked the most antiquated.

"How much do you want to bet that Miguel's former workshop is that one?" Tolu asked Daniela, gently pinching her.

"I would assume that you are correct. Let me do a quick visual scan to make sure, though." And before Tolu could ask a follow-up question, Daniela's eyes were already transfixed onto the old boat-like wooden workshop.

"What do you see?" Tolu asked. "Dani, I said, what do you see?"

"Quiet, I'm trying to concentrate!" Daniela hissed back at him.

"It looks like in the workshop there are several false walls, and one of them seems to lead down a staircase."

"Could that be where the notebook and locket are, then?" Tolu inquired.

"I'm not sure, but in a city as old as Stockholm, several of these older buildings could have compartments like that. We have to go inside," Daniela instructed.

Making their way to the workshop, Daniela finally realized Tolu's clothes, or lack thereof, she recounted later to me. "How aren't you wearing a coat? It's icy today!" she prodded him.

"Oh, I don't know, it didn't occur to me when we left the hotel, I guess. I walked out in this shirt and was comfortable, so . . ." Tolu said indifferently. "Anyway, we can talk about that later. Let's see who is currently running the store."

"Welcome, *Bienvenido, välkomna*!" the jovial store clerk greeted.

"English is fine, thanks," Daniela said, throwing cold water on his gregarious welcome.

"My name is Olaf Jorgensen. What brings you two to the Old Stockholm Boat-Building Museum today?"

"Um, we would like a tour, if possible," Tolu said nervously, reluctant to maintain eye contact with the brown-haired Swede.

"As much as I would love to host that for you two, we're currently closed for renovations, but I could answer any questions you may have."

"You know what? We do have some questions if you don't mind," Daniela said, watching the clerk closely.

Tolu told me that she was probably looking for any visual clues of deception, but Daniela neither confirmed nor denied his claim.

"This wouldn't be the former ship-building workshop of the disgraced conquistador, Miguel Alonso, would it?" Daniela asked. Her extraordinary eyes weren't needed to deduce that the store clerk took great offense to the way Daniela described Miguel. The clerk's previous jolly, free-flowing hands tightened around his body, aligned to his now defensive and combative mood.

"There was nothing *disgraceful* about what Miguel did. He defected from an empire that sought to control others and found love instead," the clerk snapped back, his arms tucked over his chest defiantly.

Finding his confidence, Tolu continued Daniela's line of questioning in a more delicate manner. "We meant no offense, sir. That is just what we were told about him. But it looks like you know more; could you tell us about him?"

"I'll be happy to correct Miguel's legacy to the uninformed," the clerk said, rolling his eyes at Daniela and focusing them on Tolu. "As you probably know, he was sent here by Isabella the First herself to learn how the Scandinavians constructed their boats so that the Spanish could learn these techniques for themselves. However, once he got to Stockholm, he grew disenchanted with the path Spain was embarking on. He met a Swedish woman here and settled for a simple yet highly rewarding life with her. Did whoever send you tell you that nonsense?"

"Yes, and I apologize for any offense that I caused. You really know a lot about him. How?" Daniela asked humbly in a more polite tone.

Olaf picked up on her changed attitude and reverted back to his more cheerful disposition. "I know because I am a descendant of that relationship, and this former workshop, now a museum, has been in our family ever since."

Daniela and Tolu looked at each other, then back at the store clerk, amazed by this revelation. When they first recounted this story to me, they admitted to not knowing how to proceed with what Miguel's descendant revealed to them. Tolu said his first thought was to do the whole *good cop, bad cop* routine again and scare him into revealing what he really knew about his ancestor's notebook and locket, but decided against that approach once he realized the clerk was more responsive when they were cordial with him.

"Well, to be honest, Olaf, we are here on behalf of a society that seeks to redeem the image of a few select conquistadors, and we think your ancestor, Miguel, would be a perfect candidate," Daniela said warmly, even extending her hand out and placing it on top of Olaf's.

Tolu gave Daniela a puzzled look, unable to tell where she was going with her cover story. Nevertheless, he followed her lead and continued her phony backstory.

"That's absolutely right, Olaf, and we would be more than happy to pay handsomely for anything that could be valuable here, granted you give us that tour we were hoping for," Tolu said, brandishing his version of Paul's wry smile.

Mikael didn't have to be there to be able to tell that Olaf was over the moon, finally able to fulfill his lifelong dream of restoring the glory of his ancestor. At least that's what he thought he was doing.

Tolu told the rest of the gang and me that after he and Daniela came up with the fictitious backstory of who they were and what they were there for, Olaf could barely stand still!

"Well, it sounds like you two would probably know more than I do regarding valuables. Please, take all the time you want and don't hesitate to find me here if you need anything. Seriously, you don't know how happy I am for this to be finally happening. I really—"

"That'll be enough. Thanks, Olaf. We'll just take the keys to the back, if you don't mind," Daniela said, cutting off the enthusiastic man.

"Are you sure you don't need anything else?" Olaf asked again.

"**Positive**!" Daniela and Tolu both replied.

As they made their way into the back room, they were mesmerized at how vast and intricate Miguel's former workshop actually was. The interior was designed to resemble a boat itself, as the corridors and winding hallways formed a concave shape just like the hull of a ship.

"Where should we look first?" Tolu asked Daniela.

"I say we try to find that hidden staircase as soon as possible and see where it leads to. One second. Let me just reorient myself first," Daniela replied.

Tolu said that when Daniela went into her *scanning mode*, her eyes became crystal-like, and her body became as stiff as a board, only moving her head like a camera on a swivel.

"Found it! It's down this way. Let's go!"

On the way, Tolu tried to pick up some knickknacks that they saw, just to continue the ruse on Olaf. They couldn't come back empty-handed, now, could they? The real priceless items would be theirs to keep. After walking around for what felt like an hour, the two of them finally arrived at the false wall that led to the secret staircase.

"Aren't you freezing?! The farther we go into this workshop, the colder it's getting!" Daniela pointed out, shivering non-stop.

Her steps and her breath became more and more labored as she struggled to get down each stair, "I . . . I don't think I can make it all the way down, Tolu," Daniela said, rubbing the sides of her arms vigorously, trying to keep warm.

"Is it really that cold?" Tolu asked, genuinely unable to discern a change in the temperature.

"Are you freaking kidding me? How can you not feel that? Your head is balder than a baby's bottom! Here, look at my breath: It is literally turning into refrigerated air!" Daniela said, exhaling forcefully for emphasis.

"I can see it, but I just don't feel it!" Tolu said in obvious confusion.

"Tolu, that means you must have some resistance to the cold. Could this be your ability kicking in?" Daniela said.

"I don't know, but if you really can't go down, how will I be able to navigate down there without your super-eyes?"

"Don't worry. Once you get down there, another false wall will be immediately to your left, and then a final staircase. It's the deepest constructed room in this workshop. The items have to be there," Daniela said.

"And what will you do?" Kofi asked.

"I'm going to go back to the main corridor where it was warmer. I'll meet you there once you get back," Daniela said, making her way back from where they came.

Tolu pressed on, traversing deeper and deeper into the nautical labyrinth that was Miguel's workshop. Once he got to the false wall, he pushed it open, revealing the final staircase, just like Daniela instructed. He was truly marveled by the beauty of the final staircase, only being surpassed by the splendor that turned out to be the final resting place of Miguel Alonso and his wife. The room was decorated with fine rubies, gold, and silver as far as the eye could see—treasures the conquistador must've stolen from the Spanish empire used to finance his Swedish workshop. However, the most notable object was the tomb of Miguel and his wife, placed right in the center of the room.

"Please forgive me," Tolu said before sliding the centuries-old tomb open. As expected, there laid Miguel and his wife, their hands still holding one another, embracing even in death. Tolu said a quick prayer and grabbed the necklace that was still on Miguel's wife's skeleton and the notebook underneath Miguel's skeleton hand. As anyone would, Tolu tried to read the notebook, but it was indecipherable, written in the same unknown language that Amir's book was.... Tolu also tried to open the locket, but it proved to be too difficult to open.

Before meeting back up with Daniela, Tolu searched the room one more time. Not for the Zaragozas, but this time for Miguel's descendant patiently waiting upstairs. Tolu said he felt like it was the right thing to do, especially since Olaf didn't even know that his ancestor's final resting place never left his beloved workshop.

"Did you find the notebook and the locket?" Daniela asked.

"Yeah, I got both of them," Tolu replied despondently.

"What's the matter?" Daniela said through shivering teeth.

"Nothing. That room . . . it was a tomb. Miguel and his wife were still there. It just didn't feel right stealing their things, that's all."

"I understand. It's all just a means to an end, though," Daniela said, trying to comfort Tolu. "Um, should we tell Olaf about Miguel's final resting place?"

"Not now," Tolu instructed. Daniela nodded, and they made their way back to the front desk, ascending back out from the workshop's inner sepulcher and outer caverns.

"My friends, so, so, tell me, what did you find?!" Olaf effused.

"Here, Olaf, these belonged to your ancestors. Instead of taking them back with us, we thought you should keep them here in your museum." Tolu and Daniela handed him several documents belonging to Miguel, as well as some jewels and a Spanish steel sword found in his tomb.

"My goodness, I had no idea these were in there! Thank you for finding these for me. I will never forget what you two have done for my family!" Olaf said warmly, giving Tolu and Daniela a big hug and two kisses on the cheek before they departed.

Tired from all the adventuring, they returned to the hotel to relax but also to brainstorm what they believed the heirlooms were to be used for.

* * *

"These heirlooms, they have to be connected in some way. It can't be a coincidence that the language written in Amir's book is the same language in our conquistador's notebook," said Daniela.

"I know they're connected; that's why Pierre and Julie desperately want them. It's getting late, though; let's pick this conversation back up at the Castillo with the rest of the ZRC."

That was the end of Tolu's and Daniela's Swedish retreat and the start of us understanding the significance of these *heirlooms*.

Chapter 21: I, Spy

Daniela and Tolu arrived back in the late afternoon when the rest of us were in the Castillo's courtyard relaxing by one of the many pools on the premises, one of our favorite places to go when we wanted out of the snug dormitory quarters.

Wasting no time, they met with us by the pool and recounted the story I've just relayed to you.

"Wait, so you mean to tell me the conquistador's body never left his workshop?" Tomor asked.

"Yes, it was still there—skull, bones, the works," Tolu said, touching his own body for reference.

"Do you think when we put all of these heirlooms together something spectacular will happen?" James asked, wide-eyed.

"No, but I know what you, Paul, or Diego will say next, so let's go find out," Sarah reluctantly said, leaving her favorite spot by the side of the pool.

We went back into our room, brought out all of the heirlooms we had recovered, and put them all beside each other, making sure to place Amir's book by Tolu's and

Daniela's notebook and locket.

"Oi! Shouldn't there be some sort of ominous humming and glowing happening right about now?" Paul blurted out.

"*Ssshhh,*" we collectively told him.

I didn't admit it, but I, too, was looking forward to something fantastical happening when the heirlooms were finally placed together, a victim of watching too many treasure-driven movie plot lines, surely. Slightly disappointed, we placed all the heirlooms back into their respective containers and started to discuss the possible ramifications of what was going to happen over the next few weeks, months, and years.

"Well, gang, we did it; we've recovered all of the heirlooms, with time to spare. There were ample levels of danger at every step, but we've proved what we're capable of and, in the process, discovered some pretty extraordinary abilities.

"When we first started, we were just a group of international scholars who thought that our lives would be forever changed by being awarded the ZNBS, the most prestigious scholarship in the world, offered by the richest family that has probably ever lived.

"In the process, though, we found out why the world knew nothing about the specifics of the ZNBS or the Zaragozas. If the world knew what they were up to, their plan for world domination would be jeopardized," I congratulated my ZRC family.

"Would it, though?" Rafi questioned, which I admitted was probably true. There are plenty of real atrocities occurring as we speak at which no one even bats an eye.

"Even still, we were right about one thing. Our lives were forever changed once we discovered what the Zaragozas were up to," I continued.

"Femi is right. Our lives are forever changed, but not in the way the Zaragozas initially planned. Their vision of indoctrinating us, breeding our abilities so that we would be indebted to them forever, enslaving us as their minions, failed," Rafi said. "Their plan of using our abilities to control the world had one major flaw: foolishly thinking that just because they raised us and countless others out of our unfortunate situations, that their profits would know no bounds," he continued.

"Rafi is right. For too long, companies and the people who control them thought that their wealth, built on the backs of people just like us, bought them infinite success. With these abilities, we'll tilt back the balance to the everyday man and woman," James said, standing proudly.

"But what we won't do is what they have done to us. We'll take that power and make sure that in our vision of a just world, everyone is treated fairly," Sarah said, standing up beside James.

"*Roight, roight,* that all sounds very good and dandy, but let's not forget that in order for us to achieve this *utopia* we seek, there may be some sacrifices along the way, and if blood is shed, let it not be in vain," Paul warned.

James, Mikael, and Kofi nodded especially solemnly at Paul's words, as they were the only ones who had personal insight into blood being spilt—an unfortunate truth.

"No matter what happens, if I had to do it all again, I would, and there isn't anyone else I'd rather do it with than you delinquents. You all have shown incredible bravery by joining the ZRC, being fully aware of what the Zaragozas are capable of, which I think even if we do fail, we should all hold our heads up high for taking a stand against such grave injustice," I said proudly.

My celebratory speech got cut short, however, because Tolu, Kofi, and Daniela received another dreaded email from Pierre Zaragoza. We knew it could only mean one thing.

"Uh, guys, come in here," Daniela called out from the kitchen.

"What is it?" I asked, being the first person that heard her.

"I just received another email from Pierre; he wants to see me again...."

Mikael, who was the second person to hear, was immediately vexed, making me worry even more if our residential *emotional expert* was feeling anxious, as well.

"Could it be because of how rebellious you were when you met with him last?" Mikael asked.

"Perhaps, but I received another message, too," Tolu added, coming into the kitchen afterward. A few moments later, we were all now standing in the ever-shrinking kitchen, wondering what Pierre had up his sleeve this time. Notably, the only person missing was Kofi, who was still in the living room, watching TV.

"Oi, mate, get in here. I know you can hear us!" Paul called out.

"Don't worry, I'll get his attention. . . ." Diego said as his mouth formed a small circle.

"Here we go again," Sarah cautioned.

Whoosh!

"Ouch! What the fuck was that!?" Kofi cried.

"Oh, we thought you couldn't hear us, so I just wanted to check your ears out," Diego said, clinching his stomach tightly, trying to alleviate the discomfort that comes with that crazy laughter of his.

"Jesus, what do you guys want?" Kofi said, rubbing out the pain in his ear from Diego's precise sonic blast.

"Nice one!" James said, slapping Diego on the butt.

"Daniela and Tolu got another email from Pierre. Did you see anything?" I asked Kofi.

"Oh, about that . . . yeah, I saw it. Why is it a big deal, anyway?"

Rafi, who was trying to keep his cool about Kofi's insolence, erupted out of nowhere like an unsuspecting ancient volcano. "Are you fucking *serious,* dude? Do you think this is a game that we're all playing? Our friends just got an email from the kingpin himself, just as we finished the Second Trials. Is the significance of that lost on your little brain? May I remind you that you *still* didn't even tell us what he said the first time?"

Kofi's audacious behavior in the living room must've meant he was ready for some sort of reproach because he wasted no time firing back at Rafi. "Yeah, I am serious, *Rapheal.* I'm sick and tired of you and Femi bossing all of us around! You know what else I'm sick and tired of? *Pretending like we can stop corrupt fucking billionaires with supernatural powers!* You wanna question my loyalty, where my allegiances lie? May I remind you, *I'm the only one who fucking got shot for all of this!*"

"Called it. I knew he couldn't wait to use that one against us!" Diego said, fist-bumping Paul in the kitchen during Kofi's tirade.

"Where were you when that flaming-hot metal ripped through my shoulder only inches away from my heart, twice? Where was your sage Native advice when I was running for my life, huh? You can all piss off. I have a meeting to get ready for." Just like that, Kofi got up from the couch and walked out of our room—but not before he made sure to slam the door on his way out.

"I've had enough of that sodding twat. Either he's out of the ZRC, or I am," Paul stated.

"Relax, man; it was really traumatic back there. He'll come around. Kofi is a good guy. He'll come around," Amir said sincerely.

"Good guy or not, he's increasingly becoming the weakest link in this little chain of ours, and you know what that means," Daniela said gravely.

"What exactly does it mean, Daniela?" Sarah questioned.

"It means that his eventual treachery could be just around the corner," Suhani said, farthest from us all. "He can no longer be trusted, guys. I hate to say it, but it's true."

"I, for one, don't get why he keeps acting like he's the only one who got hurt in all of this. Okay, fine, he's the only one who got shot, but James and I got beaten within an inch of our lives! All because of our *little game* as he refers it, and to be honest, even if only half of what we're doing is true, I'd do it all over again for the greater good," Mikael said.

"And here I thought we all shared that sentiment," I said.

Being the other person who frequently had his qualms about what we were doing, Tolu stepped up and offered an excellent suggestion. "Guys, gals, nerves are frayed right now. Let's all just try to calm down and be happy that we successfully completed the Second Trials, huh? It seems like this time around, Pierre is meeting with Kofi first. I don't know about you, but when I couldn't find Pierre's office, there was only one person I could go to."

"Oi, mate, stop beating around the bush and get to the

bloody point. What are you on about?" Paul said.

"I'm saying we ask majordomo Francis if there's any way we can find out exactly what Pierre and Kofi will be talking about, if he doesn't want to tell us himself," Tolu said.

"Pierre's office is the tallest tower, and there's only one way into it," James pointed out.

"Only one way *that we know about*, but I'm sure Francis might know of another or, at least, a way to listen in to the conversation," Tolu continued.

"That's a lot of what-ifs in this scenario, but I like how you're thinking, Tolu. How do we even know Francis would be willing to help us out?" Tomor asked.

"Well, he was overly helpful when I was trying to figure out the logistics of the party," I said.

"And like I said before, he didn't waste any time helping me find Pierre's office when I was running late."

"I'm not sure about this, guys; we hardly know anything about him, and we're increasingly relying on him," Sarah warned.

"All valid points, but I don't see any other way to find out what those two have been discussing," Rafi said.

"We don't have a choice, you all. Let's go look for the majordomo at once," I said firmly.

It wasn't particularly hard to find him, as he had quite a sizeable office in the servant's quarters of the Castillo.

"Ah, welcome, my young friends, how may I be of assistance?" the tall and slender old man said warmly.

"Señor, you remember when you helped me find Pierre's office? We need your help again."

Francis nodded firmly. "I understand. Follow me. Let's talk somewhere more private," the majordomo said, waving his hand to instruct us to follow him deeper into his office. It seemed like everyone had a false door because Francis took us into a secret passage that at first glance appeared to be a floor-to-ceiling military painting of a long-dead Zaragoza.

"Before we go any farther, you have to tell us why you're helping us," Tomor ordered.

"There's no time for that. Now, please, this way," Francis said.

"*No*! You could be leading us to our death for all that we know. We're not going anywhere till you tell us," Tomor said defiantly.

Finally, I had a chance to witness Tomor when he was dead serious! It was quite a thrill to see the change in his demeanor firsthand. I'm just glad he was on our side, powers or not.

"Okay, okay, fine. I initially helped your friend here—Femi, is it?— because his eyes reminded me of my son, my dear boy, who also had those fiery eyes: my dear boy, Jorge, whom Pierre killed himself. . . . If that wasn't enough torment, they also kidnapped my precious baby girl, all while I remained here, radiating with a vengeance, festering with rage, all while serving that monster. It pains me to even look at my reflection. But alas, I have no choice," majordomo Francis admitted. The anger and pain he was currently painted in required no interpretation. His fury was real and readily felt by all.

"Wait, wait, wait, did you say *Jorge*?" I gasped.

"Yes, that was my son's name. Why?"

Sarah immediately slapped my hand to shut me up. *"Not the time,"* she whispered.

"Oh, nothing, the name just sounded familiar," I said. *Could this be the very Jorge that Gástonio referred to, as well? The very same Jorge that Gástonio thought was me when I reentered his room that night?* Majordomo Francis said his name so casually, but little did he know, his son and our merry little band were more connected than he could imagine. . . .

"Is that enough information for you? Now at once, we must keep moving," Francis finished.

There was no further point of contention from any of us. We followed Francis deeper into the winding passage, going up several staircases, then going down, and then finally ascended up a long, serpent-like staircase within earshot of Pierre's office, the tallest tower in the entire Castillo.

"What is this place?" Rafi had asked.

"It's an old room that fell out of use long before Pierre's time. He doesn't even know of its existence. It was used by the original builders of this Castillo to store the materials used to build the tallest spires, Pierre's included. After that, however, I'm not sure, and anyone else who might've known is long dead."

The dwarf-sized enclosing was not only way too small for all of us to be comfortable, but the smell of rat feces was nauseating. They were probably snickering at all of us being crammed in their filth. Not only that, but we could barely see anything, relying only on our ears to aid us in this clandestine effort.

"Quiet. I hear footsteps approaching. It must be your friend," Francis said.

"Definitely. I recognize that sound anywhere. Kofi always drags his feet when he walks," Amir stated.

"That bloody basta–...!" Paul almost yelled out before Daniela shut his mouth with her hand.

"Sir, you requested to see me?" Kofi called out to Pierre.

"Yes, my sweet, sweet son. Shut the door behind you, dear boy," Pierre Zaragoza's deep gravelly voice rang out. "I've heard the news of your success during the Second Trials. You must know that I'm very proud, no?"

"I'm well aware, sir."

"Please, there's no need for such formalities. I know of your heroic deeds; you can call me *father* now. . . ."

Paul made a disgusted face when he heard Pierre ask Kofi to call him father, and he was correct in doing so. Although Paul made the face, we all shared his sentiment.

"If it's okay with you, sir, I'd rather . . . I'd rather n-n-not," Kofi said, his voice quivering in fear.

"As you wish. So then, let's get down to business. Have you considered my request? Will you inform me of the dealings of you and your little friends? You do still want to better the lives of your family members, no? Imagine all the good you can do as a member of the Ghanaian legislature, as the *President of Ghana*," Pierre said seductively.

"Sir, yes, I do still want to help my family and be a person who's worthy of respect back home, but . . ." Kofi said sheepishly.

"But . . . what!?" Pierre's voice thundered. "I'm tired of you brats growing increasingly disobedient. You have no earthly idea of how I can punish those who are wayward," Pierre ominously warned.

"It's not that, sir; it's just that I don't think my friends trust me anymore."

"Oh, ha-ha-ha, is that all?" Pierre chuckled, his hearty laugh reverberating even through the tight enclosure we found ourselves in.

"Yes, sir, that is it, but I'm afraid I don't understand your reaction."

"I only laugh because I thought you were going to say something more meaningful. If they do not have your trust, you will simply regain it. That's only if you love and care for your family as much as you admit, though…." Pierre said, not even bothering to obscure his threat.

"Of course, sir, I d-d-do!" Kofi stuttered.

"Then we're done here. Tell your friends I have other matters to attend to. I no longer wish to see them."

"At once, sir," Kofi replied, getting ready to leave Pierre's secret office once more.

"Oh, and Kofi, you do know that our marksmen don't miss and shoot interlopers in the shoulder, correct?" *Pierre said disinterestedly like he was in the middle of a meal.*

Kofi was silent except for his very audible gulp.

"I'll take that as a yes," Pierre said before his office grew silent once more.

"Come, it's time to go," Francis whispered.

Back in his office, we had some more talking to do with majordomo Francis.

* * *

"Let me, for one, just say that we do not even know how to thank you, Francis. What you did for me back at the party, what you did for Tolu, and now this. We are forever indebted to you," I said genuinely.

"Oh, Femi, you flatter an old man, but be careful about being indebted to others. That is the curse that has plagued my family for generations," Francis said misty-eyed.

"How do you mean, sir?" Rafi inquired.

"Oh, it's a long story, a story that's almost as old as the tale of the Zaragozas. Let's just say, an ancestor of mine made a promise to an ancestor of the Zaragozas, a promise that has bonded our families together now for hundreds of years."

"But, sir, if your families have been bonded for so long, I mean no offense by this, but why are you still serving them and not as wealthy as they are?" Suhani asked.

"Clever question, my dear girl, but you see, the arrangements of the deal were never favorable to us in the first place. We were to serve the Zaragozas eternally, until our own deaths. It was this way for my father, my father's father, and his father before him. My son, Jorge, could not willingly accept this, though. He thought that with the advancements of science and technology, old-world promises had little influence in his 21st-century life. I warned him, I so desperately tried to warn him, until it was too late, until that animal that calls himself a man murdered my boy in cold blood," the majordomo said, now sobbing uncontrollably.

"Sir, I know now may not be the right time, but we might be able to help. You see, we knew of your son through someone else we met that also had previous dealings with the Zaragozas," I finally admitted.

Wiping his tears away, Francis listened with attentiveness. "What do you mean? Who is this person you are referring to?"

"We're not at liberty to discuss that yet, but we know what your son was trying to do before his untimely demise, and we are trying to finish what he started."

"*I knew you had the eyes of my son.* Please, you all must be very careful. The Zaragozas are more dangerous than you could ever imagine," Francis warned gravely.

"We know, sir; we've become quite aware of their viciousness," Mikael chuckled, gesturing over his once-fractured ribs.

"Then you know they will stop at nothing to obtain what they believe they are owed. I know of a lot of their dealings, hidden places within the Castillo, and even some history about the Zaragozas themselves, and even I wouldn't dare to accomplish this task. But I know you scholarship recipients are *special*. Just please be careful," Francis pleaded.

We gave him our word, but now we had unfinished business for another elderly man who knew of the Zaragozas' past.

Chapter 22: Clarity

Neither Rafi nor I had to say anything. The whole group collectively knew that we had to visit Gástonio at least one more time. Paul was even the first to admit this.

"Okay, so maybe you lot were right about the brutish old man. Maybe he's not as crazy as I initially thought," Paul said indifferently.

"Well, duh, that's what I was trying to tell you, man. *You* live for over a hundred years a few miles from your previous employers who are hell-bent on world domination, see how that fares for you," Amir replied.

"This isn't the time to point fingers, but yes, Paul, we did try to tell you to keep a more open mind," Rafi teased.

"For someone saying this isn't the time to point fingers, it sure sounds like you're pointing fingers!" Paul shot back.

"Enough joking around, you guys; let's head to Gástonio's village at once," Tomor ordered.

* * *

It took us half as long to get back to the village, finding a shortcut near a small stream the last time we visited.

"What do we even say to him?" Daniela asked.

"Well, that's the easy part. He never finished his story about Arturo and his infamous ancestor, Rodrigo Zaragoza, or whatever his name was, telling him the source of their power was from supernatural entities from another world," Paul accurately remembered.

"Oh yeah. Yes, that sounds like a good place to pick back up from," Rafi agreed.

"Well, whatever we say, let's just try to be more patient with him. We know he isn't exactly all there," James said.

We got to Gástonio's village early enough for the café that we loved so much to still be open. As expected, Maria, the ever-helpful owner, greeted us warmly and even put our lattes in to-go cups, astutely anticipating that we wouldn't be there for long.

We found Gástonio outside his home, watering the many plants he had in his bucolic garden.

"Ah! You have returned! We haven't had so many frequent visitors in quite some time. Please, come in, come in!" Gástonio was even happier to see us than last time.

I didn't say it, but I was just glad he recognized us—a good sign for his current mental aptitude.

"How can I help you this time?" Señor de Guzmán said cheerfully.

"Sir, the last conversation we had, do you remember it?" I asked.

"Vaguely, but we remember it had to do with trying to stop the Zaragozas, which is as foolhardy now as it was then."

"Yes, sir, that was the conversation, and we still haven't

learned our lesson." I smiled, and Gástonio sighed. I think he realized he wasn't going to be able to change our minds so easily.

"Very well, then, what are you all referring to?"

"Well, sir, last time we were here, you were in the middle of telling us about the time Arturo told you the source of his family's power. I believe you said they were 'Supernatural entities of another realm, another world intertwined with that of ours'?" Paul said respectfully.

"Come, let's discuss within the walls of my home. We remember the conversation, and if you all are so hell-bent on your own destruction, we will do as you ask and finish the story. Sit, please sit," Gástonio instructed, lighting his pipe as he sat down in his favorite green leather chair.

"Right, so the supernatural entities that Arturo kept referring to. He kept talking in riddles, not answering any of our questions until I just came out with it. 'Señor Zaragoza, are you referring to demons? Are demons the source of your family's power?' I interrupted, unable to take the anticipation any longer. However, Arturo's face was destitute of expression, quickly making me reconsider my, perhaps, inappropriate outburst.

"'Yes, my dear Gástonio. If that's what you would like to call them, demons are the source of our familial power.' Not sure of how to act or comprehend what was just revealed to us, we remember pacing back and forth in Arturo's office, thinking, *How could this be?* Furthermore, even if it were actually demons doing the Zaragozas' bidding, why would they? How did this arrangement even take place? The thing that bothered me the most, though, was the fact that Arturo knew how important my Catholic faith was to me, and despite possessing that knowledge, he still groomed me to become an executive in his demonic conglomerate.

"'I know you must have a lot of questions, young Gástonio, and I will try my best to answer all of them. Though I warn you for the first time and the last that if you relay this information to anyone or if you ever fall out of favor with this family, *you'll surely regret it*. Do you understand?' I was shaken by such a threat, especially now that I knew of the true forces that were involved, so I nodded swiftly to display my absolute allegiance to Arturo and his family. Arturo then proceeded with how this initially came about.

"'At the onset of this arrangement, we ourselves did not know that we were dealing with a demon; however, once we did know, it made no difference to us, as the results spoke for themselves.'

"'But how did this arrangement come to pass?' we politely asked.

"'To my own limited understanding, young Gástonio, it all started when Rodrigo Zaragoza, an ancestor of ours from the Middle Ages, was nothing but a peasant peddling stolen goods from the Kingdoms of Aragon, Castile, and Navarre. On a voyage back from selling various stolen Aragonian treasure in the neighboring Kingdom of Castile, he was approached by a wanderer who offered him a deal that he couldn't refuse: unlimited success in his business through a mystical way of making others more suggestible, as well as the ability to spread this power amongst others, onto different people, *if they had what it took to control them*. All of this in return for just two things: First, Rodrigo had to promise to marry the demon's daughter and provide him with a grandchild. However, this was no business agreement or a promise you make to a friend. This agreement was made in blood. Arturo told me that Rodrigo was at first hesitant to accept this offer and asked the wanderer if he could first request a trial period lasting a fortnight to see if his supposed unlimited success would actually be true. The wanderer disagreed with this addendum, but Rodrigo's resolute greed lessened his apprehensions, leading him to quickly agree to the arrangement. The wanderer's words were true, and Rodrigo was given the success in his peddling business that he was promised. Drunk with the success the wanderer provided Rodrigo, he jubilantly returned to the wanderer to gloat that even if the wanderer's daughter resembled the backend of a goat, he would still marry her if it meant continued success in his business.

"'Astounded with how easy the whole process was to get Rodrigo to agree to his terms, the wanderer was barely able to contain his excitement. He asked my ancestor: Wouldn't you want to first lay eyes on my daughter before you give me your blood?' Arturo said.

"'Rodrigo smugly replied that it didn't matter, but he would, and emerging out from a small wooded path adjacent to where Rodrigo and the wanderer were standing, a young woman suddenly appeared, whose beauty immediately captured the attention of Rodrigo. She wore hues of violet and red to contrast her wavy brownish-black hair that perfectly accented her curvaceous body. The woman gave Rodrigo a warm smile and kindly introduced herself as Liliana.'"

Gástonio told us that this was the first moment in the Zaragozas' history in which Arturo and the rest of his family members realized how *favored* they were as a family for this opportunity. Not only did their ancestor, Rodrigo, gain the power to influence all and become as successful as he wished to be, he also got to wed the most beautiful woman he had ever met. All he had to do for this was to donate some blood to a wanderer, neither knowing nor caring about any repercussions.

"The first sign of many, warning us that this family was not one that we should have any future associations with," Gástonio said. Resuming where he left off in his story, young Gástonio had further questions for his mentor, Arturo, and the dealings his ancestor Rodrigo Zaragoza had with that mysterious wanderer centuries ago.

"We asked Arturo what had become of Liliana and Rodrigo, and he replied, 'Ah, well, that's the easy part, my dear Gástonio; they did as the wanderer said: married and bore many children, from which I am descended,' Arturo said proudly

"'And when did your family realize that the wanderer was, in fact, a demon?' we asked our mentor cautiously. 'Oh, yes, I almost forgot. Once Rodrigo and Liliana wed and bore children, the wanderer eventually came out with his duplicitous ways and revealed himself to be a supernatural being, or a *demon,* as you say.'

"'And this did not bother your family at the time?' we asked Arturo.

"'Why should it? For what reason? The initial agreement of obtaining unlimited success, which brought both power and influence to our business, was granted to us. All that had to be done was to marry a beautiful woman. What would you have done, young Gástonio?'

"'But he was a damn demon!' We desperately wanted to yell at Arturo, but fear of repercussion did not allow us to be so bold.

"'Obviously, my ancestors weren't senseless,' Arturo continued, 'Yes, they knew that the agreement may not be all that it appeared on the surface, but as any true Zaragoza understands, the end always justifies the means,' Arturo said to us. 'But as their marriage continued, Rodrigo and Liliana did something that the wanderer didn't expect: They actually fell in love.

"'Although not being a part of the demon's original plan, it actually worked out better than he initially intended. This development allowed the demon to come out with his initial deception and openly state the full terms of the agreement he made with Arturo's ancestor. In order for Rodrigo and his descendants to continue to receive the gifts promised, the Zaragozas had to produce at least two offspring each generation to keep the bloodline extant on Earth, for reasons unbeknownst to the Zaragozas, only being told, 'When the time comes, their debt would be paid by the numbers they can produce—not only through their own family but also by the ones they grant their abilities to.'

"After being overwhelmed by the information Arturo was sharing with us, we needed a break from the conversation, but not before our question was answered about why we kept seeing those flying beasts hover over the Castillo.

"'Those things?' Arturo haughtily responded. 'Let's just say they are also *beings from that other realm* who provide protection for my family and me, for when people who wish to do harm to the Zaragozas are near the Castillo. That's all I have to say about it, and I expect no further questions on the matter,' Arturo gruffly said."

Numerous questions filled all our minds as we asked each other:

What other powers could these demons grant? Why did the wanderer initially choose Arturo's ancestor, Rodrigo? What did the demons ultimately want on Earth? Are they even demons?

"There is one final thing that you kids should know about our mentor, Arturo, and the Zaragozas as a whole, something that we glossed over until now," Señor de Guzmán said to us.

"What is it, sir?" Rafi was first to ask.

"Like I just told you, the demon also granted Rodrigo and his descendants the ability to give powers to others not in their family, to supplement the number of Zaragozas, or in other words, to supplement the demon's army on Earth."

"Yes, we remember," we said.

"What of it?" I asked on behalf of the group.

"Well, kids, Arturo granted us, too, with such powers, the same way I'm sure Pierre and Julie-Marie have probably already granted them to you," Gástonio said with a crackle in his voice.

"Yes, sir, we were informed of the *special gifts* and their purpose of helping with the Second Trials."

"I see, so you kids have already participated in the Trials, we presume?" Gástonio asked in a somber tone, taking another puff from his pipe.

"Yes, we have, both of them. But during the First Trial, we had to drink some weird beverage," Sarah said.

"Ah, yes, that drink you consumed was the first step in harnessing and drawing out the powers you all have witnessed." The old man nodded sagely.

"You weren't only chosen for your scholastic aptitude, which I'm sure Pierre and Julie-Marie have probably told you. You see, we, as human beings, are all born with unique talents and abilities. However, through social conditioning, be it through life, school, or work, these abilities gradually diminish to a point where most have forgotten about them altogether. Nevertheless, there are ways to amplify or strengthen these abilities, and the Zaragozas, through centuries of experimenting, have perfected this process. That was the purpose of the potion you consumed during the First Trials. Though these innate talents and abilities are, indeed, special and unique to each of us, they are not mystical. That is where Rodrigo Zaragoza's ancient agreement with the wanderer comes in, or let me put in in a way that your cartoon-obsessed generation would understand: *That's when your natural abilities manifest themselves into supernatural powers.. . . .*

"And the power we were blessed—or cursed—with by my former mentor was the gift of superb vitality and strength of both the body and mind. We always were naturally athletic, excelling in football amongst other sports and activities. But once we started to work for Arturo, we found ourselves able to do things that did not adhere to the laws of physics!

"Wanting to use our newfound abilities to help those less fortunate around us, we helped construct most of the buildings and homes you see around you in this town and the next, but using our abilities to help the villagers infuriated Arturo greatly. He repeatedly told us these gifts were to be used exclusively for the purposes of Zaragoza Enterprises and the Zaragozas themselves.

"Our last official title at Zaragoza Enterprises was chief senior aide, reporting directly to Arturo, who was CEO at the time. But in actuality, the only aiding we were doing was helping Arturo to silence competitors through intimidation and violence! Arturo had us use our gifts not to help others but to harm.

"Obviously, we know we are complicit in doing the things that he had us do, but coming from absolutely nothing to possessing superhuman strength and intellect, not to mention considerable wealth and fame, the feeling was intoxicating, and secretly, *we loved it.* However, as time went on, we found ourselves growing disenchanted not only by working as a glorified enforcer but also in the shady and often times terrifying business practices in which the Zaragozas regularly engaged.

"Arturo sensed this change within us, too, and gradually began to groom his illegitimate son, Javier, to take over the family business, slowly reducing my role and importance within the company, a bittersweet period for me. Though we were partly glad that our dealings with the Zaragozas were starting to lessen over that time, adjusting to a life of lesser importance and reduced wealth was harder to get used to. This all ended with us finally being fired from Zaragoza Enterprises on my twenty-third birthday.

"As we went into the office to retrieve our possessions, Arturo stormed in, furious at me. 'Gástonio!' he yelled out to me, 'you had the perfect opportunity to become one of the richest and most successful people not only in Spain but in the whole world! I groomed you to take over my empire, wed my daughter, and truly become my son, but no! You spat on *everything* that I have done for you, you ungrateful street-rat!' His eyes were enraged, and his skin was a crimson red, with veins protruding out of his head. That moment, in a way, was the first day of the rest of my life, the first day *me became we.* My powers, my strength, my vitality, all of what we thought made me who we were, was used against us.

"Arturo had given me my superhuman vitality, of both the mind and the body literally making me superhuman, but stripped me of my sanity, my sound mind, my super mind, and left the vitality of my body intact, forbidding me from dying, but to suffer the torment of a fractured mind for eternity. So, although I appear to you as a frail old man, the vigor of my youth remains, while my mind continues to deteriorate. This is why I refer to myself the way I do because, after that day, I was never my old self again; I was split in two. Even now, as Arturo and his son, Javier, have all long passed from this earthly realm, I still remain here, wasting away!" Gástonio teared up.

I felt a sick feeling in my stomach listening to Gástonio's story. I tried to muster up enough courage to speak, but it was Diego who beat me to the punch.

"Wait, so how old are you, exactly, Señor Gástonio?" Diego asked in English, barely above a whisper.

It was a question we all had on our minds as the outward appearance of Señor Gástonio was quite confusing. Here was a man who anyone would be able to tell was elderly; however, he possessed this boyish charm about him that contrasted with his wrinkles and thin white hair. Likewise, he was not a frail old man, by any means. His frame easily revealed that he was quite fit as a young man, and he still looked like he could probably bench-press us all, even if we were stacked on top of each other like pancakes!

"Our age does not matter—just know that we've been on this earth longer than we should've been. But now, we realize that our true purpose in this world was not to work for Arturo as his chief aide. It wasn't even to erect the homes and buildings of this village. We believe that our true purpose is to help you kids end the tyranny of the Zaragozas, help you all more than what we could do for Jorge. I did not think it would be possible to take down an empire that the world doesn't even know about, let alone an empire with command of the unseen, but Jorge gave me hope. He looked at me the way you all are looking at me now, but our mistake then was allowing him, a mere boy with no special gifts, to think he stood a chance. But you, you all possess the gift, and now we have hope, and you kids have inspired us once more with your courage and tenacity."

The rest of the late afternoon was spent asking Señor Gástonio about his time working for the Zaragozas, the things he did for them, the things he witnessed, and delving deeper into why he grew disenchanted with his former employer. We were generally impressed at the ease with which he talked about all of these things, things that I personally would want to bury deep inside and never reveal to anyone. There was something different about the energy of Señor de Guzmán, though. Not once did he ever blame anyone for the predicament that he found himself in—not even when he was cursed to live the remainder of his life as an old man in perfect physical but not mental shape. He never directly stated this, but James and I believed this was due to his devout Catholic faith, which we could relate to from our own upbringing.

As a kid, I always hated going into the dark confessional, which was an ordeal all on its own. But the worst feeling of this whole experience was spilling your guts to the priest about your wrongdoings and feeling like complete scum for the things you were confessing. In my opinion, Gástonio sounded like a man who had accepted his past as well as his present, repenting for past wrongs and wholeheartedly accepting his curse as a form of contrition. I desperately wanted to end the curse that was bestowed on Gástonio so long ago by his former master, but what could I do? I couldn't help him personally but had an idea of someone who perhaps could: *Sarah*.

"Excuse us, sir. We have something to talk about quickly. Will you guys join me outside?" I lied to Gástonio.

The rest of the ZRC were puzzled by my actions but knew by now to follow the cue, regardless.

"What was that about?" Tomor asked.

"I was thinking, what if Sarah could, you know, heal his mind?"

"Uh, I don't think it works like that, Femi," Sarah quickly said.

"We don't know until we try. If you've healed gunshot wounds, surely you'll be able to heal a broken mind, no?" I asked.

"I'll give it a shot, but if it doesn't work, we'll look quite foolish."

"I think Femi is right. The poor guy is suffering within his own head. I say you give it a go, Sarah," Tolu added.

"Okay, fine, but if it doesn't work, I blame the both of you," Sarah said.

"And if it does, I say we try to *heal* Kofi's treacherous behavior once we get back to the Castillo," Paul said sarcastically.

Stepping back inside, Gástonio smiled warmly at us. "What was that about?" he asked.

"Well, sir, Sarah here is a healer, and we thought if she could heal physical ailments, maybe she can heal mental ones, too."

"You all make an old man's heart swell with joy again, but I'm afraid it's far too late for that. I've accepted my penance and will live out the rest of my days just as I am now."

"Yes, but what if you didn't have to?" I said, growing impatient with Gástonio's Roman Catholic guilt.

"Fine. If you all insist, I'll indulge in your request."

Sarah then proceeded to stand behind Gástonio's leather chair and place her hands on top of his wrinkly head.

"Oh, my dear, your hands are so warm, and this feeling, it feels strange, yet therapeutic," Gástonio said, moaning as Sarah worked her quite literal magic.

"Just relax; try not to talk," Sarah instructed as she kept her hands on top of his head, moving them in a circular fashion.

"Oh, my goodness, the fog, it's starting to clear. I don't believe it; I remember so much, my sister, my mother, my friends. *Oh my*!"

Sarah abruptly stopped as Gástonio cried out in terror. "What is it? Did I hurt you?" Sarah yelled.

"No, no, you haven't done anything of the sort," Gástonio said, now weeping freely.

"Then why are you crying?"

"Because we remember, *I* . . . remember. It's all coming back, the happy memories before the curse, the simpler times, *Jorge* . . ." Gástonio's voice was growing fainter and fainter as he sunk deeper into his chair, which made us all worry.

"Why is his voice growing fainter? I thought it worked!" Daniela screamed. But Gástonio called her close and told her not to worry.

"Ah, my dear, it did work. We are once again me, but before I head into this blinding light, you all must promise me to find Jorge's sister. It was to be his final mission before he was killed; please promise me," Gástonio said softly.

"We promise, Señor de Guzmán, we promise," we all said as Gástonio breathed his last breath, departing from this world, finally at peace. It was a bittersweet affair. Yes, we were obviously glad that Gástonio was finally granted the rest he so deserved, but now we were fresh out of leads on sagely Zaragoza advice.

"Well, what do we do now?" Tomor asked.

"We do as Gástonio instructed: We follow our intuition, and make sure his life and death were not in vain." I said.

We paid our respects to the old man, performed an impromptu ceremony inducting him into the ZRC, granting him the honorific title Supreme Leader, and left his humble home—but not before informing Maria of his passing so that the villagers could also pay their respects and bury him properly in his garden, a gesture I'm sure he would've appreciated.

"I can't believe it worked. I wished it didn't…." Sarah wept.

"No, Sarah, you can't think like that. What you did back there was the kindest thing anyone could ever do for him," I assured her.

The journey back to the Castillo must've been the longest we ever embarked on. Though our hearts were heavy, we at least had each other, and words weren't necessary to fill the silence.

Chapter 23: Visions

The week had come and gone, and before we knew it, today was the last day of orientation. We were to meet in the Castillo's great hall for the first time since the First Trials, all together for a final speech given by Julie-Marie. The air was different around the Castillo during this time. There was a marked difference between the amount of ZNBS recipients at the Castillo pre- and post-Second Trials. We had no clue what fate befell those scholars who had disappeared, but that was just the way the Zaragozas liked it.

These past few months had changed everyone, and that energy was felt throughout the entire Castillo. Before reporting to the great hall, we were first told to come to the banquet room to retrieve our official Zaragoza garbs and signet ring. Joining us as we donned the ceremonial robes was none other than Kofi, surely acting on Pierre's personal request from how he interacted with us.

"Hey, guys, let me just say how sorry I am for my actions the other day. It wasn't fair for me to act that way—especially since you were right, Mikael. You and James also shed blood for our cause."

"Our cause?" Paul asked snappishly. "Do you even remember what we're doing all this for?"

"Of course I do, and I'm ready to be a fully contributing member again, so just catch me up on everything you guys have been up to while I was gone," Kofi said. Unfortunately for Kofi, subtlety was not one of his attributes, and even if we did still fully trust him, there was no way he was going to get back in our good graces so easily.

"Let's just get these robes and go from there," I instructed.

Kofi looked at me desperately with those massive chocolate-colored eyes of his for what felt like a lifetime, but I was not to be swayed. We had to be extremely selective with whatever we shared with him from here on out.

The garbs were a crimson robe with purple trimmings, adorned with the crest of the Zaragoza family, a giant snake coiled around a dragon with the family motto written underneath, *Victori spoila,* pinned right on top of our hearts, while the ring also had the Zaragoza familial crest engraved, asserting our completion of orientation, distinguishing us as fully fledged members of their family, their empire….

Initially, this was the day I looked forward to most, the first day of the rest of the life I envisioned. In a sense, though, I was right—just not in the way I originally thought.

Up until this point, the Zaragozas were unusually quiet, with the only updates coming from senior ZCA executives. However, today was different. Julie-Marie was to deliver the final speech, albeit to a smaller crowd than her brother, Pierre, had previously. But this did not make the moment feel any less significant. Shortly after we took our seats, she began. . . .

"Brothers, sisters, Zaragozas through and through, you

all have just achieved what only five percent of all cohorts ever have: intellect to rival any academic; powers that would make entire nations envious; and now, enough wealth to make sure that no one in your vicinity will ever be hungry again.

"We know the road here wasn't easy. We know that you may have even more questions than you did when you originally arrived, but rest assured, now that you have completed the Second Trials, your actions have proved that you are capable of being entrusted with our deepest secrets—secrets that will be revealed to you all in due time.

"However, don't be fooled into thinking that this is the end of your journey. Some of you will now use the ZNBS to finish your undergraduate schooling, fully paid for. Most of you will apply it to your graduate, post-graduate, and professional studies, fully paid for. No matter what you choose to apply our generous scholarship for, you should all hold your heads up high because now that you are one of us, no expense will be spared in ensuring your continued prosperity, *as long as your loyalty remains steadfast and unwavering.*

"Although my brother, Pierre, could not be here today, trust me when I say he is as proud of you as I am. In one year, I will see you all again in New York City at the United Nations, where we will be announcing the next Zaragoza Directive.

"For those of you well-versed in history, you know that each Zaragoza Directive has always been where we have announced groundbreaking and innovative ideas that have changed the world for the better. But even those past directives will pale in comparison to what we have in store for this one.

"In approximately one year, every one of you will do your part and stand at the precipice of a global paradigm shift, where we, as Zaragozas, promise to end world hunger and disease; a world where governments will no longer stand in the way of impactful change; a world where we can finally look each other in the eyes as equals and call ourselves brothers and sisters of humanity.

"Ladies and gentlemen, I'm extremely proud of what you all have achieved but I promise, what you have done will be nothing to what we *will* do in the future. For those of you who have used the ZNBS to finance your graduate or professional studies, as promised, you all will be immediately employed at a ZCA location of your choice. Once again, hold your heads high, rejoice in all the things you have accomplished and the things we will accomplish . . . together!"

And just like that, Julie's speech was over, and so was our ZNBS orientation. For the life of me, I couldn't get how anyone could listen to the rancid rhetoric that Julie and Pierre espoused without feeling disgusted, without feeling like a puppet. But regrettably, I feared that their message could conjure idyllic feelings of equality and justice to some of the ZNBS cohorts. When you come from nothing, the appeal of everlasting prosperity for you and yours is incredibly appealing, as it seemed to be for my fellow American, Grace Fang.

While Julie was giving her toned-down rendition of the feudalistic speeches we had come to know Pierre for, I couldn't help but notice Grace sitting a few rows across from us.

From her puffy eyes that could barely hold the weight of

her incoming tears to the subdued but rushed applause she gave Julie after every word, needless to say, I was worried. I only met Grace a handful of times before, but after every interaction, I always walked away thinking that for her demure demeanor, she came across as a wolf in sheep's clothing, waiting diligently for her time to strike, surprising all in the process.

The fact that I would probably have more interactions with her when I returned to the States only worried me more. Being one step ahead of a genius is hard enough, let alone a genius with supernatural powers.... The only advantage I thought I had would be my power of reality-warping, but then again, I wasn't completely sure if that was what I was doing, and more importantly, I didn't know what power she possessed, either.

We still had a week and a half to pack up, and the Zaragoza private fleet of jets would take us all back to our respective countries. It was a sentimental feeling to be leaving my ZRC family, but happy that everything we planned was, for the most part, going accordingly.

To wrap up our time here in the Castillo, we got the whole gang together along with the help of majordomo Francis, Japanese cohort Keito, Swiss cohort/secret ZRC member Alfred, and some of the other ZNBS recipients that we grew close to from the Fireside Chats. We arranged one last party to commemorate our time here at the Castillo. It was genuinely exciting to see what everyone would be up to in a year's time, and we ZRC members promised to keep in touch, and I even invited everyone to come to visit me in America in a few months to catch up.

The party was insanely fun, as it usually was when copious

amounts of alcohol and gourmet food are involved, but things took a turn for the worse after our usual nightcap.

"ARGHH!"

We were sharply awoken to panicked screams coming from Rafi's room.

I rushed in to see him convulsing in bed, blanketed in a cold sweat.

"Rafi! What's wrong?!" I shouted at him.

Rafi gave me no response, still screaming in agony. Shortly after, I was joined by the rest of the ZRC as we desperately tried to wake Rafi up from his dreadful nightmare, to no avail. His tremors started to become more and more sporadic, and after a few minutes, he erupted from his bed, grabbing the first thing he could, my shirt collar, pulling my face into his. He looked at me intensely like I have never seen before, and instead of their usual soft-brown hue, his eyes glowed an orange color before returning back to their natural shade.

"I-I-I saw destruction. I saw chaos. *I saw Grace. . . .*" Rafi gabbled.

"Speak clearly, man. What do you mean?" Paul yelled from behind me.

"I mean, I saw a new world order that was orchestrated by the Zaragozas with Grace at the helm! Death was everywhere, and those who didn't submit were subjected to the cruelest of torture devices. Winged beasts flew over every Zaragoza-owned building, patrolling for potential protesters. Smoke filled the air, and the beauty of the blue sky was replaced by perpetual darkness. The calming moonlight was replaced with a sinister shade of red as fear and despair ruled the land.

"Worst of all, though, whereas most people saw this

dystopian reality as the end of the world as we knew it, Grace and the Zaragozas saw it as the beginning," Rafi stuttered in a terrible voice.

"Where were we? Where was I?" Paul questioned.

"I don't know where you were. Some of us were held captive in an underground place far from civilization, and some of us were just gone, completely. What confuses me most, though, is that before I had this nightmare, I dreamt the most beautiful dream of the world *post*-Zaragoza, a world where our differences were celebrated and treasured instead of being the seeds of division. I saw a world where the color of our skin, the beliefs we held, our sexual orientations were as insignificant as the colors of the trees. A world where humanity stood as a unified front working together to reverse the damage our presence had on the planet—*a planet united*." Rafi's tone turned to one of awe.

"How could you have such diverging visions back-to-back? One of them has to be correct; which one is it?" I demanded of Rafi.

"I don't know; I can't control these visions, Femi!" our friend said.

"Your visions have accurately predicted things before. Why can't you do the same now?" Mikael asked.

"It's not that simple. I wish it was," Rafi said desperately.

"And you said that Grace was at the helm of this evil empire. How?" I pressed.

"Yes, she comes off a bit extreme sometimes, but we all can. That type of determination and iron will is the reason we were awarded this scholarship. I don't understand," Sarah said, unable to stop pacing back and forth.

"Well, if you had both visions, does that mean both

outcomes, at this point, are equally plausible?" Daniela asked.

"We have to let this serve as a warning of what could happen if we fail, if we can't stop them. We can't let that happen; we *won't* let that happen!" I exclaimed.

We spent the rest of the early morning discussing how important it was now more than ever to be fully committed to this plan of ours. One by one, we eventually left Rafi's room, with me being the last to leave. Clasping his hand tightly, I reiterated, "We won't fail, brother. I promise, *we won't fail....*"

Leave A Review!

Seriously! It would **mean the world** to me as a self-published author if you **rate and post a review** of *The Zaragoza Chronicles: Beginnings* to Amazon, Goodreads, and wherever you bought the book.

Your review will **help others** decide whether to read this book, and your rating will help it soar to the **#1 spot!** Thank you so much for your support!

Scan the QR codes below or type the link into your browser.

Leave an Amazon review

Leave a Goodreads review

https://tinyurl.com/amazontzc1

https://tinyurl.com/goodreadstzc1

But Wait, There's More!

Short stories immediately continue in . . .

Adventures of the ZRC: Femi & the Rival

And

Adventures of the ZRC: Alfred's Tales

Now Available on Ajayeni.com

The main story continues in . . .

The Zaragoza Chronicles: Brainwashed

About the Author

Born in New York and transplanted to Atlanta, A.J. Ayeni embodies the dynamic journey of a first-generation Nigerian American. While his parents encouraged the traditional paths of medicine or law, A.J. forged his own direction, becoming a social sciences researcher driven by curiosity about the human experience.

His passion for storytelling was cultivated through years of living around the globe. From his undergraduate years in Boston to graduate studies in London, and working in Singapore, these diverse experiences shaped his worldview and ultimately inspired his writing.

Guided by the belief that humanity shares more common ground than we realize, A.J. channels his life experiences into captivating, mystery-driven narratives. His stories blend magical realism and fantasy into poignant social critiques of society and the powers that be. Offering profound insights into the human condition while drawing readers into worlds that feel both distant and familiar.

You can connect with me on:

- https://ajayeni.com

www.ingramcontent.com/pod-product-compliance
Lightning Source LLC
Chambersburg PA
CBHW030557310726
48979CB00003B/471

9781736695319